WHAT PEOPL CARG)A

I didn't want to put it down.

— *Women's Voices*, Sonoma County, CA

The Black Stone:

Ominous buildup . . . apocalyptic climax.

— *Kirkus*
Pool Party:

YAs who love thrillers may enjoy the mysterious twists. The story has romance, a weeping 'ghost', a doll that changes facial expressions, a buried treasure, and more.

— *School Library Journal*

The Dark:

Teens rarely need an excuse to stay up late, but *The Dark* by Linda Cargill would give pause for thought to even the most steely-nerved youngster. A genuinely gripping horror story. Approach with caution.

— *The Sunday Independent*, London

The Surfer:

A taut and evocative story … readers will become immersed in the challenge between good vs. evil.

— *School Library Journal*

Author Interview for *Blutige Dornen*:

I've always liked a good mystery or a good scare. When I was a kid I enjoyed the old Alfred Hitchcock movies. I still consider the famous director something of an inspiration.

— "Gruseln für 'nen Groschen," *xyz magazine*

THOSE WHO DREAM BY DAY

A NOVEL BY
LINDA AND GARY CARGILL

CHEOPS BOOKS
TUCSON, AZ

Those Who Dream by Day

A Novel
By Linda and Gary Cargill

Published by   Cheops Books
                   8746 E Wallen Ridge Dr, Tucson, AZ 85710-6235

Cover design by Kenny Cargill
Copyright © 2009 by Linda and Gary Cargill.

Side flap and title page image from *The Lusitania's Last Voyage* by Charles E Lauriat (New York: Houghton Mifflin, 1915)

Cargill, Linda.
      Those who dream by day : a novel / by Linda Cargill.
      p. cm. -- (2014)
      LCCN 2008932796
      ISBN-13: 9780979890437
      ISBN-10: 0979890438
      ISBN-13: 9780979890444
      ISBN-10: 0979890446

      1. Women--Fiction. 2. Lusitania (Steamship)--Fiction. 3. World War, 1914-1918--Fiction. 4. Historical fiction. 5. Detective and mystery stories, American. I. Title. II. Series: Cargill, Linda. 2014 ; pt. 1.

PS3553.A677T86 2009   813'.54
                 QBI08-600220

Those Who Dream By Day

A Novel of World War I

Part I

in a series

All men dream: but not equally. Those who dream by night in the dusty recesses of their minds wake in the day to find that it was vanity: but the dreamers of the day are dangerous men, for they may act their dream with open eyes, to make it possible . . .

The Seven Pillars of Wisdom by T.E. Lawrence

To my grandmother, Doris Lappe, who helped inspire this book.

CHAPTER 1

M iss Dora Benley shivered at Cunard's Pier 54 at the west end of Fourteenth Street. The weather had turned cloudy and drizzly since she'd stepped off the train from Bryn Mawr and taken a cab here. She rubbed her hands up and down the sleeves of her jacket. To ward off the rain she adjusted her summer hat of coarse straw with a bow and daisies.

Dora glanced at her watch. She was supposed to meet her parents at 10:00 A.M. They were taking the train from Pittsburgh to New York. They should have been here an hour ago.

A small party of well-dressed women chatted excitedly in front of the ship. Four large smokestacks billowed puffs of white smoke into the sky. Dora was so close she couldn't help but listen.

"Did you see the notice those Huns placed in the *The New York Times* this morning?" one lady nodded to the other.

"The Germans wouldn't dare!" hissed another.

"It must be some sort of bad joke," said a third.

Dora hadn't read *The New York Times* in weeks. She'd been too busy with exams in Greek and Latin at the end of her junior year at the Philadelphia Main Line woman's college she was attending.

"The Germans did everything except mention the *Lusitania* by name!" another lady trilled.

Dora sidled up to a group of young men in uniform smoking cigars. They were wearing dark blue suits with lapels and white hats.

"No doubt about it, she's the tallest ship afloat," one of them gazed upward at the monstrous black hull only yards away.

"Yep! I'm glad to have this job," another said. "It impresses the girls in Brooklyn. When you tell them you work on the *Lusitania,* wow! They think it's better than saying your ancestors came over on the *Mayflower*."

"It's 30,395 tons all right," remarked a serious young man. "I ought to know. I'm the assistant engineer. It's the only ship with four funnels. It really is taller at seven hundred eighty-five feet."

Another twirled his cigar, "People say it reminds them of tall skyscrapers in Chicago and New York. A newspaper, I can't remember which, called the *Lusitania* a 'skyscraper adrift'."

"She's sure fast enough," added the engineer. "She averages twenty-three knots across the Atlantic. Her top speed is twenty-five knots. She can hold five hundred forty in first class, four hundred sixty in second class, and one thousand two hundred third class passengers. That's on top of us – the crew of eight hundred and fifty."

His friend laughed. "Gee! I'm going to get pushed off the ship with all those folks."

"The Promenade Deck is over a quarter of a mile long," bragged a long-time hand.

The engineer's friend whistled.

"The *Lusitania* also has new safety features," lectured the engineer. "If the *Titanic* had been equipped with any of them, it wouldn't have sunk three years ago."

They nodded, eager to hear more.

"You ought to tell the Germans that," one of his listeners quipped.

"No other ship has her high tensile steel in the hull to make her stronger," the engineer explained. "There are electric controls for steering, for closing her one hundred seventy-five watertight compartments, and for detecting fire. If that's not enough, she has four giant steam turbine engines. That's sixty-eight thousand horsepower and like I said before – twenty-five knots tops."

All the young men's eyes got bigger the longer the engineer discoursed.

"Hello, Mom! Hello, Dad!" Dora spied her parents and waved. She hugged under one arm the package that Sir

Adolphus had sent. It was a surprise for her to give to her father on his birthday.

Mrs. Benley was dressed to kill in a town dress with an ankle-length skirt of striped silk and a solid silken tunic. Her kimono bodice was open in front. She boasted a fashionable collar and long sleeves trimmed with a row of buttons.

"Sorry we're late," her father apologized. He was the President of Benley Tire and Rubber Company. To him the clock was sacred. "Your mother wanted to do some last-minute shopping."

"I bought you something," the feather in her mother's hat waved as she talked. "It will look lovely on you at the captain's table tonight." Her diamond ring and earrings scintillated.

"When do we get to board?" Dora asked.

Her father popped open his gold pocket watch. "Any moment now." The gangplank was down but remained roped off.

"Winthrop, why don't you go see what's keeping them?" his wife rooted through bag after bag of boxes searching for what she'd bought for Dora at Macy's Department Store.

Mr. Benley strode over to the seaman posted at the bottom of the gangplank. He started discussing the matter. Her father shook his head and headed back to the ladies.

"I've never heard of such incompetence!" he thundered. "There's been some sort of delay."

"Whatever for?" Mrs. Benley asked.

"This is no way to treat first class passengers. We've paid top dollar for our tickets to England."

A man and a woman reporting team burst upon the scene with a photographer and his assistants carrying a large folding camera, a tripod, and lots of photographic equipment. The reporters hurled themselves at everybody, asking question after question.

"What did you think of the German announcement?" the male reporter pressed his nose into Mr. Benley's face.

"The Germans are always making announcements. I pay as little attention to them as they deserve."

The reporter wrote down this statement.

"The Germans probably declared war on somebody else!" Mrs. Benley dismissed the reporter with a wave of her hand. "Only there's hardly anybody left they're not fighting," she tittered. "Maybe the penguins at the South Pole." She continued to shuffle through her shopping bags.

"They've declared war on this ship," the reporter pointed at the *Lusitania.*

Her mother paled. "Winthrop, what's this man talking about?"

"Sir, if you don't mind, you'd better explain yourself!" her father growled, stepping protectively between Dora's mother and the reporter as a new-fangled folding camera flashed in his face.

The reporter pushed *The New York Times* right up to Mr. Benley's nose. Mr. Benley glanced at the headline and threw it down on the ground. "Rubbish!" he sputtered.

Dora picked the newspaper up. She quickly read the words herself under the riveting heading:

NOTICE!

TRAVELLERS intending to embark on the Atlantic voyage are reminded that a state of war exists between Germany and her allies and Great Britain and her allies; that the zone of war includes the waters adjacent to the British Isles; that, in accordance with formal notice given by the Imperial German Government, vessels flying the flag of Great Britain, or of any of her allies, are liable to destruction in those waters and that travellers sailing in the war zone on ships of Great Britain or her allies do so at their own risk.

IMPERIAL GERMAN EMBASSY
Washington, D.C., April 25, 1915.

Dora became uncomfortably aware that someone was staring at her. A stranger's eyes bored straight through her. Smoking a cigar, the man wore a nondescript dark suit. A wide-brimmed hat shaded his face. The white smoke curled upward in a lazy corkscrew. It vanished into the air several yards above his head.

CHAPTER 2

The reporter was trying to stir up trouble. "But sir," he pressed her father, "what if you were torpedoed?"

"I'm sailing to England to conclude a tire deal with Sir Adolphus Ware. Why would anyone want to torpedo me? That's Wilson's position, too. Not that you'll find me voting with the liberal Democrats," he chuckled. "As a Roosevelt man, I'd get kicked out of the Duquesne Club in Pittsburgh. Americans ought to have nothing to do with Europe and its silly wars. Imagine! Fighting because some maniac shot an Arch Duke, whatever his name was," he smiled. "What does one duke, more or less, matter?"

"Winthrop, what's all this talk of Arch Dukes? Did another one get assassinated?" Mrs. Benley asked.

"No, mother!" Dora wished the reporter would mind his own business.

Newsboys with stacks of papers cushioned under their arms had invaded the pier. They held the goods high over their heads. "Read all about it!" they shouted at the top of their lungs. "Germans threaten British and American shipping!"

"Maybe we should wait somewhere else," Dora whispered in her mother's ear.

"Do you want a paper, ma'm?" one of the boys shoved the paper at Mrs. Benley. She looked up at the gangly youth – Mrs. Benley was a short lady – in consternation.

Dora fetched a coin out of her purse. "Here," she handed it to him and hoped he would go away.

Photographers shuttled around with their camera equipment from passenger to passenger. Silver coins flashed as they exchanged hands.

"Dad," Dora tugged at his jacket sleeve, "could we get going?"

"Just a minute, Dora, I want to make sure this newspaperman understands my position."

A rotund gentleman in a sober business suit was shoving

his way through the crowd, holding up his hands. *"Silence!"* he crossed his brows like one who was used to being obeyed. Everyone turned toward him. He held a copy of *The New York Times* for Saturday, May 1st in one hand, the second most popular paper in the other. "I am Charles Sumner, spokesman for the Cunard Line. There is no danger. I repeat, THERE IS NO DANGER."

"How do *you* know?" hollered a gentleman in a straw hat.

"I make it my business," Charles Sumner asserted. "I would be fired if I didn't."

A murmur of assent swept through the crowd.

A lady in a bonnet burst into tears. "My name is Mabel Swift Moore. My husband died on the *Titanic,* and I'm to be married here in New York City tomorrow to this wonderful gentleman beside me," she hugged him. "But I'm seeing my sister off today. She's to cross to London in the *Lusitania.* I don't want to lose her, too," she wrung her gloved hands.

"Madam, this so-called German warning and threat is a hoax!" Mr. Sumner jabbed his finger at *The New York Times.*

The crowd on the pier gasped in amazement.

"When this so-called warning was read over the phone to me as a paid advertisement, I, Charles P. Sumner, agent of the Cunard Line, found it difficult to believe that it could be from the German Embassy," he announced as photographers snapped their pictures. He dropped the more minor paper and held his finger up in the air, wagging it at the crowd, while still clutching *The New York Times.*

"Hold it there!" one photographer flashed a picture with a burst of light.

"Only a few days ago anonymous poseurs demanded fifteen thousand dollars, or they would publish notices harmful to the business of this line. When someone else called wanting to place this warning I was still skeptical if it was real, even though it is a summary of the German Government's official proclamation of a war zone around the British Isles and seemed on the surface to come from the German ambassador."

"Why were you so skeptical?" a gentleman demanded.

"Countless efforts have been made to annoy the line and make its passengers uncomfortable. Several months ago an attempt was made to extort ten thousand dollars from the Cunard Line by threats of injury to its business. In this case an arrest was made. The prisoner was convicted and is now in Sing Sing."

An indignant murmur ran through the crowd.

"I try to spare our passengers such nasty details, but *The New York Times* and their yellow journalism has made this impossible today," Charles Sumner said with disgust.

A few more ladies took out their handkerchiefs and burst into tears.

"I would do anything to spare my passengers such a scene," Charles Sumner loaned his spotless white linen handkerchief to the nearest lady. "Since the beginning of this most recent war in Europe, everyone has lost every last semblance of civilization, let alone manners." He shuddered visibly at such an affront to his personal morality. "It's spreading to America like some sort of contagion."

Clucking and nods of the head followed this speech.

"This recent renewal of the threats was one reason why I found it difficult to believe that this advertisement has come from the German Embassy," Mr. Charles Sumner insisted.

"What happened exactly?" a well-dressed boy shouted at him from the front of the crowd.

Charles Sumner sighed, "I received a phone call yesterday afternoon. The caller, now being investigated by the police, tried to blackmail the Cunard Line for twenty thousand dollars. If we didn't hand over the money by early this morning, right about the time this paper was going to press, they would make sure no one sailed on any of our liners. That's what they said."

A groan sounded throughout the crowd.

"Do you have any other examples?" someone challenged him.

"I certainly do," Mr. Sumner continued. "The British

Ambassador, Sir Cecil Springs-Rice, called me yesterday. He said that on April 29 an anonymous caller had contacted the British embassy in Washington, D.C. He warned that a notice would appear in the newspapers today, Saturday. The anonymous tipster claimed that the same notice would appear in about forty other papers the same day and for the two ensuing Saturdays. The mystery person supposedly told Sir Cecil that he wanted the Allies to win, but he couldn't say who he was. That might cost him his job. He left a duplicate note signed 'Mr. 1776.'"

The crowd tittered nervously.

"Now that's the sort of prankster we have to deal with every day of the week," Mr. Sumner shook his head.

"Hooliganism!" Dora's father exclaimed to the newspaper reporter next to him who was now scribbling down everything that Mr. Sumner said.

"Did I hear you say *hooliganism,* sir?" Mr. Sumner addressed Dora's father.

"You certainly did!" Mr. Benley nodded.

"I couldn't have come up with a better term myself," Mr. Sumner praised his passenger.

Several passengers broke into loud applause. Mr. Benley nodded and smiled that so many people could be sensible like he was.

"Aren't you taking any precautions?" a female reporter, still scribbling, shouted from the back of the crowd.

"Precautions?" Mr. Sumner scoffed. "The *Lusitania* and her sister ship, the *Mauretania,* were built with extra steel in their hulls and their watertight compartments. This is no *Titanic."*

The young engineer smiled from ear to ear with satisfaction that his boss was agreeing with everything he'd said.

"Do you take other precautions?" somebody else shouted, cupping his hands. "Those Huns are awfully tricky."

"Indeed we do," Mr. Sumner boasted. "No passenger will be allowed to board the *Lusitania* today without identifying himself to the crew. I don't care *who* the passenger is."

"Even Vanderbilt?" a girl shouted. "He's sailing today."

"Yes, even Mr. Vanderbilt," Mr. Sumner assured them, "although we all know what Mr. Vanderbilt looks like."

The nervous crowd laughed. Vanderbilt was always in the newspapers.

Dora wondered about Mr. Sumner's assertions. Alfred Gwynne Vanderbilt, as everyone knew, was one of the wealthiest men in America. She doubted if anyone would question him no matter what he wanted to do.

"What other measures will you take?" a man challenged Mr. Sumner.

"Everyone must identify his baggage," Mr. Sumner announced.

The crowd whispered to each other. No one had ever heard of such precautions before.

"Every last piece of luggage?" an old woman shouted. No doubt she'd noticed that most of the first-class passengers had brought seemingly unlimited supplies of baggage and personal belongings.

"Yes," Mr. Sumner, in his immaculate business suit, assured them. "We won't allow one unidentified bag to remain aboard."

"What about your speed?" the newspaperman next to Dora's father called out his question.

"I'm glad you mentioned that, sir," Mr. Sumner nodded politely. "Our speed is our best protection. No ship doing more than fourteen knots has yet been torpedoed by the Germans. The *Lusitania* does twenty-five knots."

"What if the Huns took out one of the boiler rooms?" a man yelled.

"The *Lusitania* could still do twenty-one knots," he answered. "What's more," Mr. Sumner held up his hands, "once the *Lusitania* reaches the British Channel and the Irish Sea, the British Navy is responsible for escorting the Cunard liner into port. As we all know, the British Navy is second to none in the world, and she will take mighty good care of the

Lusitania and spoil her like a favorite daughter."

"What about the U-boats?" a lady called.

Mr. Sumner said, "I have no fear of them whatever."

He turned and strolled back down the dock accompanied by the uniformed attendant. They chatted and joked as if nothing whatsoever was the matter and this Saturday, May 1st, 1915 was just like any other day on the calendar.

"When will the *Lusitania* reach her destination?" one lady passenger started to run after the departing official.

Mr. Sumner stopped. He turned around. "On the sixth day," he promised.

"When on that day, sir?" she asked him to clarify himself.

"You'll have to ask Captain Turner for more details once you board. Now if you'll excuse me," he turned. "I'm a very, very busy man."

"That's good advice," Dora's father agreed. "Let's leave these silly nay-sayers behind." He offered his arm to Mrs. Benley. "I want to get to the state room so I can spread my papers out around me and start working on that tire sale to the British car magnate, Sir Adolphus Ware. After all, he is the real purpose behind our trip to England."

Mrs. Benley took her husband's arm with a smile. "I'd like to get my hair done before dinner."

Dora picked up several of her mother's shopping parcels, while still clutching the surprise birthday gift from Sir Adolphus. She turned down an offer of help from a boy who rushed up and asked to carry them for a tip. She didn't want to risk any extra people around to upset her mother. One never knew what they might not say, especially today when it seemed that nobody could say anything right. Maybe her father was correct. When they got on board, all this nonsense would vanish.

"Stop there!" A photographer leaped into their path. He flashed his camera in their faces. "Would you like to buy your photo?"

"Certainly not! Please step out of the way," her father

dismissed him.

"Maybe you'd like to buy it and have it sent to your relatives back home," the boy called after them. "I'm doing a booming business in the relative trade today. Everyone wants their mother, father, and sister to have a photo in case the worst should happen."

Dora shuddered at those parting words, . . . *in case the worst should happen.* She speeded up, hoping her mother hadn't heard. But as they approached the gangplank Dora caught sight of a stand displaying pictures of the ship with a placard advertising:

LAST VOYAGE OF THE LUSITANIA. BUY A PHOTO.

Just beyond the sign Dora spotted that same, odd-looking man with the extra wide-brimmed hat staring at her.

CHAPTER 3

An elegantly dressed man was unloading his luggage that several Negroes were carrying for him. He had one large steamer trunk, two dress suitcases, an umbrella bag, a silver-mounted rosewood cane, one silk American flag, one silk Irish flag, and a package.

The workers at the first class embarkation point seemed overwhelmed. They didn't ask him what was inside each bag as they marked them with his name. They simply threw them onto the conveyor belt.

The passenger opened his package. "It's my Old Rover brand tobacco. Wouldn't sail without it. Here, have a smoke!" he handed cigars around to the Cunard workers.

Dora watched his bags make their way down the conveyor belt. When they had almost reached the ship's hold, the conveyor belt shuddered to a stop. A hand reached out toward the umbrella bag and unzipped it. A wide-brimmed hat shadowed the intruder's face.

Wasn't he the same stranger who'd been eying her in the crowd?

"Dad," she alerted her father, "look!"

"What is it, Dora?"

"That man up there!" she craned her neck to see. "He's up to something."

"What man?"

"He was there a minute ago right next to the umbrella bag," she couldn't understand how he had vanished so quickly.

⇧ ⇧ ⇧

"I'd like you to meet Miss Rita Jolivet," her mother took the arm of a young lady standing next to Dora. "She's a famous actress from France, but she lives in America."

The svelte beauty with the perfect complexion giggled

in her fur coat and form-fitting skirt. Her dark brown hair was pinned back in curls on top of her head. Her pert little nose stuck out.

"She woke up this morning at eight A.M.," Mrs. Benley went on and on. "She said to herself, 'I have to return to France to see my brother off.' He's going to the Western Front, you know. Poor boy! Rita here wants to make him a nice French *cassoulet* for dinner before he goes." She dimpled as she smiled. "He won't be getting much of that in the army."

"Glad to meet you, young lady. Sorry to hear your brother's headed off to the Western Front. Seems a perfect waste of young manhood to me," Mr. Benley sighed.

"My brother is determined to fight the *Boche,*" Miss Jolivet gushed in her French accent.

"Tell him when he gets tired of trench warfare to come to Pittsburgh."

"Peetsbourg?" Rita Jolivet tried to pronounce it.

"Yes, it's in western Pennsylvania. He can work for me at the tire company," he handed Rita one of his business cards. "It'll make him forget about that nastiness on the other side of the Atlantic."

Dora clapped her hand over her mouth. The stranger in the wide-brimmed hat was chatting with one of the dock workers, lighting a cigar where the stevedores were loading baggage aboard the ship. Money was changing hands. Without thinking, she stepped behind her father.

A crowd burst on the scene. A mob of newspaper reporters was following a bald-headed, middle-aged man in a long wool coat. "Aren't you afraid German U-boats might sink the *Lusitania?*" one reporter pressed the important-looking man.

He smiled, "When you consider all the stars I have managed, mere submarines make me smile." He paused with his walking stick while they took photos.

"Who is he?" a woman in the crowd asked.

"That's Charles Frohman," another gossiped. "He's a theater manager and producer of more than five hundred plays in New York and London. I've seen most of them."

"Well, if you want to write to me, address the letter care of the German Submarine U-4," Frohman chatted with the reporters.

The reporters laughed.

Charles Frohman had no baggage besides what he was carrying, which looked like a briefcase. He continued on up the gangplank without stopping. No one bothered him. No one asked to examine his briefcase either.

Right behind him, surrounded by the same group of avid reporters, strolled a bizarre-looking, avant-garde fellow with curled locks down past his ears. He wore an eccentric, light-colored, wide-brimmed Stetson hat. His corduroy pants were unfashionably loose. His silk cravat was done up in a bow at his throat. He was swinging a leather satchel. "Speaking from a strictly personal point of view," he spoke to the reporters, "I would not mind if they did sink the ship. It might be a good thing. I would drown with her, and that's about the only way I could succeed in my ambition to get into the Hall of Fame. I'd be a regular hero and go right to the bottom."

Dora gasped. How could he say something so outrageous?

"Oh, don't mind him," an older man came up beside Dora, "that's Elbert Hubbard."

"Elbert Hubbard?" Dora thought she'd heard of him.

"The best-selling writer," a gossipy older lady said. "The country philosopher. He's got a wide following."

"Don't look so shocked, young lady," Elbert Hubbard waved a sheaf of papers at Dora. "You've got to read my latest essay. It's about how the Huns are reverting to cannibalism, as they did in the Thirty Years' War in the 1600's. I'm going to distribute it to the passengers on board the *Lusitania* when we get underway."

Everyone smelled men's cologne. A handsome, thirty-something man in a hat and shapely dark coat approached in his polished black leather shoes. He was carrying a paper that he waved carelessly about as if it meant nothing. His valet juggled two trunks.

"Mr. Vanderbilt," her father grabbed his hand and shook it firmly. "I'm Mr. Benley."

"Ah yes!" Alfred Gwynne Vanderbilt said with his million-dollar smile, seventy million to be exact. "We have an appointment."

"I'm anxious to talk about that fleet of vehicles," her father said.

"Yes, the ones I want to donate to the British Red Cross," said Mr. Vanderbilt.

"First they have to have tires!" her father joked. "Wouldn't be of much use without them."

Vanderbilt chortled. A pink carnation swayed in the button hole of his charcoal-gray, pinstripe suit.

"Etta May, this is Mr. Vanderbilt," her father introduced her mother.

Mrs. Benley burst out excitedly, "Is Mrs. Vanderbilt with you?" She stood on tiptoe craning her neck this way and that to catch a glimpse of the woman who was revered as the last word in fashion.

"No, my wife's staying at a New York hotel. She's waiting for me to get back from my trip to London. I'm sailing right back you know," he said breezily.

Vanderbilt's valet lifted his trunks onto the conveyor belt. No one bothered to search them. When they reached the hold of the ship, the same stranger inserted a gloved hand inside one of the trunks.

She dug her fingernails into the birthday package. She couldn't dare break into her father's and mother's conversation with Mr. Vanderbilt. Her mother's eyes were gleaming with satisfaction. Most ladies would consider it the peak of social accomplishment to rub elbows with Mr. Vanderbilt once in their lives – let alone share a sea voyage across the Atlantic.

"What's in your hand, Mr. Vanderbilt?" a reporter asked.

"Just a note from an admirer, I suppose." He acted as if he hadn't bothered to read it.

"May I see it?" the reporter asked.

"Of course!" Mr. Vanderbilt let it drop into his outstretched hand with a smile.

"The Lusitania *is doomed. Do not sail on her. Signed Morte."*

"Sir, this is a threat!" the reporter exclaimed.

Vanderbilt yawned, "I get all sorts of mail and telegrams."

"So you think this danger to the *Lusitania* is a hoax?"

"No human being called a man could possibly give an order to sink a passenger ship without at least giving the women and children a chance to escape," a middle-aged man in a dark suit appeared holding a bag.

"What's your name, sir?" the reporter asked.

"Charles Lauriat," he replied. "A Boston bookseller." They wrote his name in chalk on his bag and lifted it up onto the conveyor belt. He followed Mr. Vanderbilt aboard the ship.

Now it was the Benleys' turn. "Do you have to put that ugly chalk on my brand new luggage?" Mrs. Benley hissed, leaning close to the attendant. "After all, I bought it at Macy's."

The attendant smiled. "No, ma'm, we don't have to deface your fashionable bags if you object."

Dora thought that with all the exceptions being made anyone would be able to smuggle anything aboard – even an elephant!

At the top of the gangplank stood a portly, older, middle-aged man with whiskers and in uniform. He gazed off into the distance thinking his own thoughts. Every time a new family appeared, he suddenly awoke from his daze.

"Oh," he smiled down at Mrs. Benley, "welcome aboard the *Lusitania*, ma'm. I'm Captain Turner."

"I'm glad to finally be here," she stomped her feet as if for warmth, "after that long, long delay standing on the pier."

"At least on board we won't have to hear anymore of that nonsense about the Germans," Dora's father added.

The captain paused a fraction of a second too long.

"Oh yes! Good joke that! Best I've heard in weeks! Imagine a German U-boat sinking the *Lusitania!*" he forced a laugh.

CHAPTER 4

The Benleys were met by a uniformed attendant. He escorted them to their cabins amidships where sailing was most comfortable and the motion of the ship was felt the least.

"Would you like to take our elevator, madam?" The steward stopped in front of one of two black metal, box-like lifts for first class. The grille work was intricate, with gilded rosettes and medallions. The open, cage-like design reminded Dora of France. A uniformed elevator attendant opened the door. Two gentlemen stepped inside.

Her mother hesitated. "I'm rather claustrophobic. Silly of me, I know, but I can't help it."

The elevator door closed. It started up slowly toward the first-class decks. The steward led the family across the carpeted floor and up a flight of stairs. They climbed to the Boat Deck where Mr. Vanderbilt was being housed, the most fashionable address aboard. They strolled down the broad wooden promenade. Danger seemed very far away.

Bellhops brought their luggage. A stewardess helped Mrs. Benley unpack and settle into her stateroom. The assistant hung the ball gowns up and helped to choose what to wear to dinner.

Mr. Benley offered Dora his arm. He wanted her to come out on deck. She remembered that she had yet to slip her own bag into her cabin, located right next to her parents'. She hardly got a peek at it she was in such a hurry. It was a little smaller with a single berth. She dumped her satchel in the middle of the bed to unpack later.

Where should she hide the birthday parcel? On the underside where the wrapping paper gapped, it looked like something made of wood – perhaps a box? – with a strange engraving. One of her exams had been on the Near East. This looked like ancient Hittite script. How did that make any sense? She didn't have time to think about it now.

The package fit nicely behind the valance of the drapes that hung over the painted, artificial windows. It wasn't visible from the rest of the room. She'd have to remember to take it with her when they disembarked at Liverpool.

Dora rushed to rejoin her father at the rail. It was already past twelve noon – twenty minutes after twelve to be exact. "The *Lusitania*'s about ready to leave port. It's a grand sight!" her father declared with enthusiasm. The sun had finally come out from behind a cloud. The weather couldn't help but lift everyone's spirits.

The ship's orchestra played *Tipperary* from one end of the Boat Deck, not far from where the Benleys were standing. The Royal Gwent Male Voice Singers, who had been wearing identification badges when they boarded, struck up with *The Star-Spangled Banner* from the other end of the Boat Deck at the exact same moment.

"If we Americans were in charge, we wouldn't have any part of the war," Mr. Benley reflected as he listened to his national anthem. "Always remember that! Set a good example. Rise above such pettiness. And you know what the best way is?" he looked at her.

She was all attention.

"Mind your own business! That's what Germany, France, and Britain can't seem to do. If they would go into my line of work, making tires for automobiles, they'd be too busy making money to engage in medieval warfare."

That sounded so much like her robber baron father. The business of America was business, she supposed, as Massachusetts politician Calvin Coolidge had once told him. Mr. Benley thought it should be the business of the world as well. She'd grown up thinking that her father was always right.

The liner was now in the North River. The tugs eased her bow to starboard. The *Lusitania* was pointed downstream. As she speeded up, she passed the *Vaterland,* a German liner that had been trapped in New York at the beginning of the war and remained locked up at a berth in Hoboken, New Jersey.

Now she was in the Upper Bay, the Narrows. It was onward to the Ambrose Lightship. The ship paused, giving the *Lusitania*'s pilot a chance to climb overboard. The ship speeded up. She met the *R.M.S. Caronia,* an armed merchant cruiser patrolling America's neutral coastline on behalf of the British, watchful of German shipping. The ships tooted at each other. Dora watched as a cutter was dispatched from the *Caronia* toward the *Lusitania.*

"That's a mail tug. They're sending letters to go to Britain in our hold," her father explained.

The last thing she noticed before the *Lusitania* sailed out into the Atlantic was that someone from the deck of the *Caronia* had pointed a motion picture camera at the departing *Lusitania.* It reminded her of the photographers on the pier promising, *In case anything happens, we've got your picture!*

She gulped. She wondered if they had her picture, too. She looked around. At least the man in the wide-brimmed hat was nowhere to be seen.

CHAPTER 5

"You look concerned, miss," a voice said.

Dora gazed up into the eyes of a middle-aged stranger wearing that same wide-brimmed hat that she'd noticed on the dock this morning. He appeared to be the same height, dressed in the same nondescript coat, flapping in the breeze.

"Everyone can talk of nothing besides the Germans and their toy U-boats. Reminds me of something I used to float in the bathtub as a boy," he shook his head. "Personally I don't have time to worry about trifles."

Was he the man she'd seen going through trunks and bags at the pier, the one who'd talked nonstop to the dock workers? The one who'd been staring straight at her?

"Excuse me," she swallowed hard, "but do I know you?" She looked around for her father. He was chatting with another passenger several yards away.

"Frankly it's quite refreshing that you don't. I'm tired of my own celebrity. I plan to spend this voyage away from my fans revising my latest hit play, *Potash and Perlmutter in Society,*" he announced as if that would betray his identity. "I'm redoing my novelette, *The Lion and the Mouse.*"

He was a playwright. That would account for his eccentricity. Writers were always at least a little bit out of the ordinary.

"It's the latest in a long series of literary labors," he sighed. "The desperate longing to find a little time alone with my progeny is what has forced me out to sea at this grave impasse. I'm more scared of my own fans than a German torpedo."

In the distance New York was getting smaller. The city disappeared as if swallowed by the sea, like the Lost Continent of Atlantis.

"Dora!" came a familiar voice. Her mother was smiling out of her cabin door. Her hair was up in rollers. "Don't you think it's time to get dressed for dinner?"

"Ex-excuse me," Dora broke into the playwright's soliloquy, "I've – I've got to go."

"Maybe we could meet at dinner?" He gave her his card. It read *Charles Klein.*

"Perhaps," Dora smiled politely.

She departed before the eccentric playwright could follow her. She slammed the door. She leaned back against it, looked around, and thought, *This must be the wrong cabin. It doesn't resemble mine at all . . .*

When she'd left her bag in the middle of her bed, the cabin had looked immaculate. Every piece of furniture was now toppled onto the floor. Dresser drawers had been pulled all the way out. One was cracked. Sheets were yanked off the bed. The quilt was all the way across the room. The mattress had been overturned.

CHAPTER 6

D ora picked up her afternoon dress. Someone had ripped off the striped ruffles. She would never be able to wear the outfit again. She got down on her hands and knees and located her satchel under the overturned bed. Someone had thoroughly ransacked it.

She'd made the bed as if she were the stewardess. She smoothed down the sheets with the emblem of the Cunard line embossed on them – a lion gripping the Western Hemisphere between its paws. The British Empire encompassed one sixth of the globe. Today England didn't seem powerful enough to keep ne'er-do-wells out of her stateroom.

Knock! Knock! Knock!

She peered through the peephole. Her mother's face loomed large. Dora left the chain in place and opened the door a crack – just enough to talk.

"Dora, I forgot to give you the things I bought for you at Macy's!" her mother clapped her chubby little hands together. She picked up the bag at her feet, full of boxes. "I'd love to see if they fit you," she thrust it at her daughter.

Dora licked her lips. "Ah . . . I'm unpacking right now."

"I'll call the stewardess. She can help while we women have some fun."

Dora ran her hand through her hair. "Someone called on my cabin phone. I have to get back to him."

"You've met somebody on board *already*?" her mother reached through the door to pinch her daughter's cheek. "I've been worried about your wanting to go to college and all. We don't want to end up an old maid, now do we?"

"See you at dinner!" Dora opened the door enough to take the bag full of boxes. She quickly shut and locked it.

Her clothes were too wrinkled and dirty to wear to dinner without going to the laundry first. She'd have to use whatever her mother had bought at Macy's. Dora studied her profile in the mirror over her Louis XVI dresser. The hem of the white silk dress that her mother had purchased was banded with swan's-down. The skirt featured panniers bordered with white, mousseline de soie roses. The sleeves and the left side of the surplice bodice were edged in fur. The right side was trimmed with pink roses. She slipped the headband on. It featured a single silken rose.

Knock! Knock! Knock!

Dora stepped outside her cabin to greet her parents. Her mother was dressed elegantly in black net over royal blue Liberty satin with a small train. Her silk belt was decorated with cabochons.

Her father escorted each of the ladies on one arm until Charles Klein, in gentleman's evening attire, stepped out of his first-class cabin on the Boat Deck and offered his arm to Dora. A bugle sounded.

"It's the call to dinner," Mr. Klein informed Dora. "I incorporated it in one of my plays. It's so quaint, I think. Don't you? Nobody observes the old traditions anymore."

Mr. Klein seemed far too boring to be the man who'd eyed her on the Cunard dock.

As they entered the first class, two-tiered dining room with four Corinthian pillars in the center supporting an upper level, the ship's orchestra played *The Blue Danube*. Passengers were pirouetting around the dance floor. Ladies with feathers nodding on top of their coiffures, fitted bodices, and high collars brushed past escorted by gents in tails. Side buffet tables were set with hors d'oeuvres. Caviar on ice glistened next to silver plates of wafer-thin slivers of white toast and finely minced hard-boiled eggs garnished with parsley. Wedgwood china dishes of oysters were piled high on mounds of crushed ice. The ice scintillated under the illumination of the glass chandeliers.

A waiter in tails escorted Dora and Mr. Klein to one table and Mr. and Mrs. Benley to another. Each was covered by a starched white linen tablecloth and white napkins folded so that they stood up at attention like soldiers. The waiter pulled out a chair for Dora right next to a potted palm tree. Dora's and Mr. Klein's table was located directly underneath the cupola ceiling in the center of the room. It reminded her of pictures of the Sistine Chapel in Rome, though not painted by Michaelangelo. She could pick out pink-cheeked cherubs and blond cupids.

"That reminds me of another scene in my play . . . "

She picked up her menu and scanned through the list of hors d'oeuvres – Petit de foie gras, Norwegian anchovies, and Bordeaux sardines.

"We'll start with the anchovies," Charles Klein told the waiter.

Dora munched her anchovies as she studied the entrees: fillet of plaice in white wine, braised Cumberland ham with Madeira sauce, and roast gosling Normande. She smiled from time to time at Mr. Klein. At least she was practiced at this sort of thing. Her Latin professor was an old windbag, too. Seated in the first row in class, she only pretended to pay attention as he ranted and raved about Virgil's *Eclogues* being greater than the *Aeneid.*

She told the waiter. "I'll have the braised Cumberland ham with Madeira sauce."

"Me, too. Also make sure to bring us the best Austrian claret you have," Charles Klein insisted. "Two chilled glasses."

"You're the third American I've had to inform tonight that Austrian claret has been embargoed along with enemy mineral water," the British waiter smiled in a superior fashion.

"Ah yes! The war!" Charles Klein leaned his elbows on the table. "It all seems dreadfully far away tonight," he smiled into Dora's eyes. "Almost as if it has nothing whatever to do with us."

"Perhaps not, sir."

"Very well then, I'll have a bottle of champagne . . . Lanson's a good brand," Mr. Klein changed his mind.

"Very dear!" said the waiter. "Champagne's sky high since the war started."

"1906 is the best year I can think of," Mr. Klein gazed

into Dora's eyes.

"That will put you back fifteen shillings," the waiter wrote it down.

"Put it on my room tab," Mr. Klein said. "Do, sir, put it in dollars, not pounds sterling, if you don't mind. We Americans are neutral."

Dora caught sight of a man in the farthest, darkest corner of the room, seated by himself. He seemed to be using an extra large palm tree as cover – that in addition to his wide-brimmed hat, which men usually removed at dinner. He was eying her. Her heart skipped a beat.

"Well, would you?"

"Would I what?" she realized that Mr. Klein had spoken to her.

"Would you like to dance, of course?" Mr. Klein asked her for the second time.

Mr. Klein led her out onto the middle of the floor. "You know, the Kaiser supposedly won't let his soldiers do this dance. He doesn't think the Turkey Trot is dignified enough for Germans," he laughed. "I'm glad I'm an American."

"So am I!" her father led Dora's mother out onto the dance floor.

"You and Mr. Klein are getting along just fine!" Mrs. Benley whispered into Dora's ear and winked. "He's very famous and wealthy, you know."

Dora forced herself to smile.

The dance tune changed from the Turkey Trot to the One Step to the Bunny Hug and back to the Turkey Trot. Finally dinner was served. She spread her napkin over her lap and removed the dome from her dinner plate. A note stared up at her from the top of the Cumberland ham in a bold, dark hand addressed to:

Miss Dora Benley

She snatched it up and slipped it into her handbag.

Mr. Klein hadn't noticed a thing. He was still talking, presumably about his many plays. He apparently had written more than Shakespeare himself.

The stranger's place was taken by a new arrival. An older gentleman was being seated. He tipped the waiter with a hundred dollar bill that he pulled out of a big roll in his suit pocket, attracting attention from the British ladies seated nearby.

"Sir!" the waiter exclaimed at his generosity. "I mean, Mr. Kessler! I – I don't know what to say," he looked from the one hundred dollar bill back to the customer and back to the bill again.

"Take it!" Mr. Kessler pulled out a cigar and lighted it with another one hundred dollar bill. He stuck the flaming bill into his water glass and shoved it aside. "I never travel light when it comes to money. I plan to bribe the Kaiser if he comes calling in a submarine," he smiled.

Everyone in the restaurant erupted into laughter. One gentleman called, "Here, here!" A second proposed a toast.

The British lady at the table beside Dora, with her ostrich feather waving in her hat, hissed to her companion, "They say Mr. Kessler – he's the Champagne King, you know – brought two million in cash aboard. Isn't it amazing!" She took out her opera glasses and gazed in his direction as if she could detect thousand dollar bills hanging out of his pockets. "Americans care about *nothing* except money."

"They'd settle the war by paying off every side if they could," her friend nodded.

"I'll be right back," Dora assured Mr. Klein. "I – I can't wait to find out what happens to the heroine."

"But I was just telling you about the climax of *Potash and Perlmutter in Society.* I –"

Dora was disappointed to find a wash room attendant in the ladies' room, whom she had to tip. She retreated into a stall to read her note in complete privacy after she'd made sure to lock the door. The handwriting stood out in bold relief. The straight up and down letters, so dark that they leaped off the page, threatened her. She scanned the note several times before she could make any sense of it:

Miss Dora Benley –

Put what you stole on the table in the first-class lounge tonight at midnight. Don't wait for me. Our paths don't need to cross again.
Your Doom

CHAPTER 7

Who was "Doom"? A prankster like the one who sent a note to Alfred Gwynne Vanderbilt? Who had been eyeballing her on the pier? Who had ransacked her cabin? Was somebody in the dining salon laughing up his sleeve? She recalled the stranger in the big hat, whom she'd at first mistaken for Mr. Charles Klein. He'd been there in the dining room earlier. He'd disappeared. Had he penned the note?

Did the man erroneously assume that she had something that belonged to him? Was that why he'd followed her on board? He had directed her to leave "what you stole" in the first-class lounge at midnight. It was if she were the criminal – not him!

Dora unlatched the door and walked out. The uniformed attendant gave her a funny look. She reached into her purse and tipped the lady with a twenty dollar bill. The woman smiled. No doubt she would understand she was to keep her mouth shut in case Dora's mother clip-clopped her way in here.

"I thought you might have gotten lost," Charles Klein offered her his arm outside the restroom. "After all, it is a big ship. Your parents tell me this is your first sea voyage." He led her back into the two-tiered dining room with the marble columns. When they sat down, Mr. Klein signaled the waiter. "Warm this lady's food up."

"Yes sir!" the uniformed waiter said.

Mr. Klein handed the waiter a tip.

"Certainly, sir! I'll be right back!" the man's eyes shone as he tore across the dining room. It was all he could do not to knock the other waiters over.

"If you don't pay for something around this ship, you don't get it. I wouldn't have been able to get this table if I hadn't tipped the waiter when I boarded. There was a lot of jockeying for the best seats this afternoon, believe me!"

After interminable conversation about Mr. Klein's other plays – he had at least twenty of them! – dessert was served.

Dora had picked at her food for the entire meal. She couldn't help darting her gaze this way and that around the dining room to see where the stranger had gone.

Her mother leaned over Dora's shoulder. "I've got more unpacking to do to get ready for the rest of the voyage. You don't have to cut your evening short, though." She winked at Mr. Klein.

Dora lied. "I'd like to retire early, too."

Mr. Klein was obliged to escort her back to her room down the extra wide Boat Deck. She didn't want any awkwardness at the door, so she darted inside before her own mother had closed her door behind her.

She sat down on the bed and examined the note more closely. Should she confide in her father? No, that could be dangerous. The creepy character who lurked in the shadows might decide to come after him next. Should she confide in Charles Klein? No, she had just met him today. She hardly knew him. There was no help for it. She would have to go to the first class lounge tonight at midnight. She would leave a note for "Doom", explaining that he must have the wrong person.

She sat down at the desk provided by the Cunard line. She got out stationery and a pen. A ship was pictured coming right toward her prow first. It read: *On Board The Cunard RMS Lusitania.*

She wrote:

Dear Doom:

If there is any legitimacy to your claim that I have something that belongs to you, please meet me tomorrow at breakfast in the Verandah Cafe at the aft end of the Boat Deck. I will be with my parents. My father is a man of means. He will make good your claim by paying you properly by check. Then everything will be settled in a civilized fashion.

Otherwise I must ask you to mind your own business, keep your distance, and respect my privacy.

Sincerely yours,
Dora Benley

Dora listened as other passengers strolled up and down the Boat Deck. She waited until she hadn't heard anyone for about fifteen minutes. She looked for a wrap. Her clothes still lay tattered and dirty in a pile for the laundry tomorrow. She opened a few more of the boxes from Macy's.

One held a floor-length mink coat. It looked like something for an Arctic expedition. Dora put it carefully back into its box. Out of the next box she pulled a gray jacket with a gray fox collar, cuffs, and a band at the hem. Form-fitting and rather fancy, it fit perfectly once all the buttons were fastened. By now it would be nippy on deck out on the Atlantic far away from the coast. So she slipped her letter inside a pocket, glanced in the mirror over her dresser, and took off for the first-class lounge.

The deck seemed deserted at this hour. The moon overhead was obscured by clouds. Everything was shadowy. A large, dark shape loomed up overhead. It was only one of the lifeboats suspended overhead, just above the level of the Boat Deck.

She came upon a couple seated on deck chairs near the railing. The woman's ankle-length skirt was rustling. She moaned as the man kissed her. Dora slipped past the romancing couple.

It proved more difficult than she'd imagined to find the Georgian-styled, first-class lounge and music room. She'd never sailed on the *Lusitania* before. In fact, she'd never sailed on any ship except a boat on the Delaware River near Philadelphia. She'd been out on a yacht with a Haverfordian and his friends.

Soon she found herself in an eighteenth-century style room paneled with Italian walnut. The furniture looked dark and severe. Over the middle of the room hung a stained-glass, barrel-vaulted dome. An old man slouched in an over-stuffed chair in a corner, smoking like a fiend. His polished wooden humidor was laid out in front of him on a gilt table. A valet stood by to light cigar after cigar. This had to be the gentlemen's smoking lounge. She must be getting close.

Dora entered the ship's library, filled with books from floor to ceiling. Adam-style writing desks were interspersed among the other furniture. Where there were no bookshelves the walls were hung in gray and cream silk brocade. Fake painted windows were curtained with Rose du Barri silk taboret.

She proceeded to the Reading and Writing Room for first-class, female passengers. Here they could dash off notes on *Lusitania* stationery stamped with with the picture of liner and the familiar phrase: *On Board The Cunard RMS Lusitania.* Next came a barbershop complete with swivel chair and a big mirror.

She paused finally at the entrance to what must be the first-class lounge with veneered, inlaid mahogany paneling, satinwood furniture, and wood-burning fireplaces. She pondered where to leave the note. Endless double-stuffed settees and large easy chairs were arranged in groupings for cards or conversation while eating a light meal or having coffee. One chair still had a flyer from a previous voyage. It read, "Cunard Music Programme" with a picture of a stylized woman playing a harp. Towering over her rose a stained-glass ceiling depicting the twelve months of the year. The glass dome was illuminated at night by electric light bulbs. During the day it served as a skylight.

In the center of the room sat a grand piano. She lifted up the keyboard cover to conceal the note. Dora hesitated. She opened the keyboard again and moved the note to the top of the bench. On the outside it read, "To Doom." She hoped it would clear up this nonsense for good!

When she looked up to start back across the room, a tall, thin man with big shoulders blocked the doorway. He wore the identical wide brimmed hat. He'd chosen a dark spot with plenty of shadows. She never could get a good look at his face.

He stared back at her. He lit a cigar as if he had all the

time in the world. He blew out the match and threw it down on the wooden floor.

"Hello!" she ventured. "My name is Dora Benley."

"I know," came a whispery, deeply accented voice.

It took her aback. She'd assumed that the stranger was an American or British citizen. "I . . . ah . . . left you a note. It's over there on the piano bench . . . " she pointed behind her, careful not to take her eyes off him.

"Yes, I know. I was watching you . . . " came the same raspy voice.

It occurred to her that he could be a passenger from steerage, or third class. Many immigrants traveled to the United States that way. Then again the *Lusitania* was sailing to Britain, not America. It didn't make any sense.

Dora wet her lips. "Well, I hope my note explains everything. You've got the wrong person," she tried to sound casual. "So, nice meeting you! Have a pleasant voyage." She attempted to walk past him out of the room.

He pulled out a handgun. "Give me your purse."

"My *what?*" she gulped.

"Your purse."

So this had been it all along! He'd decided on the dock that she resembled a likely prospect, and he'd followed her on board. He'd searched her cabin looking for something to steal. His note had been a way to dupe her and lure her to meet him in the first-class lounge at midnight. Nobody else would be around. He could rob her. She was furious at herself for falling for it. She took one hundred dollars in cash out of her wallet. She thrust it at him.

"Give me that handbag," he snatched it, not looking at the money. He tossed everything out, from her comb to her hand mirror to her gloves to a few pens from class. There was the note that one of her girlfriends had slipped her in Latin class two days ago. It was about meeting her for tea in Denbigh Hall that afternoon.

The man turned the handbag upside down and emptied it out to the last scrap of paper. Her passport landed with a bounce on the carpeted floor. Pulling a knife out of his side pocket, he hacked away at the silk lining. He hurled the handbag over his shoulder. "What have you done with it?" he eyed her.

"I – I don't know what you're talking about."

"You must know!" he grabbed her jacket. He pulled it with such force that the buttons popped off. She slipped out of it and fled out onto the deck, leaving him holding it.

CHAPTER 8

"Come back!" the stranger fired his gun at her.

Dora slipped and fell. One of her high-heel shoes flew off. She kicked the other one off and raced away in her stocking feet. She skidded around the corner, almost colliding with a lifeboat. She ran to the foot of a narrow, precipitous stairway leading up to the bridge. A hand caught her from behind by the back of the neck. She wriggled to get loose. He ripped away the white swansdown on the collar of her gown. The bodice sagged down over her camisole.

She fled down the deck toward the lights ahead. Passengers milled about as fireworks ascended into the sky from one of the suites on the Boat Deck. She slammed into someone she couldn't see until the last moment as another sparkler exploded.

A stout, not very tall man, about thirty-eight or so, took the impact, still wearing his top hat. His finely tailored coat gapped open to reveal a V-neck vest and silk cravat over a starched white shirt with a high collar. His striped dark pants looked immaculately tailored from the most expensive materials. He grabbed her by the shoulders. She could make out the carnation in his vest pocket, though by now it was slightly wilted.

"Hey, Alfred! Did you catch a mermaid from the deep?" one of his friends wielded a Cuban cigar in one hand and a glass of brandy in the other.

Men gathered in a circle around Dora. They looked middle-aged and very prosperous, some about her father's age, others a little younger. She was engulfed in a cloud of smoke. One man gave a wolf whistle as he regarded Dora's state of half-dress. Her camisole was obvious in the light pouring out from the cabin. The door was propped open.

"I don't think Margaret will appreciate this sort of gossip. No sooner is her back turned than you are on wife number three, Alfred," one guest chuckled.

"What's your name?" asked the well-dressed man in the top hat and carnation, who seemed to be the center of attention.

"Dora Benley," she crossed her arms over her chest.

"Ah yes! I know your father. He and I were chatting at dinner about a tire deal. Alfred Vanderbilt at your service. I'm supposed to meet Winthrop Benley tomorrow at breakfast in the cafe to continue discussing the automobiles I'm donating to the British Red Cross."

Now Dora remembered. She'd glimpsed Alfred Gwynne Vanderbilt on the Cunard Pier this morning as he'd boarded the *Lusitania*. She hadn't been able to concentrate on one of the wealthiest men in America, who was always the subject of newspaper high society gossip. She'd been too preoccupied watching the mysterious stranger.

"A man I've never seen before was chasing me, Mr. Vanderbilt," Dora offered her excuses.

A gentleman whistled, "I'd chase you, too, if I was half the age I am – and my wife wasn't with me!"

The older men laughed so hard at that remark they almost cried. One got out an embroidered linen handkerchief and wiped his eyes.

"No, no, it wasn't that," Dora blushed. They thought she was running from a suitor. "This man's mad."

The iconoclastic Mr. Elbert Hubbard, the fifty-nine year old best-selling writer, approached her. He still wore his famous Stetson hat with the extra long coat, baggy corduroys, and a floppy, artistic style silk cravat done up in a bow. "Maybe it was one of the Kaiser's agents," Mr. Hubbard reached into his briefcase and brought out a copy of one of his famous essays entitled "Who Lifted The Lid Off Hell". He shoved the manuscript at Dora. "Here, read it. The Kaiser is crazy. He would do anything."

She tried to force a smile as she shoved her ripped dress up over her shoulder. "No, I don't think the man was German. He didn't sound like it."

"I hear secret German agents are stowaways aboard the

Lusitania," Elbert Hubbard lighted a cigar.

"Well, why don't you join the party?" Mr. Vanderbilt was leading her by the elbow into his suite, hopping with theater people and high society ladies and gents.

Dora stuttered, "I . . . ah . . . "

Her mother had boasted that the *Lusitania* had suites of all styles from English and Colonial, to Georgian, to William and Mary, to Empire. Vanderbilt's was the most elaborate. Vanderbilt escorted her into his private dining room. It featured moldings and a burnished gold-paneled ceiling. He led her up to the fleur-de-pêche marble fireplace. It looked like Marie Antoinette's Petit Trianon at Versailles. It was hardly the place to show up in her stocking feet!

"What's your name, dear?" Elbert Hubbard whispered into her ear.

"Dora Benley," she hissed.

"Dora Benley here has run into a German spy aboard the *Lusitania!"* Mr. Hubbard announced to everyone in a booming voice that was accustomed to making speeches.

Dora would have liked nothing better than to sink through the floor and disappear into the engine room into a big pile of bituminous coal.

"What happened?" twenty-nine-year-old Lesley Mason rested a gloved hand on her arm. She was advertising her wedding ring on the top side of her glove.

"Someone stole my purse," Dora gulped.

"No doubt it was the Kaiser himself!" Hubbard insisted. "He's aboard the ship. He wants to claim credit for sinking the *Lusitania* single-handedly."

Lesley Mason giggled and shared the joke with her newlywed husband, Stewart. "Wait until our friends back home in Boston hear about the wild honeymoon we're having!" Lesley smiled at Dora.

"Did he try to steal your clothes, too?" Lady Margaret Mackworth, the militant British suffragette, looked her up and down in disapproval. She wore no makeup, and she looked like the thirty-two-year-old prude that she was.

Dora felt a flush rising up her neck to her face, making her cheeks burn. "The man thought I was concealing something on my person. I don't know what it was," she admitted frankly.

"Whatever happened, it's nothing that a glass of wine won't cure," George Kessler, the "Champagne King", showed up at her side. He gave her a bear hug and poured her a glass of bubbly. "Pure Austrian spirits here," he stage whispered into her ear. "I smuggled it aboard right under the watchful eye of our oblivious Captain Turner. Don't arrest me for trading with the enemy! America's still officially neutral, you know," he winked at Dora.

"My dear, what happened to you!" The young French-American actress that Dora's family had met on the pier made her way over to where Dora was covering herself with her arms and Hubbard's essay. The actress looked especially lovely in her evening gown of rose de Chine Liberty silk with guipure. She waved an ostrich fan as she looked Dora up and down.

Dora tried to blend into the background, cowering next to the wall.

"Rita, you wouldn't believe it," Elbert Hubbard slipped his arms around both her shoulders and Dora's, "this young miss was assaulted by the Kaiser in person."

"The Kaiser!" Rita Jolivet fanned herself. "Is he on board?" She glanced from side to side in alarm.

"He's hiding in the bowels of the ship with his torpedo. He smuggled it on board. He gets to brag he torpedoed the ship."

Several of the women around Elbert giggled.

Frohman, the theater producer, suggested, "We'll do a play about the Kaiser on the *Lusitania* chasing young misses about. It ought to be a smash on Broadway, written by Charles Klein and produced by me."

"I'll certainly promote the book if somebody writes it," Lauriat, the Boston bookseller, seconded Frohman. "We can do a signing at the theater."

Dora tried to make herself heard, "Really, it didn't sound like German. He had a different accent, one I've never heard before."

No one would listen. They kept on joking about the Germans.

"Whether you were assaulted by the Kaiser or not, we're going to have to get you some new clothes," Rita said very low. "Come with me."

No sooner had they started down the Boat Deck than a middle-aged gent walked right out of the shadows as if heading for the party. "Miss Dora!" he exclaimed.

"Mr. Klein!" She couldn't seem to shake the forty-eight year old swain no matter what.

Mr. Charles Klein insisted on accompanying both ladies back to Dora's cabin. Her father's head emerged. "I didn't think it was time for morning coffee yet?" he said.

"Miss Benley has been attacked by some unruly lout."

"She has, has she?" her father looked Dora up and down. "Well, I'll take care of that." He grabbed her wrist, yanked her into his cabin, and slammed the door.

Her mother switched on the overhead light. She sat there in the bed with bleary eyes, squinting, her hair up in rollers. She held the bed covers up to her chin. "Dora, what on earth are you doing up at this hour? My goodness, Winthrop!" her mother finally rubbed her eyes enough to take in her daughter's state of undress. "What's she doing wandering around the ship like that!"

"I'm going to escort her back to her room," Winthrop put on his night robe and waited until the guests had disappeared outside.

"Dad, a stranger stole my purse. He attacked me in the lounge and thought I was concealing something belonging to him. I —"

"You should know better than to gallivant around the ship at night by yourself. Don't tempt the young men, and you won't get into trouble."

After her father escorted her to her cabin, Dora took off her stockings and got into bed. She pulled the quilt up to her chin and shut her eyes. Lurid images of the strange, tall, thin man in the big hat exploded in her mind. He was knocking at her door, listening outside her porthole, and rifling through her luggage. Now he was slashing at her purse with a knife. Her eyes popped open. Dora found herself staring at the ceiling unable to sleep. Her heart thudded against her ribcage. She turned over and rearranged the covers.

This was the after all, the *Lusitania.* There were lots of people on board who would protect her. She could call Charles Klein on the telephone. Not that she wanted him here, but he was better than the stalker. She remembered the tune that the orchestra had been playing at dinner before the Bunny Hug dancing started – *The Blue Danube*. She hummed its peaceful melody. Soon she was fast asleep.

CHAPTER 9

Knock! Knock! Knock!

Dora rubbed her eyes as she sat up. A piercing ray of sunshine forced its way through the slit in the drapes covering her porthole.

"Dora, it's breakfast time. We have a reservation at the Verandah Cafe."her mother chirped. "You're missing the beautiful day on deck. The crew says it's rarely this calm and smooth out on the North Atlantic. And sunny, too!"

"I'll be along in a minute," Dora opened her porthole to talk to her parents. "I have to get dressed." Dora struggled into a velvet and taffeta gown with a sash around the waist ending in a bow and a V-collar, another offering from a Macy's box. There was an under tunic with a high neckline. She hurriedly combed her hair. She tucked it underneath a black hat, a chapeau of plush sporting a feather for decoration.

Locking the door as she slipped out, she hurried in the direction of the Verandah Cafe in the aft section of the Boat Deck. She was lucky to still have her key. It had been in her pocket last night.

Uniformed waiters were serving omelettes made to order at her parents' white linen-covered table next to a Grecian style column on the deck side of the restaurant. It had the ambiance of a sidewalk cafe in Paris. Her father was enjoying his favorite cup of hot cocoa with whipped cream. Her mother sipped tea with cream and sugar. Charles Klein had pulled a chair up to the little table. Dora brushed past a potted palm and ducked underneath hanging vines to reach the chair they had saved for her.

"Porpoise to starboard!" one of the crew members called.

Her father and Mr. Klein shot up from their seats. "I have one of those new folding cameras," Mr. Klein boasted. "I'd like to get a photo. Who knows when one might not show up in a play?"

Everybody laughed.

Her father went to the rail with Mr. Klein. Vanderbilt joined them for his chat about cars. Her mother excused herself to find the ladies' room. She meandered off, stopping to chat with this well-dressed lady and that.

Dora sat alone at the table. Suddenly she noticed a thirtyish-looking man in a suit coming past her as if searching for something he'd lost. "Can I help you?" Dora asked.

He cleared his throat and looked from side to side, afraid that someone might overhear. He cautiously approached her table and said in a low, strained voice, "Have you heard that there are dangerous munitions aboard?"

"Guns?"

"Yes, guns, bombs, whatever!" he hissed as a portly matron passed him with two pink-ribboned girls in tow.

"Where did you hear all this?" Dora rose, pulled up a wicker chair, and told him to have a seat. "What's your name?" she asked.

"Michael Bidley Byrne."

Her father and Mr. Klein were coming back from the rail with the folding camera, waving to Vanderbilt as he headed in the other direction. They were chatting and laughing.

"Father, this man appears to have heard something about guns and munitions aboard the *Lusitania.*"

"Bully as TR would say! Nothing I'd rather chat about, except cars," her father took his seat. "Wonderful thing, a gun. Nothing better to make you relax than your own rifle and a nice cheroot." He took out a cigar from his humidor in his pocket and lighted it. He took a long draw and blew out the smoke

"Sir, would you explain yourself?" Mr. Klein challenged the gentleman. "We don't want to upset the ladies."

Mr. Byrne's hazel eyes flashed. "I'm on a business trip to London for J.P. Morgan."

Dora ordered Mr. Byrne a cup of coffee from a nearby waiter. She mixed sugar and cream and stirred it with a silver teaspoon. She shoved it in front of him and then looked around to make sure that her mother wasn't approaching.

"Look at the bright sunshine," her father raised his right hand to the sky. "There's hardly a cloud. A calm ocean. Even porpoises. Delightfully warm. Go play a game of deck quoits or shuffleboard. It will make a new man of you."

Mr. Benley flicked off some ashes in a tray provided by a waiter.

Mr. Byrne shook his head and sighed, brushing his dark brown hair out of his eyes.

"You don't have the *mal de mere,* do you?" Mr. Klein asked him. "If so, I've got just the thing."

Mr. Byrne stared at Mr. Klein with frightened eyes. "I got up at seven A.M. this morning to check for guns. I heard they were mounted on the ship after we left the harbor. I looked from bow to stern and on every deck above the water line. Then I went lower down near the engine room. I saw *him.*"

"Passengers aren't allowed in the hold," her father reminded him. "There's cargo space near the bow on the Orlop and Lower Decks. That's accessible only to the crew."

At the most inopportune moment Dora's mother fluttered back to the table and took her seat. "My goodness, Winthrop, what's the matter!" she gaped at the gentleman.

"This passenger's homesick if you ask me, Etta May. Talks about leaving New York behind."

"I would never have set foot on the *Lusitania* if I had known," Mr. Byrne looked off into space.

"If he had known what, Winthrop?" Mrs. Benley sat forward in her chair.

"Mother, maybe we should take a walk on deck," Dora pulled at her mother's elbow.

Mr. Benley signaled to Captain Turner, who happened to be passing by. "Captain Turner," Mr. Benley spoke. "You signed the manifest before we left port, did you not?"

"I certainly did!" Captain Turner answered. "The day before we sailed."

"How would you describe the cargo?"

"General cargo, of course. Same as always."

"Anything unusual?" Mr. Benley pressed.

"No, not one bit!" the captain replied in a belligerent fashion. He wouldn't tolerate any contradictions.

"Nothing at all that could be considered out of the ordinary?" Mr. Klein spoke up.

The captain barked, "Sir! You can trust my word."

"I didn't mean you weren't trustworthy," Mr. Klein apologized. "There's been a lot of confusion lately. Something could have slipped your mind."

"Nothing slips my mind, sir!" the captain glared at him.

"Everything you're carrying is what you carried on your last voyage?" Mr. Klein put it a different way.

"The single exception is the oil paintings belonging to Sir Hugh Lane. He's transporting them to Dublin. We don't usually sail with four million dollars worth of Rembrandts, Monets, and Rubens encased in lead in the ship's hold," the captain snorted as if he resented revealing this much. "I shouldn't mention them, but I'll do anything to assure the comfort of my first-class passengers."

"Thank you," said Mr. Klein.

The captain excused himself and disappeared around the corner very abruptly.

"See?" Mr. Klein said to Mr. Byrne. "Nothing to worry about."

"Something down there in the hold smelled rancid, if you ask me. Like food gone bad," Michael Byrne stared across the table.

Mrs. Benley's eyes got bigger and rounder.

"Sir, the pantry's up here, not in the hold!" Mr. Benley reminded him. "What would anyone keep rancid food down there? They'd throw it overboard."

"That man was standing there playing with fuses. One of them almost went off," Michael Byrne looked fixated on the empty space in front of his eyes.

"Sir, let me suggest you join the potato sack race that's about to start on the deck right over there," her father forced Mr. Byrne from his seat.

"What did this man with the fuses look like?" Dora asked.

"He had a big hat, sort of like his!" Mr. Byrne pointed at Mr. Klein. "He talked strange, too. An accent I've never heard before. He was dark. Not like you or me."

Mr. Benley was a powerful man of fifty with big shoulders. He practically dragged the distracted Michael Byrne over to the deck games, with Mr. Klein following along behind in case his assistance should be required.

"Do you think there's any real danger?" her mother asked her daughter.

Dora shook her head "no" while feeling a chill. She'd have to tell her mother "no" even if the Kaiser himself were discovered aboard. She couldn't help but think that the man with the "fuses" was the one she'd run into last night.

Her father and Mr. Klein soon returned to the table. Mr. Benley at once started talking to Mr. Klein about the unlimited future of automobiles. He envisioned a time when everyone in the world would drive one. That day would be a long time coming –- true. But it ensured the prosperity of his tire business.

Mrs. Benley was so accustomed to hearing business "chat" that she at once lost her harried look. Pouring herself another cup of tea, she smiled at everyone passing by. She raised her hand to wave at a new friend. An occasional matron would stop by her table. This sort of thing could go on for hours.

While her mother chit-chatted and her father swore to Mr. Klein that he didn't agree with Henry Ford that all cars had to be black, Dora hurried down the Boat Deck where her parents and Mr. Klein could no longer see her. Despite being extra wide, it was crowded because of the good weather. She picked her way around the passengers' lounge chairs. Socialites resting on overstuffed pillows sipped hot coffee brought to them by waiters while their legs were covered by wool blankets.

She heard shouts and easily found the potato sack race where her father and Mr. Klein had left the frantic passenger.

Looking behind to make sure no one was following, she edged her way toward Michael Byrne. He was standing in line, but he looked as if he were unaware of anything going on around him, absorbed in his own worries. He kept darting his gaze this way and that.

Dora wanted to ask more about the fuses. She was prevented by a large group of parents with children in tow hurrying past. By the time they passed, Mr. Byrne seemed to have disappeared, too. She looked around, wondering. Then she looked down. He lay on the deck at her feet. "Mr. Byrne!" she knelt next to him. "What happened?"

"Please, miss, help me up!"

She started to raise him. Her hand encountered something wet and sticky in the middle of his back. It was red.

"Don't scream!" he begged her. "It's worth your life."

She wrapped her arms around his waist. "Where's your cabin?" She pushed along the thirty-something Mr. Byrne, supporting his weight as well.

"Cabin 101 on the Boat Deck."

"I need your key."

"It's in my pocket," he whispered, wincing with pain.

She reached into his pocket, unlatched the door, and shoved him inside.

He collapsed onto the floor in front of her, unable to sustain his own weight. She rushed over, again helped him to his feet, and guided him over to the bed where he fell on his face.

A knife was stuck in his back!

CHAPTER 10

"Call the cabin steward," Mr. Byrne pleaded. "Tell him I fell on my steak knife by accident. We don't want a scandal that would attract more attention."

She picked up the room phone and called the steward. "Send the ship's doctor and fresh linens at once to Mr. Byrne's cabin 101 on the Boat Deck. There's been an accident," Dora tried to act calm.

"What's the nature of the accident?" the steward pressed matter-of-factly.

"Mr. Byrne fell on his steak knife," she swallowed hard. "I do wish you would hurry."

"Do you need anything else?" the steward asked.

"Yes, I need a new blouse. I'm Miss Dora Benley. My cabin is 110 on the Boat Deck. I'm assisting Mr. Byrne."

"We'll be there right away."

"Will you also bring me my passport? I lost it last night in the passenger's lounge. You can send somebody else for that."

Click.

"Thank you!" Mr. Byrne groaned, reaching out his hand to her, which she took "Thank you for endangering yourself for me. That man would've let me die lying out there on the deck. I saw his eyes."

"You mean . . . the one with the fuses . . . he threw a knife at you?" She stood at his wash basin set in a mahogany stand.

He nodded. "So fast that I don't think anyone else saw him. I didn't dare scream."

"Why did he attack you?" she fetched him a glass of water.

"I saw him with the fuses, that's why."

Knock! Knock! Knock!

She threw the door open. Several stewards poured in escorting the ship's doctor, who set to work on Mr. Byrne. A stewardess handed Dora a blouse. It might be one of the dirty ones, but it was better than nothing. A steward also handed over her passport. Dora stepped into the bathroom to change her clothes.

She quickly left Mr. Byrne's cabin and hurried down the deck. Her parents were still seated in wicker chairs at the Verandah Cafe. They were at a different table, right beneath a hanging vine. A waiter was serving a selection of cold meats with salad. Her father was pouring himself a glass of the American beer that had been substituted for embargoed German beer.

Dora threw herself down in a chair at the table. "You've got to do something," she appealed to her father and Mr. Klein, not caring that her mother was seated at the same table, "there's a crazy man loose aboard this ship. He was after me last night. Today he knifed another passenger," she feared the matter had gone way beyond what she could handle herself.

Her mother paused stirring her tea with her special silver teaspoon. Her eyes looked as big as the white golf balls at her father's country club.

Dora had just violated the First Commandment of the Benley household: Thou Shalt Not Upset Thy Mother. Her father had drilled it into her head from the time she was a toddler. What was she to do? If someone didn't stop the maniac soon, they might all be dead.

"Dora, really!" her father looked her up and down.

Mr. Klein was speechless.

"No need to worry anymore, miss!" Captain Turner appeared right behind Dora's chair and put a big, brawny hand on her shoulder.

"What happened, Captain?" Mr. Klein asked.

"Was someone murdered aboard this ship?" her mother shrieked.

"Madam, take it from me," the Captain addressed Mrs Benley, "no one has ever been murdered aboard the *Lusitania*. Since the ship was launched in 1907, we have never lost a passenger."

Her mother smiled, nodding and reassured.

"We have arrested three stowaways hiding in the steward's pantry near the Grand Entrance on the Shelter Deck," the Captain leaned in close to the table and whispered low. "I don't like to talk about such matters. It creates a sense of fright among the passengers, especially the lady passengers," he smiled at Mrs. Benley, "but since your daughter insists, I felt I must tell you."

"Are you satisfied, Dora?" her father looked at her severely.

"*Three?* I encountered only one of them," Dora burst out.

"You won't be encountering anymore," Captain Turner promised. "I give you my word," he thrust out his burly chest. Despite his uniform his build made him resemble a Viking, especially with his fair complexion and beard.

"How did you find out about the stowaways?" Mrs. Benley got out her fan, which she often did when agitated.

"Just a routine check," Captain Turner assured her. "We always go through that exercise on the first day of a voyage."

Mrs. Benley nodded happily. "Just as long as everything's like it always is."

"A voyage aboard the *Lusitania* should be one of life's finest experiences with not a worry, especially for our first-class passengers," the Captain exclaimed. "No more German spies or saboteurs need disturb your sleep. The captured Germans are locked up in the ship's brig below the waterline. They will be kept there until our arrival in Liverpool in five days' time. They will be handed over to the Admiralty. In effect, they are prisoners of war."

Mr. Klein shuddered, "How distasteful to us neutrals!"

"Wait a minute . . . " Dora thought hard. "The man who was after me wasn't German. He didn't speak a word of that language. He –"

"Miss Benley," the Captain stopped her, "You *will* start feeling more secure now that you are out of danger. I would appreciate it very much," he looked askance at a table of ladies, craning their necks towards them, trying to overhear their conversation, eying them suspiciously from behind their fans, "if you didn't spread unnecessary panic among the other passengers. Thank you." The Captain nodded and strode off.

Dora knew when she'd been told politely to "shut up". She ate in silence, despite Mr. Klein's efforts at chit-chat.

"Really we girls ought to stick together," the French American actress gushed in her fancy new outfit with an ostrich feather hat. She looked cozy in her pink foulard dress with polka dots and pleated cuffs at her elbows as Rita took a seat beside Dora. "You ought to room with me dorm style in my obscure, depressing little cabin, one of the worst in first-class. Oh well! What do I expect when I book at the last minute after my brother cables me from Paris? We could occupy ourselves with gossip until midnight and fall asleep exhausted."

Dora had eyes only for Mr. Byrne. Dressed in a new suit and a bit stiff, he sat down to luncheon only a few tables away. They exchanged glances.

Rita got the message and chatted with Mrs. Benley instead. Her father was trading hunting yarns with another passenger. Mr. Klein listened appreciatively.

Dora moved over to Mr. Byrne's table, leaving untouched her plate of cold meats and salad. "Mr. Byrne," she whispered low, "No one at my table will believe you were attacked."

"Fools!" he rubbed his back, wincing with pain. "That man threw a knife at my back and left me for dead all right. For all he knows I *am* dead."

"A man ransacked my cabin yesterday. He attacked me last night." She knew instinctively Michael Byrne would believe her.

"What did you do?" He turned his haunted gaze on her.

"He wants something he thinks I have," she unfolded and refolded the linen napkin standing upright in front of her. "He said to meet him in the first class lounge. I left a note for him on the piano bench, but as I was leaving I ran into him. He turned a gun on me."

Mr. Byrne looked through her and beyond as if at an

unspeakable horror. "That man is evil. I could see it in his eyes the minute I caught him with the fuses. No one who wasn't the devil could be playing with fire like that."

"He told me to give him my purse," she confessed. "I handed my money over. He grabbed for the bag as if money weren't of any interest to him. He isn't just a common thief."

"I wish he were."

Dora nodded. She looked at Mr. Byrne in silence, sensing a kindred spirit. "He hacked my purse to pieces. He acted like he expected to find something inside it."

"He's a madman," Michael Byrne concluded.

"He pulled my jacket off my back before I got away."

"Why us?" Mr. Byrne asked the obvious question.

Dora leaped six inches when she felt Captain Turner's big hand again land on her shoulder. "I heard about your unfortunate accident with the steak knife," Captain Turner spoke in a low register. "Let's keep it to ourselves, shall we? I have about five visits an hour from hysterical ladies. They want me to assure them there is no danger on this voyage. I tell them there isn't. Help me keep it that way."

"But –" Dora turned toward the captain.

"Naturally we could all have nasty accidents with steak knives," the Captain flashed a forced smile. "We want the ladies to think God himself is watching over them on the *Lusitania*. It's always been that way. If I can help it, it always shall be that way."

Mr. Byrne nodded. His face went blank.

"I'm glad we understand each other," Captain Turner lumbered away heavily across the deck, mumbling something to himself that no one else could hear.

"Dora," Mr. Klein showed up next, "shall I escort you back to your cabin?" he shot Mr. Byrne a look as if he thought the other fellow might be trouble.

Mr. Byrne eyed Dora meaningfully. The two of them spoke a secret language that no one else could understand.

CHAPTER 11

When Dora got back to her cabin she decided to clean up her room. She threw the wardrobe door open. The stranger stepped out, pointing a gun at her. "Tell me where you hid it," he warned in his thick, foreign accent. He backed her up against the wall. He frisked her, rubbing his hands up and down her sides and over her bosom.

"I don't have anything of yours. What do you think I stole?" She was beside herself.

"Shut up, woman! What you stole is unspeakable. I won't profane it with words."

He stuffed a cloth inside her mouth. He roped her wrists in front of her and tied her ankles together. He left her lying on top of her bed as he peered out her porthole. She was still lying there when it came time to dress for dinner.

Knock! Knock! Knock!

"Dora, are you ready?" came her mother's voice.

She squirmed her way over to the edge of the bed, ready to kick the bedpost to make noise. The assailant threw himself on top of her and held her down.

"Dora, are you with Rita Jolivet?" her mother asked.

"I left Dora in front of her cabin after lunch," came Mr. Klein's voice. "I didn't see Rita anywhere around."

Dora thought, *That's it! Remember that I must be in here. I can't be anywhere else. Go get a key. Break in!*

Her father said, "Dora was eating with that other gentleman this afternoon – what's his name? Perhaps she's with him in the dining room."

Dora's stomach sank to her feet. Her parents and Mr. Klein strolled off down the deck chatting.

The stranger dragged her off the bed. He threw a blanket around her and opened the door. Few passengers were milling about at the height of the dinner hour. He pulled her down the deck after him, despite her efforts to kick herself free. He pushed her into another deserted cabin, slamming the door behind him. Throwing her on top of the bed, he quickly left the room.

Though her wrists and ankles were tied, she wasn't bound fast to the bed. Dora sat up and shifted her weight until she was at the edge. She could stand up. She hopped towards the door. She put her hands on the knob and turned it, expecting it to open at her command. It was locked!

She spat the cloth out of her mouth. A bottle of sparkling water stood on a miniature tray on the top of the nightstand. She managed to raise it to her lips with her wrists still bound. She was so thirsty that she quaffed half of it. On top of a dresser sat a bowl of fruit next to a vase of cut flowers. She raised the apple to her mouth and ate it followed by the banana. It wasn't fillet mignon, but it would do.

Dora couldn't open the door, but what about the porthole? She could stand there and watch for a passenger to walk past. A well-dressed man with a walking stick strolled past with his valet. It must be Vanderbilt himself! She attempted to fling open the porthole. It wouldn't budge. When Vanderbilt and his valet were almost past her, she pounded on the glass. They stopped and looked around for a minute. They continued on their way.

Her kidnapper had planned this carefully. Her gilded cell, a first-class cabin on the *Lusitania's* Boat Deck, was escape-proof.

CHAPTER 12

She'd already removed the rag from her mouth. She struggled with the ropes that bound her wrists. Her fingers grappled clumsily with the knots. After what seemed hours of effort, she untied them. With her hands free, it was a breeze to free her legs.

The cabin phone looked back at her, scolding her for being so stupid. She grabbed the receiver. All she had to do was call a steward or stewardess, and she was as good as released from her prison. All she heard was the sound of air. Her captor had anticipated her there, too. The wire, she found by glancing under the table, had been cut.

Dora returned to standing at the door to appeal to passersby. Her mother, father, and Mr. Klein were leaving the dining room. She pounded on the wall next to the porthole, screaming, "Help me!" The walls of the cabins on the *Lusitania* were thick. The door was heavy. Even the porthole was anything except flimsy. The sound must have been muffled.

Still they stopped and stared. "Where's that sound coming from?" Mr. Klein looked around.

"Can't be Dora," her father said disgustedly.

"But it is! It is!" Dora yelled.

"That man we met at dinner said he'd seen her with that other passenger, the one she was eating with at lunch called Michael Byrne. Scandalous! Wait until I give both of them a piece of my mind," Mr. Benley declared as he stomped past.

Dora, thoroughly discouraged, lay down on the bed, pulled the covers over herself, and went to sleep. When her eyes opened, she was surprised to find that it was light out already. Sun was streaming through her porthole, striking the bed. She looked down at her watch. It was already nine A.M. Her parents would be at breakfast. Dora did swift mental calculations. They had boarded the ship on Saturday. The first full day at sea had been Sunday. Today must be Monday, May 3.

The assailant burst through the door. He tied her up

again with more rope. While the passengers were at lunch, he bundled her up in a blanket for the second time. He dragged her down the deck to still another, empty first-class passenger cabin.

Were her parents searching for her? Was that why the scoundrel felt compelled to move her from cabin to cabin?

She heard her parents tromp past out on the deck on the way back from lunch. "I never thought Dora was so irresponsible!" her father complained.

"Is my daughter ruined?" her mother asked.

Mr. Klein assured Dora's mother. "I don't think Mr. Byrne has hanky-panky in mind, if you'll excuse my crude expression. He looked like he would be scared of his own shadow."

"Where did they disappear then?" her mother exclaimed.

Mr. Klein said, "They both were possessed of some strange notion about a fellow passenger. I heard them discussing him yesterday at lunch."

"What did they say?" her father asked.

"They claimed somebody had insulted Mr. Byrne."

Dora thought, *Not insulted! Stabbed!* She tried to call it out, but the cloth stuffed into her mouth prevented her from correcting him.

"If somebody insulted my daughter, I'll have him arrested. If I can't arrest him, I'll sue him," Mr. Benley declared.

"Winthrop, we can't do anything until we find Dora first!" her mother reminded him.

"I've offered the stewards and stewardesses on board a tip for information about Dora," Mr. Benley declared. "A very generous tip. More than their wages for the whole trip."

"I've doubled it," Mr. Klein agreed.

"Why don't we hear anything?" her mother fretted.

"We'll hear something. I guarantee it," her father reassured her mother as they walked out of hearing range.

When she looked back at her captor, he was toying

with a device. Exactly what, it was impossible to discern from where she was perched on the bed. It resembled a cigar – a cigar made of hollow lead. The man was assembling it. A circular disk of copper divided the device into two chambers. The man pulled a vial of liquid out of his pocket. He took the cap off the vial. He fetched a test tube from his other pocket and took the cap off that, too. Dora recognized the pungent odor of sulfuric acid from chemistry class. The other vial smelled almost the same – but not quite. Was it another kind of acid?

Her assailant poured one vial of acid into one chamber of the cigar-like device. He emptied the second acid into the other chamber. He sealed them with wax plugs. He lifted the device up to eye level and examined it nose-to-nose. His grin broke out into a full smile.

He took out a white linen handkerchief embroidered with a "V" and wiped off the chambers. Had he lifted an expensive handkerchief out of Vanderbilt's bag on the pier in New York? To her horror, the assailant concealed the device in a drawer. He left the room promptly, locking the cabin door behind him.

Dora scrambled over to the edge of the mattress. She followed the same routine of gradually loosening the rope around her wrists, then untying her ankles. She couldn't resist peeking inside the drawer. Already the copper plate separating the two acids was becoming discolored. A chemical reaction was taking place.

Dora thought, *If I don't outwit this man, I'll never get out of here. I've got to think of something.* Dora got out a sheet of Cunard stationery from the writing desk. She folded the paper in two. On the outside she wrote "HELP!!!" in big, dark, bold letters. Dora attempted to explain her predicament. She urged anyone picking up her note to take it either to Mr. Benley in cabin 101 or straight to the stewards' office.

Dora inserted the note into the tiny space underneath the door. She pushed, but the folded paper wouldn't budge. She tore it in half, making it half the thickness and tried that. It kept on catching on the threshold. She wondered if her captor had thought of such details.

She was feeling sorry for herself when she heard a cabin boy racing down the deck. "Big reward!" he announced. He threw a paper against Dora's cabin door and continued on his way. Dora craned her neck to peer out the porthole. She could barely make out what looked like a flyer. It read:

MISSING GIRL. $10,000.00 REWARD OFFERED.

Her parents must have placed the ad!

Heavy footsteps approached. The door opened. She threw herself against the kidnapper to push him back out, but he was stronger. He shoved her down onto the bed and tied her up once again.

She lay there struggling with the ropes for awhile, then fell asleep. When she opened her eyes, she found the assailant standing over the table playing with another cigar-like device. He was pouring acid from a vial into one side of the apparatus. He poured another acid into the other side.

Liquid from one side splashed up against the liquid from the other. A huge flame shot straight up toward the ceiling. The table caught on fire. The kidnapper quickly fetched a basin of water from the bathroom. He did it again and again until it only smoldered. Smoke curled toward the ceiling in a single, wispy thread.

What kind of a device was this anyway? Was this one of the fuses Mr. Byrne had seen down in the hold of the *Lusitania?*

CHAPTER 13

Dora's captor was careful to take not one device but two with him in his pockets, lifting the other one out of the drawer. He locked the door behind him. Dora freed herself of her ropes and gags in time to hear footsteps approaching outside on the deck.

"We haven't had any leads, sir. I'm sorry. The most anybody could come up with was that they saw a man dragging something in a blanket down the deck. It might have been a girl. It also could have been a canvas all rolled up. You couldn't really tell," the crew member apologized.

"I can't believe that Dora wouldn't have gotten in touch with me in all this time. You say you haven't heard from Mr. Byrne either?" Mr. Benley questioned the crew member.

"Mr. Byrne is sequestered in his cabin. All his meals are delivered there. He says he isn't feeling well," Dora heard the crew member's voice as the footsteps receded in the distance.

"Is Dora with him?" her father sounded indignant.

"We don't have any reason to suppose she is, but we can't know for sure, sir," the crew member said when he was almost out of hearing range.

"Outrageous!" Dora heard her father explode. "Outrageous the morals young people have these days. They must get it from France, Germany, Italy or some foreign place like that."

At least her father was still searching for her. But his suppositions and prejudices were wrong. Her father never was very good at dealing with the irrational and bizarre. He valued common sense, morality, and decency above all things.

She spent that night sleeping fitfully, tossing and turning. She kept seeing the strange, dark man playing with his mysterious vials and cigar-like devices. When she opened her eyes, he had vanished. She took a drink from a second water bottle, a new one. She fell into a profound, dark, dreamless sleep. The next thing she knew it was light out. A beam of sunlight was streaming through the porthole, hitting the bed. She had the feeling of having slept for a long, long time. Her head ached dully.

Why, it sounded like a bugle! She immediately went to the porthole. She was astounded to see just that – a bugler! She glanced at the clock on the dresser. It was only five thirty A.M. Why would there be a bugler out on the Boat Deck of the *Lusitania* so awfully early in the morning?

The bugler was standing only a few feet away from her on the other side of the glass. He wore a name badge that she could barely make out: Vernon Livermore. He lifted the bugle to his lips, making a loud, trumpeting sound. She fell back a few feet, putting her hands over her ears.

Countless feet started to pound on the decks. They looked like the entire crew. She recognized waiters from her first night on the ship. Others were stewards. A few looked like cooks that she had only glimpsed in the kitchen on her way to the Promenade Cafe. Still others were sailors that she'd seen out on the deck tending to nautical chore, all racing toward the bugler as fast as they could. The men reached for the ship's lifeboats, loosening them from where they were stationed suspended eight feet above the Boat Deck. She watched while ropes, or "falls", brought them down.

By the expressions on the faces of the crew and the lack of any other passengers on deck she assumed it must be a drill. Yet at this hour of the morning? Dora watched while the crew not only brought down the lifeboats but took out the equipment stored inside such as matches, sea anchors, oil for storm lamps, and provisions including jugs of drinking water. They compiled lists, making sure that everything was in place.

Anxious passengers tripped past, awakened by the scuffling, shouts, bugling, and other odd ship noises. "Why are they swinging the boats out now?" a well-dressed matron asked. "Why didn't they do it earlier in the voyage?"

"Captain's orders, ma'm," Vernon Livermore replied.

"It's Thursday morning. We're supposed to land in Liverpool tomorrow. We should be reaching the Danger Zone any time now," the lady pressed anxiously.

"That's right, ma'm."

"That means the Germans can see us?" the lady was horrified.

"You'd better believe it!" Vernon nodded.

The lady with her daughter in hand rushed past Dora's porthole.

Thursday morning? Wasn't it supposed to be Wednesday morning, she wondered groggily? How long had she slept? She'd lost count. Hers had been a sleep without dreams.

She sniffed the bottle of water. It didn't smell right. The kidnapper must have slipped a sleeping potion into it to knock her out. She dumped the remaining water down the drain so she wouldn't drink from it again.

She felt it best to stand close beside the door. In case the kidnapper showed up, her only chance was to rush past him and hopefully make it out onto the deck. She would scream aloud. He wouldn't be expecting it. She might get stabbed like Mr. Byrne, but it was worth it to escape from her prison.

"When will the Royal Navy show up?" one gentleman passing in front of her porthole asked another.

"I hear they're supposed to provide an escort once we reach the Danger Zone," his friend replied.

"I don't see any sign of them," the first gentleman commented. He looked over the rail and shrugged.

Dora thought, *Everybody's focused on Germans, but what about the strange man who kidnapped me and stabbed Mr. Byrne? The one who plays with fire bombs? Isn't he much more dangerous?*

Pound! Pound! Pound!

She jumped a foot. She saw a portly matron nailing up a notice on the rail:

Learn How to Put On Your Life Jacket. Meeting in the Library at 2:00 PM after lunch.

Not long after she saw two mothers with a crowd of children surrounding them headed for the library. Both women carried life jackets under their arms. Looking across the room,

Dora could see that her cabin had one just like it stuffed into the closet. It was a big, bulky Boddy's Patent Jacket. It was filled with lots of fiber and would make her look like a balloon if she wore it.

She stubbornly kept her position at the door, drifting away only occasionally to eat more fruit or to pour a drink from the tap. At least it hadn't been poisoned by her captor!

Near sunset when the dinner trumpet sounded, Dora heard distinct footsteps hurrying toward her door. She tensed her muscles, telling herself, *This is my last chance.* She heard a key in the lock. She turned toward the door, ready to spring. She had a book clutched in her hand to hit the kidnapper over the head.

The door creaked open an inch. This man seemed hesitant. Had a passenger gotten the wrong room? Dora lowered her book. But then, how would somebody else's key fit this lock?

"Miss Benley, are you in here?" came a low hiss.

"Mr. Byrne!" she exclaimed.

"Sh-h-h-h-h-h-h!" he hissed. She could see him in the shadows holding a finger to his lips. "Come with me!" he whispered into her ear. "I'll explain everything."

Dora rejoiced to be free as they crept slowly down the deck, plastering themselves against the rail, and turning their faces towards the sea when anyone passed by. In this slow manner they gradually made their way to Mr. Byrne's cabin, number 101. She'd been there once before in equally odd circumstances. He quickly shut the door behind them and locked it. The drapes were already shut over his porthole. He switched on the overhead light.

"How did you get the key to the cabin I was imprisoned in?"

He took her by the elbow over to the far side of the room, glancing at the door as if afraid of being overheard. His perpetually haunted look had only deepened. "The assassin practically lived in my cabin working on his fuses every day, figuring he had me cowed after he'd stabbed me. He left his keys on the table by mistake. I picked them up only half an hour ago."

"How did you suspect I was imprisoned somewhere?"

"Your father pounded on my door. He thought you were hiding in here with me. So I figured the lunatic had you imprisoned somewhere. I tried the key with the odd room number on it as soon as I could get away."

A deckhand darkened Mr. Byrne's porthole, putting a cover over it. "Don't get alarmed!" the crew member called from outside, knocking on the door to get their attention. "Captain's orders. Don't want to light up for the Germans tonight as we enter the Danger Zone."

Dora clenched her fists. "The man was working on the fuses in my cabin. He almost set everything on fire."

Br-r-r-r-r—ring!

Mr. Byrne took a deep breath and picked the phone receiver up. "Hello?"

"If you keep hiding my daughter in your room, I'm going to bring suit against you as soon as we reach England," her father's voice rang out.

"I'm sorry, sir, I don't know anything about your daughter. Now if you'll please –"

"Don't you hang up on me!" her father threatened while her mother sobbed in the background.

"Good night, sir! I'm sorry I can't help you," Mr. Byrne hung up.

"Good grief! How long has that been going on?" Dora asked.

"Hours," he sighed as the phone started to ring again.

"Won't the kidnapper realize that he left his keys here and come searching for them?" she pressed.

"I dropped the keys in question out on the deck. A deck hand will pick them up and return them to him, assuming he's not a stowaway. I don't think he is. He must have bought a ticket under an alias. Otherwise he wouldn't dare spend so much time on the Boat Deck."

"I see," Dora said.

"The idiot's going to try something tonight. Our only chance is to stop him. I saw him headed down into the hold of the ship. Follow me."

CHAPTER 14

D ora put on one of Mr. Byrne's smaller suits. She chopped off her hair with a scissors and donned one of his hats. They waited until no one was coming and crept out onto the deck. They inched their way along close to the public rooms. In the library women passengers along with their husbands were setting up cots. Stewards and stewardesses ran about carrying piles of extra blankets and pillows.

"Some passengers have declared they are going to sleep on deck tonight," Mr. Byrne whispered. "They don't want to be caught in their cabins in case the Germans attack."

Dora glanced into the first-class salon where she had left a note with disastrous results. Passengers were competing in a talent competition. One lady was singing a aria from the opera, *Aida.* Rita Jolivet performed a skit. The orchestra played, "God Save the King." Others handed out programs. A lady held a jar labeled: *Seamen's Charities.* Passenger after passenger dropped coins into it. Dora saw Mr. Vanderbilt slip a huge wad of bills into the jar, nodding with a smile.

Everyone was clapping. It must be intermission. Captain Turner rose to speak:

"There has been a submarine warning. But on entering the War Zone tomorrow, we shall be securely in the care of the Royal Navy. Of course there is no need for alarm. Tomorrow we will steam at full speed so as to arrive at Liverpool in good time. But please, while in the War Zone we must respect the rules of the Admiralty, if for form's sake only. I would ask all male passengers not to light their cigarettes, cigars, or pipes on deck tonight."

Dora's mother was dabbing her eyes. Her father was patting her on the shoulder. No doubt they were talking about her. Mr. Klein was helping to console her mother.

"Let's hurry!" Mr. Byrne hissed.

They could see the crew taking their positions as lookouts. Men were peering out anxiously at the black water looking for signs of periscopes, as a heavy fog settled in over the *Lusitania.* Some had binoculars.

They descended to the next deck, following the crew's access route. The last sound Dora heard from the Boat Deck was the orchestra playing *America the Beautiful.* Dora thought, *I couldn't be farther away from America and home . . . This doesn't remind me of anything that ever happened in Pittsburgh, Pennsylvania . . .*

They entered the hold, strictly off limits. Now there was no light at all. They had to use a pack of matches that Mr. Byrne kept in his pocket for emergencies. He always traveled with them. They rapidly lighted one after the other. The farther they went, the warmer it got. "We're getting closer to the *Lusitania's* four steam turbine engines," he announced.

"Do we have to go all the way down *here?"*

"We have to head the rat off."

When they got off the elevator, they heard stokers shoveling coal into boilers. The coal landed with a thud. Sparks and flames leaped up in the darkness. It looked like Dante's Inferno.

Mr. Byrne fell to the floor as if struck. A hand clapped itself over Dora's mouth. The kidnapper quickly roped Dora and the unconscious body of Mr. Byrne to the same pillar. He took out one of those horrible fuses with the acids and tied it to the pillar next to Mr. Byrne. Dora could see in the dim light that the acids had begun to eat away the copper wall between the two chambers.

Dora squirmed and struggled against the ropes until she fell asleep. She dreamed of the fuses. The acids worked their way through the copper wall. They ignited a giant flame like the one she had seen in her cabin that day.

She startled herself awake. It was not only an incendiary bomb but a time bomb. The seconds were ticking away.

CHAPTER 15

"Heard anything?" one of the stokers shouted. His voice was loud from much practice talking over the machinery.

"Rumor says the Captain got lost. The fog's so dense this morning. Ordered a sounding."

"Might as well have hired a German to pilot the ship," another replied. "Turner's in a fog half the time."

"He's ordered the foghorn to sound every minute," chirped a fourth engine room worker. "Freaks the passengers out."

"Maybe he wants to alert the Germans to where we are," the first worker observed wryly.

"He might want to hand off the rotten food in the hold," the second stoker added. "Germans like everything sour, with lots of vinegar. This stuff sure smells sour! Stinks like milk and cheese gone bad."

So that was why the kidnapper had made his way down here! Dora thought. The rancid butter and cheese was where the arsonist must be storing his chemicals and supplies. That's how he'd hidden the materials to create so many fuses, without their smell giving him away.

Mr. Byrne stirred, woke and looked around. He kicked Dora in the ankle. He was glaring at the fuse tied to the pillar. The copper was nearly gone. The acid was working its way through. They had absolutely no time left. They both started kicking at the floor, struggling furiously with the ropes that bound them to the pillar.

"Fog's finally lifted," the first stoker informed the others.

"Why'd the Captain order us to slow down? We're creepin' at eighteen knots. Should be doin' twenty-five."

"He says be ready to give full speed if they spot a U-boat. But he won't fire up the fourth engine room," commented the second stoker. "I don't know how he's going to go fast enough without it."

Time kept passing as Dora strained to work her arms and hands loose.

"Order's come to change course," the first engine room worker called out.

"Where to?"

"Coningbeg Lightship. We're steering a steady course twelve miles from the Irish Coast, still at eighteen knots."

"If'n it were up to me, I'd zig-zag and go faster. That's what the engineer said. Cap'n's not obeyin' Admiralty orders," said a man with a Cockney accent.

The ship veered sharply, heeling to starboard. The sudden motion was enough to loosen Dora's ropes to the point that she could quickly untie them. She didn't have a knife, so she started working on Michael Byrne's ropes with her teeth and bare hands.

A giant thud sounded in her ears, so loud it almost deafened her. The ship shuddered, shaking the bulkheads. Water gushed into the engine room. It had a salt brine smell.

"My God!" Mr. Byrne exclaimed, shaking himself free from the ropes that Dora had begun to loosen. "We've been torpedoed. Let's get out of here."

Workers were shouting to each other. One hollered, "No one's answering. I'll go up to the bridge and ask what we're suppose to do."

Dora and Michael, both coughing, staggered out of the engine room clogged with smoke, coal dust, and water. They hurried into the elevator, the only escape to the upper decks. One other person accompanied them, the stoker headed to the bridge for orders.

They hadn't gone very far, only to the Lower Deck, when Mr. Byrne shoved her out of the elevator toward the stairs, "Let's get off. I don't like this." The engine room worker leaped off, too.

The steps of the companionway they'd entered were already mobbed with passengers from steerage, housed in the bowels of the ship. They were forcing their way up on deck, elbow to elbow. "You could see bubbles breaking the surface. It was like two white streaks, the torpedo was. That's what the steward said!" an Italian woman carting babies in each arm cried out.

A huge explosion, much louder than the first, threw Dora to the floor. Before Mr. Byrne could get his arms around her, hot, dense steam poured up the stairway in great waves, mingled with coal dust. It enveloped her, filling her lungs. She coughed so hard she thought she would choke. Everyone around her was hacking away, too.

"Mi – Michael . . . Where are you?" she reached out for him in all directions, seeing only white vapor. Passengers appeared and disappeared in the steam clouds, like tormented souls in the Underworld of Homer's *Odyssey*. Now she saw a face with eyes bulging out. It vanished, then was replaced by a baby's face red with bawling. That too disappeared. An old man's mouth with missing teeth was all that was left. He was moaning.

Arms finally closed around her and pulled her against him. Michael dragged her along. She felt her feet pass over human flesh. She was walking on skin and bones, not the steps or the floor any longer. She heard a bone crack. She winced.

"That must have been the fuse," Mr. Byrne coughed. "It – it blew!" Dora held onto Michael as tightly as he was holding onto her. He was like a lifeline.

Everything went dark. Children wailed. A lady screeched. "Where are you Rachel? Where are you Arnold? My God, I've lost my children!"

Bang! Bang! Bang! Bang!

Something was pounding on Dora's skull. The banging continued. It was hard to determine from which direction it was coming in the nightmare of darkness, screams, and steam.

"Help us! We're trapped. Get us out of here!"

Bang! Bang! Bang! Bang!

The blows sounded metallic.

"It's the elevator. They're trapped, poor souls!" Michael shouted.

Below her Dora felt something striking at her heels. A moaning and groaning so loud it appeared to emanate from the bowels of the Earth washed over Dora and Michael like another wave. It sounded like the innards of the ship were exploding and coming apart, trying to erupt through the very floorboards.

"Help us!" a muffled cry rose up.

"The crew!" Michael gasped. "They're trapped below the elevator shaft."

Cooks, butchers, and engine room workers howled. They hammered on the ceilings and bulkheads with every tool they owned, be it meat cleavers, shovels, or pots and pans.

Dora and Michael lurched to starboard, smashing against the bulkhead. The floor seemed tilted. As they dragged themselves to their feet, the bulkhead seemed the more natural place to put their feet. It had now become the floor.

"The ship's listing," Michael deduced. "At a very strange angle."

Water was all around them. Sloshing through it, Dora kept running into people she couldn't see. They seemed to be floating there – some of them face down. Others were under the water, or stuck to the bulkhead.

"Michael, are we dead or alive?" she wept.

"We're still alive, or we couldn't be talking."

Up ahead something white came into view. The closer they got, the bigger and more luminescent it became. Dora and Mr. Byrne emerged into the sun on what looked like the Boat Deck. As their eyes adjusted, a column of white water from the other side of the rail rose high into the air followed by debris. Water rained down upon the deck, drenching them and pelting them with buckets, tools, life jackets, and oars. A big, white cloud mushroomed one hundred fifty feet above the Marconi wires.

"Look out, a wave!" a woman screamed.

The bow of the ship rose out of the water. Fleeing passengers, running here, there, and everywhere, not knowing where they were going, were knocked over by the seawater spilling across the deck. Waves kept on coming, one after the other.

"Look!" Dora pointed. Bits of wood, iron, and black cinders from the funnels of the ship landed on the roof of the Verandah Cafe. The cafe's plants were falling all over the place and rolling about the deck. A palm tree headed straight for her. She had to jump over it.

"All women and children into the boats first!" bellowed a seaman.

The crew that had managed to struggle up onto the deck were working frantically with the lifeboats to launch them into the water. They didn't have proper tools. They had only knives, not axes, to cut the boat lines from the davits. Passengers crowded around them, especially on the port side that was higher out of the sea. Many had their life jackets on incorrectly. Some wore them upside down.

"Have you seen my husband?" an hysterical woman raced up to Dora, pushing her face right up to her nose.

Dora remembered the lady with the wedding ring displayed on top of her evening glove. The name was on the tip of her tongue – Mrs. Lesley Mason, the newlywed from Boston. As quickly as she'd appeared, she vanished in the throng.

"Give me that life jacket!" a passenger confronted a crew member only inches away from Dora.

"Be damned!" the crew member shot back. "It's every man for himself."

The Englishman was outraged, "That's against the law, you know. You could be prosecuted."

"What law?" the crew member spat back. "There is no law now. It's the law of the jungle."

"Hand it over!" demanded the well-dressed, first-class English gentleman, his hand gripping the life jacket that the crew member was wearing.

"You'll have to kill me first!" the crew member shoved the passenger aside. He fell and was trampled by a bunch of screaming passengers headed for the lifeboats.

Michael tried to clutch Dora more closely to him to protect her. A big wave of seawater hit them from behind. Dora felt herself being raised off her feet. She flailed her arms and legs about. When she came back down on the deck, Mr. Byrne was no longer there.

"Michael, where are you?" Dora pulled herself to her feet, reaching out for a shoulder, which she at first thought was Michael's. Turning, she saw it was only a corpse with vacant eyes leaning against a barrel. She screeched and backed away.

She looked about frantically in every direction for Mr. Byrne. Something inside commanded her to get a hold of herself. She would have to, or she would have no chance. As the crewman had said, it really was every man for himself.

"Don't lower the boats. The ship can't sink. She's all right. I repeat, the ship can't sink." Captain Turner called down from the bridge, the only deck higher than the Boat Deck. He was cupping his hands to make himself heard over the chaos.

The captain had gone insane. As Dora backed away from Turner, she ran into someone else. A well-dressed passenger had drawn his pistol and was pointing it at a crew member.

"I order you to launch this lifeboat at once, or you'll be a dead man!"

"Shoot me! Put me out of my misery," the crewman burst into tears. "I'll never see my little wife again."

The passenger put the gun to his own head. He fired. Dora turned away only in the nick of time to keep herself from seeing him blow his brains out.

She ran toward a crowd in line for the lifeboats. That must be the right place to stand. She had to get off the *Lusitania* somehow.

A boat full of passengers was being launched only a few feet away despite the extreme list of the ship and the water washing over the Boat Deck. The lifeboat overturned halfway down, spilling its load of passengers out into the ocean. The lifeboat itself slammed back against the side of the ship, smashing to death the few passengers who'd managed to hold on. The same lifeboat went into a free fall. It landed on top of the very men, women, and children it was supposed to have carried to safety, as they struggled to keep above water.

Dora picked her way along the Boat Deck. This side of the ship, the port side, was too high up out of the water. With great difficulty, she managed to push through the mobs to the starboard side, the one closer to the waterline. Dora thought it would be easier to launch a lifeboat from here.

A second later a lifeboat full of would-be escapees swung wildly over the deck on the starboard side. Dora ducked instinctively. The lifeboat knocked over a family holding onto each other. It mowed down a mother holding two babies. It beheaded an old man hobbling along on a cane. The boat struck a wall, making a gaping hole in what used to be first-class cabins. Half the screaming escapees fell out onto the deck below. Others lost an arm or leg as the lifeboat scraped against the remains of the wall. Still others were knocked unconscious and lay in the bottom of the boat looking up at the sky. The boat then spilled everybody out and swung back across the deck.

The angle of the ship was now vertiginous. Dora was about to be swept overboard. At the last moment, she grasped onto the rail. After steadying herself, she resumed crawling forward at the edge of the deck near the water line.

She collided with another passenger head to head. In front of her crouched a middle-aged man in overly loose corduroy slacks and a Stetson hat, with locks of hair down past his ears. The hat soon blew off. It was Elbert Hubbard, the country philosopher and bestselling writer, the one who'd handed Dora the essay about the Kaiser, "Who Lifted the Lid Off Hell?". He didn't look so full of bluff savoir faire now.

"I didn't think they'd do it," he admitted gravely.

She gazed into his eyes, only about two inches away. Their humorous look was gone along with his jokes about the Kaiser impersonating Satan. Stark terror had replaced them as he craned his neck upward, gawking at the smoke stacks hanging over them as the ship listed at an increasingly precarious angle.

"Would you like a life jacket?" came a polite voice, out of sync with what Dora had been witnessing.

She spun around. There crouched Alfred Gwynne Vanderbilt holding out his life jacket to her, as calm as if he were waiting for his valet to bring up alongside his own, private motorboat as a vehicle of escape.

"No – no, thank you!" Dora replied, eager to get away.

Vanderbilt turned to another lady and offered her the jacket. She gladly accepted, and he helped her on with it. Dora wondered why he wasn't trying to save himself. Perhaps he was as crazy as Captain Turner. Something had snapped. Nothing in his privileged life had prepared him for this.

Vanderbilt in his gray suit and polka-dot tie looked at Dora and smiled, his natural self-confidence unshaken. "I'm sure the British Admiralty will be along any second now. You can always depend on them."

She crawled along the rail away from him. Elbert Hubbard had disappeared.

"Dora!" called out a strangled voice. High up on the part of the deck that had turned upward out of the water stood Rita Jolivet next to Charles Frohman, the theater manager whom Dora had met the night of the party. Rita clung to the rail, shouting and waving at Dora.

"Rita!" Dora called back.

Tears rolled down the actress's cheeks. "I don't swim that well. I'm terrified of water."

"Let me help you!" Dora crawled towards her friend along the slippery deck that listed more horribly every second. No matter how hard she tried, she couldn't stand up without clutching onto the rail.

"I've got my little pearl-handled pistol with me," Rita shouted hysterically, waving it in the air. "If I land in the water, I'm going to shoot myself. I don't want to drown. There are so many bodies down there already," tears rolled down her cheeks.

The middle-aged theater producer, Frohman, was quoting line after line from the repertoire of over five hundred plays that he'd produced during his busy career. He concluded in a very resigned tone, quoting *Peter Pan,* "Why fear death?

It is the most beautiful adventure that life gives us." A faraway expression made him look spooky.

Dora extended her hand toward the actress. The young lady let go of the rail, crouched down, struggled forward, and tried to grasp it. A green wave full of corpses and debris rolled across the deck between them. It knocked Dora backward. Dora pulled herself to her knees in time to hear Rita scream at the top of her lungs as she was washed overboard. The last thing Dora saw was Rita's buttoned boots getting kicked up into the air. Frohman was gone in a second, too.

"Now everyone sit!" Dora heard a familiar voice, a voice of sanity in the midst of chaos. "Don't stand in my boat. I'll row you to shore."

Like a miracle there sat her father about eight feet below her. He must have just launched a lifeboat from the starboard side of the ship. Everyone was sitting in neat rows as he pulled away from the *Lusitania.*

"Father!" Dora screamed at the top of her lungs.

"Dora!" her mother shrieked.

"Now, Etta May, don't capsize the boat! Dora can swim. I'm sure she'll have no trouble reaching us," her father looked at his daughter with confidence.

"How can you be so sure of yourself, sir?" one lady in the lifeboat marveled.

"That time Teddy Roosevelt and I were rafting down the flood current in North Dakota, the President said, 'You've got two seconds, no one! Launch that raft, or we're gonna be dinner for that grizzly right behind us,'" her father even now recounted one of his tales. "T.R. would have thought this was all just bully."

Dora threw off her shoes so they wouldn't drag her down in the ocean. She hesitated for a second, then dove eight feet into the near freezing water, which felt like fifty degrees. She swam to the lifeboat. Her father and another passenger pulled her aboard.

Dora was shivering with cold. Her mother wrapped a fur coat that she'd salvaged from the wreck around her daughter.

"Has anyone seen Mr. Byrne?" Dora cherished a last remaining hope as she looked from one end of the lifeboat to the other.

Her mother clucked, even in such extreme circumstances, "Dora, how could you spend practically the whole voyage *in his cabin?*"

"Mother, it's far more complicated than that," she assured her. "A saboteur aboard the ship kidnapped me. He tied me up and dragged me from cabin to cabin."

Several of the passengers in the lifeboat were staring at Dora with wide-open eyes.

"Mr. Byrne rescued me. But we had to stop the maniac with the fuses."

"Fuses?" her mother was appalled.

"Incendiary bombs," Dora explained tersely. "That's what caused the second explosion in the hold of the *Lusitania*. The saboteur strapped a fuse to a pillar in the engine room."

"A German spy!" a lady screamed.

"Oh no!" exclaimed another.

"No, he wasn't German. He was too dark, and he didn't speak with a German accent," Dora shook her head.

"Dora," her father commanded, "it's difficult enough to row under these conditions," he chided her as he made straight for the closest shore instead of rowing towards Queenstown as everyone else was doing. "I'm sure you'll have a lot of explaining to do later. No tall tales for now, if you please."

He threw her an oar to give her something to keep her mind occupied. No one was going to believe her. She could see that. She rowed in silence, as the lifeboat moved through the sea of passengers bobbing up and down everywhere, crying for help and clinging to any piece of wreckage that would float.

The *Lusitania* was dragging lifeboats under the water as it went down. Passengers screamed and fell out. They tried to swim, but they were sucked backward. Dora's mother clutched Winthrop's jacket and hid her face weeping.

"Don't worry, Etta May," Mr. Benley assured her. "Our lifeboat is out of range of the undertow of the sinking ship."

Water rushed into the four, great smoke stacks of the ship

as they, too, hit the waves. Tremendous, churning whirlpools sucked victims inside. A few were ejected, blackened with soot. Propellers rose above the maelstrom. The rudder lifted higher than the smoke stacks. The ship's prow pointed down toward the deep. It looked as if the ship's nose would hit the sea bed hundreds of feet below. Green waters swallowed the decks, devouring the remaining passengers who had been clinging to her to the last second. With an audible groan the ship turned onto its starboard side and disappeared.

Dear, God! Dora thought. *It couldn't have been more than a few minutes since I left the engine room after the first explosion sounded and rattled the decks . . . Fifteen or at most twenty . . . no more . . .*

CHAPTER 16

D ora heard girls on the lifeboat nearest to theirs singing an Irish song, "There Is A Green Hill Not Far Away." A lady was reciting the Twenty-Third Psalm:

Yea, thou I walk through the Valley of the Shadow of Death,

I will fear no Evil: For thou art with me;
Thy rod and thy staff, they comfort me . . .

The surface of the ocean erupted like a volcano with clouds of steam where the ship had gone down. Waves surged this way and that, bringing up deck chairs, mattresses, pillows, oars, plates, corpses, suitcases, and clothing. They spread all across the Irish Sea. Hands and arms extended above the surface for about half a mile in each direction. A chorus of voices pleaded for help.

A hand grasped hold of their lifeboat.

"There's no more room!" a man bellowed, sitting in the lifeboat right where the fingers were clutching.

"My skirts are filling with water. I already went down once. If I go down again," a woman gasped with a pale white face that looked like a death's skull, "I won't come back up."

Where the woman was holding on, water started to enter the lifeboat. A lady passenger wept. The man hit the poor woman on the knuckles with an umbrella. "Let go!" he commanded. "You'll sink us all."

"Winthrop, do something!" Mrs. Benley shrieked.

"Etta May, you passengers will have to mind your own affairs. I'm steering this boat," Mr. Benley wielded the paddle.

The poor, rejected woman doggy-paddled out to a "reef" that had formed in the middle of the ocean composed of floating mattresses and pieces of wood. She grasped onto whatever she could. A fight broke out between her and other survivors desperately tying to stay afloat.

The corpse of a young mother floated past. She still clutched her baby on her breast. Both lay perfectly still.

"Father, isn't there anything we can do?" Dora pleaded. "If we don't help the lady, she will drown."

"One lifeboat can't save everybody on the *Lusitania*. I've got to look after your mother and you first," Mr. Benley was firm.

Dora motioned to the half-drowned woman to come to her side of the lifeboat. She figured that if the lady made it to the lifeboat again, her father wouldn't have the heart to shove her off the way the other ruffian had. When the lady struggled over, Winthrop Benley turned away while Dora and two other passengers pulled her aboard.

Someone who looked very familiar was clutching onto a nearby barrel. He kept trying to climb on top of it and slipping back.

"Look, there's Michael Byrne!"

Her father dutifully rowed towards the man with great distaste. Dora helped him into the life boat. She scowled at the passenger with the umbrella who cast her a dirty look.

"I saw the saboteur. I chased him as best I could," Mr. Byrne shivered next to Dora, rubbing his hands up and down his arms. "He disappeared down a companionway." He shrugged, "At any rate, I don't think he got off the ship."

"Mr. Klein didn't either, dear," Mrs. Benley sniffled. "He went back to get his life jacket, so he said. I think he was looking for you, Dora." She burst into tears. "We thought we lost you. Now we've lost dear Mr. Klein. We'll never know what happens at the end of the new version of *Potash and Perlmutter in Society.*" Tears rolled down her cheeks.

Dora felt remorse, though for something she couldn't have helped.

"Mr. Klein said to give you this," Mrs. Benley handed her daughter a sheaf of papers, "in case he didn't make it. He – he said he was going to dedicate it to you." Her mother burst into tears afresh.

Below the manuscript's title, *Potash and Perlmutter in Society,* Mr. Klein had written: *to Dora Benley, whom I had hoped to make my wife.* Dora slipped the papers into the pocket of her fur coat as she repressed a sob.

"And, Dora, Mr. Klein said to make sure you read the note. He put it in the *Author's After Word.*"

She nodded dumbly, too sad for words.

"And, oh yes!" her mother pulled from her purse still another manuscript. "He said to give you this new version of his novelette, *The Lion and the Mouse.* He wanted your input."

Dora didn't have time to read the *After Word* now – nor *The Lion and the Mouse.* She stuffed them both into her capacious coat pocket and continued to help row the lifeboat towards land.

After what seemed like hours, their lifeboat ran aground on the Irish shore with a big bump.

CHAPTER 17

The villagers had watched the death throes of the *Lusitania* in the Irish Sea just off the coast. They met the Benleys and their lifeboat companions on the beach with blankets, towels, clean water, and food. They hustled them into the village to have a cup of hot tea or coffee and to change their soaking wet clothes. They provided them with transport to Queenstown, the nearest large town down the coast, where both the Cunard offices and tourist hotels were located.

The Benleys didn't arrive in Queenstown until eight o'clock PM. The first of the other lifeboats had pulled up at the gas-lighted quayside in the harbor. The Benleys and Michael Byrne took rooms at the Imperial Hotel. They gave their clothes to the elderly lady proprietress to clean and dry overnight in her kitchen and collapsed into bed.

They weren't asleep yet when the little old lady came knocking on their doors with a tray of shot glasses. "Want a night cap of Irish whiskey to tide you over? It will warm you to the bones."

Dora peeped out her door to see Mr. Byrne's look with horror from his room across the hallway as he stood with a blanket wrapped around himself for modesty. "No, no, thank you!" he turned her away. "I'm – I'm a Methodist."

Dora returned to bed.

"Don't move an inch!" called out a voice with a British accent that Dora had never heard before. Something flashed in her face. She struggled to pull herself out of the covers on the bed and sit up. She realized she was wearing only underwear and pulled the blanket up around her neck.

"Who – who are you?" Dora asked the freckle-faced, red-haired young man with one of the new-fangled folding cameras in his hands standing at the foot of her bed "A newspaper reporter?" she asked as her experience of the day before rushed back on her. Only then did she realize that it was already morning. She'd slept like the dead.

"Edward Ware at your service, milady," the young man, only a couple years older than she was, advanced on Dora's bed and kissed her hand with a little bow. "My father's Sir Adolphus, the one your father's here to meet. We heard all about the disaster yesterday. I left Ware House right away to catch the Irish mail packet from Holyhead. I hired a convoy of cars in Kingstown to come down here and retrieve you and your baggage. It doesn't look like you have many possessions left," he glanced about her room as he helped himself to some of her bread and butter.

It was hard to take this newcomer in all at once, especially since he didn't stand still but kept on moving about from the dresser to the bed to the closet and back to her bed again. She wanted to rub her eyes. She didn't dare. She had to hold up her blanket over herself.

Suddenly Edward Ware and his folding camera vanished. He was knocking on her parents' door. "Good morning, Mr. Benley," he sounded as if was shaking his hand, "Edward Ware at your service. As soon as you're ready, I am. Not that I want to rush you people after everything you've been through. I'm in no particular hurry. I've got all day. Two days, if you require it."

"Oh, Winthrop, how wonderful!" her mother gushed, "I'll get my handbag as soon as I finish my tea. I'm afraid we don't have luggage anymore. And to think I'd done all that shopping at Macy's!"

"We have plenty of shopping in London," Edward Ware announced. "At least the shops that are still open."

"Still open?" her mother sounded perplexed, unable to think of a single reason why all the famous shops in downtown London wouldn't be ready and waiting for her arrival.

"Staffing problems. Our young men are off at the front," Edward apologized to his American visitors. "Young ladies are taking on factory positions for the war effort."

"Oh, my heavens!" Mrs. Benley sounded shocked.

"At least you showed up," her father said gruffly, "even if the British Admiralty didn't."

That *faux pas* caused Dora to leap out of bed, shut her door, and fall into the now dry clothes that the proprietress must have slipped into her room early this morning. She couldn't help it if they were Michael Byrne's old suit. She didn't have anything else to wear. She went racing out of her room head off a real confrontation.

To her great relief, the young English scion of the Ware family, Edward, was smiling and laughing. The freckles on his face seemed all the redder in contrast to his perfect milky complexion. He didn't take offense very easily.

"The British Admiralty's spread so thin in this war it's amazing they show up any place at all," he said. "Our First Lord of the Admiralty, Winston Churchill, is in Paris. He's planning his campaign in the Dardanelles."

Mrs. Benley packed the few items she'd salvaged from the ship, including her mirror, brush, and comb set. She threw the fur coat she had loaned her daughter over her arm. "I'm ready to go."

Dora stuffed her hands deep into her pants pockets. They were still a little chilly. She wondered if they'd ever be warm again.

"Well!" Edward looked Dora up and down in a surprised fashion. "I've heard about suffragettes, but this is beyond the pale!" he grinned wickedly. He assumed a nonchalant pose as he leaned against the door frame, lighting a cigar. He grabbed his folding camera from where it had been sitting on a chair and snapped her photo.

"Oh, this isn't my suit. It belongs to Mr. Michael Byrne. He loaned it to me," she felt flustered. "I had to wear something last night down in the hold of the ship. We were tracking the man who put together the incendiary bomb. He –"

Edward clapped his hand over her mouth. "Save it for later when we have more time. Until then, I'll reserve judgment," he winked.

She couldn't understand what it was about this Edward. He made her blush out of self-consciousness. He stared at her as if he were trying to memorize her every feature.

Mr. Klein's play fell out of her pocket where it didn't really fit. Before she could stoop down, Edward picked it up. "Amazing! *The Lion and the Mouse* by Charles Klein. Sentimental nonsense. Strange for a suffragette."

"He was our friend. He just – he just died yesterday in the sinking," she felt a great sadness settle upon her shoulders. "It's the least I can do for him."

"All in the name of the war effort."

Mr. Benley corrected Edward. "We're strict neutrals in America. It's more in the nature of a personal favor."

As they were enjoying hot tea and a dish of bread and butter for breakfast, Mr. Benley was paying the bill with a draft that had survived in his breast pocket along with his passport. The proprietress said, "They want you American survivors at the Cunard Office this morning. You've got to sign a list."

"I'll be signing all sorts of papers," Mr. Benley promised, "including one at my lawyer's office as soon as I get back to the United States. I'm going to sue the Cunard Line, thank you, along with the British Admiralty, if such a thing is possible."

The proprietress gaped at him with big eyes as if she didn't understand what he was talking about.

Dora leaned across the desk and whispered to the owner, "Have you seen Mr. Michael Byrne?"

"Right there, Miss," the proprietress pointed behind her.

Dora turned toward Michael under the watchful gaze of Edward, who made a point of observing everything she did. "Mr. Byrne, do you have somewhere to go?" Dora wrung her hands.

He shrugged as the impish Edward kept eying him. "I was coming to London on a business trip. I'll proceed with that, though I've lost the papers from J.P. Morgan. Beyond that, I don't know." He glanced from side to side as if he thought the mad bomber would show up at any moment.

"You could come to Ware House with us," Dora offered.

"Yes, yes, my good fellow," Edward extended a

congenial invitation. "Miss Dora Benley's friends are welcome at our estate."

Mr. Byrne said stiffly, "I'll be in touch with you, Dora, if anything develops. I hope you'll keep in touch with me."

They exchanged addresses and phone numbers. An awkward moment ensued as they both stood in the lobby facing each other, tongue-tied for words when they'd never been before. Finally they shook hands and waved good-bye. Mr. Byrne had arranged for his own transportation.

"Mr. Byrne!" Dora called when he'd reached the doorway.

"Yes?" he turned around expectantly.

"I'll – I'll send you your spare suit when I get something decent to wear," she apologized.

"No need to bother," he said. "I'll buy another while I'm in London."

Dora felt a tinge of loneliness when he left. She didn't know who she would talk to now. She watched until Mr. Byrne rode off in a cab, and she couldn't see him anymore.

"*Ready?*" Edward was holding out his arm for her to take. He was smiling in a way that made her forget everything else.

CHAPTER 18

The convoy of vehicles that Edward had brought from Kingstown stood ready and waiting. He helped Mrs. Benley into the backseat of the Model T Ford Touring Car that was open to the sky. He put his hands around Dora's waist and lifted her into the front passenger seat. He climbed into the driver's seat beside her. Their eyes held for a long moment.

Three Model T Ford Town Cars followed Edward through the crowded streets toward the Cunard Office. Mr. Benley entered the building briefly to list their names as survivors.

"Secretary of State Bryan cabled the Cunard Office early this morning. He wants to hear from us Americans. At least somebody's doing something!"her father rejoined them. "And Wesley Frost, the U.S. consul at Queenstown, was there distributing money to Americans in need. It was from Ambassador Page. I contributed one of my drafts to the general cause."

They drove to Kingstown, and later that afternoon boarded the Irish mail packet. That night they crossed the Irish Sea to Holyhead in Wales, with the mail packet "blacked out", its portholes covered and all lights doused on deck. The little ship tore through the water, doing 23 and half knots. A number of other *Lusitania* survivors were aboard, some still nervously wearing the same life jackets they'd used to survive the sinking. The atmosphere was one of pure gloom. The only thing that brightened the atmosphere at all was the way Edward went around and took photos of the survivors, promising to send them copies once he got them developed. He wrote down all their names and addresses. Dora saw him take out his wallet and hand over wads of spare cash to a few old ladies who were alone and had lost loved ones. They thanked him with tears in their eyes.

Early the next morning, upon their arrival in Holyhead, the Benleys and Edward Ware boarded the train to London.

They arrived at the nineteenth-century Euston Station in North London where they were met by another convoy of motor cars that had been sent to meet them by Sir Adolphus. Edward drove them to just outside London near Hampton Court. It was mid-afternoon before they turned into the Ware country estate and headed up the drive.

"Are we finally here?" Mrs. Benley exclaimed, looking around in amazement.

Edward laughed, "I'd like to say it's been our estate since Norman times or some such rot," he addressed everybody in the motor car. "Really granddad got knighted for his business. The baronetcy's hereditary, but it's hardly the old nobility. Some baron moved out of the place so we could move in when Dad was a teenager."

Dora's tired eyes took in the endless green lawns stretching out in every direction. They were shaded overhead by numerous oak and maple trees. A topiary series of ornamental trees lined the drive, shaped into reverse cones or lampshade designs.

A dark brown roof with fake thatched roof design came into view. Painted perpendicular boards were fastened over the masonry on the front of the house. Criss-crossed brown strips of wood above the front-facing, gabled windows below the eaves, created a "half-timbering" effect. Bricked-up chimneys towered above the house. Tall, narrow windows featured old-fashioned, leaded glass.

They stopped next to an arched entranceway. "Definitely Tudor!" her mother clapped her hands. "It reminds me of something back in Pittsburgh. Of course that wasn't nearly as nice."

Edward leaped out. He raced around to open Dora's passenger side door before she could get out by herself. He again put his hands around her waist and lifted her down. "There we go, m'lady," he eyed her with his head cocked just so.

"My dears, you must be famished!" a prim and proper middle-aged lady emerged from the house holding out her arms toward them. Lady Ware kissed Mrs. Benley on the cheek and then Dora. She shook Mr. Benley's hand, standing there in her putty-colored wool dress trimmed with rich embroidery in Nattier blue. She escorted them into the Great Hall. Dora was amazed to see well-polished suits of armor set up near the door for decoration. Medieval tapestries hung on the walls.

"Well, Mom, we're back for dinner!" Edward kissed his mother on the cheek. "Look at the pretty lass I've discovered," he nodded at Dora, whom he'd brought in on his arm. "I pulled her out of the sea myself."

His mother took Dora in from head to foot. "A suffragette at Ware House! The war really has turned everything upside down."

"Apparently this independent American miss couldn't find anything else to wear." The young man looked especially tall and big-shouldered standing next to his rather short mother.

His mother insisted in her cultivated voice, "I'll loan Miss Benley some spare dresses, even though they aren't exactly the thing for young ladies. They're much better than that scandalous attire."

Dora found herself ushered upstairs by the maid while the rest of her family progressed down the hallway, led by Lady Ware and Edward, who lingered near a statue to watch her ascend the stairs. Dora put on the first outfit handed to her, a blue silk afternoon dress. It was a little bit short, but it was better than nothing. She had a hard time slipping her foot into Lady Ware's shoes, which were far too small. She felt like one of Cinderella's stepsisters.

She found her way back down the grand staircase into the Great Hall with large fireplaces at each end that looked like they were never used except on the most formal of occasions.

"We wouldn't want the suffragette to get lost in the big castle," Edward offered her his arm. "I don't want the ladies picketing the estate." He led her down a darkened gallery full of endless paintings and marble portrait busts, and lined with Persian carpets. The Wares and their guests occupied the library and the adjoining parlor with the Ware coat-of-arms – a boar with horns next to a beehive hanging from a tree – right above the doorway.

Her mother sat in a chair covered with rich antique embroidery. Lady Ware was chatting with her. They both were gazing at the latest edition of a popular French publication, the last word on ladies' fashions, *La Mode Illustrée*. Lady Ware pointed dresses out and turned the pages. Mrs. Benley nodded appreciatively.

Mr. Benley stood near the roaring fireplace next to a window made of heraldic glass with a lattice-like effect. Was that Sir Adolphus wielding a cigar in one hand and another folding camera on a tripod in the other? He was shooting photos of his the newcomer from America. He looked bigger and more Viking-like than Captain Turner. His girth was positively medieval. He towered over everyone except his son. His beard came down to his waist.

Next to Sir Adolphus, on dark mahogany shelves behind glass, was exhibited an arrangement of what looked like museum objects and artifacts. It reminded Dora of the small but highly prized archaeological museum hidden away in the classroom section of the M. Carey Thomas Library, more commonly known as the Bryn Mawr College Art and Archaeology Library. She and the other classics majors spent much of their time hidden away in the dark, dimly lit, Gothic building. It had its own Great Hall, wall sconces, and gargoyles.

Dora edged closer to the artifacts, evading Sir Adolphus's camera. The first thing her eyes lighted on was a typewritten, unpublished manuscript, its title page facing forward. She leaned closer to read it in the illuminated, glass-enclosed wooden case:

CARCHEMISH
REPORT ON THE EXCAVATIONS AT JERABLUS ON
BEHALF OF THE BRITISH MUSEUM
CONDUCTED BY
C. LEONARD WOOLLEY, M.A.

T.E. LAWRENCE, B.A., AND P.L.O. GUY

Dora thought, *Carchemish . . . Yes, that was a Hittite town, wasn't it?* She remembered it from her Ancient History course sophomore year.

Hittite . . . That reminded her . . . She'd completely forgotten . . . Sir Adolphus had mailed her a package for her father's birthday, which was two days from now. She'd taken it aboard the *Lusitania*. It had been something wooden with inscriptions that resembled Hittite characters on the bottom. She'd stuffed it above the valance in her cabin. She hadn't thought about it until now. Right at this minute, it must be at the bottom of the Irish Sea.

Someone cleared his throat. Dora glanced up. A tweedy gentleman had appeared at Sir Adolphus's elbow. He looked to be in his thirties. He was keeping a close watch on her.

Next to the unpublished manuscript sat hardened clay tablets propped up by metal stands. The tablets displayed seal impressions. Ancient monarchs and officials had used seals in place of modern signatures. She could make out seal impressions of townsfolk of Carchemish in Hittite dress carrying sticks and rods. Other seals showed cattle and men with whips.

Dora moved onto the next display. A label announced:
OBJECTS FROM MIDDLE HITTITE TOMBS

Colorful beads on chains stood out. Next to the beads sat pottery and plates, most of them   chipped. There were tablets and stelae with carvings and a kind of cuneiform writing called Ancient Hittite. It resembled hieroglyphics, the ancient Egyptian system of writing. The characters were unique. They were what she'd thought she'd glimpsed on the bottom of the wooden object in Sir Adolphus's birthday package.

She pushed her nose up against the glass. She figured out that one character was the picture of a bird. Another looked like a person's face. A third resembled a shepherd's staff.

The next case featured a piece of a wall carving that had broken off a building. It could be nothing else it was so big. Attendants in priestly uniforms and wearing headdresses carried flaming torches in one hand and something that looked like a tablet with secret writing in the other. They were concealing it with their bodies. She couldn't make out the characters

"Could I assist you?" the thirtyish-looking fellow with the tweed jacket, pipe, short beard, and mustache eyed her critically, almost suspiciously.

"I was examining the artifacts," Dora shrugged.

"Leonard Woolley at your service," he nodded.

Leonard Woolley . . . where had Dora heard that name before? Oh yes! She glanced back at the first case. He'd been the chief excavator at Carchemish.

"You mean you're the –"

"The excavator and archaeologist in charge of the dig, now closed down because of the War. I'm on leave from the army and an old friend of Sir Adolphus."

"One of my boon companions. Couldn't do without him," Sir Adolphus turned his camera on Dora and snapped another photo. "We had lots of fun at Carchemish, didn't we, Leonard?"

"You mean you . . . " Dora was confused.

"Oh yes! I was there part-time, season after season when I could get away. Not that I'm an archaeologist. It's a hobby. My career is cars," Sir Adolphus nodded at Mr. Benley.

"Dad's a real rock hound, that's for sure!" Edward whistled from where he'd stationed himself at Dora's elbow.

Dora didn't know whether she should apologize about the lost birthday gift now or later.

Lady Ware looked up from her fashion magazine and cast an inexplicable, scathing glare at her husband. She returned to the magazine without saying one word.

A parlor maid entered the room, bearing a silver tray with the tea things. "Lucy, we'll take afternoon tea out on the lawn at the pavilion," Lady Ware corrected her. "We want to take advantage of the rare good spring weather."

"Yes, ma'm," the maid curtsied.

"Make sure the scones are warmed properly!" she chided the maid in advance.

"Indeed, ma'm."

In Pittsburgh the Benleys had a cleaning lady named Viola and her husband, Frank, who helped them around the yard and acted as a repairman/chauffeur. The recent Italian immigrants didn't bow and curtsy to their employers. This servile behavior made Dora wince. She felt more homesick for Pittsburgh than she'd ever been before in her life.

But when Lady Ware again cast her husband one of her dark looks, Dora couldn't help wondering what was going on. M'lady didn't seem to be in a very good mood.

CHAPTER 19

Lady Ware acted oblivious to the Carchemish artifacts. She led everyone out of the house through a side door. She showed them around her Fragrance Garden. "Look at the pheasant's eye narcissus," she pointed it out. "It's blooming. Over here we have the gilliflower." Tiny plants were growing between the bricks on the walkway. Dora lifted her feet carefully.

Lady Ware shot her a withering look. "Those are mint and thyme. You're supposed to step on them. They produce a pleasing scent."

Edward quickly took Dora's arm. He whispered into her ear, "Mother's a regular Amazon when it comes to her garden. She's afraid the War Office will requisition it and turn it into a vegetable patch for the troops."

Dora turned to Edward in shock. "As serious as that?"

He nodded, "England's running out of food. Would you believe it? I wouldn't talk about it too loudly, though. Makes mother cry."

Dora couldn't remember ever wanting for food in her life, not even in her Denbigh dormitory dining hall, at Bryn Mawr College on the Philadelphia Main Line, where the other women complained about the food all the time.

Lady Ware led them down a set of brick stairs to a red brick walkway that led to the Sunken Garden. Dora was confronted by a huge bevy of tulips of different colors waving in the breeze and nodding at her. Their little party strode past a raised pond with floating water lilies and iris. She was surprised to see carp swimming about and snails clinging to the lily pads. A frog sat on one.

Sir Adolphus had brought along his camera and tripod. He was constantly stopping to direct Mr. and Mrs. Benley to move this way or that for a photo. He loudly announced that he did so for all his friends.

Lady Ware couldn't resist feeding the fish. She sniffled

and wiped her eye with her lace handkerchief.

"Mother's afraid the troops are going to eat her carp," Edward whispered very low into Dora's ear.

"No!"

"Sh-h-h-h-h-h!" Edward winked and put his finger to his lips.

They progressed through a gateway in an otherwise solid brick wall into a sheltered garden at the end of the property, the Formal Garden. The red brick walls were decorated with espaliered pear trees on trellises. The garden was divided into four symmetrical parts growing either tulips, English daisies, tiger lilies, or sunflowers. In the center stood a tea pavilion complete with seating for a party of twenty-five. Lucy was already there with her helpers setting things up.

"Hold it there!" said Sir Adolphus. His complexion was faultlessly fair and very ruddy – that is, where it wasn't covered by his beard. The fiftyish fellow made everybody pose. A valet held out a wooden humidor of cigars. He selected one. The valet lighted it and handed it to him just as m'lord moved his folding camera around on his tripod. He took a photo of everyone standing against the garden wall.

"I want to introduce my old chum, Leonard Woolley. We excavated at Carchemish together last year before the Germans and Austrians broke it up by starting the War." He moved Woolley into the photo.

"That should interest Dora," Mrs. Benley prattled. "She's a classics major at Bryn Mawr College."

Lady Ware cast Mr. Woolley another one of her scathing looks. Apparently he didn't escape her censure either – just like her husband.

Edward pulled Dora down onto a marble bench in the tea pavilion, out of range of the lens of the camera. He leaned toward her, "Mother feels threatened by Leonard Woolley."

"She doesn't like your father to excavate?"

"She's having second thoughts."

"Why?"

"Because it's catching, I guess."

"How so? Have you been there, too?"

He shook his head, "I'm going to ship off to the Dardanelles myself."

"You want to join this crazy war?" Dora was shocked.

"*Sh-h-h-h-h!*" he motioned to her. His mother was darting suspicious glances at Dora as she poured cups of tea and added milk and sugar to each one. "You ought to understand – the land of Homer, the land of the Trojans. It's in the blood."

Dora noticed a copy of *The Times* next to her elbow on the table covered in white linen. She picked up the broadsheet and scanned it. Dora was dimly aware of Lady Ware serving the cups of tea to everyone, along with plates of warmed scones with Devonshire clotted cream and jam and another plate of savories such as tiny sandwiches and appetizers.

The paper, dated Saturday, May 8, 1915, which was yesterday, was labeled *Late War Edition.* Dora's eyes didn't know what to focus on first. She noticed a column with the heading *Serbian Relief Fund.* Another read *The Times Freight Exchange.* Still another said *Club Announcements* or *Personal.*

"Where's the mention of the *Lusitania?*"Dora asked, appalled. "You mean what we went through doesn't even merit first page attention?"

Mr. Benley grabbed the paper, glanced at it, and thrust it back at her with a "Humph!" He went on to describe to Sir Adolphus and Leonard Woolley his family's harrowing escape from the sinking ship, threatening again to sue the Cunard Line and the British Admiralty.

Mrs. Benley sat there and nodded with big eyes that looked like they were about to pop out of her head, agreeing with everything her husband said. "We were seated in the Promenade Cafe on the Boat Deck," she chattered on. "We'd just been served lunch around one-thirty, my husband, myself, and poor Mr. Klein. The man across from us was joking that he hoped he'd get his ice cream before the torpedo spoiled it all. Another man was going on and on proving that it was impossible to torpedo the *Lusitania.* Somebody screamed, and there it was! The torpedo was headed right for us."

"According to my pocket watch it didn't take more than eighteen minutes to sink!" Mr. Benley declared. "It all started precisely at 2:08 PM."

Sir Adolphus offered her father a cigar, then helped him light up.

Lady Ware continued to pour tea. She snapped at the servant who was assisting her. "I said to warm these scones until they're toasty. They look charred to me." She hurled one at the maid.

"I don't believe you English," Mr. Benley declared, "not to care that scores of Americans were drowned yesterday. After all, we are neutral in this European war of yours," her father shuddered.

"Are you going to remain neutral now?" asked Leonard Woolley, lighting up himself and taking a draw on the cigar.

"What a question to ask!" her father exclaimed. "Even Wilson declared that he'd take it very seriously if the Germans violated American neutrality. I'm sure he'll at least expel the German ambassador. Would be the only civilized thing to do. I saw appalling things in the ocean two days ago. Just appalling."

Mrs. Benley shook herself and sipped her tea.

Atop the left column of *The Times* Dora saw the subheading *Killed in Action*. She was amazed at the number of casualties. She started to read aloud without realizing it:
Butcher Killed in action on the 2nd May, Lieutenant Charles Geoffrey Butcher Dorset Regiment Aged 22, third dearly loved son of Mr and Mrs Butcher. Tregunter Road S. Kensington.

Dora glanced up to see Lady Ware drop one of the tea cups onto the brick pavilion floor. She looked red-cheeked and flustered. "Clean this up!" Lady Ware stomped her foot. "Call one of the gardeners."

Dora continued reading:
Campbell. Killed in action in the Dardanelles on the 4th May Lieutenant Malcolm Drury Campbell . . .

As soon as Dora spoke the word "Dardanelles", Lady Ware collapsed in tears. Sir Adolphus rose with a sigh and put his arm around his wife's shoulders. "Now, now, I'm sure our Edward can take care of himself. He takes after me. Didn't I come back from all my expeditions?"

His wife cast her husband a look full of reproach.

CHAPTER 20

"This man Lawrence I was telling Adolphus about, he's quite competent to serve under," Leonard Woolley sat forward in his chair and talked forcefully as if trying to convince everybody. "He used to work for me at Carchemish. You remember him, don't you, Adolphus?"

"Always had his nose in a book. Spoke languages. Don't remember how many," Sir Adolphus agreed. "An Oxford man, just like you and me."

"Now you've done it!" Edward hissed at Dora. "In your hands, this newspaper a dangerous weapon!"

Mr. Benley grabbed the paper from his daughter. "All you can do is print casualties on the front page. What a waste of young men!" he leafed through it, looking for the *Lusitania* story. "Oh, so you finally get to it on page nine. Such a minor tragedy!" He read aloud: "The *Lusitania* Sunk Torpedoed Off Irish Coast. No Warning. Many Notable Passengers. 2160 On Board. Only 658 Known To Be Saved . . . "

Mrs. Benley nodded, "And we're three of them."

Mr. Benley scanned down the column, "The *Lusitania* had a very distinguished passenger list. About four-fifths of her passengers were citizens of the United States . . . American opinion has been profoundly shocked by the wanton destruction of the ship and disregard for the lives and property of neutrals. A grave situation has been created."

Mrs. Benley sighed, "Very grave."

Mr. Benley threw the paper down. "After I sue the Cunard Line and the British Admiralty, I'm going to sue the Kaiser, too." He sat there with his hands on his waist as if he were going to defy the world.

"How on earth would you do that?" Edward burst out laughing.

"The German government owns property in the United States. I'll sue in an American court. They'll order the confiscation of that property. That's how!" her father nodded.

"Father," Edward pulled on his father's sleeve to attract his attention, "this is what it means to be an American. They want to fight in court instead of on the battlefield."

"Excuse me, sir, but isn't Benley an Anglicization of a German name?" Leonard Woolley asked suspiciously, sensitive to linguistic nuances.

Dora braced herself. Nothing made her father more livid than this insinuation. He considered it an insult or slur.

"I was born a Benner. But I am not a German," he announced proudly, thrusting out his chest.

Mrs. Benley nodded in agreement. She'd heard this, just as Dora had, a thousand times before in all kinds of company.

"How so?" Leonard Woolley crossed his brows as he smoked.

"I am an American," Mr. Benley proclaimed. "That's final! My parents left Germany on the boat in the late nineteenth century. The whole place could go to hell as far as they were concerned. I agree! Now let's get down to business. Sir Adolphus, what about those tires?" her father took out some business papers he'd managed to salvage from the wreck in his coat pocket. "Tires make much more sense than all your U-Boats, Kaisers, Arch Dukes, and whatever." He waved them away as if they were mere flies.

"In short," Edward turned to Dora, "we British have our hands full. We've got so many wars on so many fronts that we can't count them all. The *Lusitania,*" he shrugged, "gets lost in the whole jumbled mess."

"Really?" Dora felt the affront. After all, she'd almost drowned!

"Except that you were aboard," Edward ventured. "For you I'm beginning to think I could fight a whole war, my Miss Dora Benley."

Dora felt a flush rise up her neck, making her cheeks tingle and burn. She turned away and looked around the garden to escape from Edward's intense and provocative gaze.

"I want to capture that perfect pose," Edward leaped up and raced back to the house to fetch his own folding camera.

He posed Dora just so. He fixed his camera on a tripod. He attached a timer to it. He raced to sit down next to her with his arm around her shoulders before it flashed in their faces. He whispered to her. His warm breath tickled her ear.

A gardener had appeared to clean up the broken tea cup on the floor of the pavilion. He stooped down low not two yards away from where Dora was sitting. As the man rose, their eyes met. She'd felt that scrutiny before. His skin was tawny and dark, his eyes darker. The broad-brimmed hat was gone, but she was positive she knew him.

"Dora, what is it?" Edward realized she hadn't heard a thing he'd been saying.

"It's – it's . . . "

He'd never believe her. Edward wasn't Michael. He hadn't been on the *Lusitania*. All she could whisper was, "I – I thought he'd drowned."

The gardener had risen and started to walk away. She was sure he was out of hearing range, though he stopped once and turned to glance at her over his shoulder.

"Oh, that's just Ali, our gardener," Edward dismissed him with a wave of the hand. "My father brought him back from his excavations at Carchemish last year. He was one of the native workers. Not likely to drown. Swims like a fish. Saw him swimming one morning in our canal."

"Has he been here the whole time?" she whispered low while the man continued to walk away from them. He was almost out of sight.

"No, I believe he was just on holiday. Got back yesterday. Or last night."

That was as Dora had feared. She rose. "I – I have to make a phone call to London."

CHAPTER 21

When she got to her bedroom, Dora pulled out an upholstered, Stuart high back chair with a carved front rail from the writing table. She retrieved the notes she'd taken down yesterday morning in Queenstown. She looked up Michael Byrne's phone number in London and dialed.

Br-r-r-r-r-ring! Br-r-r-r-r-ring!

"Hello?" came a low voice.

"Is that you, Mr. Byrne?" Dora asked in a whispered tone that seemed natural when talking to Michael.

"I thought it might be you," he confessed. "Your ring sounded different from *The New York Times* reporters. They cable the front desk. The front desk keeps on buzzing my room."

"Something just happened. I – I don't want to say what it is on the phone."

"London would be the most anonymous place to meet," he suggested.

"The Wares and my parents are going shopping. Stay by your phone. I'll call you tomorrow morning to give you the exact time and place."

Click

Dora sat there at the desk gazing off into space. She finally picked up the *Potash and Perlmutter in Society* play by Mr. Klein that her mother had given her, turned to the *After Word*, and read the note:

Dora – I'm writing this on the night of Thursday, May 6. I don't know what's happened to you or if you are hiding out with Mr. Byrne. In case the Germans do their worst and you survive and I don't, I want you to know that I believe you. I can't convince your parents, but I saw that man that Mr. Byrne talked about at lunch. I was out on the deck late without lighting a cigarette, as Captain Turner has ordered. I was looking one last time for you as I do every night. I glimpsed the man in the wide-brimmed hat that looks very much like mine. I saw him with what Mr. Byrne described as "fuses". I will report this to the Captain on Friday before we dock in Liverpool.

Yours faithfully,
Mr. Charles Klein

P.S. I also asked your mother to give you my play as well as my revised novelette. Do with them what you will. I leave them to you. This is Friday. I'm headed back to look for you. The torpedo has struck.

Tears ran down Dora's cheeks. To hear for certain that her would-be swain had died searching for her on the decks of the doomed *Lusitania* was more than Dora could bear. She began sobbing uncontrollably.

Knock! Knock! Knock!

"Yes?" Dora sniffled.

"Are you dressed for dinner? Lady Ware stuffed your closet with some old things just as she's stuffed mine. You will have to make do until we can go shopping in London bright and early tomorrow," her mother announced.

Dora had forgotten. She had to go through with the dinner ritual. At least she'd been right about one thing – there was to be a shopping expedition to London tomorrow.

"I'll be down in a minute," Dora groaned. She opened the double-doored wardrobe. She took out a steel blue, Liberty silk dress suitable for evening wear. It was too short, but Dora arranged the V-neck bodice so it would fit on her taller frame.

She heard a wolf whistle, gasped, and turned around. The curtains around the early seventeenth century, four poster bed parted. Edward sat crossed-legged in the middle of the mattress.

"What in the name of God are you doing here?"

"I was going to protect you against that hooligan that you claim is after you," he leaped off the bed. "But after that long trip yesterday and today, I fell asleep." He stretched and yawned.

He must have sneaked into the room while she was talking to Mr. Byrne. He'd hidden himself there just to . . . just to . . . "You were spying on me!" she declared.

He bumped his nose up against hers. "I don't know if I would call it spying or part of the war effort. I have to protect the American neutrals, remember?"

Her cheeks burned crimson. "I'm going down to dinner,"she left the room.

He grabbed hold of her elbow on the grand staircase. She couldn't free herself without attracting attention. Sir Adolphus and Lady Ware were right behind them. She plastered a smile on her face, though she longed to smack Edward's.

Another surprise awaited her in the Great Hall. The long, dark wooden table had been set, the one that extended half the length of the room. It was large enough to seat a hundred people! Her attention was attracted to the Greek column-like legs carved with Corinthian decoration. The sides of the table featured fluted designs. It was past seven. The only illumination, besides the leaping flames in the fireplace, was provided by candles set in large silver candelabra in the middle of the banqueting table.

Edward pulled out a chair for her, a heavy wooden thing with velvet cushions and fringe. He pushed it in while managing to get his arms around her. He helped himself to a chair right beside her, knee to knee. Two days off the *Lusitania* she hadn't expected this sort of wild flirtation.

"Happy birthday, old chap!" Sir Adolphus patted his guest on the shoulder. Mrs. Ware handed Mr. Benley a wrapped gift. He opened it and took out a pipe to great applause around the table. He lighted up.

"Oh, my goodness!" Dora exclaimed. "That box you sent me, Sir Adolphus, I meant to apologize," Dora rushed on, looking from Sir Adolphus to Lady Ware in embarrassment. "I left it in my cabin. It's at the bottom of the Irish Sea."

Lady Ware, Sir Adolphus, and Leonard Woolley fell

silent as if she'd committed some grave *faux pas*.

"You know, the wooden object you sent me to keep for my father's birthday? I – I didn't open it up, of course. It was already wrapped. But it was gapping open a little on the bottom . . ."

Sir Adolphus and Leonard Woolley continued to gape at her. Their faces were unreadable.

"I thought it was my imagination when I saw Hittite inscriptions there. But after I saw your display case in the library, I wonder. I hope the object wasn't irreplaceable," she tried to nudge their memories.

Leonard Woolley jumped to his feet and came around to where she was sitting. "Ah, miss, I'm sure we're all sorry that you lost your package," he glanced over his shoulder at Sir Adolphus, "but we don't know anything about it."

"Of course you must!" Dora insisted. "The note attached to it was from Sir Adolphus. He –"

Leonard Woolley took Dora by the elbow and escorted her out of of the room. He led her all the way down the hall out of hearing range. She couldn't imagine what he was doing. "Mr. Woolley, I –"

"If you don't mind, miss, this sort of bold behavior may be fashionable in America, but it's considered poor manners here in England. Don't accuse Sir Adolphus of what he didn't do," his voice sounded stern.

"But –"

"If you were my daughter, I'd discipline you for such impertinence!" he stomped his foot.

"So, Dora, you have another swain at your feet, I see," Edward appeared out of nowhere and took Dora by the arm. "I'll have to be more bold, or someone will steal you from me right under my nose in my own house," he nodded at Woolley and led Dora back to the table.

"I don't understand!" Dora protested as Edward made her sit down.

"Oh, Woolley is an old tiger with the ladies!" Edward teased.

Woolley resumed his own seat across the table. He wouldn't take his eyes off her. His glare felt like a knife. She wondered, *What was wrong with mentioning the birthday gift with the weird inscription on the bottom?* Apparently doing so had been a terrible mistake.

CHAPTER 22

The ladies were chatting about household matters as if the fuss about the lost birthday gift had never occurred. "Excuse the dimness in the room," Lady Ware remarked to Mrs. Benley, "we just got electrification a few years ago. We don't use it much because of the war effort."

"I don't see how it could hurt the soldiers to turn the lights on," Mrs. Benley said. "During the Spanish American War, T.R. didn't ask us to do anything out of the ordinary back in Pittsburgh."

Lady Ware rolled her eyes toward the ceiling. "Yes, I'm sure things are quite different in America!"

"Are you Americans going to take up the call or play cowards?" Sir Adolphus challenged Mr. Benley. "Are you going to let the Germans cow you with the *Lusitania?*"

"No one buffaloes me!" Mr. Benley insisted with the emphasis on "buffaloes". He always emphasized any colorful, earthy expression he'd picked up from his frontier days with Teddy Roosevelt. "If I were Wilson, and believe me I wouldn't want to be, I'd lay claim to all those German assets in the United States. Every last one of them."

"Germans are stubborn by nature," Woolley observed. "Nothing will convince them except a good thrashing."

The server set the pork roast down at one end of the table. Dora recognized him as the gardener from today and the saboteur from two days ago. Their eyes met and held. Then he looked away with a grimace of utter disgust.

"You see, he knows me!" Dora hissed at Edward.

"Men of his race aren't used to ladies appearing in public, let alone ladies glaring boldly at them," Edward suggested.

"What's wrong with him?" Dora whispered as the older men debated the war.

"Moslems don't like pork," Edward explained. "Some such nonsense!"

"Really?" she'd never heard of it. "Why?"

He shrugged. "Old superstition. It may take awhile, but he'll become more civilized the longer he works here."

"He'll never be civilized. He helped sink the *Lusitania*," she grumbled very low.

"Ali doesn't have it in him to do anything that nasty," Edward dismissed her accusation. "He's only a poor gardener from Carchemish."

Ali continued to glance in her direction. Dora's pulse beat at the base of her throat. When Dora retired to her room, she found it been ransacked, just like her cabin off the Boat Deck of the *Lusitania*. All the drawers were pulled out. The clothes had been yanked out of the closet. The mattress was overturned. Ali had been looking for whatever he he'd been unable to find in her cabin on the ship.

She marched down the hallway to Edward's room. She knocked on the door.

"Is this an invitation?" he poked his red head out. His hair was all mussed up. His eyes looked bleary. He was yawning.

"Come and look at my room," she dragged him along by the arm as he struggled to put on his night robe and slippers.

"Is that all?" he sighed with disappointment.

She practically shoved him into her bedchamber. She turned on the overhead light and shut the door. "Ali's gone through everything. This is what he did to my cabin on the *Lusitania* – that is, before he kidnapped me and dragged me from one cabin to another for most of the duration of the voyage!"

"It's obviously one of the maids," Edward surprised Dora.

"What!"

"The girls from the village have it particularly bad. Their men are in the trenches. They have to work at any job they can find. They don't have enough to make ends meet. I'll have to tell Mother. She can discipline the girl tomorrow."

"It's obviously your Ali!" she stomped her foot. *"Why* do you defend him?"

"Why do you pick on him? He's a quiet fellow."

"He strapped a fuse to a pillar in the engine room of the *Lusitania.* He tied me and Michael up, too. We barely escaped with our lives."

"Did you get a good look at this mad bomber?" Edward challenged her. "Tell me the truth!"

"He had a big hat. It shaded his face most of the time . . . true . . . "

He stuck his nose into her face in the annoying way only he could. "You're just shaken up because of the shipwreck," he slipped his arms around her waist and pulled her against him. "I can make you forget that," he boasted. "Besides, now that your room is wrecked up, wouldn't you like to share mine?" His lips groped for hers and found them.

She unfastened his exploring hands after a few moments of blind groping. "See you tomorrow!" Dora said frostily. She pushed him out of the room and locked the door, then went to her mirror and examined her flaming red cheeks and mushed up hair. She tried to set things aright. But it didn't do any good. In frustration she turned out the light.

CHAPTER 23

Next morning early she called Mr. Byrne as she'd promised.

"I'm staying in a rented house in the Notting Hill Neighborhood in the West End. I'll give you the house number," he shuffled through a desk drawer. "It's . . . ah . . . 35 Notting Hill Lane."

"I'll be there as soon as I can." She wished she could ask for a car to drive herself, but Edward was waiting for her in a flashy red 1912 Speedster with gold fittings. Even the wheels were painted fire engine red! She wondered how many cars he owned. Her parents and the Wares were piling into a more conservative black Town Car right behind them.

"Where on earth did you get a car like this?" she was astounded.

"Dad's in the auto business in London. We trade cars off like some people trade clothes," he shrugged. "I have to have something suitable for a fashionable miss like yourself from America. Your dad's in the auto business, too, from what I understand."

"Tires," she corrected him.

"Besides, if I don't get my thrills now, I may never have another chance," his usual enthusiasm for life was dampened by a fleeting dark cloud. "I'm shipping off to the Dardanelles, remember?"

As they drove down the entrance drive to Ware House, Ali was cutting the grass. He paused and looked up as she passed. A shiver went up her spine.

"Smile!" he reminded her, reaching across the seat and squeezing her thigh.

During the eleven miles into London she kept on wondering how she was going to get away from Edward long enough to see Mr. Byrne. They stopped at Harrods, a leading department store, one of the few clothing shops still open. She watched carefully where Edward parked his car. Once they got into the store, she leaned toward him to make a comment and lifted the car keys out of his pocket. Then, after trying on a dress or two, she excused herself to go to the ladies room. She was on her way to Notting Hill in only a few moments.

Without a map it was hard to navigate her way around the crowded streets – that and the fact that everyone was driving on the wrong side of the road! She had to stop, ask for directions, and try to decipher the local dialect. Not to mention that she wasn't a very experienced driver. Her father wouldn't hear of her operating a motor vehicle. She'd done it on the sly at Bryn Mawr.

It must have taken her over an hour to get to the Notting Hill neighborhood. She parked along the street, glad to find Notting Hill Lane right away. She located a number 20. But she couldn't find either a 16 or a 24, let alone a 35.

Dora peered into the window of what looked like a library. A raven-haired lady with a dark complexion and dark eyes with long lashes was searching for something along one wall. The wall was covered floor to ceiling with bookcases made of solid mahogany. The beautiful woman with high cheekbones and a long, aquiline nose lifted out one book and now another. She opened each one, closed it, and looked some more.

Dora couldn't imagine what the woman, who seemed to possess quite a lovely figure, was doing. As she leaned over, the sash around her waist tightened. It accentuated her bosom as well as her slim waist. Dora guessed that she was probably in her early thirties, maybe her late twenties. It was hard to tell.

Dora thought, *I wonder who she is? She doesn't look English.*

"Hurry up, will you, Asalah?" came a man's voice from the other side of the room.

Dora had heard that voice before, as recently as this morning at breakfast. Only her sense of shock prevented her from verbalizing his name.

"Just a minute!" the woman shot back in a foreign

accent, pushing up a small library ladder, and climbing to the top of the stacks. She lifted out a wooden box hiding behind a row of books. She climbed down the ladder and approached the over-stuffed easy chair on the other side of the room. She placed the wooden box down on a side table. Standing in front of the middle-aged gentleman, she helped to pull off his boots one by one.

"Come here, wench!" the man pulled the sylph-like woman onto his lap. He smacked her lips.

Why, it was Sir Adolphus! He'd told Lady Ware and the Benleys that he was going to his club to meet some friends to play cards. Her father hated cards. He thought they were idle. He hadn't offered to accompany Sir Adolphus, and Sir Adolphus hadn't pressed him. Now she could see why.

The dark lady smiled, as if used to this kind of treatment. "Here are your favorite cheroots," she opened the wooden humidor that she had just fetched from the library shelf and held it out to him to select one for himself. She spoke with the same kind of accent as Ali.

Sir Adolphus picked out one, sniffed it, and then chose another. He placed the cheroot between his lips. She lighted it with a match. He took a long draw and blew it out.

While he was enjoying his smoke, the woman named Asalah closed the wooden humidor. At first it wouldn't close right. She tried harder. The box tilted a little. Dora caught a glimpse of the bottom of the box. To her amazement, it was inscribed with the same kind of ancient Hittite characters that the other box, the one left in her cabin on the *Lusitania,* had been. Dora thought, *Is that what the other box was – a wooden humidor for cigars?* It didn't make any sense. Tobacco hadn't existed until the English founded the Jamestown colony. The ancient Hittites hadn't smoked cigars.

Sir Adolphus patted his knee. "Come, Asalah!"

The young woman snuggled up to him. She wrapped her arms around his neck and kissed him. As he took another draw on his cigar, she started to undo the buttons on the back of her dress. The lady looked toward the window, noticing that the drapes weren't drawn. Dora met her gaze for a fraction of a second. She immediately hastened along the street as the mysterious dark lady fastened the drapes.

Dora concluded, *Well, it's none of my business!* But it wasn't that easy to dismiss the incident. She was so preoccupied with it, she ceased to look for house numbers. She wasn't watching where she was going. Dora ran smack into a young man hastening in her direction.

"So there you are, you minx!" Edward exclaimed. "Very clever, pinching my car keys! I had a devil of a time not losing you in traffic after I saw you slip out of Harrods." He waved off his cabbie.

"I'm busy right now if you don't mind!" she pushed past him.

"I'd like to make everything you do my business," he grabbed hold of her hand.

"I'm not your tart as much as you seem to want to make me one," she spat as she yanked her hand away. "You do take after your father, don't you?"

"Oh, so you saw *that! That's* what you're so uppity about," Edward glanced down the street at the window to the library as if he knew all about it.

"I was looking for another house number. I wasn't eavesdropping. But I see what kind of background you come from. My father would *never* do something like that to my mother!"

He sighed, "My parents were married way back in the nineteenth century. It was an arranged match. My mother was a baron's daughter. My father was new money. What can I say?" he shrugged. "This is England, not Puritan America."

"Your father doesn't have much respect for your mother."

"On the contrary, he has a great deal of respect. He keeps his mistress, Asalah, in town in this house unknown to anyone else besides my father and I. He keeps my mother in the country. They never meet. My mother doesn't have the slightest suspicion about Asalah. The girl's been here for two years.

The next to the last season he came back from Carchemish he brought her. The last season, last year in '14, he brought Ali."

Dora tried to sidestep Edward. He blocked her path. "What do you want anyway?" she smoldered.

"How about two people fall in love? Nobody has any need for mistresses," he slipped his arm around her waist and brought her up against his chest. Before she knew it, he was kissing her.

She smacked him across the face. "If you don't mind, I have an appointment."

"With Mr. Michael Byrne?"

"How did you know?" she asked frostily.

"I was listening in on the extension."

"You *are* a snake!"

"Sounds serious between you and Mr. Byrne. I shall accompany you as a chaperon," he offered her his arm with an easy laugh and absolutely no resentment that she'd just smacked him.

"You monster! Does nothing shame you?"

"Nothing!" he chortled again, pulling her along the street beside him.

He was leading her up the steps into one of the houses and opening the door before she thought to ask, "Is this number 35 where Mr. Byrne is staying?" He shut the door behind them and locked it. She found herself standing in the bedchamber of a strange house. "Where are we?"

"An older townhouse belonging to my father."

She looked around. "But –"

"Mr. Byrne will have to learn to wait his turn," he took off his coat and hung it up. "Maybe he'll have to wait for the whole damned war to be over." He turned his gaze on her.

She felt a flush rising from her chest up her neck to her face. It suffused her cheeks, making them burn and tingle. "But – but I just met you two days ago!" she read his mind.

"Haven't you heard of love at first sight?" he picked her up and threw her on top of the bed.

"I've – I've never done anything like this before," she

inched away from him toward the headboard. Her heart was thundering so hard against her ribcage, she imagined he could hear it.

"I should hope not," he crawled after her. "The next Lady Ware should be pure as the new driven snow, etc, etc, and so forth. All that stuff about Caesar's wife should be above suspicion."

"Are you asking me to marry you? I –"

"At the first opportunity," he grabbed hold of her chin and planted a kiss on her lips. She tried to pull away, but he wouldn't let her. He just kept on kissing her.

She had swum through that cold, fifty degree water in the Irish Sea. She could have gone under like countless hundreds of souls, such as her friend, Rita Jolivet, with the pearl-handled pistol, like Elbert Hubbard, like Frohman, like Vanderbilt, like poor Mr. Klein. The blood surging through her veins, her violently beating pulse that wanted to leap out from the base of her throat, told her that she was alive and not dead. When his lips groped for hers and hers groped back, when he pressed her breasts against his own chest, it was the first time she could remember feeling truly warm all over since the *Lusitania* had gone down.

CHAPTER 24

That night after dinner as Dora entered her room, the phone rang. "Hello, dar –"

"Is that you, Dora?"

"Oh, Mr. Byrne!" she was amazed that she could have forgotten for an instant that she was supposed to meet him today. She felt guilty, considering how she'd been occupying herself. "I'm sorry I didn't make it to your house. I got lost." It wasn't entirely false. She'd never found his house. "I – I couldn't locate your address. There weren't any house numbers."

"Dora, that crazy bomb thrower survived the sinking. I saw him today. He was standing outside on the sidewalk glaring in at me."

For a minute she did a double take, forgetting all about Edward. "What did he look like?" she asked.

Mr. Byrne described Ali exactly down to the outfit.

"That's what I was going to tell you today. The man's name is Ali. He works for the Wares as a gardener."

"You're kidding!"

"I can't convince them he's dangerous. Sir Adolphus brought him back from Carchemish last year just as the war started. They say he's a charity case. They defend him."

"Shocking!"

"What did he do to you, Michael?" she was alarmed.

"I locked the doors and windows. I shut the drapes. I called the police. By then the miscreant was gone. Guess what the police told me?"

"I can't imagine."

"They have enough to do besides listening to hysterical Americans."

"The British don't seem to think as much of the sinking of the *Lusitania* as we do. They claim there are lots of fronts to the war. That was just another one."

"Appalling!" he agreed.

There was a pause. "Let's keep in touch," he suggested.

"It's dangerous not to."

"Absolutely!"she agreed. "I'll call you tomorrow or the next day. I'll let you know everything that Ali does. For instance, last night he trashed my bedroom just as he did on the ship."

Michael was aghast. "I'll start calling about tickets. I'll see what ship is sailing when back to the good old USA," he promised. "I'm just about finished with my business trip. It's disgusting. J.P. Morgan's funding this war on the British side. I'd like to get out of it, thank you."

"I'll wait for your call."

Click.

Her parents' visit extended several weeks into May and many shopping expeditions into London with the ladies. It was easy for her to take off on her own, claiming that she was going to visit the British Museum, the Tower of London, or the Houses of Parliament. She always returned to Notting Hill to the special house where she could be alone with Edward.

She stopped often outside the house where she'd glimpsed Sir Adolphus and the strange dark woman that Edward called Asalah. Most of the time the drapes in the parlor were drawn. Only one other time did she glimpse Asalah. The lady was poring over the stack of books on the bookcase, lifting them out and putting them back in a curious fashion. Dora recalled that she'd taken the humidor out of the bookcase. That was a very peculiar place to keep it.

Asalah saw Dora and gave her a warning frown. The lady shook her head "no" and shut the drapes.

One day Dora was waiting for Edward to join her in their special house in London when she heard a shout on the street. She peered out through a crack in the drapes. The dark-skinned Asalah was running down the stairs from her house yelling, "Help! Help! Help! Fire!" She had a knife in her back! She fell down onto the sidewalk dead. With big, empty eyes, seeing a horror she hadn't been able to voice, she gazed upward at the sky.

Dora raced outside in time to see a fire engine arrive along with an ambulance.

Edward zoomed up in his Speedster with his father seated next to him. "Stop here!" Sir Adolphus leaped out. "Asalah called and said to come quick." He saw he was too late. He lingered a minute or two over the corpse of his mistress on the stretcher. He touched her cheek. When he raised his eyes to the house, he went white.

"Father, what are you doing?" Edward cried out, trying to stop him.

Sir Adolphus tore up the steps of the house on fire and into the entrance hall. He stumbled out a minute later coughing, with two firemen on each side of him. Sir Adolphus was holding that same wooden humidor to his chest.

"Father, why did you do that?" Edward pressed. "You could have been killed."

His father struggled with his wallet. He handed a large tip to the ambulance driver and gave him some instructions in a very low voice about Asalah's body. "Sentimental value," was all Sir Adolphus could offer as explanation as he climbed back into the Speedster with his humidor.

CHAPTER 25

T he three of them had to squeeze into the two-seated Speedster for the eleven-mile journey back to Ware House. Sir Adolphus sat clutching the humidor, not talking much, sighing. When they arrived back, he shut himself up in his room. Edward had to make excuses to his mother that one of his father's old friends from Oxford had died.

Disasters always come in pairs. Edward pulled Dora into the bathroom as she was coming down the upstairs hall. "Edward!" she was scandalized as he locked the door and yanked her into the far corner next to the claw foot tub. "What are you doing?" He'd sneaked into her bedroom often enough, but that was after midnight when everyone else had gone to sleep. She didn't want her parents to catch them like this. He lifted her into the tub. He climbed in after her, drawing the curtain around them in a big circle. "Edward, this is –"

He undid her blouse and pulled it away from her body, mouthing her breasts with his lips.

Dora couldn't understand the white hot passion that came over her when Edward was around. They had made love many times. Neither one of them was satiated. It was like an all-consuming hunger, one for the other. Nor could they keep their hands off each other at any time of the day.

It was at its worst when she had those dreams about the *Lusitania.* She was on the deck, and it was sinking. When she couldn't find any place to leap off into the waves, she would go down with the ship. She'd woken up from such a nightmare several nights ago. She had tiptoed over to Edward's room and knocked. They'd made love for hours. It had made her forget the nightmare. The rest of the night she'd spent in dreamless sleep. Lovemaking had become a kind of sleeping draught, a balm for her nerves.

He pushed her skirt up around her waist. She let him lift her up into his arms. She clung to him until the insanity passed. At last he put her down on her own two feet. Exhausted, they embraced each other. He stroked her hair, which had come undone and fallen down her back.

"Darling, the regiment's been called up. I've got to ship out," he tried to catch his breath.

"When?"she pulled away and stared at him as they stood facing each other in the middle of the afternoon in the confines of the claw foot tub. She buttoned her blouse and adjusted her skirt so she was decent.

"Tomorrow, and I've heard from your father today that you're sailing back to America tomorrow, too."

She gulped. It was news to her!

"That friend of yours, Mr. Michael Byrne, called. He bought passages on the *Philadelphia*. It's all he could find for the three of you."

"Michael? But I haven't talked to him in days," she smoothed down her hair.

"He asked for you, but we were otherwise occupied in the garden," he reminded her of the time he'd started to get carried away and she'd stopped him, afraid someone would come along and surprise them. "He talked to your father instead."

Things were happening so fast. She was stunned. "But I've never heard of the *Philadelphia*," she adjusted her waistband.

"It's a smaller ocean liner. The *Mauretania* and most of the other big ships are being requestioned as troop transports. The war's heating up, my love. The world doesn't want to wait just because we want to make love behind every bush and tree."

She turned flaming red.

"Yes, my love," Edward squeezed her hands,"it turns out there's barely enough time to get you back to Liverpool to catch the ship – and for me to catch my troop transport."

She nodded.

The rest of the day was a nightmare of packing. Dora and her mother had accumulated whole new wardrobes during their weeks in England. Last but not least, Dora got a call from

Mr. Byrne. He told her what she already knew about the *Philadelphia.* They arranged to meet at the pier.

While she was packing, Dora got a note from Edward delivered by one of the maids. It said:

> Keep the door open for me tonight.
> E.

She no longer blushed at his impetuousness. She'd grown used to it. That night she lay in bed gazing up at the canopy, waiting for him. She turned this way and that. Finally she couldn't stand it any more. Dora got up to look for him. She'd bought an older copy of *The Lion and the Mouse* at a bookshop in London, an edition published in 1906. She'd made annotations in the margins. She wanted to give it to Edward as a going away gift.

Edward wasn't in his room. So she put on her night robe and went downstairs in her slippers. Perhaps Edward had been helping himself to a midnight snack. The original kitchen was housed in a separate building. Ten years ago Edward's parents had knocked out one of the ancient withdrawing rooms on the ground level to add a modern kitchen. No doubt that was where her fiance was otherwise occupied.

She chanced to go past the library right next to the parlor, the room where she'd studied the Carchemish artifacts on the day she'd arrived. Although no light was on, she heard voices. It sounded like two men.

As her eyes became accustomed to the dark, she could make out two figures near the window. In the scant illumination provided by the moon she recognized Sir Adolphus's full-length beard. He was slouched in a chair. Woolley smoked as he stood over the master of the house. She could smell tobacco.

"Have you arranged for a burial?" Woolley asked.

"Yes," sighed Sir Adolphus in a cracking voice as if he could barely keep himself from crying, "Asalah had a Moslem maid. She has connections. She promised to get her mistress underground by tonight. I gave her money to do it. Asalah often talked about how important it was for a Moslem to be buried right away."

"And to be buried facing Mecca," Woolley added solemnly.

There was a pause. Sir Adolphus said as if it hurt him. "I feel terrible I couldn't do better for Asalah after everything she did for us – and for me in particular."

"Quite a gal!" Woolley agreed. "Quite courageous."

"She didn't deserve to die like this," Sir Adolphus exclaimed. "I feel responsible."

"Not just you!" Woolley immediately corrected him. "All of us!"

"It's been three years," Sir Adolphus marveled. "I – I thought we were safe."

"I warned you at the time, if you'll consult your memory," Woolley reminded him. "I said we'd *never* be safe."

"Lawrence said something like that, too, but he was more hopeful," Sir Adolphus remembered.

Woolley snorted, "It was his idea to begin with! He *hoped* we could get away with it. The idealism of youth! I do believe that young man would try anything. He never listens. Impetuous. Pig-headed. Wild. But he was the best damned archaeological assistant I worked with at Carchemish. Knew all the languages. Second to none."

Dora had seen Lawrence's name in the unpublished excavation report. He was the one that Edward was supposed to be joining up with in the Dardanelles. Now they were saying he was wild and impetuous, responsible for Asalah's murder. Edward was her fiance. She didn't like this.

"Lawrence should deal with this mess," Sir Adolphus said.

"For once we agree," Woolley conceded. "I'd dump it into his lap at the first opportunity if he were here. But he's always somewhere else."

"It was a close call about that package, too."

"Yes, the package . . ." Sir Adolphus sighed deeply. "I'd almost forgotten."

"I hate to think we had something to do with that ship sinking . . . "

"It was just a gift, just a good way to get it out of here . . . I – I didn't mean any harm to anyone . . . Least of all that poor girl who's engaged to my boy . . . How could I tell her I sent her daddy a package that sank her friends to the bottom of the sea? And Asalah . . . " Sir Adolphus broke down weeping.

"We'll survive somehow," Woolley assured the baronet.

They must be talking about the birthday gift. Strange that they should deny sending it and now admit it in whispers to each other. To suggest that somehow this gift had to do with the sinking of the ship . . . What did they know that she didn't?

The smoky odor from Woolley's cigar seemed to be getting stronger as if he were moving in her direction. She hurried away on tiptoes as quickly as she could. She dashed back up the stairs to her bedroom, completely forgetting about Edward until she shut the door and found herself in his arms.

"Edward! Where were you?" she asked as he scooped her up and dumped her on top of the bed.

"I was looking for this!" he shoved a sparkling diamond ring into her face as he climbed into the bed beside her.

"But I already have an engagement ring, the one your grandmother wore as a lady-in-waiting to Queen Victoria!" she reminded him, showing him her fourth finger left hand.

"This is the one I want you to wear instead," he yanked the other off impetuously and threw it over his shoulder. He didn't give her a choice. He slipped the bigger, more gaudy one onto her finger. "It was the ring that a long ago ancestress of my mother got from her Crusader husband, right on the eve that he was to leave for the Holy Land for several years. I thought it was more appropriate. I'm leaving tomorrow."

"Edward!"she could laugh at his notions. She didn't get a chance because he kissed her instead.

When they lay there side by side in her bed some time later, she remembered the scene down in the study. "Edward," she leaned on her elbow as her naked breasts glistened with sweat, "what happened to Asalah?"

Edward shrugged. "I don't have the foggiest notion. Why does that concern us?" he pulled himself on top of her and spread her legs with his own. He seemed to be trying to maximize the last few moments that they would spend alone together for many months.

She put her hands on his chest and pushed him away for just a second. "I was looking for you. I heard your father and Woolley in the library. I couldn't understand what they were talking about. It sounded as if they were blaming what had happened to Asalah on this Lawrence fellow."

"Lawrence? Ha!" Edward laughed. "He's nowhere around London. He's off in Cairo at some intelligence office. He's supposed to come and meet me in the Dardanelles. Has to make maps of the region anyway, including aerial maps. He couldn't have murdered anyone."

"No, they didn't say he stabbed her," she sat up and clutched her knees, dumping Edward onto the mattress. "Somehow he was responsible just the same."

"So what if he was?" Edward sat up next to her..

"Don't you see?" she spoke as he kissed her neck right down to her bosom. "You're supposed to join him. I don't want him to make something bad happen to you, too."

"Nonsense!" he pushed her back against the pillows and nosed her belly button.

"And the birthday package . . . It turns out your father did send it. They think it caused the *Lusitania* to sink."

Edward raised his head a little above the level of her belly. "You sound like my mother. Worry. Worry all the time. We'll have the wedding at Christmas in the chapel near Hampton Court. I'll sail to America to get you and your parents. After all, I'd like to see Pittsburgh."

Dora was so surprised she forgot about Lawrence for a moment. "Christmas? But how –"

"The War can't last much longer." His tongue found its way between her thighs. She shuddered all over. The War and Christmas were the farthest things from her mind.

CHAPTER 26

"**D**ora, did you borrow my new hat?" her mother raced into her daughter's bedroom the next morning at dawn.

Dora sat up in bed and rubbed her eyes. She'd been up half the night. "Your hat?"

"The one from Harrods, the travel chapeau with the brown velvet, knotted on one side," her mother anxiously clutched her hands. "I feel undressed without it."

"You left it in the parlor."

It struck Dora what today was. It was the day she was supposed to leave England, the day Edward was supposed to ship off, perhaps for a long time. She remembered a thousand things she wanted to say to him. Now it was probably too late.

"Miss, breakfast is being served downstairs," Lucy, the maid, appeared at her door.

Dora got dressed as quickly as she could. She half-expected Edward to be at the top of the stairs to escort her down to the last meal they would eat together in months. To her surprise, he wasn't there. She hurried down the steps by herself.

Her heart beat louder as she passed the library. She couldn't help drifting over to the glass-enclosed display cases with the electric lights. Although she'd been at Ware House for several weeks, she hadn't stopped here since the first day. She looked at everything once more as if trying to memorize every artifact. She lingered over the very last case, the one with the stone stela of the men in procession carrying tablets. A piece had been chipped out of the corner of the stela. Not only that, the glass seemed to be cracked in that one corner.

A voice thundered at her. *"Don't touch it!"* Leonard Woolley was bearing down on her with a scowl. "You should know better than to manhandle the artifacts. These exhibits are museum quality."

Dora hurried into the Great Hall, nearly running into

a suit of armor in her haste. She expected another sit down, formal breakfast, but a maid directed her into the small morning room where Lady Ware often wrote her letters and managed her household after breakfast. A small, informal repast was being served. The fireplace had been lighted. The silver coffee and tea service was carefully set out on a side board that could be rolled from room to room. The Wares and Benleys were pouring themselves cups of hot beverages and snacking on the scones and jam that the maids delivered on a tray. Normally such were reserved for high tea at five o'clock in the afternoon just before dinner.

Lady Ware was collapsed in an easy chair with Lucy in attendance. The mistress of the house continued to weep and dab her eyes. Mrs. Benley kept on urging her to take a sip of hot tea with cream and sugar. Milady would have none of it. Dora saw how it was going to be.

Dora drank her tea and wondered where Edward had gone. She glanced down at the large, gaudy diamond ring in the antique golden band that had been passed down in his family since the Crusades. Was that the last she was to see of her fiance? Had he already departed for the front? Was that why Lady Ware was crying? Dora had almost convinced herself that she was too late to see Edward off when she heard a rapid tramp of feet approaching.

"Look what arrived this morning!" Edward burst into the morning room carrying a brand new folding camera with all the latest devices. "Just in the nick of time." He handed it to Mr. Benley, who handed it to his wife. Edward's mother glanced up at him mournfully. "The U-boats didn't get it. It's from America. It's a new Kodak camera, and I'm going to take it to the front. It even has five lenses, including a wide angle and a telephoto."

Dora had seen a passenger wielding one that last afternoon aboard the *Lusitania*. Little good it had done him! She didn't know why this one was so impressive.

Sir Adolphus ambled into the room after his son. "Edward got a cable from Lawrence."

Dora gritted her teeth. It made her uneasy to hear of this Lawrence, who had disturbed her sleep even though she'd never met him.

Edward's green eyes lighted up. "Lawrence has assigned a date when I'm supposed to meet him in the Dardanelles. After all, he's coming all the way from Cairo."

Dora didn't know how she could be jealous of Lawrence and apprehensive about him at the same time.

"Lawrence really moves around from place to place," Edward boasted. "I don't know how I could get bored around him."

"Young man," chided Mr. Benley, "I don't know this nutty fellow, Lawrence. But I'll have you remember it's a war and not a vacation trip you're embarking on."

"I hope the war's not all over before I get there," Edward said.

The butler interrupted, "Sir and Madam, there's a gentleman here. His name is Mr. Byrne. He's here to see Miss Dora Benley."

"Fantastic!" Edward exclaimed. "I haven't seen Michael since we were in Queenstown." Taking big strides, Edward headed for the front door followed closely by Dora. Dora wondered what Michael could possibly be doing here. He was supposed to meet her at the pier in Liverpool.

Dora caught a glimpse of the horror on Michael's face as the tall, redheaded youth wielding his brand new folding camera with its leather case and interchangeable lenses descended upon the guest in the Great Hall. He had not been expecting Edward. If Dora had been in a different mood, she might have thought it humorous. Michael stood there stiffly in his simple dark suit with a raincoat and hat, holding an umbrella, squeezed between Edward on the one hand and a medieval suit of armor on the other, not feeling comfortable around either. The poor man didn't know where to turn.

"I've heard so much about you since I last met you!" Edward shook Michael's hand so vigorously that it looked as if he were shaking Michael's whole frame. "I'm glad you assisted

Dora on board the *Lusitania.*"

Michael nodded, confused, looking from side to side for Dora.

"Go ahead, stand there," Edward arranged things like his father. He pushed Dora up beside Michael. "I want to snap this photo of you both together at Ware House."

As they were positioned there awkwardly side by side, Dora whispered to Michael, "Why did you come here and not the pier?"

"The sailing's been moved up by an hour. I had to tell you, so I dropped by to get you," he said very low.

"Mom! Dad!" Dora raced out of the room after the photo session was over. "Michael says we've got to leave now. The sailing's been moved up by an hour."

When Mr. Benley heard, he practically dropped his cup of coffee. "Good heavens! Let's get in the car right now."

Edward packed his new camera equipment, including the film. He folded the camera up into a pack that looked like the leather case for a book.

Michael grabbed hold of Dora's arm. "Let's go before it's too late!" His eyes flashed. He pulled her out the door.

"My handbag!" she objected.

"You didn't worry about your handbag when the *Lusitania* was sinking. Why worry about it now?" Michael directed her to the rented car he'd driven to Ware House. He forced her down into the front passenger seat before he heaved himself into the driver's seat.

She couldn't understand the comparison between the sinking of the *Lusitania* and the need to leave Ware House right this second. She gaped at Michael.

Her father grabbed hold of Mrs. Benley. He forced her into the same car right behind Michael and Dora. Mr. Benley nodded with great satisfaction from the backseat, "We owe it to Mr. Byrne. He got us out of here on the first available ship. He surprised me. Maybe I haven't given him enough credit up until now."

Michael started the car and pulled away before the

Wares had gotten into their vehicles. Dora protested, "But Edward's shipping off to the Dardanelles. I won't see him until Christmas."

"You'll see him at the pier," Michael said in an icy tone, not meeting her eye. "If not, at least we don't want to miss the last liner for days. It wouldn't do to get stranded here."

"One visit is enough!" agreed Mr. Benley. "I'm anxious to get back home."

"But, Winthrop," her mother complained, "I don't have all my packages!"

"Etta May, you can buy more in New York. Lady Ware can ship the rest to you after the war's over."

Mrs. Benley regarded her husband with amazement. She never once contradicted him as they drove off.

"I may not have approved of your monopolizing my daughter on the voyage to England," Mr. Benley said to Mr. Byrne, "but I like your haste to get back to America. She's the only sane country left on the face of the earth." He settled back for the drive to Liverpool.

As Dora turned around to see if Edward was following them, she wondered what Ware House would look like the next time she came here at Christmas. Would there be snow? Would they have lights? Then she noticed that Ali wasn't in his usual place in the garden. Early in the morning he always cut the grass and clipped the hedges.

"Mr. Byrne," she tugged at his sleeve.

"What do you want, Dora?" he positively growled.

"Ali's gone. Usually he's right over there!" she pointed.

"That renegade was right outside my rented house early this morning. I think you show poor judgment to lodge with somebody who's aiding and abetting him."

She put her hand over her mouth. Mr. Byrne's attitude couldn't be described as anything less than savage. As if that wasn't enough, in Liverpool Dora hardly had a chance to say good-bye to Edward. He'd gotten there late. They didn't get another chance to be alone.

Edward wore full-length, tan slacks and a long-sleeved tan jacket, the typical Khaki Drill Service Dress for soldiers heading to the Eastern Front in Gallipoli. On his back he carried a sleeping bag. He shouldered a supply bag. A wide leather belt was strapped around his waist. His sun helmet, a tan hat, was wide-brimmed. It had a top hat-like effect. His gun, a Lee-Enfield service rifle slightly modified, was now called an SMLE, a Short Magazine Lee-Enfield.

"Give this to Lawrence when you see him," Sir Adolphus handed over the same wooden humidor that Dora had watched him salvage from the burning house. It had the same strange marks on the bottom.

"I thought you wanted to keep it!" Edward objected.

"I've got lots of humidors. But I hear that Lawrence is a particular connoisseur of cheroots. Since he's serving our country, he deserves it more than I do."

Leonard Woolley nodded. He handed Edward a letter to introduce the scion of the Ware family to his old archaeological protege, T. E. Lawrence. Woolley looked anxious to get back to his post in the military and his potsherds from Mesopotamia. "Naturally I took the liberty to cable Lawrence in Cairo to arrange the meeting to begin with."

Lady Ware embraced her son and hugged him to her as if she never wanted to let go. "Mother, it will be all right," Edward assured her, kissing her cheek. She nodded with tears in her eyes. Mrs. Benley patted Lady Ware's arm.

Everyone was watching, so Edward pulled Dora aside amidst a crowd of total strangers. He opened her lips and plunged his tongue down into it. He gave her a full-mouthed kiss just as if no one else were there. "See you at Christmas!" he finally came up for air.

She nodded, hardly able to speak with the tears cascading down her cheeks. She sniffled, "Write to me."

"I'll write every day," Edward smiled down at her, lifting her chin to make sure she looked up into his eyes. "My letters will be so long, you won't have time to read them."

Then came the last call to board the troop transport.

Dora started forward with him, clutching hands as if they were welded together with cement and couldn't let go. She even started to board the ship with him when another soldier pushed past them and parted them.

Dora kept her eyes on Edward as he finished boarding the ship, and his ship left the pier. She waved with all the other sweethearts, mothers, and friends. She pushed her way to the front of the crowd for a last look at Edward. She tried to make him out on deck She thought she'd caught a last glimpse of his red hair, freckled cheeks, and bright smile. Even that faded. She felt one last, sharp pulse between her thighs.

"Come on, Dora!" Mr. Byrne took hold of her arm impatiently. "Let's go back to America."

Dora sniffled and wiped her eyes as he led her toward the *Philadelphia,* which was now boarding.

"Amen!" agreed Mr. Benley. "Amen!"

Chapter 27

As they were walking up the gangplank, Mr. Byrne scoffed, "Frankly, I thought better of you, Dora. How could you forget after the *Lusitania,* that we're Americans – not British aristocrats! Imagine becoming engaged to some British sir!"

Dora locked herself up in her cabin and cried half the afternoon as they sailed out into the Irish Sea. She missed the location where the *Lusitania* had gone down several weeks before. She didn't leave her cabin until her parents came knocking, telling her it was time to go to dinner.

She sat in the first-class dining room staring down at her plate, feeling lost. Not only wasn't Edward here to make her smile, Michael wouldn't talk to her. Someone tapped her on the shoulder. She looked up.

"Would you like to dance?"

"Oh, Mr. Byrne, I –"

He led her out onto the dance floor. At least it was a slow dance, nothing like the Bunny Hug. She wasn't be in the mood for that. Besides, it might remind her of Mr. Klein. That would make her feel sadder – if such a thing was possible.

"You don't like Edward any better than my father does. He doesn't approve of him either." She tried to keep the tears out of her voice without much success.

"That should tell you something, Dora," Mr. Byrne scolded.

She eyed Mr. Byrne's neat linen handkerchief folded up in his breast pocket. He handed it to her without her having to ask. She blew her nose and felt a little more resigned to her fate. "Father thinks Edward's silly, immature, and oh yes, frivolous!"

"So are most members of his class in England. They're parasites, that's what! Who do you think started this war? Parasites who don't have anything better to do."

A hand reached out of nowhere and patted Michael

on the shoulder. "You give her the old what for!" Mr. Benley smiled approvingly as he led her mother out onto the dance floor. "Don't spare the rod either."

"Dad says that Edward will never grow up."

"You said it, Dora, I didn't," Mr. Byrne sighed in disgust.

She danced for awhile, feeling like the weight of the world was on her shoulders. She caught sight of Edward's diamond ring sparkling on her finger as she rested her hand on Mr. Byrne's shoulder. She heard Edward's sardonic, devil-may-care laugh, and looked around startled as if he might be in the room right now.

"What are you doing, Dora?" Mr. Byrne asked, sensitive to her every mood.

"Oh, Michael, I can't help it! I love him!" she burst into tears.

Michael stopped dancing abruptly and led Dora back to her seat. To her horror, he spent the rest of the meal chatting with her mother, leaving her father to scold her.

"Really, Dora," her father feasted on roast gosling Normande, "Edward Ware's gone to the trenches. You're on your way back to America. Write him. Tell him you've had time to consider. Break off the engagement."

"Father!"

"Dora, if *I* can't be firm with you, I don't know who can."

"But, Winthrop!" her mother protested. "The Wares have such a nice house. A Christmas wedding would be beautiful."

"A wedding at the Bethel Presbyterian Church would be even nicer, as far as I'm concerned. It has lineage, too. Goes all the way back to the Revolutionary War when we got rid of Britain and all those damned aristocrats."

"But –" Mrs. Benley tried to stand up for her daughter.

Mr. Benley held up his hand, "I know! I know! My friends who attend Bethel Presbyterian aren't lords, dukes, and baronets. They're self-made men. They're Americans."

Dora glanced at Michael. He ate his boiled potatoes and didn't look at her. They were all ganging up on her. She burst into tears and excused herself. She ran to the ladies room and hid herself in a stall.

Her mother came to get her. "Dora, they're serving the dessert. It's *flambé*. You don't want to miss it."

"I'm not hungry."

Her mother led Dora back to the table. Her father was in some sort of heated discussion with Mr. Byrne. Michael was gazing down at his plate and shaking his head. Her father was patting him on the shoulder and giving him one of his pep talks.

As her parents talked – her father was going on and on about cars while her mother nodded – Dora got up the courage to address Michael. "Though you're sitting there beside me, you might as well have gone down with the *Lusitania* like Mr. Klein."

Mr. Byrne picked at his flambé. His was melting just like hers. He wiped his face with a napkin and put down a tip. "I'm going to bed. I'll see you all tomorrow."

The next morning Dora scoured the Boat Deck for him. She wandered into the first-class lounge. She approached a gentleman who looked like him from behind. She tapped him on the shoulder and reddened when a sour-faced old man turned around and scowled at her.

She approached a stewardess. "Have you seen a passenger called Michael Byrne?"

"What does he look like?"

Dora described him as a dour, serious man in his early thirties. He dressed in dark colors and had a sober expression. He had round cheeks with a touch of red and a long nose that frequently turned red. His eyes were gray, his hair dark brown. It was trimmed just so.

"Oh, that gentleman! He was up very early. He was pacing about the deck."

"Where is he now?"

The lady shrugged.

Had he fallen overboard? She rushed around the promenade deck until she found him sitting in a lounge chair glowering out at the North Atlantic. Its gray waters seemed to match his gray mood.

"Michael!" she rushed toward him. "I feared you were at the bottom of the sea."

"All right, Dora, you win!" he rose from his seat and followed her. She was bubbling over about everything that had happened to her since they'd landed in Ireland on May 7, as they headed toward the first-class restaurant. They took a table on one side of the room. They were still ensconced there hours later. Her parents came and went.

Finally the waiter approached the table, "Would you like anything else?"

"No, that's all right," Mr. Byrne assured him.

"I regret to tell you that the restaurant's closing for the afternoon."

Indeed all the other passengers had left. So they had to move back out on deck. The sun had come out. It seemed natural to chat the afternoon away in one of the deck chairs. They joined her parents for dinner and talked some more.

"Oh, Father!" Dora said almost gaily, totally at odds with her lost feeling of the night before, "Mr. Byrne says that J.P. Morgan's son wanted him to speak to the Prime Minister. He was supposed to deliver a letter. It got lost in the sinking. They cabled him another. It was so important! It had to be hand-delivered no matter what!" The waiter came by. Dora's mouth was full. She pointed at a cake on the dessert cart with her fork and made a noise.

"Dora!" her mother was scandalized at her daughter's bad manners.

"Sorry!" Dora giggled and went on talking.

"Why don't we let Michael tell us the story himself," her father suggested. "That is, if you could stop chattering like a parakeet, Dora."

Mr. Byrne related the story he'd told Dora that afternoon. "As far as my employer's concerned, the war could go on for the next hundred years. He'll pay for it."

"Morgan is one of the merchants of death. He's funding the Brits for certain," her father nodded.

Mr. Byrne escorted Dora back to her cabin after the restaurant closed for the night. Her parents occupied the room next door. Dora stood giggling next to Mr. Byrne for so long in front of her door, that her father leaned out of his cabin. "You two might as well head back to the restaurant. It will be breakfast by the time you get done talking." Then he closed his door.

"If you like," Michael suggested, "I can bring my pillow out here and sleep in the lounge chair outside your door. We can make sure that the knave Ali can't get to you, assuming he's aboard the ship. Would you feel safer that way?"

Much of her conversation had concerned Ali and everything that she'd observed him doing at Ware House. Mr. Byrne had emphasized how many times he'd seen Ali on the street in front his his rented dwelling.

Dora clapped her hands as if it were a party instead of a watch for an arsonist and saboteur. "I'll go get my blanket. I'll join you."

Michael pulled up two deck chairs. They sat side by side looking up and down the promenade deck and glancing out to sea. They waited for Ali to strike for so long that Dora nodded off and fell asleep after her big second day at sea.

When she opened her eyes, she was back in her bed. Mr. Byrne must have carried her there. She was still fully dressed but her blanket was carefully pulled up to her chin. Her high heels were placed side by side in the middle of her dresser.

Dora sat up in bed and hugged her knees as she looked at those two shoes that Michael must have placed there. Edward had always carelessly thrown her clothes and shoes everywhere around the bedroom. Mr. Byrne was so very particular and neat. It reminded her of her father scolding Viola for not placing his newspaper in the right place on the dining room table at breakfast.

For the rest of the voyage Dora, her parents, and Michael

took every meal together. Mr. Byrne would ask her mother to dance. Her father would ask Dora. Then they'd trade off. "It's odd," she confided in Michael as they danced, "I thought Ali had drowned. Then he showed up on Edward's estate. Edward claimed he'd been there for a year and insisted the man he called Ali was harmless. Sir Adolphus brought him back from his excavations with Leonard Woolley at Carchemish."

Mr. Byrne shuddered. "Everything in Europe seems to be like that, doesn't it? Positively Byzantine, complicated, and not straightforward."

"No one investigated when Ali ransacked my bedroom at Ware House."

"Did you complain to Edward? He *is* your fiance."

"Edward insisted one of the maids had been looking for money. Apparently they've been impoverished by the war."

"Why do they bother to fight the war if it makes a pauper of everyone?"

Mr. Benley danced closer, "Because Europeans would fight over an anthill to see who could be emperor of it – even if they all had to die in the process."

Mr. Byrne declared. "I will never go back to Europe, no matter what my employer says."

"If only Dora were marrying a business man of sense like you instead of some romantic English lord who thinks fighting in the Dardanelles is a picnic!" her father shook his head.

"Winthrop!" her mother admonished her husband, something she didn't often do. "That's not very nice."

"Etta May, I can't help it," Mr. Benley groaned. "I can't wait to see that Statue of Liberty greeting us as we sail into New York Harbor. The old gal will have a smile on her face for me."

The waltz ended, and Mr. Byrne led Dora back to her seat in the restaurant. Her mother was bragging to the waiter, "My daughter is engaged to be married to a baronet's son."

"You don't say, madam!" he looked astonished. "I thought she was engaged to that gentleman," he pointed at Michael as he pulled out Dora's chair. "They're always together."

Michael resumed his own seat, folded his hands, and sighed like Job.

Dora squeezed Michael's hand. "You don't understand! Edward – he's my fiance – doesn't object to Michael. In fact, he likes him! Michael's just like . . . well," she considered, "my older brother, part of the family!"

The waiter cast Michael a sympathetic look as he picked up their plates. Michael rose and said he had some paperwork to do back in his cabin.

"Michael!" Dora objected. "You said we were going to look all over the ship for Ali."

"We might do that tomorrow. He's not the worst threat that faces us on our voyage home."

"What does Michael mean by that?" Dora asked mystified after he'd left.

Her father sighed.

CHAPTER 28

Dora and Michael made a point of meeting after breakfast every day to search the ship. They didn't wander down to the hold as they had on the *Lusitania*. Instead, they inspected all of the passenger decks – including second class and steerage.

After dinner on the last night of the voyage Mr. Byrne led Dora to his cabin and locked the door behind them. Although she had been inside his cabin on the *Lusitania,* she hadn't been in this particular room. He pulled out a chair for her, "I need to talk to you. In private."

"What's wrong?" she felt alarmed as she sat down.

"I . . ." he began.

"Yes?"

He rose to get a bottle of water. He poured himself a drink and quaffed it. He looked right at her. "What do you really think about me?"

She smiled. "You're like my right arm. I mean, you saved my life that awful afternoon on the *Lusitania.* I wouldn't have made it up to the Boat Deck without you," she rubbed her eye that had begun to tear. "I helped you, too, that time when you got stabbed and then when we had to fish you out of the ocean. After that sort of experience, we're sort of like . . . well, soul mates . . . You can read my mind. Nothing could ever separate us."

"How do you feel about this fiance of yours?"

She shrugged, feeling a little awkward to be discussing this subject with Mr. Byrne. "Edward's a lot of fun," she said evasively.

"Something else, too?"

"Michael, I don't understand why you're pressing me about this!"

"What were you thinking, Dora, when you met the fellow day after day in that house in town – practically every afternoon, in fact?"

Her jaw sagged open. "You – you . . . how did you find out about that? My parents don't even know about London," she turned deathly pale.

"I assure you I didn't enlighten them." He put his hand under her chin. He forced her to look up at him. "Take this ring," he grabbed her left hand and shook it, "and send it back to that swain of yours."

"This is the ring that Edward's ancestor gave his ladylove when he embarked for the Crusades."

"*Crusades?* Ha!" he forced the ring off her finger. He showed her the inside of the band under the illumination of the electric overhead light. The inscription read 'Harrods'. "I saw plenty more like this when I was in London."

She withdrew her hand.

"Harrods may have been the first department store in London. But it wasn't open in the twelfth century," he slammed the ring down on the table. "That young prankster's taking horrible advantage of you."

"Edward . . . well, he likes to joke around and have fun." She didn't know how to tell him that it didn't matter to her where Edward got the ring. What mattered was that it was from him.

He twisted her wrist until it hurt. "If you're not marrying him for character or honesty, which are the only things that matter in a man, what fatal attraction does that wastrel hold for you? What were you doing in that townhouse all by yourselves?"

She got up and tried to leave. He pulled her back into her seat. "Answer me!" he commanded. "Tell me, Dora!"

She swallowed hard and turned red in the face. "Michael, this isn't seemly!" she begged.

"What you did in that downstairs bedroom with the French Provincial furniture in that canopied bed with the curtains you didn't bother to shut *isn't* seemly for a young, unmarried girl."

She rose to her feet aghast. "But how . . . You weren't there, Michael!"

He stood up, still holding her arm fast. "Oh, wasn't I?"

This was worse than a nightmare. It couldn't be happening.

"When you didn't arrive that afternoon, I went looking for you, Dora. I saw you disappear into that house. I was about to knock when I heard giggling inside – and something else, too."

She burst into tears and tried to turn away from him. He wouldn't let her.

"There was a big slit in the middle of the drapes."

"No! No! No!" she screeched.

He pulled her close to his face. They were nose to nose. She was gaping into his eyes as tears rolled down her cheeks. She couldn't look away.

"That young rapscallion had his fling before going off to the front. He gave you a fake ring. He'll never marry you. He'll play you for the fool because you're so adorably naive, innocent, and romantic . . . " he shook her. "If you let him get away with it and don't send him packing, he'll make you suffer so much that you'll look back on the *Lusitania* as a picnic. He's corrupt, as all British aristocrats are. He won't care if he breaks your heart."

"You're hurting me, Michael," she struggled.

"Can you imagine the morals of a man who takes advantage of a woman just two days after she survives the sinking of the *Lusitania?* He'll make you wait for him while he has adventure after adventure."

"No!"

"Don't be surprised if he doesn't write to you."

"He will! I know he will."

"Very well, Dora," he thrust her out onto the deck. He hurled her engagement ring down on the deck next to her. "I hope your Edward will be back from Gallipoli and this Lawrence of his the next time you're in a fix and need rescued. I hope he comes the next time you're feeling down and need somebody to wipe your tears."

Michael slammed the door in Dora's face.

CHAPTER 29

That night in her dreams Dora was back on the *Lusitania*. She and Michael were making their way up the stairs from the bowels of the ship. Crew members trapped below the decks pounded on the walls and screamed to be rescued. Suddenly there was a second explosion. Steam and coal dust were all around her. She was hacking her lungs out, unable to see where she was going. Michael had his arms around her. He led her on.

They struggled up onto the Boat Deck. A giant green wave, much bigger than it had been in real life, struck them. Michael was gone. She ran here and there looking for him. She ran back inside the ship. She met Mr. Klein. He shook his head.

She headed towards the deck again, but couldn't get the door open. She was trapped as the ship went down. Dora woke up thrashing from side to side, moaning, "Michael!" She sat up in bed and started to put her shoes on to go and get him before she realized they were docking today in only a few hours. She'd never see him again.

She pulled out a piece of the ship's stationery. She wrote to Michael, telling him about her nightmare. She concluded by saying, "We saved each other's lives. Without you, I know I would have died. Can't you find it in your heart to forget about Edward and just be my friend?" She signed her name and sent for a steward to deliver her letter to Michael's cabin. She tipped him generously to make sure he did it.

"Dora, are you ready for breakfast?" her mother asked as the steward strode off.

"No . . . ah . . . I'm still packing," she said dejectedly. She went back into her cabin to dress for their arrival in New York Harbor.

Afterwards, she slowly made her way down the deck. She stopped at the entrance to the Promenade Cafe and hid behind a potted palm when she heard her father talking to

Michael at a table not far away. Her mother must have already excused herself to get her hair done.

"What did you say to Dora? She looks worse than I've ever seen her. At least she was still smiling when she waved good-bye to that English lord. She looked better when Etta May and I pulled her out of the Irish Sea," her father was saying to Michael over his coffee.

"She made it clear she prefers to marry Edward Ware. She won't give him up," Michael said.

"Did you pop the question?"

"I never got that far," Michael sighed.

"By all means, give it a try before we dock," Mr. Benley glanced at his pocket watch. "Women like that sort of thing. Or buy her a gift, flowers, etc. Ladies are impressed by trifles. Etta May has decided she wants Dora to marry that English parasite just because she fancies his house."

"I'm afraid I don't have the means to buy something that would impress a Miss Dora Benley," Michael said bitterly.

"Etta May used to wear a silly necklace I gave her when we were courting. It's only later that that the women start to look at the price tag. After we were married ten years, she wanted to replace the necklace with the real McCoy."

"I don't want to impose myself on Dora if she doesn't want me."

"Father," Dora stepped forward from behind her potted palm, "could I talk to Michael alone for a moment?"

"For heaven's sakes, daughter, let's clear up the mess!" Winthrop Benley grimaced.

"I'm afraid it's not so simple, Father," she said.

Mr. Benley shrugged in exasperation, "Women were never my specialty – just tires!" He picked up his newspaper, folded it under his arm, and marched back to his cabin.

Dora sat down across from Michael. She dismissed the waiter. "Did you get my letter?"

"Yes."

She reached out and squeezed his hand. "Are you willing to be friends?"

He glared at her. "I'm not going to be your fool while you sneak off to be with Edward at every opportunity."

She looked into his blazing eyes that hadn't changed a bit since last night.

"You're a very foolish girl who will have to learn the hard way – no matter if you have to break everybody's heart, including your own, in the process."

With that he was gone.

CHAPTER 30

T he *Philadelphia* made an otherwise uneventful landing in New York Harbor on June 3, 1915. Dora stood behind a pile of luggage on the pier while listening to her parents say good-bye to Michael.

"Why don't you come and visit us this fall?" Mrs. Benley suggested. "After all, we *Lusitania* survivors do have to stick together."

"I'll give you a call as soon as I check my work schedule," Mr. Byrne said in a polite, distant fashion.

"What about your family?" her mother said.

"I have a sister in Brooklyn. That's about it."

"Oh, well! In that case, you simply must come!" Mrs. Benley patted Mr. Byrne's coat sleeve with her gloved hand.

He nodded. Mr. Byrne then headed for a cab. Her parents headed for another. Dora joined them after Mr. Byrne was gone.

As the cab made for Grand Central Station at 42nd Street and Park Avenue, her father said testily, "Well, you made a royal mess of that, daughter!"

"Yes, I know, Father." She folded her hands in her lap and played with her engagement ring as they approached the terminal's fifty foot pediment with the statues of Hercules, Minerva, and Mercury surrounding a thirteen-foot-clock. It had been designed by architect Whitney Warren two years ago.

As they got out of the cab and went inside the station with its vast, vaulted ceiling, she looked down at her ring and realized that Edward was all she had now. Yet he was farther away than ever before. She'd been heading west all these days. He'd been heading east. She wondered if she would find a letter waiting for her when she got back to the house in Pittsburgh. After all, Edward had promised to write every day.

As soon as they arrived home, Dora raced up the front steps to the door. She shoved the door open and burst into the checked tiled entrance hall.

A chubby face peeked around the corner from the kitchen. Viola pushed her coal black hair away from her forehead. A smile irradiated her face as she thrust out two plump arms. In her dark blue, aproned dress she ran toward Dora. "Dora!" Viola hugged her. "I thought I'd never see you again when I heard about that awful ship going down," the cleaning lady dabbed her eyes with her apron.

"Viola, did any letters come for me while I was gone?"

Viola showed her the pile that had accumulated in a little more than a month. Most of the letters were for her father, of course. Others were social invitations for her mother. There were a few letters from girls at school. Dora couldn't find anything resembling a missive from Edward.

After dinner she hurried up to her old bedroom with the stuccoed walls painted white. She plopped down at her desk and wrote her first letter to Edward. She hesitated about what to say. She thought of telling him about her nightmare. Edward would never understand. He'd dismiss it or tease her. After all, he hadn't been on the *Lusitania* that day.

Dear Edward,

Why don't you write me? I'm desperate for news. Every night I wake up five times or more. The first thing I do is wonder where you are and what you're doing. You're a soldier. You have plenty to do to keep you occupied. I have nothing to do but wait for word from you.

Love,
Dora

Most of their brief but intense acquaintance had been of the most intimate sort. It seemed more natural for Edward to be kissing her arm up to her shoulder or nuzzling her neck all the way to her bosom and beyond. She should be kissing him back. Trying to substitute words for lovemaking seemed to belie the very essence of what they were to each other – lovers.

The next morning she woke up early and hiked all the

way up the gravel drive to put the letter in the family mailbox out by the road. Usually Frank did the chore, but she wanted to make sure that this letter got mailed right away.

So began Dora's vigil. She would pace up the gravel driveway to the mailbox every morning at ten o'clock. Sometimes she'd stand there for an hour or more, waiting for the clip-clop of the milkman's horses. For the milkman always came before the mailman, who came on foot.

Dora thought Edward would write any day. Then it became any week. She would never have believed at the beginning of June that she'd be waiting the whole summer without one single word!

She tossed and turned at night. She thrashed about. Every time her head hit the pillow she saw Edward's ruddy face smiling at her. At other times she would feel his fingers brushing against her breasts as they were wont to do, making her nipples stand up on end and harden even in her sleep. She'd wake up in the middle of the night wanting Edward so bad that she didn't know what to do.

Finally around Labor Day, right before she was to return to Bryn Mawr for her senior year, the mailman came racing up the road waving a letter above his head.

"What is it, Chuck?" she ran forward to greet him.

"It's what we've been waiting for so long. The guys down at the post office were real excited, too. It was all I could do to keep them from ripping the letter open and reading it. They want to find out what happened to this English lord of yours."

"Thanks!"

She grabbed the letter and cradled it against her heart as she started back down the driveway. She couldn't wait. She tore the envelope open. She almost tripped over a rock in the drive when she got to the fourth line:

My dearest Dora:

      The Dardanelles may have been ancient Heliopolis near Homer's Troy on the way to Constantinople. Alexander the Great may have come this way. But it's different now. I am one of only three survivors of over one hundred men. This is how it happened.

We landed in a small boat on the beach. We saw sand dunes meshed with barbed wire in front of us. My men were in high spirits. Before they had a chance to exit the boat, the Turks opened fire with machine guns from beyond the dunes, mowing down row after row of boys as they attempted to move to higher ground. I had to climb out on the beach on top of rows of fallen comrades. Their dead and dying bodies formed a shield.

It would be hard to imagine a terrain more precipitous with deep gullies. All the water courses were dried up during the summer. The ridges had a narrow, razor edge. Chasms were unfathomable. Our maps were totally outdated. I threw mine away, stuffing it into the pocket of the next dead man I came to. He wouldn't need it anymore. Neither would I in this land fit only for mountain goats.

I left my sword behind. It was too cumbersome to carry. Then I left my belt and even my dress shoes from my kit. Everything besides my rifle I shed layer by layer in the punishing heat and the mountain-climbing terrain that wouldn't allow me to carry much besides what was absolutely vital.

Around me I didn't see any living men. It was all I could do to pull myself forward let alone look for the other survivors of my regiment. I was scrambling through sandy soil that slid when I put my boot down on it.

When I reached the top of the ridge I didn't see any gentle, undulating country ahead. I didn't spy any waters of the Dardanelles. I saw more hills, other valleys, and precipitous slopes with scrub and brush. Beyond I saw row upon row of Turkish snipers. The marksmen fired down from the heights. Machine guns devastated the slopes . . .

The letter dropped from Dora's hand. She burst into tears at the bottom of the drive. She didn't have the courage to continue reading.

Mrs. Benley rushed up to her daughter and snatched up the note. She put her arm around Dora's shoulders and helped her up the front steps into the house. She made Dora a cup of hot coffee with cream and plenty of sugar.

She called her husband at work, "Winthrop, you ought to come home. Dora's finally received a letter from Edward. It doesn't sound very good."

"How am I going to make any money if these Englishmen, Turks, Europeans, and what not, want to tear the world up?" Dora could hear her father complaining from where she was sitting at the table sipping her hot beverage.

The Battle of Gallipoli had made it into *The Pittsburgh Press*. The British had suffered unbelievably horrendous casualties. Her parents invited a few neighbors and business associates to drop in for dinner. They chatted about it over coffee and apple pie *a la mode* served by Viola with Frank's help. Dora let the older people talk. She didn't speak up. She was too stunned and worried about Edward.

"How could anybody sustain ninety per cent casualties and still fight?" one of her father's business associates remarked. *"Are they sane?"*

Another man shook his head, "Don't know anybody in my neighborhood who would do it."

"It's not as if the damn Turks up and attacked the Brits in London. They had to go to Greece to have a battle. That's crazy! It's asking for trouble."

One of the wives broke in, "What were the Turks and the British doing in Greece to begin with?" She was clueless. "It's certainly not very American."

Dora's father sighed, "The Brits are making a mess of things. The French aren't doing any better."

"No hordes of Turks are going to come to Pittsburgh, are they?" one of the wives asked.

"Here! Here!" agreed several men. They clinked their glasses together. "We'll send them packing if they do."

Later several of the women were gossiping about a Turk who worked sweeping floors in a local restaurant. "You should see some of the odd things he eats," Mrs. Benley commented. "I wouldn't want to have to taste it."

"He's no danger," another lady replied. "He's learning English. I think he's applied to be a citizen."

"He's a political refugee."

"You can never trust a Turk," another cautioned, "or anybody from the Middle East. All they do is kill and slaughter each other. It's been that way since the Old Testament."

The guests nodded in agreement.

When everybody had gone home, Dora, still in a stunned state, slowly and hypnotically ascended the steps to her room. She sat down at her desk and got out her diary where she'd copied down Michael's address and phone number in New York City. He'd given it to her on board the *Philadelphia* before their final, cataclysmic disagreement. The old Michael Byrne, before he'd gotten so angry at her that he didn't want to have anything to do with her anymore, would have wanted to know what happened to Edward at Gallipoli. At least he would want her to share her feelings about it.

She got up the courage to dial his number. Her heart stopped beating, then thundered ahead when she heard that voice. "Hello?" Michael answered.

Her voice choked in her throat.

"Dora, what is it?" he sounded exasperated. It wasn't old times, but it was better than nothing.

"I – I just got a letter from Edward," she sobbed, letting out everything that she'd been repressing until now.

"Has he been killed?" Mr. Byrne asked.

"No, but it sounds like he could have been." She picked up the letter and started to read it aloud.

"He's alive, Dora, that's the important thing – for you, at least."

"He's – he's probably dead by now. I – I just haven't heard."

"The British shouldn't be in Greece or the Dardanelles anymore than they should be on the Western Front fighting the Germans. They shouldn't be in Africa, or India, or China. If

Edward would stay at Ware House, none of this would happen. That would be crediting your English knucklehead with too much sense."

"Sir Adolphus and Leonard Woolley sent Edward off to join this Lawrence to give him that humidor. They didn't seem to care that they were risking Edward's life."

"Didn't you tell me Edward wanted to serve?"

"Yes, but I was planning on talking him out of it."

"It's not too late until it is too late, if you know what I mean."

Dora dried her eyes. "Michael, that's a brilliant idea! I don't know if it will work, but at least it gives me hope," she said happily, running her hand up and down her arm. She stared off into space daydreaming about what it would be like to have Edward come home to her after all these months. She could imagine what it would feel like to hug him to her right now.

"So why don't you try that, Dora?" Michael prompted her.

She'd forgotten that he was on the other end of the phone. She glanced at the clock. It was almost midnight. "Oh, Michael, do you think Edward will listen to me and come back?"

There was a pause. "I would – if I were Edward," he replied.

Click.

CHAPTER 31

The next morning Mrs. Benley picked up Edward's letter and happened to read the last paragraph, which nobody had seen until now. She rushed up to Dora who was packing her suitcase to return to college. "Look! Edward says he's applying for a transfer."

Dora grabbed the letter from her mother and continued reading:

It took forever for us to be evacuated from that damned beach. Despite our losses, our commander insisted that we dig in and practically bury ourselves in a trench for safety. With the hot weather and the rains it became a miasmic bog. The few survivors sickened. My lucky fairy must have been watching over me. Maybe it was you. I was the only one to get by with a mere cold and a few bruises from falling into the damned trench, trying to escape a stray bullet from the Turks. We waited for reinforcements that never came. The commander finally cut his losses and retreated.

You can't blame me for being here. You wouldn't understand as an American. But boys I grew up with died. Imagine if all the schoolmates you knew in Pittsburgh were slaughtered in one day. I wanted to get revenge for them.

Still, even for a Brit enough is enough. Lawrence agrees with me. He has explained how he plans to win this war against the Turks another way in another place. I've applied for a transfer to join him. I hope to be leaving the Dardanelles soon. It may happen so quickly – Lawrence has connections in the War Office – that I'll be gone by the time you read this letter.

So don't despair, my love,

And one thousand kisses in all the right places from your,

Edward

P.S. You should have seen Lawrence's eyes light up when I

gave him the humidor. He acted as if he'd been waiting for it all along. It was just the right surprise.

Dora exclaimed aloud, "Now wait a minute!" She didn't want Edward to leave for another front of this crazy war right away, certainly not before he'd received the letter she'd written him. She'd already put it in an envelope and stamped it. She raced out to the mailbox at the end of the drive to fetch it. She hurried back to her bedroom. She tore open the envelope and pondered what she should say next:

Dear Edward:
If things have reached such an impasse, there's not much you can do to help. Why risk your own life for such a hopeless cause?
If you take the first troop transport back to England, you could arrive there before the really bad weather starts. You could cross the Atlantic and get to Pittsburgh well before Christmas. There's so much I'd like to show you! To think you've never been Downtown, eaten in the Tic Toc Restaurant, or seen the Kaufmann's Clock! You haven't started to live until you've ridden a trolley.
We'll have plenty of time to enjoy ourselves before Christmas when we'll sail back to England for the wedding. If it weren't for you, by now the memories of everything except the Lusitania would be growing dim. I'd be immersed in my old routine. You're the only impediment standing in my way.

Make me a happy woman and come home right away!
All my love,
Dora

P.S. I just finished your letter. I'm devastated to hear about your transfer to another front. I hope my letter reaches you first and changes your mind. Don't disappoint me, darling. Your future wife begs you on bended knees.

She raced back up the driveway. She got there as the mailman, Chuck, was strolling up the street with his mailbag slung from one shoulder. All out of breath, she thrust her letter at him.

He glanced down at the address. "Another letter for your fiance?" he asked.

She nodded.

"Greece? Sure is far away from Pittsburgh," he observed. "Seems like the other side of the moon. Doesn't have much to do with what goes on around here, does it?"

The mailman ambled his way up the tree-shaded street. He whistled as he walked.

CHAPTER 32

ora canceled her trip back to Bryn Mawr. She'd wait here in Pittsburgh for another letter, even if she had to start the semester late. Several tense days went by. She was afraid to go to the mailbox for fear she'd find the inevitable letter from Edward's parents about their son's death in battle. Sometimes it took her half the day to get up the courage to pace up the drive. She wouldn't let her parents or Frank fetch the mail. She had to make the trek herself. It would be bad luck not to.

One day she was sorting through a huge pile of mail with a dulled sense of inevitability and resignation when she came upon that familiar handwriting with the slant. The letter looked battered, as if it had suffered quite a bruising trip to her mailbox at the end of the long gravel drive. The envelope was torn and smudged. Her fingers trembled. She ripped it open.

She didn't care about the honor of the regiment. All she cared about was that Edward was safe! She read the letter over again standing there at the mailbox to make sure that her original impression was correct. There was no mistake about it. She made her way back to the house.

Her mother met her at the door with an inquisitive look. She snatched the letter from her daughter's hand and read it herself. A smile suddenly irradiated Mrs. Benley's face. "Winthrop!" she called to her husband who was home that Saturday. Her heels clicked along the tile floor as she went to find him in his study. "Winthrop! Edward's alive."

Dora walked to the kitchen like a sleepwalker, hardly aware of her mother's chirping and glad tidings to her father. She put on the tea kettle. She made steaming hot water for everyone and carried it to her father's study along with the tea cups, the cream, and the sugar. They toasted Edward's survival, even if her father did it grudgingly.

The whole time she sat there shivering, rubbing her hands up and down her arms. The chill of that trench in far off

Greece was sinking into her bones thousands of miles away in Pittsburgh. Viola's sauerbraten with Italian touches, now baking in the oven, and her mother's wild roses right outside the window climbing up the side of the chimney, failed to distract her.

While they sipped hot tea, Dora read Edward's letter aloud:

Dear Dora:

No sooner did we start the evacuation than I received word. Apparently my letter requesting a transfer must have crossed with the latest from the War Department. As it turns out, we survivors (What else can you call us? We didn't accomplish much) of the Battle of Gallipoli are being awarded the Victoria Cross. Wish you could be here when I receive it. Reminds me of graduation. Actually, cross that out. I wouldn't wish it on my worst enemy. It certainly wouldn't be fitting for a fetching thing like you. Even if a stray shell didn't get you, you'd never be able to stand the canned food and rations.
Ten more kisses,
Edward

Dora had never heard of the Victoria Cross. She supposed it was an award for soldiers. Edward talked of it as if he expected her to know. Her father looked it up in the Encyclopedia Britannica. The Victoria Cross was the highest military award given to soldier serving Great Britain.

Dora thought, *But what about coming home? He acts like he never received my letter!* She figured her P.S. must have crossed in the mail. That was too frustrating to be real. She quickly scribbled another note:

Dear Edward:

Did you get my letter? Don't you want to come home? I hate reading about the war now, and I don't want you to be part of it. Join me, and we'll forget all about it in your favorite place – in my arms.

Love,
Dora

☖ ☖ ☖

The next day the Benleys waved good-bye to Viola and Frank, who would take care of the house while they were away. They stuffed their suitcases onto the newly upholstered black leather seat of their Model T Ford Touring Car, next to Dora seated in the back. They tooted as they started up the gravel drive. After coffee at the local diner, they headed off toward U.S. Route 30, the only road to Philadelphia and Bryn Mawr College.

Route 30 wound through the countryside on a two-lane road, constantly going up and down over rolling hills into broad valleys until it gradually flattened out in Eastern Pennsylvania's Amish Country before reaching the City of Brotherly Love.

They'd soon driven from the South Hills in Bethel Borough over a bridge to the downtown Pittsburgh area. Then they'd motored on through Monroeville and McKeesport and out into the Allegheny countryside. The first part of the trip until they got past Old Bedford Village would be the most mountainous with the steepest grades.

To distract herself Dora had brought along a monograph that Leonard Woolley had written along with this same T.E. Lawrence that Edward and his father admired so much. It was entitled *The Wilderness of Zin: An Archaeological Report*, the account of Woolley's and Lawrence's 1913-1914 archaeological survey of biblical sites in and around Palestine, financed by the Palestine Exploration Fund and published in London in 1915 by Harrison & Sons. The Carnegie Library in Pittsburgh had the title in the stacks. They'd been willing to loan it to her, although they hadn't quite finished cataloging it yet.

She'd expected to be bored. Somehow the dedication seemed unusual for an archaeological report:

To Captain S.F. Newcombe, R.E.

Who showed them "the way wherein they must walk, and the work that they must do."

This quote from Exodus 18:20 galvanized her. She was swept right into the narrative, which was not only colorful, but almost literary in its pictorial quality and powers of description. It bucked the current trends to write in a bombastic, wordy style. Lawrence picked out salient points and highlighted them instead. She found herself unable to put the little volume down:

From Gaza the track to Beersheba passed through a wide undulating plain of deep, rich soil; there are no trees, and virtually no houses to be seen, but everywhere there are visible the traces of an older and more settled civilization – village sites strewn with Byzantine pottery, olive presses built of marble and cement, and broken water-cisterns. A little way from the road, on the west bank of the Wady Sharia, rises Tell abu Hareira, a splendid mound, partly natural and partly artificial, now crowned by a shrine of the saint, and covered with Arab graves.

Dora finally forced herself to close the book. She'd expected to be able to write to Edward that his new mentor was a bore who wasn't worth her fiancé's time. She hadn't counted on being put under some strange sort of spell herself. She remembered what Woolley had said in the library at Ware House: "It was Lawrence's idea to begin with . . . "

What was Lawrence's idea? She was beginning to understand the powers of hypnotic persuasion this young man possessed. *I hope this T.E. Lawrence doesn't talk the way he writes . . . If he does, I'm lost . . . I can't write to Edward using such purple prose . . .*

Still she had other attractions besides literary style. Edward should miss her in the way she missed him and want to come home right away. As she straightened her dress from slouching too much in the car, the material tugged at her bodice. She remembered Edward's fingers touching the exact same spot.

She picked up the novelette she'd also brought with

her, *The Lion and the Mouse: A Story of American Life* by dear old Mr. Klein. She settled back against her seat. The struggles of Shirley and Mr. Ryder were more homespun and everyday. It reminded her of the world back home in Pittsburgh. She'd already bought a copy of an older version of the novelette. She'd given the package to Viola to take to the post office just before she'd left for Bryn Mawr so that Edward would have a copy to read on his voyage home. She'd meant to give it to him in London, but she'd only gotten around to it now.

She was absorbed in the novelette when she heard another car swiftly approaching them from behind. She ignored it at first, used to such sounds on the two-lane highway. "Winthrop!" her mother objected. "Why does that car behind us keep speeding up, riding on our bumper, and slowing down."

"That's what most cars do, Etta May" Winthrop assured her. "It's a two-lane road. They all can't wait to get to the passing zone," he sighed. "Maybe someday they'll widen this to four lanes."

They came to a bump in the road and slowed down. The car behind them grazed their bumper.

"Did you feel that, Winthrop?" Mrs. Benley gasped.

"Yes, Etta May, I did. They let nincompoops drive on the highway, I'm afraid."

Dora turned around, putting down her book. Her mouth fell open. It was true. The car behind them, a Model T, was riding on their bumper. It seemed to be only a few inches away. "Father –"

"Not you, too, Dora!" he fumed. "Don't be a backseat driver. I'm trying to pass."

She could only hope that he'd make it around the car in front of him and lose the driver behind them, who wore a billowy wool coat and a big floppy hat that made it hard to see his face.

She happened to glance up at the rear view mirror. Her heart almost stopped. The driver glared at their car with dark eyes. She'd seen those eyes on the deck of the *Lusitania*. She'd glimpsed them at dinner at Ware House carving the pork roast.

They'd haunted her dreams ever since.

How on earth had *he* gotten into back country Pennsylvania along this quaint, old, two-lane road where he was as out of place as a Martian would be? How had he even discovered that this was where she lived?

She hunched down in the backseat and tried to hide her face. Her father finally got around the car in front of him. Dora relaxed a little, thinking they'd escaped.

"Look, Winthrop, it's that car again!" Mrs. Benley pointed.

Those were the words Dora dreaded most to hear. The stranger named Ali was really following them. She wanted to say something, but she knew that would violate the rule against upsetting her mother, who already seemed to be in a state.

They stopped first at Jeannette and then at Greensburg. The road curved and wound among hills. It went up steep inclines and down again. No matter what, they couldn't seem to shake the man.

Mr. Benley pulled into a gas station at Youngstown. Dora didn't see Ali as she paced up and down the dirt parking lot with her books. Her father filled the tank and had the station attendant look under the hood as her mother used the facilities. Dora stayed away from the main road. If their pursuer drove past, she didn't want him to catch sight of her.

Dora, like her mother, took the opportunity to use the restroom. There was no shelf for her purse so she placed it on the floor next to her in the stall. No sooner did she flush than she looked down. Her purse was gone!

The scene with Ali grabbing her purse and slashing it apart with a knife in the first-class lounge of the *Lusitania* flashed through Dora's mind. She raced out of the stall and over to the sink. She searched the other stalls. She rushed up to her mother outside the restroom. "Did I leave my purse with you?"

"Your purse? You never leave your purse with me!"

Had somebody stolen it? She knew things like that happened to other people. It had never happened to her before.

She'd thought she was safe here in rural Pennsylvania if nowhere else on earth!

She kept her composure while going back to the car. She fished her new Russian boot gaiters with pointed toes out of the backseat. It had just rained. The dirt parking lot was a little muddy. She strode around observing whether any other woman had by chance picked up her purse.

No one else seemed to have her Pandora bag. They had every other style of purse. She saw velveteen bags, leather bags, pin seal bags, imported beaded bags with fringe which were all the rage right now despite the war.

Dora turned to see a tawny-skinned man in a long wool coat charge across the parking lot and leap into his car. He was carrying something in his hand. She couldn't quite get a clear view of it. He slammed the door and started the engine. Then he was gone.

Her father was signaling to her from the other side of the parking lot. She couldn't stand here gaping after the disappearing car much longer. She had to go.

Mr. Benley grumbled as she climbed into the front seat. "The station owner is crooked. He and his whole family live behind the lot. They'll rob you blind if you let them."

"I suppose you didn't let them, Winthrop," Mrs. Benley commented as she powdered her nose in the rear view mirror.

He complained about this and that all the way down the road past Ligonier. They were approaching Old Bedford Village, just off Route 30, by the time her father switched subjects.

They had reservations to stay at the Bailey Boarding House and Auto Court. The main building was an old two-story log farm house built by Pennsylvania Germans in 1762 and later renovated. It was remarkable for the notching of its corners, called V-notching. The main building also featured a two-sided fireplace built of lighter colored stones from the area plastered together.

They pulled into to the small parking lot. Mr. Benley went to check in and get the key.

"We'll go shopping, Winthrop. We'll be back in about an hour," Mrs. Benley assured her husband. "I'm sure Mrs. Millrose will have shown you to our room by then."

Dora and her mother entered Furry's Basket Shop. A buxom German girl wove baskets together for tourists. Mrs. Benley bought one of the baskets hanging overhead. She could rarely resist shopping of any kind.

As they were leaving the shop, Dora tripped on something lying on the ground. What was her purse doing here? She checked inside. There was her comb and mirror – and her wallet!

A shadow fell on her. She looked up. Not far away, leaning against another building, stood Ali. At this distance it was impossible to mistake him for anyone else. He eyeballed her. The corners of his lips, which naturally turned downward, rose into a sort of half-grin before resuming their normal position.

She turned into the first shop she came to, the Dutch Corner. She plunged into a crowd of people. "Dora, where are you going? Wait for me!" her mother rushed after her.

She shoved her mother into line in front of the counter. She hadn't been planning on buying anything to eat quite yet, but why not? Anything to get away from Ali. A Pennsylvania Dutch girl with blond pigtails leaned toward her and asked, "May I help you?"

"What do you think, Mother? We can bring something back to the room for Dad."

Her mother, who was always an expert on buying things, felt right at home. She stepped in front of her daughter and took over. She gave directions to the cooks about exactly what she wanted for dinner.

"It looks like they have quite an assortment of everything," her mother clapped her hands and exclaimed in a jovial fashion. "I see shoo-fly pies, whoopie pies, jams, pecan buns, jellies, home made breads, hand-made pretzels and mustard, funnel cakes, brittle, and lots and lots of chocolate fudge."

"Funnel cake!" Dora replied mechanically. She shivered. She didn't have the nerve to turn around.

"You *must* have something to hand over to me," Dora heard the overly familiar gruff and highly accented voice right at her elbow.

Dora's mouth opened and closed. She glanced down at her purse.

"It *has* to be somewhere," said the voice from beside her.

She darted her eyes to the side. She couldn't quite see him.

"Is that man bothering you, miss?" asked the Dutch girl from behind the counter, frowning at him.

Dora didn't know how to answer. She kept her lips sealed.

"They don't serve that kind here anyway," exclaimed a lady who was standing next to Dora and her mother in line. "He looks like a foreigner."

The blond girl glowered at the stranger behind Dora. She left the counter to talk to an older man who seemed to be her father. The girl's father picked up the phone. "Hello, sheriff, there's a foreigner who looks like he has no business here harassing the customers," the man said loudly enough for all the other shoppers to hear.

Dora glanced over her shoulder. Ali was gone. He'd disappeared into the crowd the way he'd vanished into the Irish Sea.

"Would you like anything more, ladies?" the Dutch girl pressed as if nothing had happened.

"Winthrop, that's my husband, loves your pretzels. I'll take a bag," said Mrs. Benley, who had missed the whole proceedings in her intense preoccupation with the food.

"With mustard?"

Mrs. Benley nodded as they handed her several packages and she handed over a wad of dollar bills.

As they left the building Dora couldn't help noticing an ugly scene going on. A muscular Dutchman, with football player-like shoulders, had pinned a man to a tree. It wasn't Ali. It was someone who looked like an Eastern European. The Dutchman was socking the man in the jaw.

Dora wanted to say, "Can't you see he's not the right suspect?" But her mother was oblivious to the whole incident as she strode on past with her packages for dinner. Dora remembered the Eleventh Commandment, "Thou shalt not upset your mother!" and kept her own lips sealed. She averted her eyes.

Her father met them at the door to their room at the auto court. Dora showed him the bag full of pretzels. His eyes lighted up. It reminded him of the food his own mother used to make.

Mr. Benley glanced at the victim tied to the tree. "The war seems to be spreading. When it gets to rural Pennsylvania, now that's serious!"

CHAPTER 33

They arrived at the Bryn Mawr campus the next day. She kissed her parents good-bye for the next several weeks. This would be the first time she'd been apart from them since the morning that she'd met them at the Cunard pier in New York on May 1.

Dora had dinner with some of her old friends on campus who gathered around to admire her engagement ring. Then she took a stroll through the Cloisters. Bryn Mawr College had been modeled after Oxford University in England – on a miniature scale. It was awash with dark stones, gargoyles, and medieval terminology. She perched herself on the edge of the lily pond and gazed down into the water, wondering what Edward would think of the place.

A man's face was reflected in the water between the green pads floating on the surface. She turned. Nobody was there.

"Is someone here?" she asked.

No one answered.

She peered into all the dark corners. She couldn't see another soul. Had it been her imagination? Perhaps she was tired after the long journey. She should return to her dorm room in the abbey-like Denbigh Hall and retire early.

Her first night back at Bryn Mawr, Dora wrote another letter to Edward:

Dear Edward:

I've seen the saboteur again. He's come to America to chase after me. I felt much safer when you were there to protect me. You should ask your parents if Ali is still at Ware House. I don't think he is. I'm sitting in my dorm room at Bryn Mawr College. I keep on telling myself that this is America. Things like this can't happen here. But they are happening anyway.

After my mid-terms I'm going home in mid-October for Fall Break. Mother and I will be shopping for the wedding gown.

She's been in touch with Lady Ware. They are coordinating the wedding invitations for Christmas. I haven't heard from you yet. Did you ever get my letter about coming home sooner than expected? I'm getting very lonely here without you. Every night when I climb into bed, it feels chilly without someone beside me to keep me warm.

Yours forever,
Dora

P.S. I'm going to buy a surprise for our wedding night.

She fell asleep that night dreaming of Edward. The next day she thought of little else when she was in class. Her archaeology professor was discussing Leonard Woolley's dig at Carchemish. She was able to raise her hand and volunteer that she'd been to England and had seen the study of Sir Adolphus, one of Woolley's friends. He had lots of artifacts there.

She ended up doing a report on Woolley's dig before the war. She'd buried herself in the Art and Archaeology Library for the next few weeks, often late into the day. She wasn't allowed to check out all the books she wanted. They were part of the rare book collection. So one afternoon she waited until the librarian had left so she could smuggle them out to her room.

As Dora darted across the grassy area in front of Taylor Hall, headed for Denbigh with her stash of rare books, a man loomed up beside her. She didn't get a good look at him. She cut and ran as fast as her feet would take her back to her dorm.

When she opened the door to her big single room with a bay window and window seat, she immediately noticed that somebody had been there in her absence. Furniture was overturned. The mattress had been dragged down onto the floor and hacked to pieces with a knife. The stuffing had all been shaken out. The box springs were exposed. All the sheets and pillow cases had been torn off the bed. The fiend had even hacked her pillows to pieces as if she were hiding something inside them.

All her books on the book shelf that she had carefully arranged, had been thrown down onto the floor. They'd been kicked about. She noticed an ugly shoe print on the cover of her Woolley and Lawrence book, *The Wilderness of Zin,* that she'd been reading on her trip back to Bryn Mawr. Even *The Lion and the Mouse* had been smudged! The rug she'd shipped to the campus in a big trunk was torn to shreds. It would have to be thrown away.

Her closet was flung wide open. Her entire wardrobe had been hurled about the room. Most of her school dresses had been torn apart with a knife. It was the same sickeningly familiar scene that Dora had encountered twice before in the past few months – once on the *Lusitania* and once at Ware House. Now Ali had left his mark at Bryn Mawr, too.

She reached down to start picking things up, when she happened to glance out the window of her second floor dorm room. There on the window ledge, crawling along on his hands and knees, crouched Ali himself! He was just outside the double hung, wooden frame windows, overlooking her window bench covered with the cushions that her mother had made specially for her dorm room. He was impaling her with his gaze.

CHAPTER 34

D ora realized there was only a flimsy metal screen between her and the saboteur. She slammed both windows shut and locked them. She raced out of her dorm room, stopping only to lock the door behind her from the outside with her key.

She charged down the hallway yelling, "Help!" She wondered why none of the other girls were responding to her cries. She stopped cold at the end of the dark, dimly lighted hallway of the old dorm building. It was the October evening chosen for the Step Sing. All the girls on the campus had brought their Bryn Mawr lanterns with the red glass and the owls to the steps of Taylor Hall, where the bell tower was located, to sing "Akoue" in classical Greek. It was a Bryn Mawr tradition.

Surely the house mother must be in residence. Dora flew down the wooden staircase to the ground floor where the "bells desk" was located. But the dorm mother had gone to the Step Sing. No one was manning the desk. Dora grabbed the dorm phone. She dialed the police with shaky hands. She tapped her fingers while they took their time about answering.

"Hello, this is Dora Benley. I'm at Bryn Mawr College at Denbigh Hall. Please come at once. There's a man prowling about outside, and –"

"The police don't respond to campus calls. That's for the college to take care of," replied the dispatcher.

"But – but you don't understand," she darted her eyes about, "this isn't some boy from Haverford College. This is an arsonist and saboteur. He was involved in the sinking of the *Lusitania*. I know. I was on it, and –"

"Miss, the police have better things to do than participate in campus pranks. Go call your sorority sisters instead."

Click.

Dora gaped at the phone. She couldn't believe the police weren't going to answer her cry for help.

The double wooden doors at the entrance to the hall

creaked. Someone was pulling on them from outside. That must mean . . . She raced forward and locked them from the inside. Only Denbigh residents knew the "tricks" for opening the old, balky door. You had to hold one door up with your foot while you pulled the other with your hand. Ali wouldn't know the "tricks". But he might have discovered them soon enough.

Dora raced from window to window in the front lounge, locking them. She hurried back to the bells desk, wondering what she should do next. Maybe she should call the police again and plead with them? No, that would be a waste of time. And her parents were too far away to help. That left only one person . . .

Although she'd called him only once when she'd gotten Edward's letter from Gallipoli, she had Michael's phone number in New York memorized. Her nervous fingers had trouble dialing it.

"Hello?" he picked up the phone on the first ring, answering her prayers.

"Michael!" she wept.

"What's happened, Dora?" his voice dropped the mocking, sardonic, bitter tone that he'd adopted with her lately. He sensed her panic right away.

"It's Ali. He's here right now outside my window."

"Where, Dora? Tell me where."

"I'm in my dorm, Denbigh Hall, in Philadelphia."

"Yes, at Bryn Mawr College," he finished her sentence for her.

"I'm all by myself. I called the police. They think it's a prank. They won't come. And –"

"I'll be there in two hours. Maybe an hour and a half. The station's right across the street from where I live. A train leaves in seven minutes."

"I'm locked in."

"Go to the bathroom. There aren't any windows there. Right?"

"Right," she gulped.

"I'll find you. Try to hold on. Arm yourself if you can."

"Yes, Michael, yes!" she hung up.

She didn't know what to do for a weapon. Then her eyes lighted on the silver service for the dorm's dining hall, located next to the bells desk right next to the entrance to the now silent eating area. She grabbed a fork and stuffed it in her pocket. She raced back upstairs to hide herself in the girls' showers.

She locked the door with her key. She pushed a chair against it to make sure it would hold. Then she disappeared inside a shower stall and pulled the curtain across the rod. Her heart was thundering in her ears. Her pulse was racing. She hoped Ali couldn't hear her ragged breath. She crouched there for she didn't know how long before she heard footsteps.

"Michael?" she whispered, hoping against hope. When she consulted her watch, she saw it had been only an hour. Much too soon. Michael was coming from New York City. It was too early for the Step Sing to be over with.

It must be Ali. She couldn't imagine how he'd gotten into the dormitory. She'd closed all the windows and locked the doors. He was making a lot of noise searching for her. Finally she heard him trying the door to the girls' showers. When it didn't open, he ran against it.

There was no window for escape except one high up on the wall above the sink. It was a slim chance. She pushed off the faucet, turning it on in the process, and pulled herself up to the ledge. She had her hand on the window handle when the door to the shower room gave way.

Ali seized Dora by the ankle. "Help!" she called out the slit of a window that was now open. "Help!" She could hear the Bryn Mawr girls singing in the distance. They couldn't hear her.

He yanked her down before she could holler anymore. He backed her up against the wall. She felt his big hands on her for the first time since she'd been his captive aboard the *Lusitania,* when he'd dragged her from cabin to cabin. "All right, where have you hidden it?"

"Do you mean a wooden humidor?" she guessed. Back

on the ship she'd had absolutely no idea what he was talking about. Now she had some vague notion, though it made no sense.

"What else could I mean?" Ali shot back. "I wouldn't be here for anything less."

She remembered Edward telling her that these Moslems had strange customs, such as the one about not eating pork. She wondered if this was another bizarre tradition. Did they worship cigar boxes or cigars?

"I don't have the humidor anymore," she admitted the truth.

"I went to your cabin on the *Lusitania* while the ship was sinking. I found it above the drapes over the painted window. *"It was a fake!"* he hissed.

Dora remembered Sir Adolphus saying to Leonard Woolley that the gift he'd sent her father was a "good way to get it out of here". What had the baronet meant? This whole business was getting more confusing all the time.

"What is the significance of the humidor?" she dared to ask. She had to play for time. She hoped Michael would arrive before this madman killed her.

Ali's eyes flashed. "It is not for such as you to question."

"Did it have to do with the ancient Hittite script on the bottom? I –"

Ali started to pound her against the wall, heaving her back and forth with his hands. "Where is it? What have you done with the real humidor?" Ali demanded.

Dora remembered the humidor that Sir Adolphus had rescued from the burning house. He'd given it to Edward to take to Lawrence. Edward had written that he'd given it to him. He'd said Lawrence had been expecting it. But she didn't dare tell Ali that. She didn't want to endanger her fiance.

She screamed at the top of her lungs instead. She hoped that someone would hear her. It was the wrong thing to do. Ali stopped pounding her against the wall and got out a knife. He pointed it at her.

Dora remembered the whole set up at Ware House – how Woolley and Sir Adolphus had the library made up to look like a museum. They were all artifacts from the dig at Carchemish. Did she dare to ask about that? She hadn't tried that tack. "They told me you were a helper at Carchemish," Dora tried to distract Ali from using his knife. She got her hand around the fork in her pocket in case he attacked her again.

"What about it?" he hissed at her.

"What wrongs did Sir Adolphus and Leonard Woolley commit?" she asked.

"What wrongs indeed!" he shook his head. "You Englishmen think you can do anything, spit on us, and get away with it."

"Did they steal sacred artifacts? Is that what this humidor was somehow?"

"Ha!" he laughed in her face, startling her. "Englishmen steal ancient artifacts all the time. Do you think we Arabs care about those? My family sells them in the market for money. How else do you think I bought my ticket on the *Lusitania?* How do you think I got here? Pah! I spit on your precious ancient trinkets!"

She was so astounded she didn't know what to say. "What other wrong could they have committed against your religion?" Dora asked, trying to force herself to keep calm. Time was still passing, but all too slowly.

"Only the greatest wrong of all –- *the great forbidden!"* he glared into her eyes with such intensity she wanted to shrink back, though she was already smack up against the wall and couldn't move an inch. "The thing the Prophet said to guard against above all other things."

"Sir Adolphus sent me the fake humidor as a birthday gift for my father. I didn't know what was inside the package until after the ship sank. I –"

"You deserved to drown, but you escaped," Ali interrupted her.

"Even Sir Adolphus wasn't the one who started this."

"He lies!"

"Leonard Woolley himself said it was Lawrence's idea to begin with, and he even advised him against it. Lawrence wouldn't listen and . . ."

She stopped talking when she saw the change that came over Ali's face when she mentioned Lawrence's name. Before he'd at least been able to voice his grievances. Now his face turned into a ghoul's mask. He plunged his knife at her. She ducked. He missed, leaving his knife sticking in the wall.

She fled to the door and raced out of the bathroom. She ran down the hallway with Ali in hot pursuit.

"Anyone who deals with the diabolical Lawrence *deserves* to die," Ali shouted.

Dora heard footsteps racing upstairs ahead of her. "Michael!" she screamed, flying right into his arms. "Ali's right behind me."

Michael pulled out a handgun he'd brought with him. He fired at Ali just as the man ducked into one of the open dorm rooms. Michael entered the dorm room as Ali disappeared through the window. He fired again.

The gunshots had done what Dora's screaming had failed to do. Girls suddenly rushed back to the dorm in their Lantern Night costumes carrying their red-glass-paned lanterns with the Bryn Mawr owl symbol. Michael grabbed Dora's hand and guided her through the crowd of screaming females down the stairs to where the house mother had now appeared.

"What is your business here, sir?" the woman confronted him, looking him up and down.

"Doing what your police refused to do. Defending the life of this young woman, Dora Benley," he insisted. "I think I can speak for her father, Winthrop Benley. It isn't safe for her to stay here. Dora," he turned to her, "go get your things. We're leaving – now!"

CHAPTER 35

Dora rushed back upstairs to throw a few clothes into her damaged suitcase. They marched out of Denbigh Hall side by side as a crowd of girls in Lantern Night costumes lined the hallways and the front entrance gawking at them.

"Michael, where are we going?" Dora pleaded after they started out to the darkened street that ran through the campus, illuminated only by gas lamps.

"There are no more trains until tomorrow, when I intend to take you home to Pittsburgh. We'll have to spend the night at a hotel, I suppose."

They took a cab. They talked about how Ali could have gotten to America. They couldn't figure out how he'd discovered her address – unless it had been through the Ware connection. Maybe he'd snooped in Lady Ware's address book in her morning room before he'd left Britain.

Michael asked for two rooms at the hotel front desk.

"Really, sir!" exclaimed the check-in clerk. "Is this really quite proper?" he eyeballed Michael.

"This is my cousin, sir!" Michael blustered, not quite meeting the man's eye. "I'm escorting her home to Pittsburgh."

Dora couldn't help but raise her hand to her mouth to conceal her smile.

The check-in clerk scowled at Michael. But he handed him two keys.

"Here is yours, Dora," Michael made sure to hand it to her in front of the gentleman.

Dora couldn't sleep. She kept on seeing shadows outside her window. She heard strange, suspicious sounds in the hallway. She knocked on Michael's door about one A.M.

He poked his head out the door, bleary-eyed, "Yes?"

"I – I can't sleep. Could I come in?"

He ushered her inside after making sure there was no

one else in the hallway to observe what was going on. She sat down on the bed and wrapped his blanket around herself. Michael slumped in the easy chair and dozed off right away.

"It's a good thing you had that gun, Michael."

"Oh, yes, yes," he roused himself and adjusted the chair's pillow to fit in the small of his back. "Quite so."

"I don't remember you had it aboard the *Lusitania.*"

"I bought it when I got back to New York. The *Lusitania* makes you think more about defending yourself," he could barely keep his eyes open.

"Did I impose upon you by calling you to come to Bryn Mawr?" she asked after a few more moments.

"What? Oh!" he straightened his spine and crossed his feet, still with his street shoes on, for he hadn't packed. He'd come the way he was, just as he'd promised. "It wasn't exactly my idea of fun, Dora. I was worried I wouldn't get there in time. I ran the whole way from the Bryn Mawr train station to the dorm. I didn't stop once."

"You did that all for me?"

"Yes, Dora," he sighed, "I did it all for you. Here, let me get you another blanket," he struggled up from the easy chair and went to the closet where the maids had been kind enough to store a spare blanket. He brought it over to her and threw it over the bed where she was ensconced.

"I keep on thinking I hear Ali creeping down the hallway."

He slumped down on the bed in a sitting position right beside her. His eyes were shut as if he were already asleep. "Fine, Dora, fine . . . "

"You were the only other person in the world who would believe me about Ali."

"You did the right thing, Dora, when you called me," he sounded as if he were talking in his sleep. He yawned.

"I'm glad to hear you say that. You haven't had anything good to say about me lately, you know."

"Oh, you're a good girl, Dora. You're a good little girl," he sighed after a pause, as if he were so far gone that he didn't know what he was saying.

She sat there so long that her eyes began to close.+ She fell asleep, thinking this was the first time she and Mr. Byrne had been together since that horrible morning of June 3 when they'd gone their separate ways after disembarking from the *Philadelphia*.

She woke up some time later. Michael was snoring. Dora pushed him down onto the bed and pulled the blankets up around him. He must be a sound sleeper. He didn't wake up. She hesitated only a second before lying down right beside him. After all, it was only Michael . . . She rested her head against the pillow. She felt so warm now it was like paradise.

She woke up when the sun first started to come through the drapes. She rested her head on her hand and supported herself on one elbow as she watched Michael. She listened to him snore. She couldn't resist leaning towards his ear and whispering, "Michael!"

He roused himself a little. His eyes opened and closed.

"Michael!" she tried again, leaning on her elbow. "You know what? I didn't know you snored!" She laughed a little.

He opened his eyes in horror and gaped at her. He leaped out of the bed as if it were on fire. She couldn't help but sit there laughing and pointing at him. She laughed so hard she started to cry. Michael stood there with mussed up hair and a morning scowl, staring at Dora as if she'd turned into a witch.

"Michael, forgive me, but I can't help myself!" she fell back against the pillows laughing so hard she couldn't stop.

"Dora!" he backed away from the bed scandalized. "What would Edward say?"

"I think – I think –- " she laughed. "I think he'd die laughing."

"Scandalous!" Michael took off for the bathroom. "What can you expect from a decadent member of the British aristocracy? He's corrupted you enough that you act like this." He slammed the door and locked it. The water was running. He was slapping himself with something. It smelled like her father's shaving cream.

"Michael," she tapped on the bathroom door, leaning her ear against it, "guess what?"

"Can't you leave me alone long enough to shave?"

"You remind me of Bernard."

He cracked the bathroom door and gaped out at her. His face was covered with shaving cream, gratis of the hotel staff. "You mean you . . . with Bernard, too?"

She nodded.

"When did this happen? When I left you alone in Pittsburgh?" he came out of the bathroom and grabbed her by the arms. With shaving cream all over his face he gaped down at her.

She nodded again.

"Dora, is this what Edward did to you?" he looked at her in horror.

"I slept with Bernard all this past summer. But I slept with him before the *Lusitania,* too," she confessed.

His eyeballs looked as if they would pop out of his head.

"How often did this happen?"

She shrugged. "I don't remember."

"You don't remember! Dora, were your parents in the house?"

She nodded. "Oh yes, they were the ones who brought Bernard to the house for me. They introduced us, you could say."

"How could you let this happen?" he started to pace back and forth.

"Bernard was irresistible. We slept there really cozy like, cheek to cheek. I put Bernard's big black nose with all the fur right next to mine."

"Wait a minute," he pushed her away from him, "what did this Bernard look like?"

"Oh, he was this long," she spread her arms wide, "and this wide," she demonstrated. "He had fur all over, and two button hole eyes."

"You mean he was a *dog?* " Mr. Byrne exclaimed.

She nodded. "My stuffed dog toy. His name was Bernard, and he was as big as a St. Bernard. When I was a little girl and I was lonely, cold, or I was unhappy, I'd take Bernard to bed with me. Then I could sleep. You're like Bernard."

Mr. Byrne smacked his forehead with his hand and slammed the bathroom door. He went back to shaving. At breakfast down in the dining room Michael continued to scowl at Dora. "You really can be a minx, can't you, Dora?" Michael buttered his toast. "Your father should discipline you."

"Why don't you tell Father all about it when you get me to Pittsburgh?" she whispered across the table. "I'm sure he'd like the part about how you snore. He snores, too, you know," she giggled, her spirits as high as they'd been in weeks.

Michael blushed and fell silent.

CHAPTER 36

When they arrived back in Pittsburgh by train, Mr. Benley was scandalized by the lack of response of the Bryn Mawr police department. He called the mayor and complained. He phoned the police chief. "I'm going to sue them, too!" he declared at breakfast.

"You really do have to understand that Ali represents a great danger to your daughter," Michael explained to Mr. Benley over scrambled eggs and hash browns.

"I didn't believe either of you at first. But after the *Lusitania,* one's inclined to believe almost anything of Europeans and their wastrel allies," Mr. Benley shook his head and finished his pancakes.

"Ali followed me to Bryn Mawr, Father," Dora emphasized.

"There was that awful driver who bumped into us!" Mrs. Benley exclaimed.

"That was Ali," Dora announced to her mother.

"You don't say!" Mrs. Benley's eyes grew as big as saucers.

"Well, my daughter's dropping out of that school! At times like this, she should stay close to home," Winthrop Benley decided.

"Wait a minute!" Dora protested.

"That's a wise decision, sir," Mr. Byrne looked at Dora.

Since she was getting married in December and moving to England, she didn't bother to protest very much. Besides, it was the beginning of Fall Break. There was time to decide what to do next. And she was distracted, to say the least.

On the second day back, after Viola had spoiled her with a hash browns, sausages, and scrambled eggs breakfast complete with everything, the doorbell rang. Frank opened the front door. Excitedly he raced back to the dining room that was set for four for breakfast.

"Viola!" Frank cried to his buxom, portly, raven-haired wife with the big smile and the apron tied around her waist. "Set another place. Quick! We have a guest."

A sylph-like young woman with a perfect face not much older than Dora entered the room carrying her suitcase, which Frank took from her immediately. *"Rita!"* Dora rose to her feet, clutching the table for support. It was like seeing a ghost risen up from the grave. "I – I didn't know . . . I didn't know . . . "

Rita threw out her arms and ran for Dora. Dora knocked her own chair over running for Rita. The two young women hugged each other and broke into tears. "I didn't know you had survived either," Rita wept, "until your mother called me two weeks ago and invited me down to your house."

"I read about Rita in the newspaper. They were talking about how she's going to star in a new film," Mrs. Benley explained.

Viola set another place next to Dora. The two young women had so much to talk about. They ended up never leaving the table all day long. Viola served lunch while they were sitting there. Many hours after that she served dinner. The two girls hadn't budged an inch the whole time. Instead they chatted like twin sisters.

Rita was telling her friend, over meat loaf with a variety of garden vegetables and some Italian touches that Viola had sneaked in all by herself, "I've always been scared to death of drowning as I told you. I swim, but I don't swim that well," the French-American woman gesticulated.

"I don't swim all that well myself," Mrs. Benley added. "If it hadn't been for Winthrop, I don't know what would have happened. Winthrop's always so ingenious!" his wife smiled. "He got that lifeboat launched when the crew didn't know how to do it."

Mr. Benley declared as he ate his baked Idaho potato with lots of butter and bacon, "Teddy Roosevelt wouldn't have had it any other way."

"I wish you could have saved me!" Rita shuddered. "I stayed next to Mr. Vanderbilt and Mr. Frohman until the very last minute. I didn't think someone as important as Mr. Vanderbilt could drown," she shook her head. She looked off into space as if she could see it all happening over again right now. "My God!" she crossed herself. "He was the richest man in America. I thought those distinguished Robber Barons knew what they were doing. They kept on hanging onto the rail and climbing up the Boat Deck as the waters washed up after us. They kept on saying we'd be rescued, that the ship couldn't sink."

Viola paused with a serving dish of buttered mixed vegetables in her hand. Her mouth was open. Her eyes were bulging out of her head. She leaned closer. She looked as if she couldn't imagine such a horrible thing. Frank peered out the kitchen door, hanging on every word.

"I didn't hear what happened to them until later, because a big green wall of water swept me off the deck."

"Yes, I remember that," Dora nodded.

"I never got to shoot myself. My pearl-handled pistol got knocked out of my hands," Rita gesticulated.

"Thank goodness!" exclaimed Mr. Byrne.

"I went under," Rita turned pale as if reliving the experience. "I got dragged down, down, down. I thought I was dead. Then I got spit back out on top of the ocean. I found a floating board to cling onto. I stayed there for hours. My legs were so numb and cold I couldn't feel them anymore."

"The water was exactly fifty-two degrees that afternoon at ten after two when the torpedo struck," her father said. "I found that out later. This is why I am suing the Cunard lines," her father stirred his coffee self-righteously.

"I didn't get picked up until it was dark," Rita wiped her eyes.

"Here, have plenty of extra hot coffee," Viola ran back to the kitchen to fetch some. "Drink this, and your toes will never be cold again, no?"

"At least you're here now," Dora hugged her friend. "Just in time to be my bridesmaid, if you will do me the honor."

"Wonderful!" Rita clapped her hands. "Are you finally

marrying Mr. Byrne?"she asked hopefully, looking up at him. "I remember you two were together on the ship all the time."

Mr. Byrne looked down at his coffee cup. He was a long time about stirring it.

"She would be if I could knock some sense into my daughter's head!" Mr. Benley sighed.

"Winthrop!" his wife chided him.

"Mr. Byrne and I had quite an adventure, didn't we, Michael?" Dora winked at him, changing the subject.

"Amen!" said Mr. Byrne. "I'm not sure it's quite over yet."

"But how is that possible?" Rita leaned closer, her eyes agog. "We're on the land right now."

"Haven't you told her, Dora?" Mr. Byrne turned to her.

Dora shook her head. "I've been followed by a stranger ever since I boarded the ship. He plagued me in London and at Ware House. He showed up at Bryn Mawr College, too."

Rita's eyes grew bigger and bigger. "Is he a German spy?"

Dora shook her head.

"He's definitely an exotic," Mr. Byrne said. "Someone from the other side of the world. He has dark skin and eyes. According to what Dora says, I think he's Middle Eastern. He was hired at Ware House as a servant named Ali."

"I go to England to cement a profitable business deal, and this is how I get rewarded," her father complained. "First I get sunk by a German torpedo, even though America's neutral. Then my daughter is plagued by some British colonial – and that's after she gets engaged to a mad British lord."

"British colonial?" Rita's eyes got bigger.

"All those Middle Eastern types are British colonial subjects. If the British don't keep them in line, who will? I'll sue the British Parliament and even King George himself if I have to," Winthrop Benley shook his head and made a fist.

"Winthrop would take on anybody," his wife smiled and nodded.

"Britain didn't have to set a bad example and enter some

stupid war that Austria-Hungary started with Serbia. What kind of backwater is Serbia anyway? Who cares if some crackpot assassinated Archduke Ferdinand and his wife? Never heard of them before! This war madness keeps on spreading. I'm glad that America has the good sense to keep out of the mess!"

"Wilson did say he wouldn't tolerate any German aggression," Mr. Byrne reminded him.

"Yes, since the *Lusitania* went down with all of us aboard save only Frank and Viola, thank God!, Wilson's made the Kaiser himself apologize and recant."

Viola was a good Catholic. She crossed herself when he said that and grabbed the rosary beads hung around her neck.

Mr. Benley continued, "Wilson's promised no more nonsense on the high seas with neutrals and civilians, especially with women and children involved."

"What if the Kaiser doesn't keep his promise?" Rita threw out her arms.

Winthrop Benley looked personally offended. He stuck out his chest and growled, "He'll have me to deal with then."

"Winthrop!" even Mrs. Benley was amazed.

"What am I to do if I wake up tomorrow and the whole world has turned to monkeys, apes, and chimpanzees except for the USA? Do I have to turn into one, too?" Mr. Benley exclaimed.

Later when the girls were alone up in Dora's bedroom, Dora filled Rita in about her new fiance, Edward. "He says he'll be back at Christmas. The war has to be over by then at the latest. He's going to come here to Pittsburgh to fetch me, though I've asked him to come sooner. We're going to Ware House to get married."

"How wonderful!" Rita clapped her hands. "But after the *Lusitania,* I don't know if I want to live anywhere but right here in America."

Dora said, "Well, I just assume we're living in England. He has an estate there and all. But who knows? Edward says he's dying to see Pittsburgh."

She showed Rita her engagement ring. She didn't care

if Mr. Byrne had proved it to be a fake. She thought it was a wonderful romantic gesture, and the very memory of it kept her warm at night.

Rita moved a little closer and whispered, "But poor Mr. Byrne, he looked so down at lunch!"

"Yes, I know, Rita, I know," Dora bit her lip. Michael weighed on her conscience in a way that Bernard never had.

CHAPTER 37

The next day Mrs. Benley, Rita, and Dora took the trolley into downtown Pittsburgh on a shopping expedition. Dora tried on several different wedding dresses. They settled on the new style, a bride's dress of white satin and *mousseline de soie*. The trim consisted of garlands of orange blossoms that wreathed the tulle veil. Even the ladies behind the cash registers came out to view it. They thought it was the most magnificent dress for sale at Kaufmann's Department Store that autumn of 1915.

Rita decided to buy her bridesmaid's dress at the same time. Before they'd finished, they'd invited half the store to the wedding at Ware House outside London. Dora had the store photographer take a picture of her with Rita standing side by side in their new dresses. She would send it to Edward to remind him of where he should be and when.

They lunched at the Tic Toc Restaurant at Kaufmann's and then left by the door nearest the Kaufmann's Clock at Smithfield Street and Fifth Avenue, ready to wave down the first trolley. They were so overloaded with packages they could hardly carry them, each sporting the Kaufmann's logo.

"Bang bang, pow pow!" Rita laughed as they emerged from the store. "We can barely climb out of the trenches with all our gear. We're going over the top anyway, as my brother says in his last letter from the front."

Dora hadn't giggled like this in a long time. "The war can't go on forever." So it seemed that day as the women met Mr. Benley and Mr. Byrne for dinner. They traveled only several blocks down the street to the Duquesne Club.

Mr. Benley and Mr. Byrne were driving up when they arrived. They'd come from Mr. Benley's office, where Mr. Benley had given his daughter's friend a tour. They talked shop as two doormen hurried over to open the car doors for the gentlemen. The ladies descended from the trolley, and they all entered the Richardson Romanesque style building together.

They were escorted into a lounge where they were served hors d'oeuvres for a couple of hours before the dining room opened for dinner.

As they were being served the main course, the head waiter approached their table looking grim. Dora felt cold prickles up her spine. Could it be about Edward? Mr. Byrne exchanged glances with her. She could tell he was thinking the same thing.

"A cable for your party, sir," said the waiter, presenting the message to Mr. Benley. "It was delivered to your house. Your cleaning lady's husband brought it to us."

Mr. Benley tipped the man and read the cable. He grimaced. "Humbug! It's from Lady Ware," he thrust the paper at Dora.

Dora paled as she took it. She could think of only one thing. Rita grabbed it from her. Dora's hand crept under the table, looking for Mr. Byrne's. She found it.

"What does it say, Rita?" Dora pleaded, unable to stand the suspense any longer. "Has Edward been killed in action?"

Rita shook her head. "Lady Ware is asking if you've heard from her son, Edward. She hasn't heard a thing since he left in late May."

Dora decided to cable back immediately. She would copy Edward's last message for his mother and affix a date to it. Now that she counted, she hadn't heard from Edward in weeks and weeks herself!

When they got back to the house, Viola shuffled through an old pile of papers and mail. She brought them an old letter dated at the very beginning of September right after the last one Dora had received. She must have just missed it, going back to Bryn Mawr when she had. Dora grabbed and opened it. It was very short:

My dearest love,

I got your letter! Of course I'd be glad to come home sooner. I'd leave right this minute except that I'd feel like I was betraying my company, my parents, and my country. I'd be a coward, and I want to be a hero for you, my love. Wouldn't you rather be married to someone you could be proud of instead of someone who makes you ashamed?

My new assignment won't take any time at all if Lawrence is to be believed. You should be seeing me in just a few more weeks.

Love and kisses – and more!

Edward

Dora threw the letter down on the floor in front of everybody and stomped on it. "But it's more than a few weeks already, and we still haven't heard from him!" She charged up the stairs to her room in a rage. Rita raced after her.

Just before Dora slammed the bedroom door behind her, she caught sight of Mr. Byrne's gaze. He was looking up at her from the bottom of the stairs. He was saying, *I told you so,* without having to move his lips.

CHAPTER 38

That evening everyone sat outside on the patio until dark. Dora, Rita, and Michael took up one whole cushioned bench with Michael between the girls. Mr. and Mrs. Benley occupied their usual white-painted, wooden Adirondack chairs under the maple trees, which had already shed most of their leaves.

"Michael," Dora sighed with her eyes shut, listening to the cicada during the last days of Indian Summer, "I'm glad you don't want to be a hero." She yawned. The war seemed very far away.

"No, Dora, I just want a little peace and quiet. I want to earn a living," Michael confessed with his arm resting around her shoulder.

"If everybody in Europe thought like that," Mr. Benley smoked his cigar, "we wouldn't have so much trouble in the world."

Everyone else retired for the night. They left Dora and Michael sitting there alone. Dora raised her hands as if to fend off his unspoken words. "You don't have to tell me again how irresponsible Edward is, about how he's going to have adventure after adventure and forget I ever existed."

"You're saying it better than I could, Dora."

"You act like we're two old folks who've been sitting on the patio forever and ever – older than my parents. You must be about eighty years old you're so wise," she said sarcastically.

"I'm really not so smart. If I were, I wouldn't be sitting here next to you," he looked back at her pointedly.

"That's not a very nice thing to say!" she said reproachfully.

"If I had any sense, I would have meant it that day I slammed the door in your face and put you out of my life forever."

She moved a little farther away from him on the bench. "You don't say!"

"No, Dora, I'm afraid I'm in it for the long, long, long haul. I can't walk out on you in a world that's so topsy-turvy you can call me from college because you're cornered by a saboteur. No, as Rita says, we *Lusitania* survivors have to stick together. As the old Chinese proverb says, when a man saves your life, you owe him yours. In that sense we two pledged each other our lives months ago."

"Michael, what are you –" Mr. Byrne's arms closed around her.

He pressed his lips down against hers. She quickly pushed him away. She didn't want to hurt his feelings. But how did she explain to him that her own feelings for him weren't the same as what she felt for Edward? She thought he was just her best friend and someone who understand her the way nobody else did.

"I'm ready any time you are to make you my wife, the mother of my children, and to live with you until we both die as your parents have done all these years. I love you, Dora. I can't run away out of jealousy as I tried to do this summer. I have to face up to it. I have to have patience."

"Michael, I don't want you to think that I'll get tired of waiting for Edward and change my mind. Edward will be coming home, and –"

He got up, ready to go to bed. He started toward the door. He turned. "And if he doesn't come back, if somebody shoots Edward dead, who else would you marry then?" he asked pointedly.

She bit her lip. She didn't like to think about it, but she guessed he had a point.

"I thought so," he said and closed the door behind him.

"Michael!"

He opened the door. She said, "Would you marry me on such terms?"

"What terms, Dora?" he leaned out of the door in the shadows.

"I mean, well . . . knowing I really loved another man?"

"A dead man isn't a man anymore, Dora. He's six feet under. If he cuddles up to anybody, it's the worms. I can hardly be jealous of them."

He closed the door with a note of finality. She shivered sitting there all alone. "Edward, where are you?" she asked the mums, the owls, and the rustling dead leaves of autumn. "How can you leave me all alone like this?" But even though a tear rolled down her cheek, only the night was left to wrap its arms around her and keep her company.

CHAPTER 39

Rita stayed as long as she could. She took the train back to New York to appear in a play and then a movie. She promised she'd call before Thanksgiving, which was when their little group would have to start for England to get there in time for the wedding.

Dora finally agreed with Mr. Byrne and her father, though Mr. Byrne had left the day after Rita. She took a leave of absence from Bryn Mawr College until the war ended. She resumed her grim, summer-time ritual of trekking to the mailbox every day for news about Edward. It got to the point several weeks later that they were sending cables back and forth to Ware House on an almost daily basis. Both Lady Ware and Dora were frantic. It was hard to say which lady was more frantic – Edward's mother or Edward's fiancée.

"For Christ's sake, how is a man to get any work done around here with all this female prattle and melodrama!" her father pounded his fist on the table one evening at dinner when Dora and her mother did nothing except worry aloud about Edward's whereabouts.

"But, Winthrop, no one's heard from the boy in months!" Mrs. Benley exclaimed.

"Etta May, am I supposed to be in the tire business or in the business of keeping track of wayward British lords?" he thundered. "And there aren't enough of them left to make a business out of that, no matter what I charge."

"But that leaves Dora in an impossible position!" her mother continued. "She's supposed to be married on December 22 in the chapel next to Ware House. That's a little over a month from now. We've got tickets on the *Tuscania* next week. Do we sail or not?"

"How the hell should I know!" Winthrop pounded the table again. *"Frank!"* he yelled.

"May I help you, sir?" Frank appeared in the doorway.

"Bring me the phone. I'm going to call my lawyer."

"What are you doing, Winthrop?" his wife protested. "You can't sue the British army, can you?" she asked big-eyed.

"Hello, Frederick, yes, this is Winthrop again . . . Yes, I know you have several ongoing suits already. Well, I want to add another task for you to do . . . No, it's not another suit. At least not right away it isn't . . . I want you to cable the British War Office. I want it done every day until you get an answer. I want the whereabouts of a Lieutenant Edward Ware traced. Yes, he's British . . . Yes, he's the lord my daughter has set her sights on marrying against my better judgment."

"Winthrop!" Mrs. Benley protested.

Mr. Benley motioned to his wife to be quiet.

"Yes, this British lord was last seen leaving the Dardanelles in September, which is the only smart thing I've ever known him to do. He was headed . . . Just a minute . . . Where was he going next?" Mr. Benley asked his daughter.

Dora shrugged. "He was shipping out with Lawrence, an acquaintance of Leonard Woolley. He didn't say where he was going, only that he was applying for a transfer."

"Nobody knows. That's just the problem. But you can put a trace on a T.E. Lawrence, too. Apparently he's part of this mess, whoever he is. Never heard of him before . . . Yes, I know it will be a lot of work. I'll double your retainer. No, I take that back – I'll triple it effective immediately!" he got out his checkbook. "And I won't use the mails. I'll have Frank bring it to you."

They waited for countless days without any word. Finally Frederick Bognar, the lawyer, appeared at the house one night at dinner time. Viola set another place. He looked grim as he got out a cable and handed it to Mr. Benley. Dora couldn't stand it. She raced around the table and stood behind her father, breathing down his neck:

Have never heard of a T.E. Lawrence. STOP. STOP. Don't know anything about a Lieutenant Ware either. STOP.

"Oh, Father, what are we going to do?" Dora clapped her hands over her mouth. "They don't know anything about them. They could be dead."

"Didn't Edward promise to write?" her mother said.

Dora nodded. "Unless something's preventing him. That's what I'm worried about."

After several more days of listening to weeping, screaming, wailing women, Mr. Benley was ready to tear out his hair – even though he had a receding hairline and couldn't spare any of it. "That's it! I've had enough. I'm calling Wilson."

"Wilson?" his wife exclaimed.

"Yes, Woodrow Wilson."

Immediately the man whose image Dora had once glimpsed in a black and white photo rose up before Dora's mind's eye. He was a five foot eleven, skinny gentleman with a long, gaunt, oval face and a grim smile. His lips were always pursed tightly together. His nose was long and pointed, held high in the air. He'd been wearing a gray suit with a black overcoat and a black top hat.

His wife and daughter watched in speechless amazement as Mr. Benley called the White House. It took a day or two, but he finally got through to Wilson's private secretary after he reminded him that he was a survivor of the *Lusitania* disaster *and* a prominent Pittsburgh businessman.

"Yes, President Wilson, glad to meet you. Not that I pretend to be a Democrat, mind you. I'm an old Rough Rider through and through. But I can cut you a deal about your White House fleet of cars. Yes, I'm just the man for that."

Wilson replied. Dora and Mrs. Benley couldn't make out his exact words.

"I need for you to put me in touch with someone who can locate soldiers in Europe engaged in that wild fracas over there."

Wilson answered again.

"Yes, I know we're neutral, and thank God for that! But you see, my daughter here is engaged to a Lieutenant Edward Ware. His father's Sir Adolphus Ware, a baronet of Rufford, Bart to be exact," he read it off a piece of paper. "It seems that Lieutenant Ware's disappeared into the Wild Beyond with a

T.E. Lawrence."

Wilson spoke.

"Yes, I've tried the British War Office. I might as well consult a Swami. They pretend not to know a thing for reasons of their own. They claim they've never heard of either fellow, which is of course an outright lie."

Wilson said something else.

"You want me to talk to the British Ambassador? Very well, I'll call him in the morning. If this lead turns out to be good, you can expect a large contribution to your political party for your trouble, even though I'm not a Democrat. Yes, Mr. President, thank you."

A few days later Winthrop Benley was on the phone with the British Ambassador. "I want you to contact the British War Office to look up a T.E. Lawrence and a Lieutenant Edward Ware."

A few days later at dinner the ambassador called back. Viola acted flustered. She had answered the phone herself and couldn't wait to hand it to Mr. Benley. Everyone – including Frank and Viola – clustered around Mr. Benley and leaned over his shoulder. Dora was biting her nails. Mr. Byrne was visiting at the time since it was a Saturday. Even he put down his fork and knife and listened respectfully.

"Simply put, you've committed a diplomatic *faux pas* by inquiring into the whereabouts of your son-in-law to be and T.E. Lawrence," the gentleman's impeccable British English could be heard on the other end of the phone very clearly even though he was in Washington, D.C.

"*Faux pas* or not, just give me an answer. Where the hell is Edward Ware hiding out?" Mr. Benley was impatient.

"That's what I'm trying to explain to you. I'm not at liberty to tell you."

"Not at liberty is different from don't know, I suppose?" her father was blunt.

"I'm going to be frank. Both Lawrence and Ware have been sent on a secret mission. It's not being publicized in the press in Britain either. The High Command wants it that way for reasons of their own. Lord Kitchener doesn't want the enemy to have any advance notice."

Dora exchanged desperate glances with Mr. Byrne.

"Are you suggesting that my daughter communicates with the enemy?" Mr. Benley sounded insulted.

"I'm sure she's a red-blooded American girl," the ambassador said. "But war is war, and this one seems to be a particularly nasty one."

"You can say that again! It never ends," her father shook his head.

"Well, we're giving Lawrence his chance at ending it. He has a plan that everyone thinks will work. He wants only a chance to put it into action. I can't tell you anything else except that both he and Edward are alive. That's the very most I am authorized to say."

Dora grabbed the phone. She would never have had the nerve if she hadn't been so desperate. "Mr. Ambassador, Edward and I are supposed to be married at Christmas. Is Edward coming home in time?"

There was a pause. "I don't think so, miss. You'll have to put it off, postpone it until after the war. I'm grievously sorry. Now I understand the reason for your concern. Yes, I really am dreadfully sorry for you all."

Dora handed the phone back to her father. She sat gazing at her vanilla ice cream as it melted all over the apple pie. Mr. Byrne squeezed her hand. Dora smiled at him through her tears. "Yes, I know, Michael, you told me so."

"Bastard British," her father cursed after hanging up, "all this secret dealing, secret treaties, all this diplomatic hanky-panky, that's what started this damn war to begin with. Don't they ever learn?"

"You should have been in charge of the British navy instead of this Churchill," Mrs. Benley declared. "You should have been named First Lord of the Admiralty. Then they wouldn't have sunk the *Lusitania.*"

"All it takes is some right thinking instead of all this deviousness. Mr. Byrne," Mr. Benley paused with his pie fork halfway to his mouth, "you're looking for a job, right?"

"Yes indeed, sir."

"You're a God-fearing man. I can tell."

"A Methodist, sir."

"That's the best kind next to the Presbyterians," Mr. Benley decreed.

Mrs. Benley smiled, cutting another piece of Viola's freshly baked apple pie. "Winthrop, we only attend that church because it's the nearest one and you don't like to waste time on Sunday mornings. We were both raised as good Lutherans, Mr. Byrne."

"You're hired, Mr. Byrne. I don't have time to deal with all these ladies and run a business at the same time. I need all the help I can get," Winthrop Benley decided in an instant.

"Thank you, sir," Mr. Byrne smiled. "I couldn't hold off my employer about going to England any longer anyway. I handed in my resignation on Friday."

"To tell you the truth, I thought you were a troublemaker at first, shacking up with my little girl on the *Lusitania*. By golly, it turned out you really were hot on the tail of some fugitive from justice. You saved my little girl to boot."

Mr. Byrne's cheeks flushed.

"Besides, I like your loyalty. You've proved to be a good friend." The two men shook on the deal. Viola brought in the after dinner mints. "In uncertain times, one needs somebody he can trust and count on."

"That's certainly Michael," Dora sighed, thinking of someone else with red hair, bright reddish-orange freckles, and wicked green eyes.

CHAPTER 40

D ora called Rita the next day. "The wedding's been postponed," she groaned.
"What happened?"
"Edward was sent on a secret mission. They won't tell me where or for how long. He hasn't written. My Dad had to drag it out of the British Ambassador."
"I'll hold onto my bridesmaid's dress. I'll keep it freshly pressed to use at a moment's notice."
"You're a friend."
"How could I be anything else after all we've been through together?"
Christmas came and went. Dora tossed and turned, waking up thinking she was married and on her honeymoon only to discover that there was snow outside her window and she was all alone. She thought, *Edward! Why don't you at least write me? Are they really preventing you from telling me where you are and what's going on? Can't you guess what I must feel?*
Lady Ware was getting the same treatment. Dora received a letter every week from her future mother-in-law lamenting the lack of news. Lady Ware described how she carefully pored over the *Killed in Action* column of *The Times* every day looking for one name and one name only.
Dora lived in suspended animation. She was unable to really go forward, unable to focus on anything. Her attention was constantly distracted by the coming of the mail and then the disappointment of not hearing anything – only to build up to the same crescendo tomorrow, and the day after that, and then the week after that.
Spring came. Spring went. Now it was the summer of 1916, more than a year since she'd stood at the pier in Liverpool and waved good-bye to Edward as he departed for the Dardanelles. Chuck, the mailman, came racing down her driveway early one day as she stood pruning rosebushes with

her mother. "Dora, here's the letter from Edward!" he shouted. The whole community of Bethel Borough in the South Hills of Pittsburgh had been galvanized. They knew all about Miss Dora Benley's plight.

Dora dropped her pruners and tore it open. The envelope fell to the driveway and blew away. It caught on the branch of a rhododendron now in bloom. She sucked in her breath to brace herself for the worst. Her eyes scanned the letter quickly, trying to devour it all at once. Was he wounded? Was he coming home soon? Instead of important news, the letter bogged down in a morass of words. She would have to slog through it line by line to decipher it. Worse, he seemed to be going on and on about *something* – and it wasn't her, his feelings for her, or anything worth reading! She remembered the style of *The Wilderness of Zin.* She thought, *Wait a minute! Is this Edward or Lawrence writing?*

"Is Edward all right?" the postman's voice broke into the fog of confusion and sudden revulsion that had consumed Dora's brain.

"What?" she looked up, dazed, to find not only the postman but her mother and several neighbors gathered around her in a tight knot, wringing their hands.

"Is the wedding to be soon?" her mother pressed.

"I – I don't know!" Dora threw the letter at her mother, burst into tears, and raced up the steps to the front door. She ran right into Viola holding a wicker laundry basket full of clothes. She knocked them all over the oriental rug in the foyer.

"Dora!" Viola exclaimed.

Dora charged up the stairs to her bedroom.

Sharp tongues whispered behind her, talking about the strain visible in every line of her face. "How long has this been going on?" asked one neighbor, entering the house after her mother.

"How much more can she take?" asked another from the bottom of the stairs.

As soon as she got to her room, Dora picked up the phone.

"Benley Tire and Rubber," answered the receptionist.

"Give me Mr. Byrne!" At least she could trust Michael not to talk like an archaeological monograph!

"Yes, Dora," said the receptionist.

"What happened this time, Dora?" Michael answered immediately.

"Edward's letter finally arrived," she sobbed. "After all these months!"

"It doesn't sound as if it's the big moment you've been waiting for," he observed dryly.

Dora pounded her fist on her nightstand. "He writes purple prose about strange, foreign people saying bizarre things. He sounds so serious all of the sudden," she ran her fingers through her hair, "like he was twenty years older. It must be the influence of that horrible Lawrence, the war, or who knows what. Edward writes like he doesn't know I'm alive! He could be writing to you, my mother, or to Chuck, the postman!"

"You're father's about ready to leave. We'll be there in about half an hour."

Click.

"Oh, Michael," she said with tears in her eyes as she put the phone down, "why can't you be the one who's far away fighting a war and Edward be in your place?"

CHAPTER 41

Viola was the one to retrieve Edward's missive from the bottom of the front steps. She brushed it off with her apron and arranged it neatly and in order at Dora's place at the dining room table.

Dora wouldn't come down to dinner until Mr. Byrne went to get her. He sat her down right next to him in front of the dining room windows, where Viola had carefully drawn the curtains for privacy. The neighbors had been sneaking down the drive and peering in to see if they could figure out what was going on.

Dora stared and stared at the pages, turning from one to the next. Her parents and Mr. Byrne said grace and started to eat without her, though slowly. Viola kept on tiptoeing into the dining room to see how Dora was doing. Then the cleaning lady reported back to Frank in the kitchen and one of the peskiest neighbors at the kitchen door. They gossiped in hushed whispers.

Dora gripped her fist as she read and pounded it on the table. Her mother got so curious that she picked up the pages and scanned them for herself. She handed them to Winthrop, who lifted his eyebrows, shook his head, and handed them off to Mr. Byrne, who knew enough to arrange them in a neat pile once again. He didn't bother to even glance at them.

"Damn!" exclaimed Mr. Benley. "You can't eat dinner with this war going on. It spoils the digestion."

"Dora," Mr. Byrne nudged her, "why don't you start from the beginning and read it aloud?"

"Oh, Michael, do I have to?" she looked vexed.

He nodded.

She sighed and began to read:

Dearest Dora:

For many months I wasn't allowed to write you. Now General Murray, who commands the Arabian sector, says the situation is stable enough.

The other day we destroyed a railroad belonging to the Turks. It was hit and run. That is Lawrence's new style. It works like magic. The Turks are too well-equipped by the Germans to attack them head on in battle. This kind of thing wears them down slowly but surely.

No sooner did we ride up to an empty section of track than the Arabs dismounted and chopped at the railroad ties with axes, disarranging them so that if any train came that way it was certain to jump the tracks.

Lawrence was grinning from ear to ear. He's making me unlearn everything I ever thought I knew about wars and battles. When his Bedouins had finished with their work, he planted one of his "tulip bombs" out of sight next to the track. When the train hits it, it will blow sky high, twisting the tracks so they can ever be straightened again. Lawrence always says that it's the most beautiful sight he's ever seen – one of his hand-made tulip bombs exploding with a flourish.

After such a hectic morning, when we got back from our raid on the railroad, I resumed entering letters from the British War Office. I found the latest one missing. It had arrived early that morning. I had laid it aside carefully by placing it under the paper weight on the desk which almost covered it entirely.

You might remember how good I am not when it comes to keeping things in order. I looked everywhere – under the desk, around the inside of my tent, around the outside, and then all over the periphery of our encampment. At the last minute I checked my pack that I'd taken on the raid in case I'd put it there instead of where I thought I remembered.

When I still couldn't turn up anything I thought I must tell Lawrence. It was my duty, even if it cast me in a bad light. It reminded me of when I was in British public school at Harrow. I was asked to fetch the paddle.

One disadvantage with these tents was that I couldn't knock. Colonel Lawrence was seated in front of his desk. I cleared my throat. He didn't look up. Lawrence reminds me more of one of my professors from Oxford than an army officer. He's always writing something down, taking notes, composing letters, keeping journals, reading aloud, or orating to himself, to me, or to a group. Sometimes I see him doing any one or more of these things on camel back.

He seemed to be totally absorbed in some papers. Perhaps Lawrence himself had "borrowed" the missive. All I had to do was ask about it.

"Colonel, I'm sorry to bother you, but an important letter has been lost," I interrupted Lawrence.

"I'm afraid a lot more than that has gone astray," Lawrence sighed as he went on reading.

"So, you have the latest from the War Office?"

"Ours is the civilization of Napoleon, Caesar, of the Magna Carta, of Marco Polo, of white men who have ventured to the darkest corners of the globe," Lawrence read while he talked. "As Kipling wrote, it's the White Man's Burden. How do we treat the natives who become dependent on us and our enlightenment? Do we then lead them astray, cheat them, rob them, and then expect them to bless Western civilization?" Lawrence looked troubled. "We should reward them and let them participate in the blessings we ourselves enjoy. But not the British War Office!" He shook his head. "They don't listen to me."

"The War Office doesn't make policy," I consoled him. "It's the Prime Minister and Parliament."

"Yes, and that's where all the treachery comes from!" he threw the letter down and paced around the tent.

"But – but we are only soldiers. It's not up to us . . . "

"What do you think has gotten them nowhere on the Western Front?" he stood nose to nose with me and thundered as if I had turned into the British War Office. "Secret treaties. Dirty treaties. Stalemate. Why, I visited Gallipoli . . . "

"I was stationed there . . . " I reminded him.

"Soldiers drowned in the trenches from the winter rains. Unburied corpses washed into the lines. Frostbite. Snow. Men killed from exposure because they were ordered to sit there in a trench and shoot and shoot until everyone on both sides was dead and nothing was accomplished," he whipped about like a fury. "A dysentery epidemic. The young physicist Henry Moseley killed. The poet Rupert Brooke dead of a septic mosquito bite. Altogether over seventy thousand young men from the United Kingdom dead in one battle. One hundred fifty thousand for the allies – in one stupid military operation that accomplished nothing for anybody."

The Colonel is so fearsome when he gets in a mood like this, I was rooted to the spot.

"I'm going to actually win this war even if only on one front! I'm going to DO SOMETHING – regardless if they put me in front of a firing squad for treason or disobedience."

Most of the missives from the War Office are rather boring. What on earth had been in this one?

He snatched up the letter on his desk. "They should make Leonard Woolley the Prime Minister. They should make him General Woolley. I would sooner listen to him." Lawrence stood there distracted for a few moments leafing through the missive to find a particular passage.

"Yes, as Woolley writes to me right here, 'I've often had occasion to remark that much of the character of the Arabs comes from the Tigris and Euphrates Rivers and their shifting courses throughout the whole of recorded history. They had nothing to rely upon. They did not have their Nile River which seemed eternally the same to the Ancient Egyptians. They had no Tiber River like the ancient Romans or anything like our River Thames. Cities would be created and destroyed in the course of a mere generation or two because of the capriciousness of nature. No stability of one strong government was allowed. It led to the strengthening of the tribal system with local potentates of this tribe or that making do with whatever they could . . .'"

It was slow to dawn on me. This was not a letter from the War Office. It was a letter from Leonard Woolley. It was about their excavation – along with my father – of the Hittite City of Carchemish before he'd joined the Army.

"So my forces will forge ahead and ignore the British War Office. We won't let them betray the men who depend on me. I'll try to compensate them for the generations that they've spent wandering in the wilderness, looking for their own Promised Land. We'll bring them freedom from the Turks and give them the blessings of liberty as the British people have liberty . . . "

I nodded.

"This little tribe has hegemony over this little area over here," Lawrence got out a map and started jabbing at it with his finger. "That little tribe has hegemony over there," he jabbed again. "What we could teach them is to get together so they could start exerting a force for good in the world," he went on and on. "It's past the time to divide and conquer . . . "

"Since you are talking about the War Office, I wanted to mention that a letter was delivered here this morning while we were eating breakfast. I'm afraid –"

"A letter from the War Office?" Lawrence looked at me.

I nodded.

"Well, I'll tell you what to do with that," he proclaimed.

"I can't do anything with it. You see, it's mis –"

Lawrence picked up a sheet of paper. He ripped it into shreds in front of my face.

My mouth dropped open.

He threw the pieces of paper at me. He kicked the shreds of paper around on the dirt and sand on the floor of the tent. Clouds of dust rose up.

This was not the sort of thing I had learned at Oxford. Since Lawrence was an Oxford man, I don't think he'd learned it there either.

"Let me get this straight. You want me to tear up any letters I get from the War Office?" I repeated.

"Now we're catching on, Lieutenant."

I wet my lips. "Shall I reply to them first?"

Lawrence paced around the tent some more, obviously considering. Then he stopped short. "Yes, why don't we have a standard reply. Don't bother to read the boring, repetitive stuff. Just reply, 'Proceeding as usual . . .'" He looked off into space as if seeing the faces of the British War Office generals. He laughed and rubbed his hands together with glee.

"Proceeding as usual?" I repeated what he had said.

"Exactly!"

"Shall I still enter them in my register, sir?"

"Amuse yourself if you like! Don't bother me with them," he ordered.

"Is that all, sir?" I wanted to take my leave so I could collect my thoughts.

He went to fetch his SMLE rifle, an exact replica of my own. He took it to the flap of the tent and rudely shoved it aside. Colonel Lawrence aimed straight up at the sky. Without any ado, he fired.

The English officers visiting our camp came charging out of their tents, wondering if we were under attack. Somehow the Arabs intuited what he was really up to. They knew Turks didn't attack in such a manner.

"Has something happened?" one officer asked.

Lawrence said, "Just proceeding as usual," with a wry wink.

The British nodded and departed for their tents.

"I dedicate this rifle to the true task that I have set forth," he told me. "I won't play the War Department's games. I will give the Arabs what they have never had for centuries – a way to hold up their heads among nations."

There is very little moisture in the air here, and the swings of temperatures are extreme every day, varying on average between thirty and forty degrees. Right now, of course, my shivering had more to do with my fears than the actual temperature of the air.

So you see, my love, I have my hands full. I am doing things I never dreamed possible before. I feel as if I have been saddled with a grave responsibility. Lawrence, as I have come to realize in the past months, is no mere commander like all the others I met at Gallipoli. He is a great man with a unique vision all his own – sort of like Genghis Kahn, Caesar, Napoleon, Attila the Hun, and Hannibal all rolled into one. Like other great men, he takes big chances and dangerous ones, too.

I hope you will understand why I have not written up until now,

Edward

P.S. I reserve you for my dreaming hours when I am in bed alone. That's also when I'm reading the volume you sent me by Mr. Klein, whom I understand was your first swain. If he was anything like Mr. Byrne I should have liked to meet him. Michael is so amusing. I wish he was here now to make me laugh. Ditto with Mr. Klein. *The Lion and the Mouse* reminds me of your American way of thinking – so prudish and severe!

P.S.S. I'm sure you can also understand why I can't get away now. I know it's a few months longer than we had planned. Maybe by this coming Christmas? Yes, you look fetching in your wedding dress. I got your photo. I daydream about ripping it off you piece by piece, including the veil. Now that would make a photo! Speaking of photos, I haven't had much of a chance to use my camera yet.

P.S.S.S. I was finishing up this letter when there was a commotion outside my tent. I ran out to check on it. A Bedouin had arrived hawking wares. The others were gathered around him and haggling for a deal. The Arabs love nothing better than this sort of thing. Lawrence makes sure they have plenty of coins, most of them stolen in raids, so they can amuse themselves.

This particular merchant claimed he had lots of cigarettes, pipe tobacco, and cigars. The men love nothing better than a good smoke after a day of raiding. But low and behold, there came Lawrence out of his tent. He made his way through the jostling crowd. They stepped back when they saw who he is. He threw down a bag of Turkish piasters and said, "Give me the best cigars you have."

"For that price we *can* give you the best!" said the Bedouin named Mohamed, searching through his wares. He gave Lawrence a handful of fat cigars that I could smell from where I was standing.

Lawrence then astounded everyone by throwing down those cigars and stepping on them.

"Pah! I want more than that for my money."

Mohamed grinned at him and said, "You drive a hard bargain, *shereef,* but so do I. That will cost you more money."

"I don't have anymore money right now," Lawrence insisted with his arms akimbo.

His men laughed.

"Well then, no more cigars!" Mohamed shrugged.

Lawrence headed back to his tent. He soon returned with the humidor that my father and Leonard Woolley had given him. He shoved it at Mohamed.

"I used all the cigars up. I'm willing to trade it for more. I don't need the box."

Mohamed examined the cigar box that my father fancied so. He shrugged. "All right, here are ten more of my very best cigars."

He and Lawrence shook on the deal. Lawrence went back to his tent smoking. His men applauded.

Such is life in the desert. I bet it's nothing like Pittsburgh.

When Dora got all the way to the PS and PSS, she blushed and stuttered a little, skipping over Edward's racy remarks. She smiled that he had indeed remembered her and then colored again to realize Mr. Byrne understood what she was doing. She read the PSSS rapidly, trying to get to the end and not interested in hearing more about the ubiquitous humidor and how it kept on showing up every place under the sun.

She finally put the letter down and let loose with a sigh of indignation. "Christmas again!" she moaned. "I don't believe it."

"Is that when the wedding is to be?" her mother looked bewildered.

"And that Lawrence character goes and gives away the humidor as if it didn't mean a thing to him – just so he can get a few more cigars!"she shook her head. "Ali was willing to stab me for it. Well, if I see him again, I'll have to inform him that a Bedouin by the name of Mohamed has it now."

Her mother and father excused themselves to go to bed. Only she and Mr. Byrne were still sitting there together.

"Dora, you realize, don't you, that this can't go on forever?" Mr. Byrne asked. "Your father wants me to press you to reconsider if you will marry me and move into the house I'm renting."

"Oh yes! I know how father thinks," she sighed, "and he's so right! Nothing would make me happier than to marry you, Michael," she stared down at her half-eaten plate of food and spoke without enthusiasm. "Everything would be on schedule and on time then. Everything would be very rational and very right."

"But what about Edward, Dora?"

"Yes, what about him indeed!" she leaped to her feet. She paced back and forth, back and forth. "And that Lawrence boy would I like to get my hands on him! I hope he gets killed in one of his raids by one of his tulip bombs. Beautiful indeed! Then Edward will come home."

She grabbed a vase full of her mother's best mums. She smashed it on the floor. The water splashed on her feet. She raced upstairs to her bedroom and slammed the door behind her. She even took a cold shower to forget. But she kept on returning to Edward's insinuation that he would like to have a photo of her without her clothes on, perhaps clad only in her wedding veil.

That night when she was all alone she went to sleep clad only in her wedding veil. And she woke up weeping. She didn't close her eyes again until dawn. Her last thought before drifting off was, *Michael, you may understand many things about me. But this you will never understand . . .*

CHAPTER 42

E dward surprised them all. His next letter arrived the very next day. The mailman knocked on the front door. As soon as she answered, Chuck put the letter right into Dora's hands. She ended up reading it standing there with the mailman watching:

Dearest Apple of My Eye,

Lawrence and thirty-five of Prince Feisal's rag-tag force of tribesmen set out to attack the Turks directly. Prince Feisal went first in white. The headman of one of the seven tribes, Sharraf, was on his right in a red head cloth and henna-dyed tunic and cloak. Lawrence was on his left in white and red. It looked like the Middle Ages.

Behind us men carried three banners of purple silk with gold spikes accompanied by drummers playing a march. Last but not least came one thousand two hundred camels of the bodyguard, all packed as closely as cattle being driven from place to place. These men wore whatever pleased them. Everyone was singing in Arabic. I didn't know the words. But I could guess from the repetition of names that they were singing paeans to Feisal and his family. Feisal is the son of King Hussein, and he's the Emir of Mecca. He's the one Lawrence is trying to place on the throne to end the Turkish domination.

It didn't look like a surprise raid to me, but Lawrence managed to capture the town of Weijh. The Turks had been weakened enough in that sector that the village was ripe for plucking, and Lawrence plucked it.

On the way back we encountered that trader named Mohamed. The men were stopped, preparing a celebration feast. He noisily barged in among us, hawking his wares. Lawrence was seated cross-legged near the fire. Mohamed stood over our *shereef,* looking down at him.

"So, you give me this box, and it's worthless!" Mohamed complained, waving the humidor about.

"How did you come to such a conclusion, friend?" Lawrence was nonplussed. He hardly moved a muscle. He only looked up at the Bedouin.

"I took it to a bazaar. They said it's a fake, a forgery. It's made of cheap pine wood even though it looks like mahogany."

Lawrence smiled. He stretched by the fire. "Isn't beauty, my friend, in the eyes of the beholder?"

Mohamed glared at him. He threw the box at Lawrence and stomped off. All the other Bedouins broke into raucous laughter. They clapped their hands, thinking Lawrence had gotten the better of the trader.

Mohamed consoled himself by making a few other trades and sales before he left the encampment.

"Did you just make an enemy, sir?" I asked Lawrence when the laughter had died down.

"I have so many enemies already, another one hardly counts for anything," Lawrence helped himself to a platter of dates.

"You do take chances, don't you?" I commented. "To offend somebody like Mohamed just to get ten more cigars is like . . . "

"Gambling?" he turned toward me. "To live in the desert is to gamble. Every day you throw the dice and hope for the best."

When we got back to our more permanent encampment and I was approaching my tent, I saw a figure dart out of it. I ran to catch up with him.

"See here, you vagrant!" I called out.

The man disappeared into the desert. One of the Bedouins came up to me, "Don't worry about him, Lieutenant, he's a petty thief!"

"What if he's a spy!" I suddenly remembered how one of the letters from the War Department had never been found. Had this scoundrel stolen it?

Later I asked Lawrence about the thief. He shrugged, meaning he wasn't listening but was preoccupied with his own thoughts. At that moment Prince Feisal came into the Colonel's tent. Lawrence joked, "My secretary is nervous about some vagrant. Thinks he's a spy."

Much to my shock Feisal laughed and said something in Arabic to Lawrence. They both enjoyed a laugh at my expense.

When Feisal left, I asked Lawrence what I had missed. He explained, "Feisal says, 'Oh, you think he's one of those British army or navy native spies, the ones who are spying for so many sides at once that they can't even remember who is who.'"

After a blank look from me, I remembered that he must be talking about the Lebanese and Armenian exiles, hired by the War Department, and put ashore, then picked up by warships for regular reports. They sold so much misinformation as triple and quadruple agents, riding about on flea-bitten camels, that they'd become universal figures of fun.

Prince Feisal declared an impromptu feast to celebrate Lawrence's victory over the village of Weijh. I had the privilege to sit beside Lawrence during the meal. The servants got a fire going outside the tent, and we watched something that smelled delicious being prepared. The servants then brought in a platter of *kharuf mahshi*.

You may ask what this is. It is baby lamb stuffed with rice. It was so delicious that I later loitered and asked a servant in my halting Arabic (I am being tutored by Lawrence, who learned the tongue before he arrived) how it is prepared. Not that you would want to prepare such an exotic dish in far off Pittsburgh where it would be considered barbaric, but you might be curious how your fiance is spending his time and how I will naturally expect to be served by you wearing only your veil after we are married. Apparently it is stuffed with not just rice but nuts and raisins as well. It is rubbed on the outside with a paste of onion crushed with cinnamon, cloves, and cardamom. These spices are native to the part of Arabia that borders on the seacoast and in ancient times was called *Arabia Felix*. It is cooked over a roaring fire on a spit until browned all over in bubbling goat butter. We washed this all down with Arabian coffee *(Qahwa Arabeya)* flavored with cardamom, which they claim is more famous and stronger than the better known Turkish variety. It was certainly enough to make me open my eyes. Maybe I'll be able to package it and bring a sample back to you as a gift. This is what the noble savages drink instead of wine and liquor, which is forbidden by their religion.

They have a ceremony here that certainly competes with my mother serving high tea in the garden at Ware House. Here even the prince gets involved. It has to do with ancient rules of hospitality in the desert. Prince Feisal actually roasted the beans over a separate fire himself while we were waiting for the lamb on the spit. When he considered them sufficiently browned, he cooled them in water. A servant brought him his grinder. He used a mortar and pestle. Instead of sugar, which they don't have here, he added cardamom pods in equal measure to the coffee beans. After all that labor, all the prince needed was boiling water and Arabian coffee mugs.

While I was sipping the coffee, my neighbor turned to me and said something I didn't understand in Arabic. Later Lawrence told me he'd remarked, 'Feisal makes coffee from morning until night.' That didn't make much sense considering that he was a prince and not a cook. Lawrence explained that it was great praise honoring Feisal's hospitality.

Lawrence remained silent throughout the whole meal. Everyone talked to him. He replied only when spoken to. You could tell he was the honored guest. He sat at Feisal's right hand.

Lawrence rose to propose a toast. "As your poet Abu Tammaam al-Taa'ee says, "More truthful in its tidings is the sword than are books . . . So I honor you, Prince Feisal's army. You have made today possible."

After the men clapped, I asked Lawrence, "Is that really what the poet said?"

"It's all in the translation," he told me. "Translations are far more important than you realize. A few words here or there can make all the difference."

"I didn't know you were a translator of Arabic!" I confessed.

"It was my ambition once," he said. "Now I'm fulfilling the same mission in a different way."
Love and kisses,
Edward

P.S. I wish it could have been our wedding banquet. You could learn to do a belly dance like some of the women in Turkish countries – not that I have seen any of them, though! And we could dance together all night after that.

I don't mind telling you that I'm as lonely for you as you are for me. And there's no female Michael to keep me company in the meantime. I haven't so much as seen a woman anywhere for months. You haunt not only my dreams but my waking hours. Perhaps you could send me something of yours to keep with me when I am off-duty – something that would remind me of you?

Dora hurled the letter to the floor and stalked off, leaving the mailman gaping at her. Viola picked it up and made her excuses to Chuck, inviting him in for a cup of coffee for all his trouble. Only later did Dora get enough control over her temper to write to her fiance:

Dear Edward:
You promised me that we would be married Christmas, 1915. Now you say maybe Christmas, 1916, but I have less reason to expect that you'll keep your promise this year than last. You seem to think I'm supposed to wait for you forever while you ride around the desert on a camel and pretend you're in the Middle Ages along with this crazy man Lawrence who deals in antique humidors and spouts ancient Arab poetry!

You got one transfer. Can't you get another? Can't you work in the War Office back home in Britain so you could keep your promise? Or aren't I as important to you as Colonel Lawrence and all his Bedouins? Honestly, Edward, I don't know what to think!

Sincerely yours,
Dora

    But before she sealed the letter, she hesitated. She slipped a pair of her stockings into a brown paper envelope, looking from side to side to make sure no one else saw her. She wrapped them well and stuffed her letter in next to it. Blushingly she sealed it and put it in the mailbox. It would remind Edward of their time in London. That's what he had been asking for — a memory of her.

CHAPTER 43

D ora had to get away. She decided to go shopping in downtown Pittsburgh. Frank drove her to the trolley stop. She was meeting Mr. Byrne for lunch.

On the trolley she was perusing the collected works of Elbert Hubbard, the madcap writer she'd met aboard the *Lusitania*. He'd handed her a polemic tract, "Who Lifted the Lid Off Hell?", about how the Kaiser was going to resort to cannibalism next. She'd found the essay had been published by *The Philistine* in October, 1914. After the sinking of the *Lusitania,* Hubbard's followers had held a big memorial service for him. His body had never been found. She felt a strong affinity with all these passengers such as Hubbard whom she'd never met before the voyage, especially the Americans who hadn't known what to expect.

She soon switched to re-reading Charles Klein's *The Lion and the Mouse*. Dora felt more than a twinge of guilt. It hadn't been her fault that the saboteur, Ali, had tied her and Mr. Byrne up to a pillar in the engine room, next to one of his diabolical, chemical time-fuses. Still, if she had stayed close to Charles Klein the whole voyage as her parents had originally intended, he would still be here today. He would have exited the ship with her father and mother in that lifeboat.

Her real distraction, though Dora didn't like to admit it, was the book she'd started on the way to Bryn Mawr and never finished, *The Wilderness of Zin* by Leonard Woolley and T.E. Lawrence. She kept on trying to figure out what made this lunatic Lawrence tick. She needed to break the magnetic hold he had on Edward – or her happiness was doomed.

She kept on coming back to the dedication to Chapter 1, entitled *Our Route In The Desert*, which was a quote from an old English ballad, *The Nut-Brown Maid:*

> *If ye go thyder, ye must consider,*
> *When ye have lust to dine,*

There shall no meat be for to gete
Neither bere, ale, ne wine,
Ne shetes clean, to lie between.

Was this some sort of male thing, this wilderness experience, this living close to nature? She'd always been interested in ancient history and archaeology, but she supposed that was because she could admire polished finds in a museum and didn't have to go trudging through the wilderness to get them.

As she skimmed through the notes at the end, discovering lots of classical Greek inscriptions, she wondered about the nature of T.E. Lawrence's mind. If he was scholarly – and hadn't Edward said he reminded him more of a professor than a general? – what was he doing riding around with a bunch of Bedouins? How many languages could one fellow know? So far it was seven and counting. Besides his mother tongue, there was Middle English, Ancient Hittite, Greek, Latin, modern Arabic, and now Ancient Arabic, too, if Edward's last letter was to be believed.

A sudden bounce knocked the book out of her hands. She held on to the back of the seat in front of her. The trolley car jounced along the track at a fairly slow pace, jostling her from side to side, winding in and out of a woodsy area on a hill elevated above the road level.

It was then she felt eyes on her, burning a hole through her skin. Across the aisle sat a man wearing an ordinary business suit. He favored a big hat with a wide brim to conceal his face. Those were the same dark eyes that she'd seen at Bryn Mawr, in Denbigh Hall's shower room. The corners of Ali's mouth turned upward into a menacing grin before he went back to reading a copy of *The Pittsburgh Press*.

Smoke from the steel plants along the Monongahela River was blowing toward the downtown that day. Dora covered her nose with a handkerchief as she got off at Kaufmann's and disappeared inside the store. She headed for the hat department. Her mother had suggested she start building up her wardrobe while she waited to get married. Her trousseau would then be ready at a moment's notice.

She picked up the first hat she came to, a garden or travel chapeau style. It was made of straw, edged with brown velvet and dotted with cream foulard trim. The ribbon on top was tied on one side. The sales clerk pushed a mirror in front of her so she could appreciate the effect. When she peered into the glass, she saw Ali behind her.

Dora paid for her purchase in cash. The sales clerk wrapped it up in a fancy bag with the Kaufmann's logo and handed it to her. Ali edged closer.

She dashed down the aisle, weaving in and out of crowds of shoppers. "Oh, excuse me!" She leaped onto the escalator and began running up the moving stairs. Two fat ladies got on behind her. Ali forced his way past the fat ladies, taking two steps at a time.

Dora jumped off at the top. She fled toward the entrance to the Tic Toc Restaurant.. The clean-shaven Mr. Byrne stood waiting for her in his conservative suit, holding his hat and umbrella.

"Dora! For heaven's sake, what's happened now?"

She pointed behind her, jabbing her finger at a crowd of strangers. "Ali! He's following me."

Her father might scoff at her. The other shoppers in the crowd might think she was eccentric. Michael Byrne always believed her. He shoved Dora behind him and stalked out into the crowded restaurant lobby to look around.

He returned to her side. Taking her arm, he led her over to the table by the window. He pulled out her chair and made sure that anyone trying to reach Dora would have to run into him first.

"Is this the first time you've seen the miscreant here in Pittsburgh?" Mr. Byrne pressed.

"The last time I saw him was at Bryn Mawr. I thought I was safe here in Pittsburgh," she nervously tapped her fingernails on top of the table.

"I'll make sure of it," he scanned the room for any sign

of the intruder.

"Have you decided what you want?" a waiter stopped beside their table.

"Two specials," Mr. Byrne ordered for both of them.

"Would you like a glass of wine with –"

Mr. Byrne scowled like a good Methodist, "Coffee."

The coffee gave Dora something to do with her hands. She sipped it with lots of sugar and cream, waiting for Ali's next move. She could hear the ticking of Mr. Byrne's watch.

The specials turned out to be two enormous cheeseburgers on toasted buns accompanied by steaming hot bowls of chicken noodle soup. Neither of them touched their food. They just sat there.

"Is there something wrong?" the waiter returned in a few moments.

"Oh, no, no!" Mr. Byrne said. "It's just fine." He handed Dora the bottle of Heinz ketchup and a jar of Heinz pickles left on the table for them.

"If this Colonel Lawrence is so great a desert fighter, why can't he keep the Bedouins where they belong in Arabia? What are some of them doing running around Pittsburgh?" Michael squeezed more ketchup on his cheeseburger.

"Michael," she hissed, "Ali's just gotten seated."

Michael summoned the waiter to his side and whispered something into his ear.

The waiter went to talk to the manager of the restaurant. The manager headed for Ali's table. "I'm afraid, sir, that the restaurant located just down the street would be more suitable for someone like you. It's called Solomon's Temple."

"That's for Jews!" Ali objected in his heavily accented voice.

"I don't really care where you lunch. But you won't lunch at the Tic Toc."

Ali stalked out of the restaurant. He stopped at the door to glare at Dora and Michael.

"Normally I would go back to work," Michael glared back at Ali, "but I insist upon escorting you home – right to your door," Mr. Byrne paid the bill and tipped the waiters for their cooperation.

CHAPTER 44

It was already the middle of the afternoon when they emerged onto the street in front of the Kaufmann's Clock. They caught the first trolley out of town, the Shannon Drake line. Ali started to board, using the door in the middle of the trolley. Mr. Byrne complained to the trolley driver.

The driver paced back through the trolley, past businessmen in suits and women with shopping bags and little children. "Are you some troublemaker?" the man confronted Ali.

"I am here visiting friends," he said in his accented voice.

"We don't allow Huns, spies, or foreign-types on our trolleys. Get it?"

"I am not German," Ali stated flatly.

"No, but boy, you look like one of them sinister Turks."

"I am certainly not a Turk!" Ali glowered at him.

"*Pittsburgh Press* says the Turks are the allies of the Huns. No friends of ours. Get out of here, or I'm going to call the police!"

The other passengers were eyeballing Ali. Some made dirty hand gestures. Others snickered. Two blast furnace workers from United States Steel rose. They approached Ali, picked him up, and muscled him out of the street car. He landed right in the middle of Fifth Avenue.

The crowd inside the trolley cheered as they took off.

"See what we Americans can accomplish if we work together?" Mr. Byrne smiled at Dora and patted her hand.

Dora looked behind her. Ali was boarding the trolley behind them unchallenged.

The trolleys slowly made their circle of the downtown area on their way to the bridge, the tunnel, and home. Once they left the city, the tracks narrowed. They headed over a tall, makeshift bridge over a roadway. Dora couldn't take her eyes off the streetcar behind them that was so close it was practically butting them.

Both streetcars stopped constantly to let passengers on and off. Sometimes the trolley halted before entering another track. They had to wait for a trolley coming in the opposite direction. In some sections the track bed wasn't wide enough to permit trolleys to go in two different directions at the same time.

On certain stretches they gained speed. They bounced and jounced along through the woods. She was thrown against Mr. Byrne. He was thrown against her. Branches smacked against the sides of the trolley. They slowed down. The trolley behind them slowed as well. She craned her neck. Ali leaped off. *I wonder what he's doing that for . . .*

They were stopped forever at that junction waiting for a trolley coming from the South Hills suburbs into town. Finally it passed. They edged their way onto the next intersecting track. No sooner had they gotten under way than Dora smelled something strange. The trolley bounced, then lurched sharply to the right. It ran off the track and crashed, wedging itself against a tree at an extreme angle. The tree sat at the edge of a cliff looking directly down onto a busy road more than a hundred feet below.

Ladies were screaming and crying. Mr. Byrne pulled Dora out of her seat. They made their way toward the front door of the car, where broken glass was lying everywhere. They climbed along the edge of the seats as if they had become the new floor. The trolley had developed a fatal list – just like the *Lusitania.* "C'mon!" Mr. Byrne urged Dora as they shoved their way toward the front door. "If we can survive the wreck of the *Lusitania,* we can survive this!"

A lady screamed, "Fire!"A tall, flaming tree along the side of the tracks crashed down on top of the streetcar.

Mr. Byrne yanked Dora through the door at the last minute. She saw something that looked like a note sticking there. She grabbed and stuffed it into her purse without reading it. Behind them was mass chaos. Other passengers were smashing the windows open with canes and walking sticks. People crawled over others, fighting their way toward an exit. Mr. Byrne shoved Dora ahead as they ran up the tracks to escape the burning wreck. Fire totally engulfed the car.

Dora pointed up at the hillside overlooking the tracks. "He did it!" From behind another tree Ali was glaring down at them.

CHAPTER 45

They escaped up a steep flight of wooden stairs that scaled the hillside. They hailed a cab as soon as they reached a road. Mr. Byrne rode with Dora all the way back to her house. While stopped at an intersection she retrieved the note she'd pulled off the front of the trolley.

"Look, Michael!" she handed it to him. It read, "Compliments of Colonel Lawrence."

"Ali's saying that he made your streetcar jump the rails and crash the way Lawrence makes Turkish trains derail and crash – or some such nonsense."

"If he thinks I have any influence with Colonel Lawrence, he must be nuts! I can't write to Lawrence and tell him to give back the humidor."

"I thought you told me Lawrence had traded it to a merchant called Mohamed for cigars."

"Yes, but another letter came. Mohamed gave the humidor back to Lawrence. He complained that it was made of worthless pine wood."

"I see," said Mr. Byrne. "Another mysterious development."

"What do you mean?" she asked him with big eyes.

"Simply this – I think this Colonel Lawrence has something up his sleeve. He knows more than he lets on."

"You mean what goes on in the Arabian Desert and Pittsburgh is somehow connected?"

"It's a world war, isn't it?" Mr. Byrne paid the cabbie.

The Benleys came running out to meet them. They'd heard about the trolley wreck by word of mouth and feared the worst. Mrs. Benley hustled Dora off to a hot bath. Mr. Benley and Mr. Byrne sipped coffee prepared in a hurry by Viola. They commiserated with each other at the table until the ladies joined them for dinner. Viola served a nice steaming roast beef with a few Italian spices and a dish of buttery mashed potatoes with gravy.

"Why does that man keep on following our daughter, Winthrop?" Mrs. Benley passed the gravy. "If you could get us off the *Lusitania,* you must be able to do something about it."

Her parents had gone from being great skeptics about Dora's tales of her pursuer to firm believers. The evidence had grown too strong, and Mr. Byrne backed up everything that Dora said.

Mr. Benley wrote a cable and brought it to the table to read aloud:

Sir Adolphus:

My daughter, Dora Benley, has been attacked and nearly killed by a man named Ali. STOP According to Dora, your son, Edward, her fiance, told her that Ali came back with you from Carchemish. STOP He worked for you at your estate for about a year. STOP I assume he must no longer be there. STOP He has followed Dora to America and made her trolley jump off the tracks. STOP He set a tree on fire and crashed it into the trolley, killing several people. STOP The incident is being reported in The Pittsburgh Press. STOP What do you have to say about this? STOP

Please answer right away. STOP

Yours,
Winthrop Benley

Two days later Sir Adolphus replied by cable:

Dear Mr. Benley:

Indeed Ali is no longer with us. STOP He seems to have run off about the time Edward left for the Dardanelles and you went back to America. STOP I don't know why he would be pursuing your daughter, Dora. STOP. It makes as little sense to me as it makes to you. STOP

I am sorry I cannot help you further. STOP

Yours,

Sir Adolphus Ware of Rufford, Bart

"So he's going to play innocent!" Mr. Benley threw the letter down. It shows you how much you can trust any of those damned Europeans, even Englishmen!"

Dora had been confined to the house since the trolley incident, under a kind of virtual house arrest. Her only adventure was to pace up the gravel driveway toward the main road to get the mail and trudge back again to the house. The rest of the time she was closely supervised. Her father now took the further step of hiring a security guard to patrol the grounds at night. Mr. Benley didn't think Ali would be stupid enough to mount an attack on his daughter in her own house during daylight hours.

Dora wrote to Edward:

Dear Edward:

I've been attacked by Ali. He followed me to downtown Pittsburgh. He made the trolley car I was riding jump the tracks and then set it on fire. I do beg you to come home. I'm sure Lawrence can do without you. I can't.

Love,
Dora

CHAPTER 46

The trolley incident occurred in the late fall of 1916. Dora was not to hear from her beloved Edward again until the early spring of 1917.

My dearest:

Lawrence got the idea to disguise himself as a woman. He insisted I do likewise. We sneaked from our encampment to Damascus, four hundred British miles from here, to see what they had in the way of troops and guns – on a dare one day after breakfast. Feisal bet that no British officer would have the nerve. Lawrence replied he was on his way. We had little time to prepare. We were on our camels in less than fifteen minutes.

As soon as we were within the gates, I hissed low, "That looks like you!" I was pointing at a wall displaying Lawrence's picture. Beneath it was a notice in Arabic advertising that the Turkish authorities wanted Lawrence dead or alive. They called him "El Orens, Destroyer of Railways". They offered 100,000 Reichsmarks as a reward. Lawrence got himself a cup of coffee and sat down underneath the sign, sipping it quite casually as if he did it every day.

I kept darting my gaze from side to side in fright. Turkish officers were walking the streets in droves. Surely they knew what the famous *El Orens* looked like with his rosy complexion and blond hair? Even wearing a woman's *abaya,* an occasional wisp of blond hair would inevitably escape.

"Have some coffee, Lieutenant," he said in a normal tone. "Stop dancing and prancing around. You destroy my view, and I'm enjoying myself."

"No! No! No!" my voice strangled in my throat in my effort to keep quiet. "You shouldn't have come here. Now that you've seen their fortifications outside the city gate, for heaven's sake, let's go!"

At the end of the alley I saw a pair of dark eyes staring right at us. A group of men were strutting past. I waited on tenterhooks until I was sure they were out of sight. I hissed in the Colonel's ear again, "Lawrence, someone recognizes us."

"How do you know, Lieutenant?" he asked as if taking high tea on the verandah back home in England.

"He was staring right at me."

"How do you know he doesn't find you fetching?" Lawrence winked with that wicked wit which is always in evidence when he's in a good mood. "I mean, he probably thinks you're a girl in that outfit."

I could feel myself blushing to the roots of my hair.

Two Turkish officers rapidly paced down the street in our direction.

"Lawrence," I leaned toward his ear, "let's go now! They're coming to get us."

"Lieutenant, go buy yourself coffee," he gave me a few Turkish coins. "Stop whining in my ear."

The Turkish officers were almost upon us. If Lawrence refused to listen to reason, there was little I could do. I dashed into the nearest coffee shop and bought myself a mug of steaming hot, Turkish brew.

I took a sip. Then I took another and another. Soon I got up enough courage to look out the window. Sure enough, there sat Lawrence sipping his coffee as he had before. The Turkish officers were nowhere in sight.

Looking both ways, I rejoined Lawrence. "Where did they go?" I was afraid to ask.

He pointed straight ahead. They were pacing off in another direction.

"How much longer do we have to stay here?" I clenched and unclenched my fists underneath the *abaya*.

He got up from where he'd sat for the past hour or so. "Let's take a stroll," he strode deeper into the city away from the gate.

"That's not what I had in mind," I had no choice but to scurry after him.

The alleyways in Old Damascus grew narrower. Walls on opposite sides of the "street" almost touched. Sagging buildings leaned inward toward each other. Clotheslines were strung from window to window on the second and third stories. Down below in the middle of a blazing, sunny day it was dark and cool. Shadowy figures from above wearing identical abayas peered down at us with their faces covered and only their shifty eyes visible.

Suddenly something wet and smelly landed on top of my head. Lawrence turned toward me. "You're very popular among the Turks, aren't you?" He elbowed me and laughed.

Someone had dumped a bucket of slops on me. I didn't know what to do but continue to pace onward in the best British military tradition. Lawrence impulsively stopped at a street vendor's stand. He paid several piasters to buy a flask of Syrian beer. Moslems weren't supposed to drink alcohol, but this passed the test among the common people by long tradition. Without as much as a, "May I?" he dumped the contents of the flask over my head. At least the stench of beer was more bearable than slops. I considered myself lucky – all in the line of duty, naturally.

I was continually troubled by those dark eyes that always sought me out and always seemed to be at the end of some impossibly shadowy alleyway. "Lawrence, I think someone's following us," I warned.

"You're a schoolmarm," he said. "You don't know how to have any fun with our enemy."

When we couldn't go much farther and were about to turn around, we heard a giant explosion. The city walls near us caved in as if exploded by a bomb. Rubble and shards of rock went flying in every direction. Another explosion in the harbor fronting the south bank of the River Barada went off almost simultaneously. Before we had a chance to react, a load of viscous golden, gooey matter, which must have been packed in the hull of a ship, came streaming towards us. It smelled like something familiar, but I wasn't going to stand there and gape. Lawrence gawked a moment too long. A big wave of golden goo toppled him.

I ran and ran without looking over my shoulder.

Women screamed behind me. Barrels toppled. They cracked and splintered on the pavement. Donkeys brayed. Camels hissed. One wad of goo took a side course and streamed on ahead of me way over to my left. An old man was picked up and carried for some distance yelling and screaming before someone rescued him.

When the wave finally subsided, when I didn't hear anymore barrels being knocked over or donkey carts overturned, when the screaming receded farther behind me, I slowed my pace. This whole area of the city was covered by a sweet-smelling, golden-colored goo. I stuck my finger in it and tasted it. Honey, of course! Only the emergency of the moment had prevented me from recognizing it right away. How had it gotten here? Had the explosions been an accident, or had they been deliberately planned? At once I remembered the man with the dark eyes wearing the cloak. Had we been recognized? Had someone tried to assassinate *El Orens?*

How should I proceed when the alleyway was covered with viscous sludge? I lowered my booted foot into it. It stuck in a nasty sort of way and made it very slippery to try to go forward. I tried the next street to the left. That one was filled with honey also. So I tried the one after that. I kept on going until I found one that was clean. I proceeded back up the alley until I got to the place where I remembered last seeing Lawrence.

"May I suggest you try this alley instead?" asked a voice. He looked a little the worse for the wear with honey all over his robe. He was no more dead than I was.

"Lawrence!" I hissed. "How did you manage –"

"I saw an empty barrel. When the honey knocked me down I climbed into it and turned it upright. When the wave subsided, I stood up and walked away. Very simple."

The amazing thing was how he could think on his feet. He didn't panic like the rest of us. He kept his head. That's probably the chief reason why he's so successful. "But, Lawrence, I think someone tried to assassinate you," I told him seriously.

"Yes, we know you're an old woman, Lieutenant. You love to see conspiracies in everything."

Somehow Lawrence found a Turkish laundry. Don't ask me how, but he managed to run through the place, shedding his old robes and taking on entirely new ones. When we left the city, his attire was sparkling black once more. He didn't show any sign of having been knocked over and almost drowned by a wave of honey.

When we got back to our position, the Arabs crowded around and begged *El Orens* to tell them about his adventures. He stayed up until almost dawn, spinning yarns about how he'd embarrassed the Turks by waltzing into Damascus unobserved. Everyone was in stitches about the honey incident. One of the sheiks listening to him that night turned to me and complimented the Colonel. He said, "*El Orens* is the greatest of the sheiks."

I fell asleep in the wee hours. I opened my eyes to see the same cloaked figure that I'd chased out of my tent before. When the first ray of sunlight hit my cot, he vanished as if he'd been a specter and not a real man.

I wish it had been you instead, Dora! I wouldn't have chased you away.

Always,
Edward

P.S. I miss you, too – and how! – but I can't desert Colonel Lawrence. He can't take care of himself. I'm sure you can see that after my letter of today. Besides, his war against the Turks is the only successful military campaign the British are waging. My future wife will understand.

As far as your suspicions about Ali are concerned, you must be hallucinating. What reason could he possibly have for following you to America? It must be someone else. The war has created countless deserters, vagrants, and homeless people. I'm sure your father can take care of it. What about that Mr. Byrne fellow you used to associate with? Do you still see him?

He seemed to be very resourceful as well as loyal.

Until we meet again, all my love and kisses – and a lot more, too!

P.S.S. I got your little gift. Oh, how I cherish it! It's just what I had in mind. And I promise to keep your secret, too. I won't tell anybody else.

CHAPTER 47

"**E**dward prefers this Colonel Lawrence to me," Dora's fingers trembled with rage as she finished the letter. "Lawrence must be very fetching in his desert attire." The part about her "little gift" hadn't mollified her in the least!

She ripped the letter to shreds and tossed it over her shoulder. She was sitting on a picnic cloth on the front lawn of her parent's house on April 1, 1917 during an exceptionally warm, early spring day in Pittsburgh. Pacing up the drive was the security guard that her father had hired.

Dora lay down on the cloth in front of Michael and placed her hands underneath her head. She stretched and kicked off her shoes, running her toes through the grass. On impulse, she plucked a daffodil growing next to a tree stump. She stuck it behind her ear without looking at Michael. "I suppose I shall have to marry you after all, Mr. Byrne. Edward has left me to you. He says you're both resourceful and loyal." She sighed.

Mr. Byrne reached for the bowl of German potato salad that Viola had made and helped himself to another serving. He took a bite of his ham and mustard sandwich on rye.

"It's been almost two years since I've seen that bastard Edward. I'm going to end up an old maid. For heaven's sake, I was twenty-one then and now I'm twenty-three!"

Michael yanked her up into a sitting position. He took an empty plate, filled it with potato salad, and one of Viola's sandwiches. He thrust it at her.

"If you were serious, you'd take off that silly Crusader's ring from Harrods and send it back to Edward," he spread more mustard on his sandwich. "You'd write to him and tell him you're breaking off the engagement and marrying me. You won't do that, now will you, Dora?" he eyed her knowingly.

"Oh, Mr. Byrne, one of the problems with you is that you know me too well! You spoil my fun!" she eyed him reproachfully as she took a tentative bite out of her sandwich.

She leaned back against the tree stump where her

mother had planted pansies. While she ate, the redheaded imp named Edward played around the edges of her consciousness, tormenting her, evading her, making her feel as if she, too, were lost in a vast desert without an oasis to quench her thirst.

That night before bed she wrote a letter, not to Edward but to Colonel Lawrence himself. He must be at the same address, just a different name.

Dear Colonel:

You are a barbarous man to keep Edward from his family and fiancée. Lady Ware writes me all the time. She's distracted with worry and grief. I've been engaged to Edward for two years, and we're not married yet. Of what use is it to keep Edward by your side night and day? You yourself said you didn't want any more orders from headquarters. So why do you need a secretary? Release him! I'm sure you and your Bedouins will be very happy together.

Sincerely yours,
Dora Benley

The next morning, April 2, Dora almost mailed the letter. At the last minute, before pacing up the driveway still again, she threw it into the wastebasket. It was useless to send it. Lawrence would simply ignore her. He seemed the cold-hearted, cold-blooded type.

When she got to the mailbox, there was another letter from Edward. She devoured it immediately:
Dear Dora:

Lawrence has been captured by the enemy. This is how it happened:

We'd been trying to set up explosives. The rest of us ran when we heard the train coming. Lawrence lingered, fiddling with the mess. We shouted at him to retreat, but he acted like he didn't hear us.

I had advised Lawrence that he should obtain the assistance of a British explosives expert. He wasn't an expert in munitions, though he acted like one. Sometimes the explosives went off prematurely and came near to killing someone. At other times they didn't go off at all.

He only stepped back from the tracks just in time as the train lumbered past at a sluggish speed. Lawrence condescended to stand behind a nearby sand dune. He dared to wave at the Turkish soldiers as they rode past in their lamb's-wool kalpaks, their red fez, and kabalaks. Apparently they didn't recognize *El Orens, Destroyer of Railways,* because they waved back. He wouldn't have stood a chance if they'd recognized him and remembered that *El Orens* commanded a reward of 100,000 Reichsmarks dead or alive.

"Lawrence!" I hissed.

Either he didn't hear my stage whisper, or he was ignoring me.

"Lawrence!" I practically shouted.

He continued to wave at the train as if daring the Turks to shoot.

Something moved behind a taller dune some distance away. Something silver colored was poking out slightly. Now it was poking out more.

"Lawrence!" I screamed at the top of my lungs. "Get down! There's –"

A shot rang out. Lawrence fell to the ground. He must have been struck!

The sniper disappeared behind the distant dune. As a party of Arabs pursued him, I raced toward Lawrence, keeping low to the ground. I saw your worried face, Dora. I remained as alert as possible, seeing danger behind every clump of dune grass.

Someone up ahead laughed wickedly. Assassins must have fallen upon Lawrence, not just one culprit. I got out my gun and held it tightly. I might not get more than a second or two to react.

Imagine my surprise when I found Lawrence rolling on the ground holding his belly, laughing until tears appeared at the corners of his eyes. He pounded his clenched fist on the ground as if he couldn't stand it and laughed anew.

"Lawrence!" I stepped forward, scandalized. "What on earth. . ."

"I'm sorry, Lieutenant," he finally sighed. "Don't you see? They might as well not have wasted their bullets. They can't kill me," he boasted.

"Of course they can," I snapped. "They will, too, if you just keep on rolling around on the ground. The tragedy of the matter is that, even if you don't care, I do. So does my fiancée. I'll probably be killed along with you."

A smile irradiated his face, as he sat up, clasped his knees, and breathed in the desert air deeply that so agreed with him. He suddenly looked very serious, showing how his emotions could shift on a dime. "I was borne for this," he went on looking off into space. "I was always fascinated with Near Eastern archaeology and languages. That's why I excavated at Carchemish with Leonard Woolley. I thought it was because I was going to be an archaeologist myself. But no! They needed me here. God sent me to them."

Had the sun gotten to his brain? He sounded more like an Old Testament prophet than a British Military Officer! He looked more like one too, with that pale complexion, those intense blue eyes, and the ruddy cheeks, his uncut hair blowing out from underneath his headdress.

"Those men on the train didn't shoot you only because they didn't recognize you, not because of any divine mandate."

He turned those burning eyes on me. I fell back a couple of paces. I didn't believe in ghosts or the supernatural, at least not since I've been about eight. But I swear – maybe it was a trick of the light – I saw two fires flaming in them. They spooked me.

"Don't you know it wasn't those Turks on the train who shot at me?"

"It was a sharpshooter behind a sand dune over there," I pointed.

"That proves my point," Lawrence nodded. "Whoever

he was knew me for what I am. He couldn't kill me no mater how hard he tried."

"We were shooting at him after he fired. He had to flee if he valued his life. It wasn't any divine protection, it was the British Army!" I insisted.

"If he hated me that much, he would have made sure that his bullet was well-aimed," Lawrence exclaimed with absolute conviction. "He would have put everything he had into it. Some Power deflected that bullet, and that's what scared him away," he proclaimed.

"Look here, Lawrence, if you don't come with me now, I'm going to call for help. We'll carry you away if you won't use your two legs. No God will help you then."

Lawrence smiled. He laughed. His laugh became a chortle. "No, Lieutenant, no Edward," he said, using my Christian name in a way he usually didn't, "I won't cause you all that trouble. Far be it from God to defy the British Army." He chuckled some more. His mood shifted slightly. He strode beside me back to the lines. On a whim on the way back Lawrence, being very full of himself, said, "All right, men, I spy a Turkish unit over there. Let's put the fear of Allah into them!"

A cheer went up. The motley crew of Arabs under Prince Feisal and some other petty tribal chiefs loved nothing better than to plunder and pillage. They followed Lawrence's example to button their mouths the closer and closer they approached the enemy (after all, this was to be a surprise attack). You could tell it was unnatural for them. They were bursting to make as much noise as possible. They sneaked up on the Turks as best they could, then charged. They scared the unprepared fellows so badly that they dropped everything and ran. These Turks weren't in uniform. Most were preparing food over open fires, and they hardly knew what had hit them. Many were taken prisoner.

Lawrence couldn't prevent the Arabs from seizing what pleased them. It is in their natures, this sort of child-like behavior. Worse, Lawrence's Arabs will fight with each other if they find some trinket they both wanted to possess. Instead of planning military strategy, Lawrence has to spend precious time refereeing the fights that break out.

Two men pulled at a woman's necklace strung with emeralds. They were each yanking in opposite directions. The strand of gold links gave way. The emeralds spewed out all over the ground. The two rapscallions threw themselves to their knees trying to gather up the greater number of precious stones. When they got too close and knocked elbows by mistake, they shoved, kicked, and spat. One would think they were Turk and Arab instead of two Arabs on the same side and brothers at that. Customs in this country are strange – as far from what Englishmen and Americans would expect as you could get.

Lawrence came upon these two men. They were at fisticuffs. He shoved them apart and took them to task.

One of them pointed at this brother and proclaimed, "He has the Evil Eye! He was bewitching me so he could steal my emeralds."

The other brother shook his head vehemently, "No, he has the Evil Eye! He was putting a spell on me."

Lawrence cried, "Silence! You both know I am famous for curing cases of the Evil Eye, aren't you?" he said with the sternness that Arabs all respect.

They nodded. Their eyes grew bigger. They had all seen *El Orens* in action.

"First you and then you!" he pointed at one brother and then the other.

They both shook their heads "no" and started to back up away from him.

"Return to your former self or die!" Lawrence was dramatic in his role.

Both brothers fell to their knees and pleaded with Lawrence not to kill them. Naturally he had no such intention, but the simple-minded folk had no inkling of that. Lawrence made them line up in order.

The first brother squatted down on the sand in front of Lawrence, who assumed a Buddha-like position reserved for sorcerers and magicians. The Colonel managed to look severe and unapproachable. Lawrence made sure that his lips turned downward. He crossed his arms. The first brother quaked. He made a whimpering sound like a dog, but he didn't dare move when *El Orens* fixed him with his famous stare. All men must blink, but some don't have to as much as others. Lawrence was one of the few gifted with the talent. So he was able to level a steady gaze directly into the poor man's eyes.

"Mercy, Great *El Orens!*" the first brother bowed down in front of him, throwing himself to the ground and groveling.

"Rise!" Lawrence commanded. "You are cured. You no longer have the Evil Eye."

The man was eager to crawl away to a safe distance. Lawrence summoned the other brother, who shook his head and begged for mercy. Lawrence would have no mercy on him either.

My gaze roved a little beyond our camp. I was startled to see another pair of dark eyes hiding behind a gray plinth not far from us. I stood stock still. It could be an animal such as a goat or a bird of prey. When it didn't move after many minutes, the silence interrupted only by the moans from the second brother whom Lawrence was now fixing with his maniacal stare, I inched slowly to the left. I paused, then moved again. I was approaching the shady side of the plinth where something was hiding. I gripped my rifle tightly.

 Something bright flashed near the plinth. I remembered the sharpshooter who'd fired at Lawrence a couple of hours before, the reason for Lawrence's collapse into mirth and megalomania.. He must be back.

Lawrence posing as a Buddha was a perfect target. Evidently this man, whoever he was, didn't care anything for Lawrence's fabled abilities against the Evil Eye. He was biding his time, figuring he had only one more chance.

I thought, *This assassin is really determined. He's willing to risk his life to kill Lawrence . . . Even the Turks can't pay that much money . . .*

I was edging closer to another outcrop of rock. I was

almost there. I prayed he wouldn't move in the moments it would take to cover the last few steps. I didn't see him glancing in my direction. I congratulated myself for staying out of his range of vision. My hand shook as I quietly loaded my SMLE rifle. I tried to steady my hand as I rested the rifle on the top of a rock. I peered through the sights.

Now I could see clearly that the intruder was disguised in Arab clothing from head to foot. His face was concealed completely under a hood. I saw only an empty black gap of material where his visage should have been. The tip of his rifle glinted.

I deduced that I couldn't shoot him from my position. He was too well-concealed. All I could hope to accomplish was to warn the infiltrator that he'd been spotted and scare him away. I hesitated, waiting for him to present a better target.

"You have been cured!" Lawrence announced back in camp. "You will no longer suffer from the Evil Eye." The second brother backed away on hands and knees, bowing his head to *El Orens.*

An old woman, a laundress who worked for the rag-tag troops, stealthily approached the little group. She was staring at Lawrence fixedly, gazing into Sidi Lawrence's eyes as intensely as he'd been gazing into the brothers' eyes. She shook her head, "You have horrible eyes like bits of sky shining through the eye-holes of a skull lying in the desert."

"Do I indeed?" Lawrence was amused as he answered in the local vernacular.

She nodded. "I've never seen anything like it, eyes of such power in a man so young! Was your father a Gin or an evil spirit?"

"No, but I could have acquired that power when I was in Carchemish with Leonard Woolley, a man of great powers . . ."

You could tell she was hanging on Lawrence's every word. She leaned closer until she threatened to fall into his lap as he sat there cross-legged on the ground.

"Carchemish was located on the West Bank of the

Euphrates, south of Turkey, up on an acropolis. The site had been occupied for several thousand years. Around 605 B.C. the Babylonian army of Nebuchadnezzar II defeated the army of Pharaoh Necho II of Egypt there. To commemorate the victory, great stelae were carved in gray granite."

"Yes, I can see it . . . " the lady nodded eagerly as if it were being carved before her that very day.

"Leonard Woolley and I dug up a great stele depicting an officers' procession. The men were carrying spears and long, carved wooden bows that they had proudly strung. I rather liked the find. As I cleaned it, I kept on staring at it intently," Lawrence spun his always incredible, exotic tale.

I wished he wouldn't be so long-winded at the expense of his own safety. I wanted to warn him that an assassin lurked nearby. But I dared not speak. I hardly dared to breathe.

"The Hittite officer nearest to me, wearing a long, short-sleeved tunic down to his ankles, met my eye," Lawrence continued. "I couldn't look away."

"Yes, the man in the stele was an evil spirit. You got the power from him," the woman understood in her own terms, as Lawrence had no doubt intended. "That's why you must never go near a burial site," she spoke fearfully. "They will try to lure you into the grave if they can. Either that, or you will become evil like them."

The intruder behind the plinth stirred. I couldn't tell what he was doing for sure. But he must have moved his rifle, if only a fraction of an inch. The sun was so blinding that anything metallic acted like a mirror. If you were watching closely, it was like a signal.

Should I shoot now? I stooped down and got my hand around a rock without once taking my eyes off the sharpshooter behind the plinth. Hoping my aim was true, I threw the rock toward where I knew the Colonel was positioned. I hoped it would either strike Lawrence in the back or at least fall near him to give him warning.

I heard the rock fall with a distinct thud. I could not spare a glance that direction right now to judge its location. It didn't sound as if it had struck a person. The lady didn't remark on it. She and Lawrence went on talking as if oblivious of my deed. The rock must have fallen wide of its mark.

The sharpshooter's gun glinted in the sun once more. *I thought, I can't wait any longer. If I do, he'll shoot Lawrence right in front of my eyes.*

"They were sinners indeed to make the graven images to begin with. The Prophet forbids it. You associated with idolaters and heathens," the old crone accused the Colonel, talking of the Islamic religion that censures making images of people for artistic purposes.

"I'll agree the Babylonians and the Egyptians didn't come to a good end. I'll agree they tended to be idolaters. They did worship calf's heads, snakes, half-dog/half-human gods," Lawrence expostulated. "One of the reliefs next to the soldier's relief was of an ancient Babylonian King and his son, the Prince."

The old woman shuddered. "Avoid that at all costs! Ancient kings and princes were like devils." She made the hand sign to ward off the Evil Eye.

My hand had been poised on the trigger for so long that my fingers throbbed. The old lady's voice whined in my ear like a never-ending nightmare that I couldn't wake from. When I heard what I thought was a clicking sound emanating from behind that plinth, I fired. I managed to fire again in rapid succession before the explosive power of my gun knocked me backward.

The old lady shrieked and fled.

There was a shout from the camp. It was Lawrence's voice. "Who goes there?" Lawrence darted out into the desert beyond the plinth faster than I could react.

"No!" I shouted. "No! Get back, Colonel!" I had myself wedged into a crevice between two rocks. It took some time to extricate myself so I didn't break my neck. By then, Lawrence had disappeared. "Law –" I ceased calling out. I didn't want to make my position known as I didn't know where the gunman was hiding. He could be anywhere and everywhere. For all I knew, he could have friends and compatriots.

I crept along as close to the ground as possible, as we had been taught to do, hugging the cliffs and rock outcrops. I didn't see moving shadows, and I spotted birds, who wouldn't be perched there if some interloper was hiding in the same place. I heard nothing but the sounds of the desert – the call of the dove, the munching of a herd of camels chewing on grassy stubble emerging from the reddish soil. I didn't want to venture too far. Lawrence might be in trouble. I should head back to the camp and round up the Bedouins to help me.

They roused themselves from their midday nap at once at the slightest suggestion that *El Orens* might be in danger. They threw themselves onto their camels half-dressed. Others were clearly drunk. That didn't stop them. We rode out into the desert in the direction I'd last seen Lawrence. We charged around the perimeter of the camp. The Arabs searched the washes and the rocky outcrops. They climbed anywhere that anyone could insert himself. They came back empty-handed.

The Arabs suddenly looked to me to make the decisions. Since I hadn't a clue where he'd gone, I decided to split up. Splitting up is terrible for a military force under battle conditions. But we were reconnoitering and spying, if you will. Only by splitting up could we cover more territory. I was getting the scary idea that Lawrence had fallen into enemy hands after foolishly wandering out into the desert by himself.

Of course with Lawrence one could never be sure. He might be up to something that none of us could guess. No doubt he would make himself known in his own good time. Still it was my duty to assume he'd been kidnapped.

"Capturing *El Orens* the Destroyer of Railways would be a big deal," I assured the men in halting Arabic. "I don't think they'll execute him right away. They would want to get the maximum publicity value out of it. We need to be all ears to find out who took him and where. Above all, we want to know how we can free him."

They nodded.

I appointed an Arab for each group who would serve as

a liaison. They would bring any news about what they'd found to me once every three days. None of the watering holes or towns in the desert were farther apart than that. Then I would give new orders to each liaison to take back to the group.

I commanded the largest search party. We headed toward the coast in the direction of Damascus. I figured that if the Turks had captured Lawrence that was where they would take him.

We came upon an old Roman ruin, for you know that Romans settled the coastal part of Syria – as they settled all over the coast of the entire Mediterranean. It looked like an impressive theater with the pillars still standing, which must have been a rarity.

The men were weary. They wanted to eat. I agreed this was as good a place as any to make camp for the night. I took a stroll as the men prepared dinner over a fire. First I strode through the amphitheater where the seating was located. I climbed the steps to the back of the theater, where it grew considerably darker.

I heard footsteps. "Who goes there?" I called.

It couldn't have been one of my men. They'd been taught to answer promptly, or someone might shoot them by mistake. So I didn't say anything further. Instead I crept near the wall and waited with heart pounding for the next sound. The intruder's step was very light. He fled across the floor in the pitch black toward the exit at the back of the theater. A robed figure disappeared. In a few moments I tried to follow. By the time I reached the exit, no one was there.

That night I didn't fall asleep until very late and then I slept only fitfully, tossing and turning. I couldn't get comfortable on my cot no matter where I put my pillow. I was used to Lawrence giving the orders and was unaccustomed to command. I thought it was a nightmare when I heard someone whispering into my ear. I paid little attention – that was until it became persistent like the buzz of a fly that won't go away no matter how I swatted at it. It grew louder, then was accompanied by a touch on my shoulder.

I looked up startled. At first I couldn't make out anything in the pitch black of the tent. Then I saw a shadow. I've never believed in apparitions since before I went away to school. Public school had drummed such nonsense out of me for good, I'd thought. I began to have a few doubts now until out of nowhere I heard a woman's voice.

"Oh, British officer, I know where your Sidi Lawrence is hiding," she hissed.

Now that I was fully awake, I could make out more than a shadowy form. I could begin to make out the face of a young woman or at least the part of her face that could be seen beneath the hood and above the veil, which wasn't much. Mostly I was aware of her dark eyes and the tip of her pointed nose.

"Who are you?" I rose from my cot and brushed myself off.

"I work in Deraa. I saw your Sidi Lawrence. He handed me several coins, which is more than a month's wages for me and my family. He told me to come here and alert you. I am supposed to guide you back to town."

"So that's where he's at!" I said. "Not Damascus, but Deraa?"

She nodded.

"How did he get there?"

"He was captured," she kept her voice low, "and taken there forcibly. He's been flogged and is set to go to trial soon. That trial must never take place," she shook her head as she whispered her story to me, "because then he will be executed."

"We'll set out at once," I grabbed for my pistol, my rifle, and all my things.

"Not so fast!" the lady put out her hand and touched my sleeve, then quickly withdrew it. "Wait here." She departed the tent and came back right away. She handed me an armful of robes. "Sidi Lawrence says you and the men you choose must wear these when you come after him."

I examined them in the half-light of the tent. I'd lighted my lantern. I was horrified to discover that they were once again women's dark-colored, formless *abayas*.

"What else did he tell you?" I said, almost afraid to ask.

"He said you were to come to the jail and bring lots of money with you."

The last British pounds sterling we'd seen was many weeks ago. Most of the local money, the Turkish piasters Lawrence came by, were stolen in raids. It had been distributed to the men. Many had gambled it away. Others had whored it away in the small towns we'd visited. Some had lost it or had it stolen by brigands.

"He said to bring British pounds if you could find them. Otherwise bring piasters. He told me you would know where to get the loot."

"I see. I'm to bring lots of money. Yet I must leave here and follow you right away."

She nodded again. "He said you would know how to do that, too."

Lawrence had more confidence in me than I had in myself. "Very well, just wait here."

I blew a horn that I'd brought from Lawrence's tent. It was his way of assembling the troops at night or when they were otherwise occupied. Soon the men were stumbling over to my tent in the dark, falling over each other in their haste.

"How many of you still have some of your loot?" I asked.

They looked at me with blank stares. One eyed the other. No one was going to divulge such information.

"I'm going into Deraa myself tonight to rescue Colonel Lawrence. I've received information from a spy."

They were all over me in a second, volunteering to accompany me. I could now see that the armful of robes was merely one robe. Lawrence had never intended any of the men to follow me.

"No, this is a mission that calls for only one man," I insisted when I had quieted them down. They respected that. "Now you all sit out here and keep watch while I'm away. Don't go back into your tents," I cautioned them, "at least until it gets light out."

They nodded and sat down where they were. Some got out stacks of cards. Others got out dice, a game more native to their culture. Still others leaned elbow to elbow and sang ditties.

"Don't light fires unless you must," I reminded them. "I'll be back as soon as I can."

Since they were out of their tents, I sneaked into them. I was able to collect enough loot in this way to bring to Deraa. If you think this a questionable tactic, I'll remind you we were in the desert – not in London or New York. I told myself that the "loot" really didn't belong to the Bedouins. They'd stolen it. So it was free for the taking. It was for the best of causes – not as if I were taking it for myself.

I'd provided myself with two full canteens of water – a necessity for any trip in the desert, even at night and at any time of the year. Watering holes were a matter of local knowledge only, not often shared with British officers. I made sure I had my pistol and rifle.

I quickly slipped into the woman's *abaya,* so I wouldn't have time to dwell on how distasteful that costume was to me. I took off, reminding myself that it was better to travel by night than by day in the desert. It was cooler, and I could travel undetected on my secret mission.

"Ps-s-s-s-s-st!"

I slowed my camel down and looked around. I was beginning to think better of it. What if it was a trick and somebody was ready to waylay or attack me? After all, Lawrence himself had been captured alone and unattended in the desert.

"Englishman!" came the sound of the same woman's voice that I'd heard earlier.

Out of the shadows slipped a woman in dark robes with a cavernous hood. She darted up to my camel in such a way so as not to spook the animal. "I am here to show you the way. I didn't want to let myself be seen in your camp."

She couldn't possibly be a plant by the Turks. She'd

brought me news of Lawrence. Besides, I'm not sure they knew about me. Even if they did, I doubt if I was important enough to capture.

She rode ahead on her own camel, which she'd concealed in the shadows up until now. I followed at a distance. She led me straight to Deraa in the wee hours. We both tied up our camels. I made sure mine was some distance back away from the walls, in a darkened corner which I judged would be shaded even during daylight hours. She slipped into the city by means of a back gate. I followed close behind.

She headed for the regiment that was garrisoned in the city. They had housed themselves in what looked like an ancient palace. No sooner had she opened the door into the darkened interior than she picked up a broom that was resting against the wall. She turned quickly and handed me one.

Now I could see the genius of her plan – or rather Lawrence's plan. I was to pretend I was a cleaning lady robed from head to foot in a plain, black *abaya*. Here I really did have to trust the girl. I followed along where her broom led. She swept around a table of Turkish officers sharing beer. They shouted for more. She took their pitcher and raced off to refill it. She was back in a hurry.

After we'd cleaned in what looked like the mess hall of the barracks, we moved on to the next room where more Turkish officers were playing games of cards. Others had dice, just like my men back in the desert. Even if they were not Arabs, they were still followers of the same Mohammedan faith. They were not allowed to drink hard liquor, so they proved wastrels in every other respect.

We swept the floors. When no one was looking in our direction, the lady quietly opened the door leading to a narrow, darkened hallway. She motioned for me to follow. We tiptoed along, picking up the soles of our feet to make as little noise as possible.

Not long after that, with a glance to either side, she darted to the left. I followed her down what proved to be a stairway to the lower level. The only light was provided by sconces on the walls along either side of the passageway. I'd only my broom to feel my way along and to ascertain how far away the walls were.

Soon I became aware of shadowy figures behind bars along one side of the wall. They rattled their cages as we swept past, calling to us and asking for food or water.

"Ignore them!" she hissed.

We continued on down the interminable passageway in what I now knew was a prison. Since this building had once been a palace, it came equipped with one. Up ahead I heard a voice that sounded familiar. Oddly enough it wasn't pleading like all the others, asking for food and water. It seemed to be declaiming something. Closer still, I could begin to make out the words:

> *"O Man of Shuruppak, son of Ubar-Tutu,*
> *Tear down this house, build a ship!*
> *Give up possessions, seek thou life.*
> *Forswear worldly goods and keep the soul alive!*
> *Aboard the ship take thou the seed of all living things.*
> *The ship that thou shalt build,*
> *Her dimensions shall be to measure.*
> *Equal shall be her width and her length.*
> *Like the Apsu thou shalt call her."*
> *I understood, and I said to Ea, my lord:*
> *"Behold, my lord, what thou hast thus ordered,*
> *I will be honored to carry out . . ."*

When I forced myself to really listen, I thought, *It reminds me of Christ's College! We were reading that passage. In fact, my don asked us to write an essay about it. It sounds like Noah, but it isn't . . . Why, it's the Epic of Gilgamesh!* It didn't take me long to figure out who would be declaiming ancient Near Eastern poetry in the bowels of a Turkish palace in a squalid jail cell. It could be no other than he.

"Lawrence!" I made my way to where he was housed. "I've found you at last!"

Lawrence said in his normal tone, "I was trying to get an inspiration. I kept on thinking that to escape here, I needed a flood of epic proportions. Like Gilgamesh I could build a boat and sail away to the sea. Instead the Sister Fates have sent you to me." He held out his hand for the money he knew I would bring. At once he called, "Suleiman!"

A Turkish guard immediately looked around the dark corner.

"Come! Come! I have a little going away gift for you."

Suleiman smiled as Lawrence, through the bars of his cell, poured the piasters into his greedy palms. Lawrence stopped halfway. "Now, Suleiman, if you want the rest – and I know you do – first let me out."

He took out his keys and let Lawrence out. The young lady handed Lawrence another *abaya*. He slipped it over his head and hurriedly threw the bag of coins at Suleiman. He didn't glance back over his shoulder as we dashed out the nearest exit.

We slipped out of the city pretty much the same way we'd come with the aid of the young cleaning lady. She went as far as the walls. I located my camel. She let Lawrence have hers. Lawrence and I rode back to the encampment.

On the way, I couldn't restrain myself from commenting, "I was trying to warn you that a sharpshooter was lurking about our encampment. You didn't take my hints. Instead you went wandering out there all by yourself. No doubt you're lucky to be alive."

"The sharpshooter can't harm me," Lawrence stated flatly.

"Obviously he almost did. He arranged for you to be captured and dragged into Deraa."

Lawrence shook his head. "A group of Turks caught me by chance. They're the ones who dragged me off and threw me into prison. That other one in the shadows wanted me dead. He wouldn't be satisfied with anything else."

"Good heavens, Lawrence! If you knew that, why in God's name did you wander off into the desert and give him a chance to take aim at you?"I protested.

"I want to convince him to stop following me. It won't do him any good, you know. He has to realize that."

How could anyone in Lawrence's position think like him? I suppose that's what had made T.E. Lawrence, the archaeologist and scholar, into the fabled figure *El Orens,* or "Lawrence of Arabia" as he is now being called by everyone here.

"Do you have any idea who he is, the assassin I mean?"

Lawrence considered carefully. "He could be any one of a number of thugs hired by the Turks to kill me. Then again he could be someone else I don't suspect. Still, that's not important. The important thing is to shake him, to act more bold than he does. That always discourages them."

"Yes, Colonel, I'm – I'm sure it does," I took his measure.

When we got back to his tent he took out his humidor, which I hadn't seen since he got it back from Mohamed. He must have traded for new cigars in Deraa while in the prison. He lighted one and smoked it.

Hugs and kisses – and lots of them, too!

Yours,
Edward

P.S.   I'm beginning to worry about you, my love. You distract me when I'm tending to my duties. You make me want to quit and come home to you, though that would mean the death of both Lawrence and the Arab Nationalist Movement. You must realize that would be the death of me also. I could never live down the shame of it. Surely you can wait a little longer. The passion that binds us is not the sort of thing that can die that easily. I think it grows stronger with each passing day.

P.S.S. Last night the most peculiar thing happened. I was awakened late at night. I heard noises outside my tent and went to investigate. The same brigand dashed away into the distance. I went to Lawrence's tent, thinking to awaken the commander. Instead I found him poring over what looked like strange inscriptions laid out on his desk. The first thing that occurred to me was that it resembled some sort of secret code.

"Colonel, are you communicating with spies?" I sneaked up on him.

He grabbed the few papers that I'd barely gotten a chance to see. There were some other things there, too, that looked dark and shiny. He stuffed them into the top of the humidor and closed it. "Lieutenant!" he hissed, "you should be asleep."

"The same man keeps sneaking around our camp at night. I just saw him."

"I haven't seen anyone," he dismissed me.

I returned to my cot, but kept my eyes fixed on his tent flap. Not too many minutes later I saw a flame. The fire was confined to an ashtray. It quickly burned down and flared up when Lawrence put another torn up or crumpled piece of paper on top of it. He was burning those papers I'd glimpsed. The same inscrutable marks teasingly flashed past my eyes.

The flame died, and I went to sleep. The next morning Lawrence's tent was empty. The humidor was sitting on the floor beside his cot, now totally empty. There was no trace of last night's papers or the strange, black, shiny strips of whatever. I turned the humidor upside down and tapped it. Nothing came out.

The box was not made of cheap pine wood as Mohamed had claimed. It was fashioned of the best solid mahogany – heavy, substantial, hand-carved, and expensive. Holding it in my hands now – and I hadn't held it since I gave it to him – it didn't feel as heavy. It was somehow diminished.

"Lieutenant, what's keeping you!" came the call. I put the humidor back where I'd found it and dashed off. That night on the way back to my tent I glanced inside Lawrence's. The humidor was gone.

CHAPTER 48

Dora felt a moment of triumph. Edward was beginning to worry about her. She penned him a quick note, hoping it would make him jealous:

Dear Edward:

You are so preoccupied with your Colonel Lawrence that's it's incredible you remember that you have a fiancée. You may not have to worry about me much longer. Mr. Byrne keeps on pressing me to marry him. I am considering his proposal seriously. I have waited for you for almost two whole years! I'm not getting any younger, you know.

Maybe you should ask Colonel Lawrence if he has a sister. You could settle down with Lawrence and his sister and never have to worry about us Americans again.

Sincerely yours,
Dora

Br-r-r-r-ring!
"Hello?" Dora answered.

"It's me!" exclaimed Rita. "Guess what? I've just been cast as the star in a film about the *Lusitania.*"

Dora gasped, "Wonderful!"

"I need moral support. I was wondering if you and your family could come up to New York City. That's where it's being made. You could visit the studio and see what you think. The director says it's all right. I told him you were all survivors, too."

Her mother phoned her father and Mr. Byrne at work. They at once bought train tickets. They were off the next day to the big city where they hadn't visited since June of 1915.

They entered the studio inside the Austrian liner, the *Martha Washington,* tied up in New York Harbor, where it had been interned at the beginning of the war. They were immediately confronted by a giant poster of Rita with her picture at the top featuring her beautiful, angular face, pointed nose, dimpled chin, and locks of black hair. Beneath that was the title:

LEST WE FORGET
Semen Classics
Presents
Beautiful Rita Jolivet
In an Eight-Act Special Production Deluxe

"No, we *Lusitania* survivors never will forget," said a middle-aged man standing next to them. "With all the war talk in Washington, I don't think America will either."

"I recognize you," said Dora. His name was on the tip of her tongue.

"Charles Lauriat at your service," he shook hands with Dora, Michael, and Mr. and Mrs. Benley.

"You're the Boston book seller, right?" Dora said. "I remember meeting you."

"You were traveling with your parents."

"You wrote a book."

"Yes, *The Lusitania's Last Voyage*. Published in 1915."

She remembered that an illustration of the *Lusitania* with its four prominent smoke stacks was the book's frontispiece. The book related the harrowing narrative of Lauriat's escape from the ship and its immediate aftermath.

At first she couldn't place the next survivor. Then she remembered meeting him at Vanderbilt's party the first night at sea. "You're the one with the roll of hundred dollar bills!" she burst out.

George Kessler, the Champagne King laughed. "I'd give up all those hundred dollar bills gladly if everyone who attended Vanderbilt's last big bash could be alive right now."

Other *Lusitania* survivors were milling about the set, including some Dora hadn't met aboard or had only glimpsed at a distance. What was chilling were the passengers who were not present such as Vanderbilt, Hubbard, and Frohman. Dora learned for the first time that the honeymoon couple she'd met the night of Vanderbilt's big party, Lesley and Stuart Mason, had not been among the survivors. It made her shake all over, though it was two years later.

They got to watch Rita, all made up, being filmed in scene after scene. In one sequence she was falling overboard, which Dora had actually witnessed her doing in real life. An actor playing Frohman stood beside her on the reconstructed deck making his famous final statement from his *Peter Pan* play, "Why should we fear death? It's the most beautiful adventure life presents to us."

There was the fictional plot, too. Rita was captured by the Germans. She was sentenced to the firing squad as a spy. She insisted that she did not want a blindfold. She escaped and looked for her estranged fiance, who had broken up with her, thinking she was a German sympathizer. In the end she proved her loyalty by strangling the villain, a Prussian baron, with his own bed sheet.

"I can't wait to see it at the Nickelodeon Theater across from Kaufmann's," said Mrs. Benley.

"The part about the sinking was really chilling," Mr. Byrne insisted. "I keep on expecting Ali to show up at any moment with his fuses."

They visited the Hudson River. A crew was filming a group of hundreds of extras who'd been hired to flounder about in the water and pretend that the ship was sinking. The production crew had built an expensive replica, smaller of course, of the doomed *Lusitania*, complete with the requisite four smoke stacks.

The visit brought back all sorts of memories for the little group of survivors. That night they were up late discussing them at their hotel. Someone had gotten copies of a new book that had come out, entitled *As the Lusitania Went Down*. On the cover were pictured a bride and groom in full wedding regalia. They were standing on top of the sinking ship. In the background was pictured a lifeboat. They even sang a popular ditty about the subject:

> *The sun was sparkling brightly*
> *upon the ocean foam*
> *The Lusitania speeding fast,*
> *was very nearly home.*
> *Then came the blow so sudden*
> *that pierced the vessel's heart.*
> *But while the crowd surged o'er the deck*
> *A young man stood apart . . .*

They didn't get to bed until very late. Somewhere in the middle of the night Dora heard a scream coming from across the hall. She leaped out of bed, put on her robe, and raced over to Rita's room. She knocked on the door. "Rita, it's Dora. Let me in."

Rita flung open the door and threw herself into Dora's arms. "I was on the ship again," Rita sobbed. "That green water was coming for me. I even lost my boots."

Dora hugged her friend.

"I don't know how many times I've lost that same pair of boots!" Rita sniffled. "Maybe one million. I'll never get over it."

"Your movie's well named, Lest We Forget. I don't think we survivors can ever forget," Dora agreed with tears in her eyes. "I've had nightmares, too."

The next morning Dora was awakened by shouting down on the street in New York City. "Read all about it!" the paper boy cried.

Dora groaned. She thought, *Read about what now?* Mr. Byrne knocked on her door. She answered groggily. He shoved the newspaper into her hands. She stared at the bold headline of the *New York Times:*

PRESIDENT CALLS FOR WAR DECLARATION,
STRONGER NAVY, NEW ARMY OF 500,000 MEN, FULL
CO-OPERATION WITH GERMANY'S FOES

Below that was the text of the President's address from the previous day when he'd spoken before Congress. At the bottom of the page it read: *The War Resolution Now Before Congress.*

"We're in. Wilson's done it. He's declared war."

Dora gasped. "Not us, too!"

He nodded grimly.

Her father came charging into her room next. "I'll have Wilson impeached. I'm going to start getting signatures today. I'll send them to my congressman and senators."

Dora thought, *So your war has spread to us, too, Edward. I hope you're happy. I'm sure it will make your Colonel Lawrence do an Irish jig for joy. Maybe he'll get another fit of the giggles.*

Her father exclaimed, "It's enough to make you want to move to the Alaska Territory!"

They were in New York for the whole day. Part of it they spent in the studio. That evening after dinner they went to the movies. Rita wanted to see the just-released big hit movie entitled, *Mystery of the Double-Cross.* It had been out almost a month already. It drew standing room only crowds. The Benleys, Michael, and Rita were lucky to get the last seats in the entire theater.

"It's supposed to be better than *Intolerance.* And it makes *Civilization* pale by comparison," Rita assured them, naming hit movies of 1916.

"Not another war picture!" Mr. Benley groaned. "The less people talk about that war over there, the better." He got out some work papers he'd sneaked along in his pocket.

"Ah, Mr. Benley, wait until you see the opening sequence!" Rita clucked. "Even you'll be impressed."

Mr. Benley didn't look at the screen once while they showed newsreels of the Great War in Europe with the notice that had become customary:

President Wilson has asked Americans to preserve absolute neutrality during the war abroad. Please refrain from partisan applause in viewing this picture, thereby complying with the President's request . . .

"Traitor!" Mr. Benley grumbled. "He's gone back on his word."

He didn't look at the screen again while the notice flashed up on the screen:

Just a minute please while the operator changes a reel.

As soon as the movie started, Dora noticed that her father couldn't take his eyes off it. An elegant matron strolled up to the rail of her cruise ship holding her two little dogs and looked out at the ocean. The lady immediately sighted a submarine surfacing. She screamed and pointed at it, alerting the other passengers.

The word spread on the Boat Deck like a wildfire as the matron ran crying and weeping into the restaurant. Everyone rose from his seat and fled out onto the deck in a mad mayhem to save their lives. It turned out to be an American submarine in the movie, but in real life everybody knew what had happened.

"Well, Mr. Benley, what do you think?" Rita asked when the movie ended.

"Warmongering!" he shook his head. "I say the sinking of the *Lusitania* is the best reason NOT to go to war. It's the best reason of all not to have any contacts with Germany or Europe. We don't want to get pulled down to their level."

The next morning when they were at Grand Central Station buying tickets back to Pittsburgh, a newsboy was hawking papers. Another outrageous headline appeared in *The New York Times:*

SENATE, 82 TO 6, ADOPTS WAR DECLARATION;
ITS OPPONENTS SCORED; HOUSE ACTS TODAY;
BERLIN FEARS OUR INFLUENCE ON RUSSIA

Charles Lauriat stood beside them buying his ticket back to Boston. "I think war was fore-ordained as soon as the torpedo struck the *Lusitania*. Wilson hesitated for two years.

Now he's being pushed into it against his will."

"Against all our wills," concluded Mr. Byrne. He glanced at a newspaper for sale, being hawked by another paperboy. It was called *Leslie's Illustrated Weekly Newspaper: The War in Pictures.* Everyone seemed to be buying it. They were devouring it all around where the Benleys and Michael were standing.

The next day Dora, Mr. Byrne, and the rest of her family boarded the train back to Pittsburgh. The paperboy on the platform was waving the newspaper over his head. Mr. Benley handed some change out the window and grabbed one:

HOUSE AT 3:12 A.M., VOTES FOR WAR, 373 TO 50;
$3,000,000,000 ASKED FOR ARMY OF 1,000,000
NATION'S GIGANTIC RESOURCES MOBILIZED

"That's it," said Mr. Byrne. "It's history."

Crowds were reading the headlines on the platform. Some erupted into cheers. Others were grumbling to each other, looking stone-faced, or saying nothing, huddled next to a recruitment poster that blared:

REMEMBER THE LUSITANIA.

"Oh, Michael!" Dora whispered solemnly. "I'm glad you're thirty-four. You're too old to be conscripted."

It reminded her all the more poignantly of Edward. America was just getting into the war. Edward had been in the thick of it for two whole years. Who knew how much longer it would last?

CHAPTER 49

It was past Christmas and into the new year, 1918, before the postman rang her doorbell in the snow and excitedly presented Dora with Edward's next letter. It was late in the afternoon. A blizzard had delayed the mail.

After she poked the fire once, Dora sat down in front of the fireplace in the living room. A large oil painting of her father presided over the mantel. Viola brought her dinner there. The fire flickered and went out. Frank came to restart it.

My dearest darling:

Mohamed, the merchant, who only now and then grudgingly visits our camp, was spitting into the sand and grumbling about how he'd been cheated by Sidi Lawrence in the matter of the cigars.

"I hope that column of Turkish soldiers I saw about a quarter of a mile from your camp destroys you," he proclaimed.

"What?" objected Lawrence. "The Turks don't usually travel in such large groups. They are too afraid of me."

The Arabs laughed over coffee and unleavened bread baked over ashes, which they consume by the pound beside the campfire every morning.

Mohamed shrugged and opened a tin of beef, obtained during our last contact with the British Army and shipped all the way from Chicago. He carefully inserted his knife into it, repeating the customary phrase, "In the name of Allah the Merciful and the Compassionate!"

When he'd gobbled his fill, he said, "Whoever wants to come with me, we'll see what's going on with those Turks. I'm supposed to meet a caravan coming from that direction."

He'd spent the night at our encampment, selling his wares. He had only empty camels to ride back into the desert. Several men volunteered to ride with the trader. They promised to come back within the hour.

Mohamed declared as he prepared to leave, "I'm finished with you, Lawrence, you and your cheapskate band of Bedouin warriors. Unless you agree to pay for your ten free cigars, I won't come back."

"Good riddance!" said Lawrence.

The Bedouins gave an enormous war cry and charged out over the desert.

We kept ourselves busy pacing about, tending to this and that. Everyone could not help but look over his shoulder toward the far horizon in the direction Mohamed had led Lawrence's men.

As the minutes ticked by and no one returned, the situation grew more and more tense. The men kept on nervously glancing toward the horizon and then at Lawrence. He was occupied reading letters from Leonard Woolley as well as Sir Arthur Evans's latest news from Crete. Lawrence, without seeming to pay any attention, was watching carefully out of the corner of his eye. He suddenly leaped up and said, "Let's go after them!"

The Arabs cheered. They never could sit still for long, always wanting to be up and about. They couldn't understand how Lawrence managed to sit there and read.

Lawrence mounted his camel. Within five minutes everyone was after him charging away in the direction of the unseen Turkish column.

"El Orens!" one man rode up to him. "Is that the Turkish column over there, the one Mohamed was talking about?"

Lawrence was eagle-eyed, but even he had limits. This was too far away. It must have been five to ten miles. At that distance something seeming to move could be anything from a column of Turkish soldiers, to a group of traveling camels, to a dust storm, to a mirage.

Lawrence decided instantly, waving a letter about that he'd been perusing, "Turks are moving into that area. We need to beat them to it and push them out. Even if it's not the Turkish column, we're headed the right way."

We traveled not by good old British miles but by watering-holes. We would make camp when we reached the next one and the next. As many days as it took, they would be called our "first water", our "second water", and our "third water". Before reaching our "first water" that evening, Lawrence sent swift camel riders off to reconnoiter and find out where the other men were. They came back and reported that they could not find a trace of the missing men. Lawrence concluded that they'd wandered too close to the Turkish lines. They'd been captured, along with Mohamed, and taken prisoners. This was all the more reason why we should hurry and catch up with the column.

By the time we made camp for the night at our "first water", the column had vanished in the distance. Lawrence relaxed by the camp fire. He got out a book as well as the humidor of cigars that my father had given him. He had been rationing them out so they would last. He allowed himself one only every few weeks.

I got out a rasher of bacon and started sizzling it over the fire. I'd taken it out of a can I'd found among my supplies in my pack. Perhaps I'd overlooked it. It wasn't like fresh bacon, but I figured it would taste better than any other kind because we were down to unleavened bread and coffee supplemented by what we could shoot.

I didn't think the other men were paying much attention. They were having a wild time singing, playing games, and shooting off their guns into the night sky. Even Lawrence couldn't prevent them from acting like a bunch of school boys.

When they smelled what I was doing, they dropped their guns aghast and backed away. They pointed at the flames and shouted, "That's unclean!"

"My nostrils!" another pinched his nose tightly with his fingers.

"Yuck!"

They made such a fuss about it that I threw the bacon to the jackals, who weren't so picky. Had some trickster planted it to create a scene? I had the same uneasy sense I'd had for months that somebody in the shadows was trailing Lawrence and trying to create as much trouble as possible – that is, if they didn't plan to do away with the Colonel.

That night I worried that the Turkish soldiers were going to hear us and descend upon us en masse. When the men weren't shouting about "unclean bacon", they were firing their rifles off into the night until almost dawn. I went from man to man and motioned them to be quiet. Lawrence slept, which turned out to be the wiser course.

At dawn we trekked to the northwest. Great walls of sheer rock rose up before us made of red and white sandstone. The sun glinting off them blinded me. I searched for soldiers concealed behind the rocky plinths. Lawrence rode up to me, "About twenty miles to the north is the valley of the Dead Sea. This is where Moses was supposed to have been when he made the water gush from the rock. Don't you recognize the peaks ahead of us?" .

I shook my head "no".

"They are the sacred mountains of Edom. We've got to penetrate them."

"We're going to climb up *there*?"

"We're following in the footsteps of Alexander the Great and the Roman legions of Titus. The Crusaders were here, too," his eyes shone.

That was Lawrence for you! He could be blind to everything going on around him because he thought he was trotting along in the footsteps of the Caesars of the first century A.D. He'd gotten himself captured once. Next he could be assassinated. We could all be mown down. That was all right by him as long as Titus would approve.

"Lawrence, over there in the far distance," I pointed, "do you see something moving?"

Lawrence considered. "It must be a mirage. We never get any closer. It's always there."

"You don't think it's that Turkish column?" I puzzled.

He waved it away. "If there ever was a Turkish column

and it's not some trick to draw us on!"

I looked at him in surprise, "You mean Mohamed is a spy, a plant? He tricked us?"

He looked at me with that enigmatic smile as if he'd suspected Mohamed all along.

When we descended from the high plateau into what appeared to be a valley, the walls of stone rose on each side. The valley must have been ten to twelve miles wide. As we progressed, it narrowed rapidly. The Arabs balked. Their camels whined and stopped. Only Lawrence rode on ahead. "Come along!" he shouted. "I came through here as a student and then as an archaeological assistant in my Carchemish days."

One objected, "Sidi Lawrence, we can't go this way. It's cursed."

"Cursed by whom? The Turks?" the Colonel tried to rouse them.

"No! No!" the objector retreated several steps. "The spirits of the Pharaohs haunt the place."

The other Bedouins nodded.

"There's a secret treasure buried here," one Bedouin paled. "Whoever finds it, the mummy will come after him."

I didn't see any pharaohs or mummies. I saw only towering sandstone cliffs that were starting to take on a reddish hue as it grew later and later in the afternoon.

"I already dug up that treasure when I was excavating with Leonard Woolley and Sir Adolphus," Lawrence confided in them. "We sent a great horde of gold coins and statuary to the British Museum."

The men's eyes grew bigger as they listened to Sidi Lawrence in awe.

"I met an officer who was connected to the Middle Eastern Department of the British Army. That led to my being here today. All the good things I have wrought sprang from your pharaohs and curses."

They whispered low to each other. Slowly one after the other started to follow Lawrence, who rode at the head of the column. I galloped up next to Lawrence. "Is that what really happened? Where did you find all this loot?"

He smiled. "It could have happened." He winked at me. "As far as what started these tall tales among the men, you will soon see."

The passage we were following grew narrower until we could ride only one man abreast in single file. We were funneled right through the rock wall in front of us, a pathway everyone called the Siq. To judge by the face expressions of the Bedouins in line behind me, most of those men would follow Sidi Lawrence into the jaws of Hell itself.

The Siq was by now only twelve feet wide. Sheer rock walls rose up on either side. They were not smooth but very rough and worn away by winds, freezes, and sporadic rain storms through the centuries. The rock walls were marked by rivulets that resembled the fingers of a giant's hand. Down the channels escaped the rain from the monsoon season.

Finally the reddish, striated rocks closed in on top of us, darkening our way and making it seem cave-like. Only a narrow slit remained above us so that we could peek at the blue sky over our heads.

When the Bedouins saw lizards darting about among the rocks, when snakes appeared suddenly in front of their camels, startling them, one man after the other got out his handgun. They shot at the reptiles. They couldn't really hit one, but they thought it great sport to try.

I whipped around with my pistol firmly clutched in my hand. The sound I'd heard was only that of the camels brushing against a wall of pink oleander blooms and small fig trees. They grew near the base of a crashing brook cascading down from the top of the ridge.

Bedouins threw themselves to their knees and refilled their skins in the brook. One never missed such an opportunity in the desert. Lawrence wisely let them splash themselves and water their camels. He got out a book that he always carried with him on campaign.

I nervously shifted my weight from side to side of my dromedary. "Lawrence, do you think we ought to linger about so long in this narrow gorge?"

He shrugged, "Alexander sent Demetrius with an army to conquer this place. His troops lingered in this gorge. He didn't conquer anything. We don't intend to conquer much either – just chase the Turks away."

I never could get anything sensible out of him. "Why would Alexander want to conquer a pile of rocks?"

"This is the gateway to Petra, of course," he laughed.

"Petra?" I exclaimed. "Never heard of it."

"The ancient kingdom of the Nabataeans. Before Alexander."

When the afternoon siesta ended and he gave the order to march onward in single file, I saw the shadow of a man above us reflected on the rock wall in the glinting afternoon sun. The unknown, unseen man had something clutched in his hand – no doubt a pistol. His shadow lingered there for only a second, so that I couldn't be sure I really saw him.

It wasn't long before the Siq ended and we ran smack into a temple right in the middle of nowhere. The Bedouins stopped and whispered to each other, pointing superstitiously at the thing. Lawrence rode up to the temple in delight.

"Look at these columns, pediments, and friezes. Look at the ornate, Corinthian style," Lawrence loved to play school teacher when he wasn't playing general.

I kept a sharp eye out for the intruder while commenting, "It's hard to make out the design. Is that erosion?"

Lawrence shook his head. "It's the work of the *Wahabbis,"* he frowned in distaste.

"The *who?"*

"They're a vagabond sect of the Sunni branch of the Moslem religion. They hang about in the farthest reaches of the Arabian Desert with a man who claims the rights we are fighting for in the name of Prince Feisal and his father, King Hussein."

"What man is this?" I was surprised. "I haven't heard anything about him."

"All he can do is perform spiteful, petty acts of

destruction."

"It looks like the temple has been defaced. What does that have to do with Islam?" I pressed.

"Ib'n Saud and his *Wahabbis* think that you can't make a graven image of anything, let alone of nude men and women clad in togas and pallas, even if they were pagans. In fact, they don't like buildings of any kind. They are iconoclasts. They frequently knock them down as soon as they see them if given a free hand."

"Very uncivilized!" I shuddered, amazed that there might be other menaces in the Middle East besides the Ottoman Turks.

"It seems to be some prejudice of theirs that harkens back to their days as nomads wandering in *Arabia Petraea,* the Roman province that encompassed all the Arabian Desert, even the part far away from the coast, which the Romans called *Arabia Felix,* or Arabia the Beautiful. Technically *Arabia Petraea* was the rocky part, the wasteland. In fact, that's what the name means literally in Latin – Arabia the Rocky."

"It certainly is that!" I looked around at the desert rock formations.

"These *Wahabbis* count the plinths or rocks around here as holy," Lawrence explained. "They think no building should overshadow them. If they find one that does, they topple it. They prefer tents."

"They sound like a bunch of cave men."

"They have a favorite rock called the Black Stone that they keep hidden in the *Kabba* in Mecca. You know, the site of the yearly pilgrimage to Mecca, the *Hajj?*"

I nodded.

"They think that the cloth-covered *Kabba* is about the right size for a dwelling. It's wrong to have anything bigger or more substantial. They don't believe in grave markers, let alone mausoleums or tombs."

"Savages!" I agreed. "At least the Moslems we're dealing with are more intelligent."

"That's why I picked out King Hussein and Prince Feisal

to work with. They are enlightened. They want the Arabs to unite under one flag and one government under the supervision of the British. It goes without saying that they want to live in buildings." He wriggled his nose. "Besides, do we have time to worry about a few vandals when we have the Ottoman Turks to fight? We must concentrate on defeating the once mighty empire that rode up to the gates of Vienna and knocked twice."

He toured the temple with distaste, scowling at the destruction the *Wahabbis* had wrought. "There's no future for the Arab world in this kind of behavior," he sighed while viewing a satyr with his legs chiseled off. "I'm glad the *Wahabbis* are such a small sect. I hope they will soon have died off."

"Who built this temple?" I changed the subject.

"Hadrian," Lawrence brightened up. "He visited Petra in A.D. 131."

He snorted when he saw how some recent visits by the iconoclasts had resulted in obscene words being carved next to the monuments. "Without a team of crack Italian sculptors, I can't do anything about the satyrs and Pans. I *can* do something about this, though."

The archaeologist prevailed for a few minutes over the Colonel. He halted the march and had his men polish away the obscene words.

On the periphery of the temple and amphitheater I could make out a campfire that didn't look very old. In fact, it looked like someone had used it only the night before. That reinforced my fears that somebody was indeed following us. Picking up a stick, I poked at the ashes to see if I could uncover more clues. A piece of unleavened bread appeared, charred at the edges, the type all Bedouins favor as their trail food. Only a few hours ago someone had been nibbling at it. The teeth marks were easy to make out.

I thought, *If someone spent last night in this temple, they were either coming from the opposite direction, or they got ahead of us.* I remembered the shadowy Turkish column that seemed to always be on the horizon and which Lawrence figured was a desert mirage or a trick. I also recalled the shadowy form I'd seen above us in the narrow pass at the entrance to Petra Canyon. Were they about to jump us at any moment?

I stepped back to study the outlines of the ruined temple. I examined every standing column and a few that were lying on the ground. I stared down at the vast amphitheater with the steeply rising rows of seats overgrown by patches of wild desert grass. Something rustled through the reeds. At first they vibrated. Then they flattened themselves. I hid behind a column, trying not to topple it. I watched the movement closely. A giant lizard peeked its head out.

A hundred feet above our heads stood a Greek urn. Excitedly the Bedouins pointed and chattered away in their own language. That urn was called the Treasury. According to legend it had belonged to the Egyptian Pharaohs. Bedouins took aim and fired at it.

Lawrence continued on away from the temple, farther down the plain of the oval valley that seemed to be a mile and a half long and half a mile wide. We entered through the city gate that once must have housed more than one hundred thousand souls, carved from native rocks. We came upon the ruins of ancient fortresses, palaces, and tombs. We entered the Senate House carved from a hillside of red rock and found ourselves in the lower part of the city.

While wending our way through narrow, twisting alleys, I lingered whenever possible to listen for slight sounds. Once, I lingered too long. "Lawrence?" I thought I'd heard the Colonel call me.

Lawrence was nowhere to be found. Neither were his Bedouin troops. I was lost.

CHAPTER 50

Dora heard the chime on the clock. She looked up. It was twelve midnight. Everyone else had gone to bed. She continued to read Edward's letter, sitting on the edge of her seat:

"Lawrence!" I shouted. I listened as my voice rebounded off the soaring red walls around me. It echoed many times until it was finally still.

"Lawrence!" I tried again, wondering if my voice could escape the immediate confines of the rock canyon. Again I listened while it echoed for many moments. No answering cry could be heard.

A bullet whizzed past, hitting the red rock wall behind me. I hunkered down as I scanned the edges of the cliff, looking for someplace for a marksman to hide. Did they think I was Lawrence because I was British and not Bedouin?

Directly ahead rose a magnificent Roman building carved out of the solid red rock. It resembled a public building in the Forum. I darted inside the empty, darkened doorway for cover. Inside I slid back against the wall the way a hunted animal would do. I waited there for countless moments. I planned to make a dash for it across the empty square. Just as I stepped softly out onto the front porch, I saw a message on the side of the building.

Countless graffiti had defaced all the buildings and rock walls in Petra Canyon over the past two millennia. This one was very recent. A skull and crossbones wore what looked like a British Army helmet. Below the graffiti the lurker in the shadows had carved, in bad English and with horrendous spelling:

GOE WY, EL ORNS!

It didn't take much imagination to fill in:

GO AWAY, EL ORENS!

I hadn't gone two steps into the cleared area in the center

of the road, bright with sunlight, than the sniper let loose with another round. I was reduced to slithering along the red rock wall at the edge of the street. I made myself as thin as possible, as if I were an insect not wanting to be seen by a bird. I had to watch my step. I was continually tripping on rubble, rock slides, stones littering the way. Once I plunged backward and nearly hit my head. Another time I caught myself from falling down into a crack in the earth and breaking my ankle if not my leg. Then I would be left here to die of thirst, unable to make it back to my comrades.

The rock wall ended abruptly. The streets widened in a vast open area full of sunlight. Buildings and houses were everywhere. It looked as if I might see someone hurrying along the street from the local water well or a delivery boy looking for a coin as a tip. Perhaps I might run into a centurion from Rome wearing his horse hair, crested metal helmet.

Fingers from behind grabbed me by the hair. Someone had been shadowing me all along, waiting for the opportunity to pounce. I could imagine the steel blade against my throat like a sacrificial lamb, seeing my last ray of sunlight before my eyes were darkened forever. I caught a glimpse of you, Dora. I wished only that you could find out what had happened to me, that you could see the surroundings in which I'd died and been hastily buried in an unmarked grave next to unknown Roman bones.

I didn't hear breathing. Slowly I turned. The pressure on my hair increased. I felt as if my locks were being forcibly yanked from my head. I found myself face to face not with an assassin but with a oleander bush with beautiful pink blooms. A branch had seized upon my hair and torn out a lock or two.

I dashed across the street. Reaching a door, I found that it was a false one. It had been carved to look like a door, but didn't open. Right above my head, next to a fig tree, sat an open air shrine charred black from ashes. It had been used to sacrifice animals and take the omens. Though none of the ashes had survived the desert winds through the centuries, the charring had been so deep it had not been erased after all this time.

I ran quickly along the alleyway, hunkering down as low as possible. I couldn't judge exactly how far behind me the footsteps were. Perhaps a hundred yards. Perhaps fifty or less. I was racing along through deserted streets paved with stone. Sounds were magnified out of all proportion.

Somehow I had to shake my pursuer until I could figure out how to rejoin Lawrence. I dashed inside the first door I came to. This particular house had a gaping crack in the back of it. A rat let himself out that way. I followed.

A dark form loomed up in front of me at the end of a long alleyway. Whoever it was skulked there waiting for me, hoping I wouldn't see him until it was too late.

I darted down the first passageway between the houses, hoping there would be an exit. It grew so narrow that I was wriggling along with the brick walls brushing against my back and belly. I was beginning to think I would have to stop and go back the way I'd come, risking running into the shadowy gunman who lay in wait for me.

This ancient city was like the Minotaur's labyrinth. All I needed to get around was a ball of thread provided by Ariadne. Since I obviously wasn't Theseus of Athens, I was hard put to know where to go next.

Ahead a roseate temple ascended grandly from the street, carved by some long ago sculptor from a solid rocky mass. Pink steps started up abruptly. I fled up them, falling over my own feet, picking myself up, and disappearing into the rock fortress. Powerful Corinthian columns with fig leaves sculpted at the top towered above me as I entered under the protective portico. Statues of unknown gods and rounded urns flanked me on either side. Above me loomed a hideous, sculpted head of a woman, very much like Medusa, with writhing snakes for hair. Her wide open, staring eyes were ready to pop out of her head at any moment. Her lips were open, revealing sharp teeth. It had to be my imagination that, as I passed beneath on the stairway, the creature's eyes turned downward and stared straight at me, freezing my blood despite the desert heat.

You may think the rose stone softened Medusa. But it made her more horrible still. Bathed in a half-light, neither white nor red, sometimes this color and sometimes that in the dying light of day, glinting with sun and now darkened in growing dusk and shade, she seemed alive and breathing. She was an ominous presence closely watching me below.

The first flight of stairs leveled out. After a brief landing that might have once been furnished with benches and urns, I ascended the second flight. A ceremonial doorway rose to many feet over my head. It led into darkness. Was I like Antigone, being trapped in a cave as a tomb? Would those doors close behind me? Would I suffer the fate of Aida? Would I end my life singing?

I found a crevice in the wall. I squeezed myself in, hunkering down there, hardly daring to breathe. Seconds later someone else came past. I could hear him only a few feet away. I wanted to say, *Who are you? Who sent you?* I imagined he must be a Turk from Ottoman army headquarters. They naturally would hire someone to assassinate *El Orens,* the Destroyer of Railways.

As the man paused in front of me and then continued onward away from my hiding place, I thought maybe he'd lured Lawrence to Petra to begin. He'd used the so-called disappearing Turkish column so he could pounce upon him.

This man had observed me staring at his campfire. He had read my doubts. He'd decided to lure me away from the group by making sounds and attracting my attention. I'd fallen for the trick. That same killer was now attempting to do away with me so Lawrence would be none the wiser. The assassin had no intentions of letting me rejoin the group so I could spread the alarm. He did seem to be in great haste to get his work done. He didn't want Lawrence and his Bedouins to find me before I was dead. Dead men tell no tales.

I'd chided Lawrence often enough for wandering away from the pack. He'd even been taken prisoner doing it. Now here I was not following my own advice. I could kick myself.

I fled back into the darkened main chamber. Then I

sped out the entrance. As far as I could tell, I no longer heard footsteps behind me. I dared to hope I'd eluded my would-be captor. Upon reaching the main street I immediately veered sharply to the left and hunkered down in a shady, shadowy passageway between buildings.

I couldn't win at this game if it continued much longer. I was no Bedouin. It didn't come naturally to me – surviving in the desert. My opponent could go on playing for days, knowing exactly when and where to take a cat nap, knowing where to find water, knowing how to prepare food over a campfire and extinguish it quickly. No doubt he'd grown up doing such things. My only hope was to reach the rest of the Bedouin army as soon as possible.

The building ahead beckoned me. A rectangular hole led into blackness. It looked like the perfect hiding place. Looking in every direction to make sure I wasn't being followed, I disappeared inside it.

My feet were standing on air. I was dangling my legs, kicking and flailing for a handhold or foothold. I found myself grasping a stone ledge, hanging over a precipice that extended I didn't know how far downward.

CHAPTER 51

Dora paused only long enough to glance at the clock. It was one A.M. She continued to read:

My handhold was slipping. I attempted to find a crevice in the rock for the toe of my boot so I could give myself a boost upward. When I put my weight on it, my boot slipped. I plummeted onto a dusty floor and rolled.

I got up and measured the room. It was about twenty paces one direction and twenty paces the other. There were no furnishings of any kind nor anything hanging on the lower walls. I failed to detect the presence of another living being.

I got out the last of my rations for dinner. I swilled the last of my water. If this was to be my tomb, so be it. The light soon died in the hole above me through which I had plummeted. Night came on. It didn't take long for me to fall into a deep, profound slumber.

Suddenly a bright light shone above me. I'd slept the whole night through and well past dawn. Instead of the sizzling bacon and kidney pie whose aromas wafted my direction every morning during the summer while I was home on holiday from Oxford, there was only dust to make me sneeze. Instead of lying on a soft mattress covered with my grandmother's heirloom blanket, I lay flat on my back in the dust on the cold, hard ground. With a groan it came back to me at once – where I was and why.

I uncapped my water skin and turned it upside down. A few drops landed on my tongue. They served to torment me about what I didn't have rather than to relieve my burning throat and parched mouth. I lacked so much as a bit of hard, unleavened bread to gnaw on.

I figured today was it – do or die. Without water it would be certain death to climb up into the sunlight and start running all over the place. I resolved to stay where I was and wait for Lawrence to find me. Without him and the Bedouins, I was a dead man.

I tried to look on the bright side, if there was a bright side about dying of thirst. At least here it was shady. The walls were thick enough that it would remain cool throughout the day – if I lived that long. I'd never tried to go without water before. I didn't know how long one could last. I'd heard stories, which I didn't like to think about now.

It was hard to sit still and do nothing except wait, counting the minutes and seconds. I could hear my gold pocket watch ticking, though I couldn't read its face in the dark. My hand would slip around it and feel its pulse, like my own heartbeat, measuring out the time for me to live. I was willing to trade the watch for a long quaff of chilled water from a well. The gold timepiece, presented to my great-great-great grandfather by Wellington after the Battle of Waterloo, was worth nothing here.

The sunlight above me had changed its angle, illuminating more of the chamber. I was astonished to see an engraving on the wall above me of a camel caravan making its way through a landscape that looked very much like the Great Arabian Desert. It was easy to recognize the outlines of the rugged, red sandstone jagged cliffs and mountains.

Where had I seen a wall mural like this before? I remembered trekking through the mountains. We'd come upon some etchings in the rocks. That had led to a cave where we'd had lunch. The Bedouins had not wanted to join us. They'd said it was taboo. The cave had been elaborately painted with murals. There had been recognizable donkeys and horses, also pictures of fires and weird-looking demons and spirits.

Lawrence had said the cave spooked the Bedouins because it was a burial chamber. Could this be another of a much later time period, albeit a more expensive and well-built one? Could that be why it was so empty? Why it was under the surface of the street?

I heard voices. Two men were lowering themselves down into the chamber. It was too late for me to escape, even if there had been way to do so. I hunkered back against the wall in the shadows and lay perfectly still. I closed my eyes and peered at the men through cat-like slits.

A shaft of sunlight thrust its way down to the floor. It had a strange, three-dimensional quality that resembled the finger of God pointing down accusingly at the interlopers, who by now had reached the floor. The middle of the tomb was illuminated, sweeping away the dark shadows.

Along the opposite wall lay a corpse, a shriveled up mummy with leather for skin. He still wore rings and traces of finery, persevered by the dry desert air. He lay stretched out on a bier with his hands folded over his chest. He was looking straight up at the ceiling in tattered shreds of cloth that had survived the centuries.

The two men crept past the corpse, kicking him to one side irreverently. One of them spat at him. "You!" he cursed. "You caused all these evils! If it weren't for you, we wouldn't be trekking across the desert hunting down Sidi Lawrence."

Why, it was Mohamed, the merchant, the one who'd led the party of Bedouins after the Turkish column some days ago, the one who had never returned!

"Abdullah was a rich man in his day," said his companion, whom I immediately recognized as the rascal whom I'd chased out of my tent on innumerable occasions. "He thought he was doing something important to put the Holy of Holies in his tomb." He shook his head.

"Author of all the plagues of Egypt!" Mohamed exploded and threw an empty tin can at the corpse. It grazed the mummy's bony nose, breaking it off.

"He's dead. He can't hear us," sighed the thief. "He's probably sitting in Paradise right now surrounded by Virgins. If you could eat grapes, figs, and dates, would you listen to such as us?"

"Allah cast him into hell," Mohamed swore. "Abdullah should have known better than to steal such a Holy of Holies out of the mosque and put it here for troublemakers to get their grimy hands on."

"Ah! You mean *El Orens!*" said the thief.

"Who the hell else should I mean?" Mohammed's dark eyes flashed. "As it was, Abdullah defaced the Holy of Holies beyond all recognition. He defied the Prophet's wishes and the express decrees of his lawful successors."

"Let's get to work. We don't want *El Orens* to beat us to it again."

"What about him?" Mohamed spied me lying there in the shadows playing dead, hardly daring to breathe. He pointed right at me. His eyes consumed me.

The thief cast me a glance and then waved in dismissal. "The fall into the chamber killed him. He broke his neck."

"I'll make sure he's dead!" Mohamed drew his knife and started across the chamber toward me.

His fellow in crime grabbed him. "Remember what Prince Ali told us? We would be paid only if we destroyed the last traces of the ancient desecration and brought him evidence of it."

"He also wanted *El Orens* dead. We have failed," Mohamed sighed, putting his knife away.

"Prince Ali told us that the Holy of Holies was more important," he caught onto the edge of Mohamed's robe. "Besides, the British officer dropped his gold watch over there. We can take that to Prince Ali to prove that one's dead."

"Yes, my Osama!" Mohamed rubbed his hands together, giving the thief a name at last. "Or we can sell it in a bazaar for ten times what it's worth," he picked up my heirloom gold pocket watch, "for it looks like it's made of solid gold." He fingered it with experienced hands, slavering over it.

Osama took out a large wooden box from a crevice in the wall above the corpse. I wondered if it was the coffin of a child. When Mohamed threw it open, I saw scrolls resembling those I'd once seen in the British Museum – the thick paper made from papyrus plants along the Nile which was the first cloth upon which anything was written in the ancient world. They were covered with mysterious characters. They reminded me of the letters I'd seen Lawrence copying down in his tent that night, the inscriptions which he then proceeded to burn.

These were finer still and looked very valuable. Lawrence would love to get his hands on them. To my horror, Mohamed and Osama no sooner dragged them out of the wooden box, than they hacked them to pieces.

"Let's build a fire!" Mohamed squatted down. They'd brought charcoal and matches. They lighted the fire and hurled the papyri into it, letting the smoke drift up through the opening. I had to keep myself from coughing or sneezing. I didn't want to tip them off I was still alive.

"Here, I have part of Abdullah's scroll with me!" Mohamed held the paper above his head and waved it in the air. "We will send it to Prince Ali so he can see it came from the tomb of this long ago King Abdullah of Petra – the heretic who escaped from Mecca to this obscure place in the desert."

"How will Prince Ali know it's the right scroll?"

"See?" Mohamed showed Osama. "Each of the pages is marked with the king's official seal. Abdullah retained it even when he fled Mecca in the seventh century to escape Muhammad's successors. And he took these scrolls with him, heretic as they are, to far away Petra that had long ago seen its glory days. He thought he was clever to bury them in his tomb."

"It's like he foresaw the coming of Sidi Lawrence," Osama said.

"No one could imagine a villain like him," Mohamed declared. "And after we kill him, no one will ever exist like him again."

"But we can't kill Lawrence until we steal what he's hidden from us," Osama sighed.

"That wily desert fox is playing a game of cat and mouse with me. I take the humidor. But nothing's in it. He's hidden the loot somewhere else. He knows I'm looking for it, but he plays on and on."

"That's Sidi Lawrence for you. He's not like other white men. He's far too clever."

Mohamed shot a look upward, exclaiming, "Put out the fire. I hear footsteps."

Osama threw himself at the rope and quickly climbed to the top. Mohamed lingered only a moment to give me a swift kick in the buttocks. Then he, too, disappeared.

CHAPTER 52

D ora heard the clock chime once more. She looked up to see it was 2:00 A.M. She couldn't go to sleep yet. She had to finish the letter:

"Edward, for heaven's sake, is that you?" came a familiar voice.

At the opening to the chamber shone the face of Colonel Lawrence, part in shadow, part in the sun, highlighting his long, pointed nose and his high cheekbones. A lock of his wavy blond hair peeked out from underneath his headdress. His clear blue eyes sparkled with mirth. "Edward, what are you doing down there? Practicing some Near Eastern burial ritual?"

"Lawrence!" I shouted. "I wondered whether I'd see you again in this life."

"We've been wasting time looking for you," the Colonel declared, "ever since one of the men saw you wandering away from our ranks yesterday. He went after you, but you vanished. What on earth could you have had in mind?"

Two Bedouins tied a rope around a pillar near the opening and shinnied down to the bottom of the burial chamber. They gave me a drink from their skins. I grasped onto the rope and climbed up.

"Hamid says he called you. You didn't answer," Lawrence gave me a crust of unleavened bread. "He went back and got Abdul. They both chased you about the city. You ran away. About dusk they came back and reported to me. I couldn't credit it. I sent the night patrol to hunt for you. When they couldn't find you, I ordered the whole troop to come search for you this morning. Here we are," Lawrence volunteered with a sweep of his arm.

"Lawrence, it couldn't have been Abdul and Hamid. It had to be . . . " I pulled Lawrence aside and spoke in a low a whisper. "Mohamed and Osama – he's the thief I saw about camp – were after me. They were down there in the burial chamber," I pointed toward the tomb, "burning scrolls that they pulled out of a crevice in the wall. They said they were working for some prince. I –"

Lawrence threw back his head and laughed. "Really, Lieutenant, has the sun gotten to your brain? It's bad enough with the men imagining mummies, ghosts, and goblins. Now you come up with ancient burial chambers, geniis, and buried princes with hordes of gold." He slapped me on the back as if it were a joke and sauntered off.

I'd heard the wastrels talk and had watched them closely. Mohamed had administered a parting kick to my buttocks, which I could still feel. I was lucky to be alive, and here Lawrence was making light of it. I was expected to mount the camel that Hamid offered me. I followed along in stunned silence.

"Edward!" Lawrence called from the back of his camel as our dromedaries carefully picked their way around the stone monuments. "You should have become a crime novelist like Sir Arthur Conan Doyle or an adventure writer like Haggard. When we're gathered around the fire one night, huddling to keep warm, I'll call on you to entertain us."

I'd no choice but to follow Lawrence and his army wherever they were going. Exactly where, I hadn't the presence of mind to wonder. Only when the camel next to me spat rather nastily, another spat back at him, and some of the spittle landed on me was I alerted to look around. We were ascending. I realized that we were beyond the city gates and had been so for many minutes.

Lawrence turned to one of the Bedouins and said something rapidly in Arabic. I'd learned enough to survive. But I was rather slow, and I couldn't translate dialogue spoken at that speed.

Suddenly the Bedouins dismounted. They let their camels pasture on stubble growing nearby. Some went to fill their water skins at a springs pouring between the rocks. Others took the opportunity to chew on the unleavened bread or nuts they carried with them.

Not knowing what else to do, I tied my camel up – just in time. Lawrence was off up the mountain slope. Bedouins scrambled up behind him, leaving only me to gape after them. I wished I had a walking stick with me. Some of the older Bedouins had brought theirs. I had to struggle along as best I could.

Lawrence didn't seem to be troubled by such problems. The Bedouins, like goats, could climb anything, the more rugged the better. They'd grown up in the desert. They'd skipped up and down steps like this as boys.

Only when we'd climbed a mile or more did Lawrence disappear within a great gray stone facade. It must have been one hundred and fifty feet high and many feet long. How had anyone built something like this so far above the city? Daring to look behind me at the way we'd come, I judged it to be at least a thousand feet above the town.

"What on earth is this?" I exclaimed.

"El Deir," one Bedouin explained.

"What!"

"The Co-ve-nant," another Bedouin tried to pronounce the word carefully, repeating something that Lawrence had taught him. "High place."

I craned my neck to see to the very top of the building. I could make out what looked like a giant Greek urn. Carved in it was that face of an ugly woman with bulging eyes and snake-like hair writhing around her head. I thought, *What is Medusa doing here?* She gaped straight down at me. That must be part of the effect the sculptor had been trying to create.

I thought, *Maybe the ancients were used to such heights. They didn't fear them. Nowadays, at least among white men, what a place of foreboding!*

All somebody had to do was take a fraction of a wrong step in any direction. Down he would plummet, falling thousands of feet to his death, crushed by rock long before he reached the bottom of the slope.

From behind the big urn with the Medusa head, someone peeked out. His cloak left only a black and seemingly empty space where the face should be. A cold hand clutched my stomach and closed in a tight fist. Was that Mohamed? Was that Osama? It had to be one or the other.

Lawrence appeared at the entrance to the magnificent building. "What are you up to, Lieutenant?" He started down the pathway with the grace and swiftness of a mountain lion.

From behind the Medusa something flashed in the sun and edged outward. It glinted and glowed, pointed downward at an angle. Its barrel was aimed toward Lawrence. It kept moving ever so slightly as he strode toward me all unawares.

"Lawrence, watch out!" I jabbed my finger in the air in the direction of the Medusa. "Get down!"

Lawrence fell and rolled almost at the same moment that the shot went off. I fired back while dashing toward him, forgetting my own safety on the rocks. I hunkered down as close to the ground as possible. At the same time several Bedouins converged on *El Orens.* They tackled him in their anxiousness to be the first to aid him.

"Don't worry about me," Lawrence held his arm and winced, "somebody misfired, that's all." He took a cloth and bandaged his own arm. One of the Bedouins helped the *shereef.*

"Lawrence!" I crouched next to him and whispered into his ear. "What did I tell you? They're after you. I heard them say that they wanted to kill both you and me. They've been hired as assassins by some Prince Ali."

The Bedouins took off in the direction of the shot. Staircases around the building led straight up. I followed the Arabs in their race up to the very top. The staircase dead ended at the face of the mountain. The peak rose high above me. Nearer to me, carved into that solid rock face, stood a flat platform a little over the height of my chest. Above that was a domed-shaped kind of roof that was charred and blackened. It was just like the ancient altar in the town of Petra. This must also be a sacrificial altar high in the mountains surrounding the city. Worshipers once brought animals here to sacrifice and take the omens.

A bullet came whizzing straight for me. I ducked. Someone had been waiting to catch me alone, or perhaps they'd mistaken me for Lawrence. I fired in the same direction.

"There he is!" A group of Bedouins appeared from around the corner. They swarmed about and escorted me down the steps back to where Lawrence was standing. They were chattering a mile a minute like parakeets. I could make out little of what they were saying.

The Colonel held up his hands for silence. "So, Lieutenant, it was you all along."

"Me all along – what?" I asked.

He thumped me in the chest. "You were the one shooting. I told the men that's what I saw. They were to come and get you before you hurt somebody else."

"I fired back at the gunman up there if that's what you mean. I did it while you fell to the ground," I defended myself against I didn't know what charge. "You must have seen that."

"Yes, but they tell me there's no one up there," he glanced over his shoulder at the building and the urn with the Medusa design.

"But – but what about the bullet that hit you?"

He put his hand on my arm. "You have a happy trigger finger."

"You mean – you mean you think I fired that bullet as well?"

"I don't hold it against you," he wrapped his arm around my shoulders and led me to a vantage point overlooking the area. "Hunting down the Turks takes its toll on everybody after awhile."

"Colonel, surely you can't imagine that –"

"Hush!"

"I was coming back down the stairs and wondering where to turn . . . "

Lawrence nodded, half paying attention to what I was saying, "You're always getting lost, aren't you? It seems to be an affliction of yours lately. We all need some rest. After this coming battle, perhaps we can get it. The Turks are massing on

Petra. We have to defend it."

"Oh?"

Again he smiled. "Lieutenant, look down below."

I stared down where he was pointing.

"This is the best vantage point around Petra. That's why I came up here. I want to study the layout of the land. The best defense of the city is from where we entered it. You can see the Siq from here."

So he was dismissing not only me but the threat on his life!

"Remember that camera of yours, Lieutenant?"

I gaped at him. This was hardly the time to bring up my camera!

"Take a photo of the city below us."

"Colonel?"

"That's an order, Lieutenant."

I groped for the equipment in my pack. As I got out my folding camera, he leaned closer to me as if peering through the lens. "Lieutenant, even if that were true that assassins were hunting me down, I was brought here to help the Arabs achieve their independence from the Turks. God didn't intend for me to come here in vain. If I were you, I'd think the same way."

He was back to his Messiah philosophy! "Lawrence, the Messiah himself was assassinated, if you want to call it that. He was crucified. They have something much worse in mind for me and you."

He guffawed as if I'd made a joke, patted me on the back, and strutted off to talk to somebody else. He walked as if his arm had not been bandaged, as if a little assassination attempt now and then meant nothing to Lawrence of Arabia.

CHAPTER 53

Dora heard the clock strike three. She barely glanced at it as she continued to read, resolved to stay up as long as it took:

At dinner the men roasted game on a spit over a blazing fire. Jackals howled in the distance. A cool night wind gusted around Petra, making everyone draw nearer to the flames. "We've got to secure the port of Akaba," Lawrence stated flatly. "It's the most important city on the west coast of Arabia. It's been that way for thousands of years."

"Why are we in Petra to begin with?" I couldn't help but keep watch on the dark distance beyond the campfires. I couldn't shake my terrible feeling of foreboding.

"We have to hold Petra to hold Akaba," Lawrence said with finality. "Petra is the high place in the region. You have to own the high ground."

The Arabs amused themselves firing rounds of ammunition into the still night sky. Lawrence always supplied them with fifty to one hundred rounds each day. Much of it was wasted in this fashion. Others smoked much cherished cigarettes, or "gaspers", which made them cough and laugh all the more. Still others toyed with wrist-watches, field glasses, and other trinkets which they would pass around among themselves. Lawrence never ran short of amusements. He kept two or three camels busy carrying "toys" of such kinds at all times.

Lawrence was off the next morning for Akaba, where a Turkish garrison was housed. "How are you going to break into an armed city? We don't have that many men?" I protested, riding next to the Colonel.

He grinned. "Remember, not only Alexander the Great but the Roman legions march with us."

The Arabs who overheard us chuckled like Sidi Lawrence. So I would have to trust him. He didn't like to confide in anybody. He kept everything to himself – all too much, I think, if I am to judge by my encounter in that tomb in Petra.

First we came to Gueirra, a Turkish post in King Solomon Mountains. What I remember from the map was that this was twenty-five miles from Akaba. I braced myself for the worst. As soon as we drew near, out streamed the Turks with their hands up. The Arabs cheered and rode up to collect their weapons. Lawrence grinned broadly at me. He dared to wink.

"What the devil?" I asked, dumbfounded as we rode into the outpost unopposed.

"Sidi Lawrence, his reputation goes before him. It makes a loud noise," one of the Bedouins banged two pots together to illustrate his point.

No sooner did Lawrence station a few Bedouins to hold the fort, than he was off toward Akaba. "Don't we get to stop for lunch?" I asked.

"Not if you want the advantage of surprise."

Soon we'd ascended into the mountains and were squeezing ourselves single file through an extremely narrow pass called the *Wadi Ithm.* "What are we doing this for?" I asked.

"No one will expect it."

"Yes, and no one will know where to come looking for us when we starve or get lost." I had an intense feel of what this would be like after my night spent alone in the underground chamber.

Soon we were coming down out of the pass directly into the Kethura, another Turkish outpost, the only land approach to Akaba. Lawrence and his Bedouins, mounted on racing camels and Arab stallions, charged the Turkish garrison. He sent the Turks running at the same time that other Arabs appeared out of nowhere to join us and swell our numbers. The whole desert was in revolt, having heard of our success. "It's the *Shereefian* army!" one Bedouin declared. Another echoed him and another and another down the line. Of course what they meant was that Lawrence was the *"Shereef"* and we were the *"Shereefians"*, or his subjects.

"I suppose we will make camp here?" I suggested to the Colonel.

"Hardly," he replied, "we have to make one more call. Akaba."

"Today?" I couldn't believe it.

"We have to be ready to make our appearance right on time," he said ambiguously.

I had no choice but to follow or be left in the middle of nowhere in the blazing sun with no supplies and mostly captured Turks for company. Lawrence was insane to head straight up over still another mountain pass in the King Solomon Mountains. We had to scale an old Roman wall with camels in tow. Lawrence directed us over the lowest part of it. That was one of the advantages to having an archaeologist guiding us. That night we got almost as far as the descent into Akaba where Lawrence was forced to make camp.

I woke up in the middle of the night. The campfires were glowing orange embers. A shadowy figure hovered over me. "Is that you, Colonel?" The man fled. He scaled the mountainside looming above us on silent, cat-like feet.

I fired into the dark. Arabs sprang up and joined me. They loved nothing better than to fire round after round of ammunition at any owl, lizard, or snake, let alone at an escaping villain. Soon the night air was filled with bullets. It sounded as if we were fighting a battle. Lawrence appeared at my elbow. "Shooting practice? I didn't think you were the type, Lieutenant."

"Anybody would be the type if they awoke and found a stranger standing over him. It was probably that Osama I was telling you about."

He shrugged and yawned. "We've got bigger bad guys to deal with."

Next morning I examined the hillside for a body. Whoever it had been, had managed to escape without a trace. Not even the low brush had snagged a thread of his robe as he'd crept past.

"Can't wait to find yourself a Turk?"

I turned to behold a man wearing a *kuffiyeh* of white silk and gold embroidery. It was held in place over his head by an *agal*, consisting of two black woolen cords decorated with silver and gold thread. Over his shoulders was thrown a black camel-hair robe, or *abba.* Underneath all he wore a pure white robe coming down to his feet. He tied the robe in place around his waist with a gold-brocaded belt. In the belt was fastened a curved sword. Only Princes of Mecca were allowed to wear such fine attire.

After my initial surprise I noticed that the apparition out of the desert with the sun shining behind him was scarcely more than five foot three and talking in a familiar tone of voice. "You've put on that costume?" I asked, dumbfounded. It wasn't the one he wore everyday. It looked newly laundered, not the least bit dusty or dirty.

"Certainly! I want to give the Turks a scare," Lawrence admitted, every bit the showman.

"I see . . . " No wonder everybody called him Sidi Lawrence, the blond *shereef*, the uncrowned King of Arabia!

"Come!" the Colonel beckoned me to follow him.

Everyone had risen early. Bedouins were showing off their best outfits, donning baubles, whether captured or not. Others had decorated themselves with their wife's jewelry. Many had spent the wee hours polishing their knives and pistols. They wanted to resemble riders from Arabia's fabled past.

Lawrence took his place in the lead. "Let's follow the footsteps of Moses toward the Promised Land!" As the men cheered, he wove his way down out of the narrow pass through the mountains. It was still so early that he managed to hurry past the Turkish artillerymen – waking up and rubbing their eyes in the dawn light – posted on the outer perimeters of Akaba. They must have thought of Lawrence as an apparition from their dreams.

Lawrence charged right into the main square of Akaba that morning of July 6, 1917. It was surrounded by mud huts, narrow streets, and bazaar stalls with merchants hawking their wares. No one took any notice of Lawrence and his desert hordes until they had gone quite some distance.

Finally a German officer stepped out of a building and gaped at him with a monocle. He hurried right up to Lawrence and saluted him. "Who are these men of yours?" he asked. He could tell quite naturally that Lawrence, dressed in such a costume and with such a sense of "presence" about him, must be the leader.

"They are the army of King Hussein, the Grand Shereef of Mecca, and his son, Prince Feisal," Lawrence answered at once.

"Who?" the German officer asked as if he came from another world, which he did.

"King Hussein is Emir of Mecca, as I said," Lawrence repeated.

"What does that make me?" the German was perplexed as he scratched his head.

"Our prisoner," Lawrence grinned.

"Are you taking me to Mecca or somewhere else?" he asked.

"Egypt."

"Do they have provisions there? We don't have many left here," he confessed, wriggling his nose at the flea-bitten, fly-infested bazaars across the street.

Lawrence assured the man, "The British military supplies them with treats from all the way across the Atlantic, straight from America."

"The Land of Milk and Honey!" the German sighed, doing everything besides licking his tongue.

"Lead the German prisoner away!" Lawrence gave the order.

His men complied and shackled the man, who only smiled as if quite content to drink a bottle of Coke with the aura of America about it instead of staying in Akaba.

Lawrence wended his way back to Petra, leaving men behind to hold the fort. The Bedouins surged out of Petra to greet and congratulate us. For the nomads have channels of communication all their own. News travels as fast as it does in Europe, though in different ways. Since Lawrence had unified almost all the Arabs under one banner, nearly everyone he saw now was on our side.

"After you took Akaba, why would the Turks bother to follow us here?" I asked.

"Revenge," he explained. "Even if the Turks won't fight, the Germans will make them."

Lawrence let the Bedouins rest for several days in Petra, cooking over campfires, telling tales around them, and exercising their camels and stallions around town. He let them brag.

He left very abruptly early one evening for a raid on a chalk mountain fifteen miles northeast of Petra. We approached the old Crusader Castle known as Shobek up a steep hill while Lawrence discoursed about Baldwin I, King of Jerusalem, an occupant of the castle. He'd done an undergraduate thesis on the subject of Crusader Castles while at Oxford.

The whole way was winding and precipitous. I wondered that Lawrence dared to do this at nightfall. We might lose our footing. It was still guarded by the Turks. Wouldn't we be spotted and captured? Eyes peered out at us through the desert trees and bushes. Someone was moving through the brush on either side of us. I rode up ahead to alert Lawrence. "We're being watched. Shouldn't we turn around?"

"Patience, Lieutenant," he waved me off. He seemed unimpressed, thinking himself the Messiah of the Arabs and being assured that no one could harm one hair on his head – not the Turks or the Germans, or even Mohamed, Osama, and the unseen Prince Ali.

Suddenly a bunch of men rushed out at us. I said my prayers and thought of you, Dora. Not a shot was fired. No alarm was raised. The men either leaped on other men's camels or provided their own. They blended in with our party.

Lawrence turned his camel around and shot back down the mountainside. I followed, not wanting to stay behind in such a place. Lawrence did not cease galloping when we reached the bottom of the hill. The riders continued charged across miles of desert, stopping only to water their camels once.

We arrived back at Petra long before dawn. The men acted like they didn't need any sleep. They broke into song and merriment.

"What did we accomplish by this raid anyway?" I confronted the Colonel.

"Wonderful things!" he proclaimed.

"Who are these strange men who returned with us?"

"If you weren't so preoccupied with spooks, with thinking we're being ambushed by secret assassins, you might have paid attention. They're Syrians."

"But they came from the Turkish stronghold!"

"They were being held there as slave labor. We liberated them. Better yet, they've joined us. I've doubled my forces, for they are Arab patriots, too."

"Some of them might be spies."

"*You* might be a spy for all I know, Lieutenant."

"So might anyone, for that matter," I replied. "But someone's been following us all the same as I warned you."

"I don't have time for such spooks and frights, if you'll remember what I told you!" he dismissed me. "I've got business to attend to."

The next day a raiding party of Arabs, including the liberated Syrians, attacked the same chalk mountain. They destroyed three hundred rails of a side line of the Damascus-Medina Railway near Aneiza. No sooner did they accomplish their objective than Lawrence called them back to Petra to prepare for battle.

"They will attack us here next," he proclaimed. "When they lose here, they will have lost Akaba for good. If they can't recapture the city, they can kiss Holy Arabia good-bye. They might as well sign an armistice with the Allies."

I shouldn't be astonished at his daring or his broad, sweeping vision. I lived with it every day. I lived with the danger that sprang from it as well.

Lawrence set up his headquarters at the Temple of Isis, which he kept ablaze at night with a bonfire. Other bonfires answered it from all the high places. The whole deserted ruin of a city took on an eerie atmosphere with the leaping flames from the altars as well as the campfires that the Arabs built. At sunset it looked oddest when the flares competed with the last, dying rays of the sun reflecting off the roseate stone.

. "Here," Lawrence offered, "have a cigar." He held out my father's elaborately carved, wooden humidor. It had materialized out of nowhere.

"Lawrence, how do you expect me to take a cigar from that thing when it's caused so much trouble!"

He lighted up himself and blew smoke in my direction.

"Mohamed says he kept on looking in that humidor and couldn't find something associated with that ancient King of Petra, Abdullah. He says you know where it's hidden. *Do you?*"

Lawrence held up his hands. "Can't I even enjoy a smoke without you spewing your Gothic fantasies?"

"Mohamed claimed –"

Lawrence sighed and turned the humidor upside down. He poured out the few remaining cigars. He showed me the empty box. "What could possibly be hidden inside here besides cigars? Isn't that what a humidor's for?"

I leaned forward. "I caught you red-handed that night, you know!" I hissed. "You were copying down inscriptions with cryptic characters. You burned them and –"

He closed the humidor with a bang and stuffed it into a pack behind him. "Lieutenant," he turned his eyes on me, "neither you nor I ever saw such inscriptions or characters. I never copied them down. You never approached my tent to ask me about them. It was all one of your ghoulish dreams, *do we understand each other?*"

"Yes, Colonel," I realized for the first time how determined he was to keep up his front at all costs, even at the cost of human lives, "I believe we do." I rose.

"Now won't you have a smoke – *on my terms?*" he

leaned back in his chair and took a draw on his cigar.

For the first time I saw him for what he really was. Beyond the white flowing robes and the desert attire, T.E. Lawrence had the instincts of a poker player, like a gambler in your Western films. He could keep a straight face no matter what the odds. He wanted to bluff, outplay his enemies, and win the wager in the end. He had the endurance of a bull and nerves that couldn't be shaken.

"No," I turned, "I'm going to write my fiancée. I'm going to tell her my days are numbered."

Yours,
Edward

P.S. I worry that Prince Ali is Ali the gardener who once worked at Ware House and has disappeared. He could be the saboteur you've told me about, the one who helped sink the *Lusitania* and vandalized your room at Ware House. If he's tried to murder you, it must be because my father and Leonard Woolley sent you that birthday package that went down to the bottom of the Irish Sea with the ship.

I don't know why my father would have done such a thing, but I saw him with my own eyes run into Asalah's burning house in London to rescue the humidor. At the time I accepted his explanation. He associated it with his mistress. Now that I've seen the bones of King Abdullah and heard what Mohamed and Osama had to say, I wonder if there wasn't a lot more to it.

Lawrence, my father, and Leonard Woolley seem to be engaged in a conspiracy. Lawrence is the kingpin. It has something to do with that now long ago dig at Carchemish when Ali and Asalah came home to England with my father. I wonder if my father, Lawrence, and Woolley didn't make a side excursion to Petra. Lawrence brags to the men that he was here before in his student days. I wonder if the three of them didn't descend into the tomb of King Abdullah and find something they shouldn't have.

Exactly what did they find? I'd like to know before I'm murdered for it.

What I can do, though, and must do with great reluctance, is to break off our engagement. It's the only way to protect you. That man you used to go around with, Michael Byrne, is a far safer person for you to marry.

You needn't write me anymore. In fact, I forbid it! The less you have to do with me the better. Let me carry my own doom to the grave. Remember the short, happy time we spent together.

Until eternity unites us in a better world,
Edward

P.S.S. During the few brief weeks of our courtship I never felt the way I do now. You were a pretty girl. I wanted a fling before I left for the front. Yet since I've been with Colonel Lawrence, I've fallen in love with you. You've grown on me day by day. The photo I took of you standing there in that suit in Queenstown, Ireland sits on my makeshift nightstand. I talk to you every night. You reach out to me, and I am quiet in my heart if only for a few hours. I remember the feel of your hands on my cheeks. I pretend that you put your hand in mine, and I kiss it. Then I can sleep.

Why do I say this now? I want you to know I'm not breaking off our engagement because I don't love you *but because I do. I really, really do!*

Good-bye,
Edward

CHAPTER 54

Dora glanced around the living room bleary-eyed to see the dawn streaming through the window. The embers were now extinguished in the fireplace. The painting of her father still presided over the mantel.

"Dora, my goodness, are you still up? Didn't you ever go to bed?" Viola rushed into the room.

Dora merely gaped at the cleaning lady.

"Mrs. Benley, Mr. Benley, Dora was up all night!" Viola rushed up the stairs.

Mrs. Benley hurried downstairs in her night robe, "For goodness sakes, Dora, you'll make yourself ill if you don't get any sleep."

Dora looked at her mother blankly.

Her father came trudging down the stairs. He took the brass poker in his hands and stirred the ashes in the fireplace. He cursed and lighted the fire again. "Don't you have any sense, girl? You don't sit here on a cold March morning without the fireplace lighted! Or is your brain in a deep freeze over this British lord of yours?" he looked down at the voluminous pages of Edward's letter that Dora had allowed to fall to the floor at her feet.

Her parents both stared at her, expecting some sort of reaction. They got none. Dora spooked Viola, who paled as she knelt beside her young mistress. She picked up all the pages and tried to arrange them in some sort of order.

"I'll put Mr. Edward's letter on the table for you while I fix breakfast," Viola assured her. She backed out of the room without taking her eyes off Dora for one second. The cleaning lady practically tripped over the door jamb heading into the kitchen.

"Winthrop, I don't like the way Dora's acting. It's not like her. Usually she chatters away about these letters, or she fumes, or breaks into tears. I – I don't remember her just sitting there staring into space."

Her father had retrieved his newspaper from the doorstep. Viola had been too distracted to place it on the table for him. He was already annoyed as he glanced toward his daughter. "Women!" he spat and headed into the dining room for his morning coffee.

Mrs. Benley hesitated in the living room watching her daughter for a few more moments. "Dora, won't you speak to me?" she pleaded. Then she scurried into the kitchen. "Viola, we'd better call Mr. Byrne. Only he knows how to deal with Dora when she gets like this."

The aroma of sausage and freshly scrambled eggs with butter assaulted Dora's nostrils. It wrapped itself subtly around her. She ignored them like alien substances that had nothing to do with her. She rose from her chair. She made no attempt to fetch Edward's letter from the dining room table. She glided across the floor like a sleepwalker, staring straight ahead as she ascended the stairs.

"Viola, where has Dora gone?" her mother scurried back into the living room. She ran into the foyer in time to see her daughter disappearing into the upstairs hallway. She gaped after her, not knowing what to do.

Dora shut the bedroom door behind her. She slumped down on her bed and sat there looking through her window, whose curtains had never been drawn last night because she'd never slept here. Soon she didn't see the window. She didn't even see her bedroom. Instead she saw a fair-complexioned man with blond hair, blue eyes, and an intense stare approaching her. He looked vibrantly alive, almost radiant, as if his skin itself were glittering. He was wearing the white silken robes of the Sharif of Mecca with a belt and a Bedouin's headdress. A sword was fastened to the belt. He held a rifle. He was pointing it at her ready to shoot. He vanished. She kept on staring ahead just the same. It didn't matter if she saw him or not. He was always there like some ghostly presence.

Br-r-r-r-r-ring!

She glanced at the phone and let it ring. Then it was silent once more.

Br-r-r-r-r-ring!

It started up again, then was silent.

Soon it was afternoon. It was too late to go to bed. She went out to the garden where yesterday's snow was melting in an early spring thaw. She strolled around the walkways deep in thought. She didn't eat dinner with anyone else, even though Michael came over. She avoided his company. Her mother, father, and Mr. Byrne peered out the window at her, no doubt discussing her and her actions.

Edward had a picture of her in Mr. Byrne's suit that he'd taken in Queenstown the day after the *Lusitania* sank. She had no photo of him. After all these months – no, years! – it was hard to remember what he looked like exactly. She recalled the redhead and the orange freckles, the pale complexion. Other than that, it was impossible to be sure of his eye color. Sometimes she imagined Edward with blue eyes, sometimes gray, at other times green. Sometimes he had a pug nose, at other times an aquiline one. And the shape of his chin . . . well, that was a total mystery. All she had was a "Crusader's ring" to remind her of her fiance. Yet somehow the bond that joined them was forged with iron and steel. He had his teeth in her and wouldn't let go.

Dora remembered the bare rooted tea rosebushes that she'd bought the other day. They were soaking in pails of standing water in the garage, taking up water in their roots before getting planted. It was late and getting dark out. Michael had gone home reluctantly after attempting to talk to her with no success. Her parents were upstairs in the anteroom to their bedroom reading. She decided to start planting the roses. Usually that was Frank's job. But what did it matter?

Dora had never been fond of yard work until recently. Since being confined to her house and grounds, there was little else to do. It was a short stroll up the gravel drive to the shed above the garden. In the distance she noticed the night guard. Once he'd paced off in the other direction, she opened the door and reached for the spade.

She couldn't quite put her hand on it. So she flicked

on the overhead light. On the far side of the shed sat a man slouched against the wall next to the bags of soil and manure. She recognized his face in an instant, though she hadn't glimpsed it in many months.

CHAPTER 55

A li's feverish eyes focused on Dora's. With one hand he grasped his other arm, which was tied up with a strip of cloth. He'd been wounded.

"What – what are you doing here?" Dora backed away so quickly that she ran into the wall of the shed. A watering can and garden tools fell to the floor with a clatter.

"You win – for now," he glared at her with hatred in his eyes.

"Win? What do you mean win?"

"You and your friends have stolen the Holy of Holies," he said. "And you've gotten away with it."

Dora remembered Edward's letter. Otherwise she wouldn't have understood what Ali was talking about.

"No one meant to steal it," she persuaded him. "When that humidor arrived in the mail at Bryn Mawr, I was in a rush to get to the train station. I didn't open up the package. It was supposed to be a gift for my father's birthday. I didn't know what it was. I only knew that you were eyeballing me in the crowd on the Cunard Pier."

"Your Colonel Lawrence stole it on purpose," Ali eyed her still.

Dora didn't know how to defend the Colonel. "Lawrence's motives are his own. He won't share them with anybody, not even Edward despite all his loyalty."

"Then you must all suffer equally – his friends and family alike. That is the law and the way of the Prophet."

Dora stomped her foot. "Edward was tricked. His father and Leonard Woolley sent him to Lawrence with the humidor you're seeking, the real one," the truth spilled out of her as she tried to appeal to Ali, "because they couldn't handle the humidor and whatever it represented anymore. I overheard Sir Adolphus and Woolley agonizing about it one night at Ware House. They said it was Lawrence's idea to begin with. They wanted to get rid of it and give it back to him."

"Make Lawrence give it back to me then!" Ali tried to move forward, but the pain in his arm prevented him. He clutched it and winced.

"I – I can't make Lawrence do anything," Dora wanted to weep, "and neither can Edward. Edward has tried. He's written me about it. Lawrence won't listen. The Colonel's hell bent on playing his game of cat and mouse with you Arabs to the last."

"You will die!" he hissed. "So will Sir Adolphus! So will Leonard Woolley! And so will Edward and Colonel Lawrence himself," he vowed. "No one can profane the Prophet and get away with it." His eyes were dilated, making her wonder how long he'd been holed up in the shed.

"Wait here!" She raced back to the house. She grabbed Edward's last letter. She also stopped in the kitchen to get a drink of water for Ali as well as grab some tapioca pudding that Viola had made and forgotten to put away. She hurried back to the shed to find Ali still slumped in the same position.

She knelt next to him. She held his head and let him sip the water. She fed him tapioca with her own hand.

"Won't you please show me mercy," she begged with tears in her eyes. "I'll call an ambulance. I'll have them take you to the hospital. I'll even pay for it. I won't tell anyone who you are. Please look at this letter!" she thrust it in front of Ali's eyes. "Edward explains everything here. You can read it for yourself. He says that he was surprised to find Mohamed and Osama in King Abdullah's tomb. He fell into the tomb only because he was chased there. Please call off your killers. Please spare my Edward if you will do nothing else. You *are* Prince Ali, aren't you?"

He looked at her and nodded.

"Then will you please do as I ask?"

"It's too late even if I wanted to," he sighed. "Mohamed and Osama have instructions from me and my father to kill Edward and Lawrence on sight and at the first opportunity. I could not take those orders back without bringing disgrace upon my name and my whole line."

"Then I could speak to your father? What's his name?"

"My father is Ib'n Saud, the rightful Shereef of Mecca. Hussein parades around with my father's title," he scoffed.

That name struck a stab of fear in her. She dropped the pages of the letter. They fell to the floor of the shed. She remembered from Edward's letter that Ib'n Saud was the iconoclast who loved to destroy all buildings and monuments, the one Lawrence said was uncivilized. Dora despaired of being able to reason with someone like that.

"Besides," Ali managed to summon a laugh, "it's not just me, it's my younger brothers – and they are legion. We're all sworn to avenge the honor of our good name and the mandates of the Prophet Muhammad. Either that or we will die trying to do so. And we are sworn to do this for the next five generations."

"Five generations?" she scrambled to her feet. "Why?"

"Even if we get back the Holy of Holies, you must all be punished. We must set an example so other heathens will never again offend against us."

"I've never heard anything so horrible."

"Such is the law of the desert. Such is the *jihad,* the holy war everlasting. It is indiscriminate who it will kill. Even my sister Asalah died because of it – *at my hand."*

If he could murder his own sister over some Holy of Holies, it was hopeless. He would never listen to her. He would never have pity on anyone.

"Such is the whirlwind that this Lawrence of yours has unleashed!"

Dora turned to leave, but didn't make it farther than the door to the shed. She heard a noise in the distance getting closer. To her astonishment her driveway was being invaded by a group of nameless men in white, loosely fitting robes with pointed white hats and masks. They were carrying what looked like white crosses in one hand and flaming torches in the other. A big, burly man carried an even larger cross, which he planted standing up in the soft earth of the driveway. Another set it aflame.

"Who are you? What are you doing?" Dora ran to meet them, noticing that her father's guard was slumped against a tree.

One shouted, "We caught a dark-skinned thief hanging around here the other night. He was stealing food from the garden. We shot him, but he got away."

The cross was flaming high. She backed away. Now she understood what was happening. These were the men who'd shot Ali. "No – no one is here," she lied.

Ali attempted to flee out the door.

"There he is!" shouted one of the leaders. A hooded man took out his rifle. He aimed and fired. *"Allah Akbar!"* Ali cried. *"Allah Akbar!"* He slumped to the ground. His eyes were staring up at the sky, at nothing. He was dead.

Dora screamed and burst into tears. She stood for she didn't know how long weeping.

"Dora, what on earth are you doing outside at this hour?" her father in his night robe and slippers made his way up the driveway. Her mother was peering down from her bedroom window. Her light was on. She was holding the telephone.

Dora ran to her father. He caught her in his arms. "Look!" she pointed down at Ali's body. "There he is. He's the man who's been chasing me ever since the *Lusitania.*"

The men in white robes had fled. They'd left only their burning white cross at the head of the driveway illuminating the scene.

"What the hell . . . " her father looked up at the cross. "What was the Ku Klux Klan doing here?"

"The *what?*" Dora was confused. She hadn't been keeping up with local events. She'd been too preoccupied with Edward.

"Never mind!" he knelt down next to the lifeless body of Ali. "So this is the man who tried to kill you on the streetcar?"

She nodded. She could see her mother dialing the police from her bedroom window. Mr. Byrne arrived before anybody else. He lived down the gravel drive two houses away. Michael hadn't bothered to get dressed. He was making his way in his slippers and robe. He gagged when he saw the flaming cross. He sidestepped his way around it and flew to Dora's side.

"What's happened here?" he slipped his arm around Dora's waist.

"Ali's dead!"

Michael Byrne stooped down to get a better view. "Well, so he is!"

"Is this the man you saw on the *Lusitania?*" her father asked.

Michael nodded, "Yes, the one who stabbed me when I discovered him with the fuses down in the engine room on May 2, 1915. He's been my nemesis and Dora's ever since. I can hardly believe it. But what's that thing doing there?" he turned toward the flaming cross. Its dark, flickering shadows reflected on his face.

"The Ku Klux Klan shot Ali," Dora explained. "He was hiding in our shed. I came out to get a shovel to plant the roses. I couldn't sleep after Edward's letter, and I discovered him there. He was already wounded in the arm and delirious. What he said didn't make a lot of sense. Then the Klan showed up again and shot Ali dead."

Just then a Bethel Borough police car drove up.

"There's been a murder," her father approached the officer. "A Klan killing."

"Where's the victim?" the officer asked.

Her father pointed at the ground while Mr. Byrne led Dora back to the house where her mother was waiting at the door.

Dora heard the officer say, "Don't these foreigners know to keep out? They've caused enough trouble. My cousin just got killed in France. Imagine that! He couldn't find the battlefield on a map. Now his bones are part of a giant mass grave."

Viola and Frank, who lived behind the Benleys' house, had heard the commotion. They hiked over in their nightclothes to prepare lots of hot coffee with cream and sugar. Mr. Byrne sat up with Dora the rest of the night until she finally fell asleep in his arms from pure exhaustion.

CHAPTER 56

When Dora woke up the next morning, the first thing she did was write a letter to Edward:

My dearest darling:

The Ku Klux Klan killed Ali in my driveway last night. Before he died, I talked to him in the shed at some length. Ali claimed that he was going to come after me, you, and Colonel Lawrence – all of us! – for five generations. He said his brothers and his whole family were sworn to do this. He admitted that he was Prince Ali. Mohamed and Osama work for him. He said his father was Ib'n Saud, the iconoclast.

I pleaded with you before to come home. Now I'm telling you to desert. Leave Lawrence's camp at night. Go to the first British settlement and tell them your story. They must believe you. It's up to your Colonel Lawrence if he wants to be chased around by a band of cutthroats and murderers. I don't want you to be part of that company.

I am packing my bags today. You may think I'm mad. I probably am by now. I have no idea how I'm going to find you. Your Arab friends don't sound too friendly to American women. I'm sure that British military regulations prohibit civilian women in the battle zones.

When I get to the nearest friendly city I can find, I will write to you. Maybe you can come to me.

I hope I will find you before this letter does.
 Dora

Dora took the letter to the post office herself. If there were no war, she would be married by now. She would almost certainly have children. She would have gotten on with her life. Now everything was stalled. The whole world was listening to distant gunfire. She had read that the shops in London shook when canons fired in France. She imagined she could hear Arabian guns on this side of the Atlantic, too.

Dora spent the rest of the day packing her satchel. She threw in everything she had. Her mother entered the room. "What on earth are you trying to do, Dora?"

She bit her lip. "I'm sailing to Europe. I want to find Edward."

"How could you have forgotten the *Lusitania?*" her mother gaped at her.

"The *Lusitania?* Yes, yes! I remember," Dora said mechanically, grabbing for a girdle.

Her mother took her by the shoulders and turned her around to face her. Her forehead was more lined than Dora remembered. "You say you remember the *Lusitania.* We were on it, honey. We almost lost our lives. That's the main reason we've gone to war."

"Edward's more important than any ship." Dora was so absorbed in her own thoughts she went on pulling slips and corsets out of her highboy and afternoon dresses out of her closet.

"Winthrop!" her mother pounded out of the room, her high-heeled shoes clomping along the wooden floor. "Come here and talk some sense into your daughter. She's going to Arabia to find Edward."

Dora had to steel herself. She'd figured getting out of the house might be harder than sailing the Atlantic. She was almost twenty-four. She had the right to go where she wanted. They couldn't stop her.

She heard her father's footsteps pounding up the stairs to the second floor of the house followed by her mother's lighter steps. She could count the footsteps approaching her room down the hallway. She knew that it would take fifteen. She remembered from when she was a little girl.

A shadow fell on her. "I absolutely forbid it!" her father stated flatly as if she were one of his employees and not his daughter. "I would never sail across the Atlantic again even after this interminable war ends. I wouldn't trust one of those

Huns not to have a grudge against the United States. All it takes is one submarine commander with one stray torpedo. Hundreds of people will be dead floating in the water. From now on if business calls me to Europe, I'll send a subordinate."

"That's you, Dad. I'm different," Dora managed to get out.

"You're still my daughter. The chances that Lord Edward will come back safe and sound from this war, I would judge to be about ninety-five to five against."

She gasped at his cold-blooded statistics.

"Then you'll have to marry some nice, red-blooded American with a sense of responsibility like Michael. Soon there won't be any other young men left. Europe's bleeding itself white. The population will decline by half."

"That's why I've got to go, Dad. I don't want Edward to be just another casualty."

"If his number's up, his number's up," her father stated matter-of-factly.

Her parents wouldn't understand. She could see that now. Her attempts to confide in them were worse than useless. Winthrop and Etta May Benley were from a different century, the nineteenth. This was the twentieth, the new century. Things were different now. They were all mixed up.

"Edward's breeding won't let him get out of there before it's too late," Dora pressed down the clothes in her traveling trunk decisively. "I want to find him and talk some sense into him. I can't do it from six thousand miles away."

"Haven't you heard that American women aren't welcome in Arab countries?"

She nodded. "Yes, I know. I may have to . . . " She caught herself. She was about to blurt out "disguise myself in native dress". But that would outrage her parents even more. Her father in particular would be irate about her running around in an *abaya* with only her eyes showing. Her mother might think it was irreligious.

"You may have to *what?*" her father growled.

"I may have to . . . well . . . take up residence in Italy

and communicate with Edward from there," she stated what she thought might be minimally acceptable to her father. "I may have to hire a messenger to take letters back and forth to him."

"You'll do what!" he exploded. "Italy's at war, especially northern Italy up in the mountains. There are all sorts of troops stationed there. Do you think you can waltz through in your Easter bonnet and your new frock?"

"Dad, really!"Dora said. "I don't intend to go anywhere near the fighting. Besides, civilians aren't involved."

"Civilians aren't involved, and you're a survivor of the *Lusitania!* I'm ashamed of you," he tapped his foot. "My daughter ought to have more common sense."

Her mother nodded in agreement.

"If that young man you're engaged to had any brains he'd come over here. He'd have my blessing then."

"But, Dad, Edward's from an old English family. You know that."

"Not many old English families left. They killed each other off in this damned infernal war," he growled. "One duke gets assassinated over here. This country has to have revenge on that one. That country declares war. Somebody else has a treaty to defend them. Some other country has a treaty to defend his opponent." He shook his head. "They lose five hundred thousand men here and another five hundred thousand over there. Pretty soon no one will be left – only us to do the clean up work." He cursed under his breath.

"England has an empire. Edward thinks it's his duty to defend it. He was raised on that kind of thinking."

"Damn the empire! If I had a son, and I don't, I wouldn't sacrifice him in the name of any damned British Empire. I certainly don't intend to sacrifice my daughter to it."

"I agree with you one hundred per cent, Dad. I don't want to sacrifice my future husband to the British Empire either."

"So you're not going to give up this lunacy?"

"I can't keep my sanity if I stay here and read Edward's

letters."

"Then we'll burn his letters. I've been wanting to do that for a long time."

"Sorry, Dad," she turned back to her traveling trunk.

Her mother burst into tears anew. "Come on, Etta May," Winthrop said. "Let's leave Dora alone."

Winthrop stomped out of the room in the same manner that he strode around the house – like the king of the manor. He slammed the door behind him. She heard him lock it.

CHAPTER 57

Viola brought a luncheon tray up to her room. "Sorry, Dora, it's your father's orders," Viola arranged the big meal of the day on top of her writing desk. She laid out the china and silver ware. She'd brought a white linen tablecloth that her mother always insisted upon complete with a matching napkin. She poured water with ice cubes from a cut glass pitcher.

"That's all right, Viola," Dora tried to keep her composure. She was biding her time, waiting for the right moment. She had her bag packed and hidden underneath the bed.

"Make sure you eat the cookies. You're mother sent them. She'll be offended if you don't gobble them up."

Dora smiled.

"Sorry, but Mr. Benley told me I had to lock the door. I'm sure you'll understand," Viola turned the key in the lock as she left the room.

Dora hurriedly ate a few things. She wasn't very hungry. Then she went back to packing Edward's letters to take with her in her handbag.

"Do you want to go with us downtown to the Duquesne Club?" her mother knocked.

"No, I'd rather stay here by myself."

"Viola's going to stay on late until we get back," her father barked at her. "Remember, I don't want any shenanigans."

She listened for their footsteps going down the stairs and out the front door. She went to her window and watched them on the driveway. Winthrop climbed into the driver's seat of the Model T Ford. Her mother got into the passenger side. Mrs. Benley looked up at Dora's bedroom. Dora waved down at her. Her mother waved back. Her father didn't cast her a glance, which made her feel a pang. She kept the smile plastered to her face until they'd rounded the bend and were gone up the drive that led out to the main road.

She looked at her clock. She forced herself to wait ten

minutes to make sure that her parents weren't coming back to fetch something they'd left behind. She sat down at her desk and got out a pen. Quickly she scribbled a note:

Dear Mom and Dad:

Sorry you don't approve of my expedition to find Edward. I hope you'll understand that I had to go anyway. I will contact you by cable as soon as I reach Europe.

Yours truly,
Dora

P.S. Don't blame Viola. She didn't have any part in my escape. And tell Michael I couldn't help it. He'll understand.

With that she turned on the water in the bathroom full force to make noise so Viola wouldn't hear her. She tied a bed sheet to her bedpost and pushed her bed against the window. She threaded the sheet over the windowsill and let it hang down. She made sure it would support her weight. She pushed her travel bag out the window first. It landed on a patch of thick green myrtle vines that cushioned its fall. Next she let her handbag drop. She'd put on the most comfortable pair of shoes she owned. She climbed slowly and quietly out the window. There was about eight feet to jump, the same as between the listing deck of the *Lusitania* and the water line with its waiting lifeboat. She jumped down holding onto the sheet. She found herself dangling in the air kicking her legs. She let herself drop the rest of the way.

She picked up her satchel and carried it up to the work shed behind the house, the same place where she'd last seen Ali. Her bag was heavy, but she didn't dare let it drag on the ground.

"Dora, what am I going to tell your parents!" Viola emerged from the back door of the house as Dora climbed into her father's spare car. The big Italian lady in the dark blue dress was wringing her hands.

"Go back inside, Viola, and pretend you didn't see me leave. I wrote a note. I explained you didn't know anything about it."

Viola nodded, worried.

"Turn off the water in my bathroom. You know how my father always yells at us for leaving it on. For God's sake, take the sheet down," she pointed to the sheet hanging from her windowsill.

Viola followed the direction she was pointing. Her eyes widened in horror as she realized that Dora had let herself down that way. She looked from the sheet to Dora and back again, scandalized.

Dora started the motor. She knew Viola well enough to be certain she would go directly inside and agonize for a few moments. Then she would pick up the telephone and call her parents at the club. Dora had to be well away from here before that happened.

Dora hadn't had much time to plan her trip. She'd only decided to leave earlier that day. Most of her time had been occupied arguing with her mother and father. The rest had been spent packing her satchel and plotting her escape from the house. She had some money with her. She had Edward's letters. She had her passport. But she'd have to visit the bank before she left. That would slow her down.

She parked the car near a trolley stop. She was headed to downtown Pittsburgh to catch the train, the first leg of a long, long journey. She would stop at Mellon Bank where her family did business to get a few drafts that she could cash in Europe.

No sooner had she parked than a mail truck drove up behind her. "Hey, Miss Benley, I've got another one of those letters from your English lord," Chuck came right up to her car door. "Been searching all over for you. You weren't back at the house the way you usually are."

"Th – thank you," she stuttered. This was the one thing she hadn't planned for.

"At least I think it's from him," the mailman handed it to her. "It's from the British War Office like usual. But the handwriting on the address isn't the same."

Dora looked at the mailman blankly, then glanced down at the envelope. Edward always addressed his letters to her in a cursive that looked very elegant and was full of loops. She'd read so many of his letters she'd grown used to it. This handwriting she'd never seen before. It looked odd, eccentric, hard to describe.

She didn't want to open it in front of the mailman. "Here, Chuck," she handed him a tip. "Thanks! It looks like a long one."

"Bed time reading!" Chuck waved as he leaped back into his truck.

She crossed the parking lot. What if the worst had happened and it was already too late? What if someone else had written informing her that Edward had been killed? She reached out to grip the railing as she seated herself on a bench to wait for one of the new "yellow trolleys". They were painted orange but had started to fade to yellow despite being introduced only a couple of years before in 1915.

Should she read the letter now? Or should she wait until she boarded the trolley and walked down the sloping floor to take one of the rattan seats near an open window with a shaded light bulb perfect for reading? Dora couldn't stand it. She tore open the envelope.

Edward's handwriting leaped out at her just as if he hadn't ever written her that letter breaking off their engagement. She soon forgot her doubts as she was drawn into his narrative. She missed her trolley as it lumbered past unheard and unseen.

CHAPTER 58

D earest Dora:
      Lawrence called me to him one morning. "Lieutenant, we need more soldiers."

"What!" I countered. "You always claim you like to lead small forces. They're more agile and swift. You can hit and run quickly."

He waved away my objections. "That's when we're doing the attacking. In Petra we will be defending our position. The more soldiers the better."

"What do you suggest?"

"Go recruit some Arab youths. I've turned some young men away over the past months just because I thought they were too young. Now we need them."

Next morning Petra was swarming with adolescent boys. Lawrence took each of them aside and taught them how to play messenger. He wanted them to ferry notes back and forth from where he planned to be on the North Ridge to each of his units stationed at a different position in or near the ancient city.

Still Lawrence wasn't satisfied. "We still don't have enough soldiers. We need live bodies to man the approach to the city, you know, the one through the narrow gorge. Get the women."

I stood there gaping at him, *"Sir?"*

"The Arab women."

Was he joking? I'd been fighting in the Arabian Desert for many months. I had yet to encounter a woman in uniform. "Colonel, the Arab women are the last on earth I could imagine as Amazons."

"The women are fierce. Sometimes the men abandon certain prisoners to the women to make sure they are tortured thoroughly before they die."

I informed the soldiers with some diffidence that Lawrence demanded they recruit their wives and mothers as soldiers. Much to my amazement, they came back in no time with a battalion of barefoot women wearing long blue cotton robes, gold bracelets, and rings in their ears and noses. Under the leadership of Sheik Khalil's wife, they practiced climbing the rocks that overlooked the gorge. Lawrence gave them guns, and they didn't shy away from those either.

Later that night, while the torches burned in the ancient altars and men gathered around campfires to boast what they would do to the Turks, the women sewed, wove, and made butter with churns. As the women worked, they sang. There was a strange noise, like a cry in the night. It was taken up here and there and repeated again and again.

"What on earth is that?" I asked. "It sounds like a jackal howling, but it isn't. It hardly sounds human."

Lawrence smiled. "Didn't I warn you that Arab men hand over their prisoners to be tortured?"

"That's the women?" I could feel the hair standing up on my head.

"They're *ululating*. It's a special word just to describe the incredible sound they make. They do that before battles when they fear great calamities." He showed me what they did with their tongues, lips, and vocal cords. He couldn't make quite the same eerie sound. He wasn't female. And he was only one man.

I was to manage the sheik's wife and all the ladies who'd decided to respond to Lawrence's call for troops. I was also to be in charge of sending boys with reports about the advance of the enemy to Lawrence on the North Ridge as well as to sub-commanders in all the other positions around town and out of it.

I sent one of the boys at my disposal to report to me if he could find anyone who shouldn't be in our encampment or whose name he didn't know. I gave him a piaster for his trouble.

As I waited, the night grew very quiet and still despite the incessant chatter of women only several yards away. The women blended into the nearly constant hooting sound of the desert owls and squawks of the birds of prey, who waited longingly for their next corpse.

I sent a second boy after the first and bade him hurry up. As I continued to wait – I couldn't move out of this position near the Siq – my eyes blinked shut. I fought to keep them open. They shut again and again. It had been before midnight when I'd sent the second messenger. Now it must be near dawn. Not only had Venus disappeared from the sky, the waning moon was setting.

The women had fallen silent. That was a sure sign it must be almost dawn on this morning of October 21, 1917. I tried to make out the time on my new watch, which I'd picked up from a bazaar. There wasn't sufficient illumination.

Just the first purple rays of dawn appeared, I could hear a distinct buzz. It grew louder. It made me reach instinctively for my binoculars and train them up into the sky.

Out here in the desert I could be one of Richard the Lion-Hearted's knights ready to fight Saladin in the Third Crusade. Or I could be back in ancient times riding as one of the legionaries in the army of the Roman Emperor. Only our guns themselves anchored us at least in the fourteenth century. Very little, except a can of food from the British provisions office, anchored us in the early twentieth. For many weeks in a row we lived off the land and went without modern conveniences – even so much as a fork.

Now I saw an airplane and a German one at that bearing the insignia of Kaiser Wilhelm. It was flying low over Petra. I threw a rock against a stone column. A boy immediately leaped into my presence, rubbing his eyes as he also had been asleep.

"Go at once. Tell Lawrence that the Germans are attacking by air," I slipped a piaster into his hand.

He darted off faster than I could speak, climbing rocks with the agility of a mountain goat and slipping through rock carved tunnels with the swiftness of a jackal.

I waited several minutes, never taking my eyes off that airplane. It appeared overhead and then disappeared into the gloom. It never strayed so far that I lost track of the low buzz and hum in the still, early morning air. The plane, when it reappeared, was lower in the sky. It looked like an Albatros, a new German model introduced in 1917. It had a double wingspan, one wing lower than the cockpit and one above it doubling as a kind of roof. The plane was painted bright red with black Iron Crosses outlined in white on the wings. The propeller in front was going around and around. It looked very much like one of the planes piloted by the infamous Red Baron, Manfred von Richthofen, on the Western Front. The pilot was wearing the requisite dark flying suit, head gear, and goggles. No doubt he was waiting until he could see us as well as I could see him.

I threw another rock against the same pillar. Another young boy sprang up seemingly out of nowhere. "Go wake the women," I directed him. "Tell them to take cover under the rocks in the pre-arranged place. Remind them to bring their guns and ammunition."

As the sky gradually grew brighter, the plane flew lower, dropping an illuminating torch to better see what was on the ground. I thought about taking cover myself. The plane could strafe us at any moment. Being in the desert, there wasn't lots of natural cover.

We were next to the King Solomon Mountains. These were "sky islands", tall, pointy, sculpturesque ridges of rock that rose straight up from the desert floor at a much lower elevation, making them seem all the taller. Right now the sun was trapped to the east right behind one of these enormous ridges. That's why only a small amount of light was able to escape from behind the mountain. The sky was getting lighter by the most infinitesimal, gradual degrees. As soon as the sun rose high enough, which could be any minute now (if I could only catch a glimpse of my watch), then it would burst out all at once. It would go from being dim to practically blinding you with its sudden brightness. I'd spent enough time in this treacherous desert to figure this out. Naturally that would be when the plane would attack.

I gathered up my few belongings and crawled along the

ground, keeping to the darkest shadows. I paused whenever I could, for the only things that moved in a desert besides those tumbleweeds propelled by the wind were living beings. That was what the German pilot was patiently looking for.

Crawling on my belly, I found the ladies. The women were squabbling. One wanted this place on the rock. Another wanted that. Their babies squalled, too. The Turks would capture me amidst an army of wrangling women. They looked ready to fire their guns at each other to judge by the tones of their shrill voices, the way they screamed and wept, and the way they flung their arms about. Still I had no choice but to stay with them near the rocky caves and tunnels.

The dawn broke almost at once. I heard Lawrence's gun go off five miles away right outside the town of Petra. Where I was now positioned I had a pretty good view. Lawrence had only two mountain guns and two machine guns. One of the machine guns exploded into action, shooting fire toward the sky. It just missed the plane.

The plane banked sharply and came back again, dropping a bomb not far from Lawrence's position. It hit one of Arab machine guns dead on. The men manning it vanished in an instant. When the smoke cleared, nothing remained except charred rubble.

The plane dropped bomb after bomb. I could hear them landing much closer to me. I climbed out of a deep crevice in the rock long enough to peek up over the ridgetop. A bomb hit a temple. Several columns toppled. A cloud of dust rose into the sky. The Turks and Germans thought we were all stationed in the hills outside Petra. That's where the aircraft kept on returning. That's where the battle raged.

About six hours later all the Colonel's guns went silent.

CHAPTER 59

A trolley was stopping next to Dora. The front door opened. The driver looked at her. She could wait for the next one. She waved the man on and continued reading:

Had Lawrence been hit? About half an hour later I saw his men retreating back to Petra by twos and threes, in as small groups as possible while keeping to the hills, ravines, and desert dune grass cover. They surfaced about where I was hiding with the women.

"What's happened?" I confronted the first group.

"Sh-h-h-h-h!" they kept on crawling along.

"Where is *El Orens?*" I asked the next group of what looked like stragglers.

They turned and pointed, then continued crawling along on their hands and knees as if this were great sport.

The next bunch didn't understand English. My Arabic was poor, and in such a tight situation I forgot the few words I knew. I kept on making hand signals at them, pointing backward, and saying again and again with a question in my voice, *"El Orens? El Orens? El Orens?"*

One of the Bedouins merely waved, then burst into speech when a woman ran up to him. She hugged him. A baby crawled into his arms. They all kissed each other.

Perhaps Lawrence hadn't been able to recover from the direct hit on one of his best gun positions. After all, his specialty was hit and run guerrilla warfare, especially blowing up railroad tracks. Defending a citadel was hardly his kind of thing.

This retreat kept going on for the better part of an hour. Soon it seemed that Lawrence's whole army was here, falling back to what they thought was the protection of the high rock walls of the ancient city of Petra.

I heard a horrific sound. It was the tramp of boots. Lawrence's men wore boots, but they didn't march in formation.

I could tell these boots were doing just that, with practiced discipline. I crept forward to see if I could discern anything from the next boulder.

Not only did I hear the tramp of boots marching in formation. I heard shouts that sounded like orders in a very harsh, nasty voice, amplified by a horn. When I listened closely I realized they were speaking German. It was a tongue with which I was familiar from my Oxford days. My father spoke it fluently from tromping around as an amateur archaeologist.

I shouldn't be so surprised that the Germans were marching on Petra. After all, a German airplane had been dropping bombs. The Germans were the chief allies of the Turks. That would make it all the more difficult to fight them. The Turks might be supplied by the Germans. But the Germans were almost as well-equipped as the British.

Turkish voices mingled with the Germans. Where was Lawrence? Was I left to fight the Battle of Petra all alone and unaided? I was the only other Englishman present. The Arabs would expect me to act as second in command as I'd done when Lawrence had been kidnapped by the Turks.

I motioned to the Bedouins to move behind the rocks with their guns. A few waved back at me. Others picked up their belongings and did as I said, though very reluctantly. Most seemed to be occupied in climbing to the highest rocks to catch a view of the advancing troops.

"Don't you realize the Turks and Germans are coming?" I advanced upon a group of Bedouins lazying around on the ground and drinking coffee. Their rifles lay beside them instead of clutched tensely in their hands the way I would expect. One poured a cup of hot coffee and handed it to me. The steam lazily wafted upward toward the sky. The man said something I couldn't understand.

"Did *El Orens* give you any orders?" I pressed.

They smiled at me and kept on chatting. One threw his head back and laughed at what sounded like a joke from his friend.

"*Orders?*" I repeated. "Do you have orders?"

One nodded and laughed. I didn't know if he was answering my question or chatting with his comrade. I wasn't sure if he understood what I was saying.

I hastened over to where the women were congregated. To my shock, some of them were busy changing diapers, or at least what passed for diapers among the Bedouins. Others were chatting while boiling something over a fire. Steam curled upward past our hiding place out into the open.

"Put out that fire!" I ordered, rushing up to the women.

They looked at me blankly.

I tried to stomp out the flames with my boots. I picked up a nearby pail of water and hurled it at the conflagration. That created even more smoke. I coughed, trying to disperse it by waving my hands and arms about. Finally I accomplished my aim. The fire was now only smoldering.

All the women were still gaping at me as if they didn't understand. A few shook their heads and whispered to their friends.

"You can't light a cooking fire when the enemy is almost upon us. Do you want to let them know exactly where you are so they can come and get you? I'm sure you've seen how the Turks treat Bedouin women." I winced to remember the corpses I'd seen lying along the roads of various desert towns where we had come too late to save them.

The sounds of the advancing Germans and Turks were by now so loud it seemed like they were marching practically right beneath us into Petra. I took as many rounds of ammunition with me as I could carry. Climbing up through a rocky shaft, I reached a perch right above the tunnel that formed a narrow entrance into Petra. I was so well-concealed that, while I could see everyone below me, none could see me. Even if I leaned over the top of the rocky perch to get better aim or a better view, I would remain well hidden in the shadows.

It wasn't just a regiment or two. It looked like the whole Turkish Army along with more Germans than I could count all advancing into Petra. One German enlisted man joked to another, "Lawrence of Arabia is finally beaten. I'm going to get a photo of him surrendering to us on my new camera. My mother sent it to me for my birthday in one of her packages from home."

The soldier then proceeded to hold up his camera and brag. Three of his friends laughed and cheered.

"This camera's a folding Kodak from America. My mother bought it right before the British blockade. I'm one of the last soldiers in Germany to get one," he continued to brag in his cocky fashion.

"Why don't you make this Lawrence of Arabia autograph your photo of him?" another friend called back.

"I'll do that," he promised and held his camera proudly above his head.

"This famous *El Orens,* or whatever the Arabs call him, may be good at sneaking around the desert blowing up railroads. When you engage him in a real battle, he turns tail and runs back into Petra. He's probably hiding in a hole in the ground. We might have to excavate the ruins to find him."

The whole troop guffawed.

"By now he's probably turned into a mummy. We'll have to yank all the bandages off."

Again they all chortled.

There must have been at least a thousand of the enemy troop in the narrow, rocky gorge leading into Petra. The gorge was so narrow the troops started to back up. They had to slow down to nearly a crawl. Then they stopped all together as if waiting in a long line. No doubt they'd been forced to squeeze through the narrowest point in single file, which was not very good military formation.

Suddenly a rocket flew up into the air overhead. It exploded into many colored fragments. The still and silent rocks on every side of me exploded into gunfire. I had thought all the Bedouins were lying around smoking and chatting with the women. I'd no idea that others with guns had concealed themselves around me. The gunfire rained down upon the heads of the Germans and Turks.

The enemy at first didn't know what was happening.

They looked up and saw nothing but rocks.

The women around me pushed boulders down through the crevices between the rocks. Others emptied slops pans or kettles of hot oil on top of the enemy soldiers. The ladies shrieked and ululated like banshees to make it all the more horrifying. They alone could be heard above the guns.

The enemy troops below scattered. Bedouins were throwing bombs from above and from the left and right. Arabs had descended down to the level of the road to stop up all the exits from the tunnel itself.

After the massacre had gone on for who knew how long, as the sun declined behind the mountains, a second rocket burst into flames in the sky. Lawrence himself rose up from behind a rock not too far away – the first I had seen of him since yesterday – and called, "Rise! Sons of the Prophet!"

With a deafening cheer, the Bedouins sprang up from behind the rocks and boulders all around me. They leaped up and down in place, throwing rocks up into the air. Then they tossed their guns. A few of the young men picked up women and threw them back and forth while the ladies chortled. Others held up babies and infants in one hand and rifles in the other.

"Pursue! Bring me prisoners!" Lawrence commanded in Arabic.

The men leaped down from the rocks. Kissing the women and children, they mounted their camels and galloped down the dusty road away from Petra. They chased the few German and Turkish soldiers who had managed to escape the trap that Lawrence had obviously set for them.

"Go all the way to the nearest towns and cities!" Lawrence urged them. "Don't come back without your weight in booty!"

I raced up to Lawrence. "Why didn't you tell me what was going on?" I asked. "I sent messengers, but I never received any answers."

He shrugged. "We didn't want our strategy to leak out. The boys could be captured and tortured for information."

"But –"

He clapped his hand down on my shoulder. "Besides, you were to manage the women and those in your sector in case we didn't make it."

"But they were just lounging around. They didn't obey my orders. They acted like they knew about the big surprise all along."

Lawrence chuckled. "You can't beat any Arab for wiliness. They're the trickiest creatures alive. Guess it comes with the territory." He looked about him at the pinkish-red ridges of rock. I guess he was referring to the desert itself.

There was much celebrating late into the night as the men on camels straggled back with both prisoners and plunder. Apparently they'd captured an entire Turkish transport, a field-hospital, and taken hundreds of captives. It was all because of Lawrence's genius for surprise.

As I sit here late at night after the Battle of Petra, as it will no doubt come to be known, I am writing you this overly long letter. Once again the whole camp is lighted with torches where the ruins of the old altars still stand. The men are excitedly chatting around the bonfires as the Bedouin women roast calf and lamb over spits such as the ancients would do. The aroma is floating in on a night breeze. It wafts around my nostrils. I thank a Bedouin woman with a toddler on her hip for bringing me a plate which I am now enjoying as I write to you. I think you will be able to discern the grease stains that my fingers make on the paper.

Now down to business – our business. I have a plan that I concocted out of the depths of despair in which I last wrote you. I no more want to break off our engagement than you do, my love. You haunt my dreams as you do my waking hours. Life without you would be a long death sentence without joy of any kind. So I have confronted my father with my idea in a letter. He agrees with me. He's just sent me the money in pounds sterling – in cash. I have left a note for Osama who still hangs about our camp like a wily snake. I've told him to meet me tonight at the Tomb of King Abdullah of Petra. Perhaps Mohamed will be there, too. Since I can't get Lawrence to budge, I've taken it upon myself to try to bribe the brigands.

I want them to stop pursuing you and me. I want to see if I can settle this issue in a civilized fashion. This will be a better ending to the story of King Abdullah and his Holy of Holies than any other I can think of. Remember, this is a hefty bribe. And they can't get all of it until they show me evidence of having complied with my terms. My father had to mortgage half his estate to manage it. But it will be worth it if it means that we can meet again and at last be married as we had so long ago planned.

Pray for me, my angel! I am doing this for you, Dora, for us – because I love you.

Your husband in all but the law,
Edward

Dear Miss Benley:

Edward disappeared two nights ago from our encampment at Petra. Within hours the boy he paid to mail the letter to you brought it to me. He suspected that Edward was up to something. I'm sure you'll forgive me the liberty I took of perusing what he has written to you for clues about his disappearance. I was appalled to read that he went to the Tomb of King Abdullah to meet with two unprincipled wretches who go by the names of Osama and Mohamed. Naturally we followed Edward right away. But when we arrived, we were too late. Edward was not there. There were no signs of anyone having been there. We have mounted a search of the surrounding countryside in vain. There is no ransom note or news from the caravans of his capture. Perhaps when Osama and Mohamed didn't show up that night, he decided to go somewhere else to meet them. I have gone through channels to contact the thieves themselves. So far there has been only silence.

British officers don't tend to disappear without word in the Arabian desert. I'm sure we'll hear something soon.

Sincerely yours,

Colonel Thomas Edward Lawrence

CHAPTER 60

For endless minutes Dora sat gaping at the letter. When she looked up she realized that the last possible trolley had long since come and gone. She stared down at the empty tracks and saw a vast desert in front of her instead — one that stretched off to the horizon and beyond, one that engulfed everything in it.

Edward was gone . . . He'd vanished . . . She had feared that something like that would happen. That was why she had rushed out of her house. She wanted to snatch him away from all the nasty cloak and dagger stuff in the wasteland he was fighting in. She was too late.

Dora clutched her fist and wished herself back in the past. She would give anything, even years off her life, to make this six months ago. If she'd left Pittsburgh then, she might have prevented this. She glanced at the satchel by her side. She'd been filled with such purpose only an hour ago. She hadn't cared what obstacles she would encounter. Right this minute, in light of this letter, it looked like her plans had turned to dust.

"There she is!"

Dora heard that all too familiar voice, full of hysteria and tears. She saw her mother racing toward her across the parking lot with her handkerchief in one hand. Tears were rolling down her cheeks. Behind her mother came her father. He was tromping along like those Turkish and German soldiers must have been as they entered Petra – full of confidence and purpose. Hanging back near her parents' car stood Viola, still clutching the door. She glanced at Dora, then looked away with guilt in her eyes.

Her mother grabbed Dora in her arms and hugged her, crying and protesting that she was running away from home.

"Dad," she stepped away from her mother, "this letter. You've got to read it. It's Edward. He's disappeared. Colonel Lawrence says –"

"Damn it! I can't always have this fiance of yours destroying our family life. Dora, what nonsense it this? Look how upset you've made your mother."

Edward had written that it was October 21 when he'd woken up to the sound of a German airplane overhead, an airplane that had dropped bombs all around him. Now it was already March, 1918. Anything could have happened during the interval – anything at all. The newspapers got the news faster by telegraph. But they never wrote about Lawrence of Arabia or his troops. Their dispatches were mostly about the Western Front in France. She wondered if they would report if Colonel Lawrence himself had been killed. For all she knew, his whole force could have been annihilated.

"Dad," she attempted to impress her urgency on him, "we've got to do something NOW."

"Viola told us that you let yourself down from your bedroom by a bed sheet. I've never heard of anything more ridiculous in my life. Then she says –"

"Dad," Dora tried to make him understand, "none of that matters now. You've got to get on the phone and –"

"Get back in the car!" He grabbed her handbag, confiscated her car keys, and handed them to Viola. Viola turned them over to Frank. Frank was to drive Dora's car back to the house behind Mr. Benley's Model T.

Dora tried to reason with him from the backseat while he drove home in a silent fury with her mother sitting in the front passenger seat dabbing her eyes and weeping. "Cable the Wares. Sir Adolphus and Lady Ware may have better connections at the British War Office. They could probably get an investigation launched."

"Stop babbling!" her father pounded the steering wheel with his clenched fist. His knuckles had turned white.

"Please promise me that you'll at least send a cable to Edward's parents tonight," she begged.

Every time Dora spoke, her mother cried more loudly. Her father clammed up more.

"And, Dad, you have other business connections in

Britain," Dora gripped the back of her father's seat as she leaned over his shoulder. "You could contact them. They might be willing to hire a detective who –"

"Detective?" her father scoffed. "Do you think this is a grade school romp? This is a world war! Private detectives don't tromp across battlefields to find someone no matter how much you pay them."

They were getting close to home. They turned off Bethel Church Road into the long gravel drive that led up to the main house. Dora had to fight back her tears. "If you won't help me, I'll have to carry on by myself." She stuffed the purse under her arm and grabbed hold of her satchel. She thrust open the back door and started to get out.

"Winthrop, Dora's running away again!" her mother screamed at the top of her lungs.

Arms closed around Dora's waist. "What's happening?" said a familiar voice.

"Oh, Michael," Dora turned in his arms, "you've got to help me." She grabbed hold of his lapels and shook them. "It's Edward. He's vanished."

Her father scowled as he left the driver's seat and trudged around towards the rear of the car. "I found her at the trolley station with this damned letter in her hand." He showed the letter to Michael.

"Mr. and Mrs. Benley, I think I can handle this. You folks go about your business," Michael took Dora by the arm and led her over to his car, which was stopped to one side of the gravel driveway. He put Edward's letter into his lapel pocket.

"We were headed downtown," her father growled.

"Enjoy yourselves. Dora won't run away from me. I promise you."

Mrs. Benley dabbed her eyes with her handkerchief. "We always trust you, Mr. Byrne."

Michael shut the car door behind Dora. He climbed into the driver's seat himself. He started the car, but he just sat there until Mr. Benley's Model T disappeared down the gravel drive. Michael turned his car around in a perfect three-point turn. He headed back out to the main road.

"We're not going back to the main house, are we?" Dora read Michael's mind.

He reached into his suit pocket and handed her two tickets.

She looked at them dumbfounded. "Why, these are two stateroom tickets on a troop transport headed for Liverpool!"

"My bag's been packed for weeks," he looked behind him into the backseat. "And a troop transport's the best I can do. All the old liners have been requisitioned for the war effort."

"But –"

"There won't be any peace until you have your opportunity to go find Edward," Michael said. "I intend to help you."

"Oh, Michael, I love you!" Dora threw her arms around his neck and kissed his cheek. She settled down against his shoulder and hugged him to her. She liked the feeling of the warmth of his coat against her forehead.

He slipped his arm around her waist.

"What about my father?" she looked at Michael horrified. "He might fire you! Besides, he'll be after us."

"I've handled that, too," Michael assured Dora. "I handed Viola a note to give to your parents that ought to take care of everything."

CHAPTER 61

After a long voyage, escorted at first by the U.S. Navy and then by the British Admiralty once they reached the War Zone, as they had not been in 1915, they reached Ware House in late March 1918. Lady Ware met them at the carriage entrance. She stood there alone, majestic in solid black with a veil over her face.

"What happened?" Dora leaped out of the car and raced up to the woman who was to have been her mother-in-law. All she could think of was that Lady Ware had heard about Edward, and it wasn't good news.

Grim-faced and without a word, Lady Ware led them to the family graveyard next to the rose garden. She looked down at the newest stone there. The epitaph read:

Sir Adolphus Ware 1860-1918
May he rest in peace

Lady Ware stood over the gravestone and said, "He got your cable from the ship saying you were coming at the same time the letter arrived from the War Office telling us Edward had gone missing in Arabia. He came out here into the garden and blew his brains out."

Dora burst into tears. Michael put his arm around her shoulders. "But why?" Dora pleaded.

"I suppose he despaired of ever finding Edward alive," Lady Ware snapped bitterly. "We're losing the war anyway. The Germans are winning. He probably thought what's left to live for?"

"We're here to look for Edward," Dora assured her. "We'll write or cable you about whatever we find."

Lady Ware gave Dora a startled look as they drifted back into the main part of the garden. They were standing beside what had once been the pond full of carp. Dora remembered Edward joking back in May 1915 that his mother feared the British Army was going to eat her prize carp. Now the fish were all gone – along with the gardeners. The topiaries were overgrown. Weeds had sprung up everywhere, including between the stepping stones. Not even the lawns were mown.

Dora and Mr. Byrne didn't stay for high tea, if there was to be a high tea today. Lucy was nowhere to be found. They drove the rest of the way to London and found lodgings at a hotel.

They needed to travel to the Continent to make their way to the Middle East. When they applied to the Admiralty, the clerk looked them up and down, "Americans! You think you can do anything, don't you? Just because we're all bled white and there are a million of you advancing on us this summer to join the war . . . well, we'll see what you're really made of."

"Yes, I guess we will, won't we?" Mr. Byrne replied.

They went back to the office every week to see if the situation had changed and they would be allowed to proceed onward to the Continent and then to the Middle East. Every week the situation only got worse. They kept up with the news in *The Times*. It was all they could do.

Of course there were no references to Edward or any mention of his disappearance. She looked for his obituary in vain. For that matter, there were absolutely no reports about Colonel Lawrence himself.

The same situation continued all spring and into the summer. American troops continued to arrive in France. There was much cheering in London. As far as Dora was concerned, it was just a big distraction.

They were still in London on November 11, 1918. They woke up early to the chiming of bells throughout the city. The Great War was over. There would be no more fighting. With difficulty Dora found out that Prince Feisal, the son of King Hussein of Mecca, had entered Damascus in triumph with Lawrence during the fall of 1918.

Dora finally decided that Lawrence himself was the man she had to talk to. "Ask the War Department how I can speak to Colonel Lawrence," Dora told Michael one day.

"I suppose I knew it would come to this," Michael sighed.

He got through by his usual channels. By now he had a nodding acquaintance with just about everybody at the War Office. He returned from the phone with the news, "Lawrence will be escorting his Arab friends to the Paris Peace Conference starting in January."

"January?"

He nodded. "Wilson's coming from Washington. Everyone has to wait for the President of the United States to arrive."

CHAPTER 62

D ora and Michael took a train from London to Dover. The authorities finally allowed them to cross the English Channel during the first few days of 1919. They took another train from Calais to Paris and were among the first tourists to arrive in the City of Light after the end of the Great War.

They were pushed into a boarding house near St. Gervais. Dora was astounded to see the church there had been demolished by a single shell, fired from a huge German cannon nicknamed "the Paris Gun," that had fallen on the church on Palm Sunday the previous April. The roof had collapsed. Over a hundred people had been killed. It reminded Dora of the seriousness of her mission, not that she needed reminding.

Dora insisted on standing outside the French Foreign Office at three o'clock in the afternoon of January 18 when the Peace Conference formally began. As bugles sounded, delegates streamed into the gilded and ornamental Salle de la Paix. She had Michael keep watch for anyone in Arab robes who looked Anglo-Saxon while Dora used her spattering of college French in a vain attempt to ask where "Lawrence of Arabia," as the Colonel had by now been dubbed by the press, could be found.

The delegates were numerous and polyglot. Not only did two presidents attend, there were nine premiers, countless foreign ministers, emirs, maharajahs from India, emissaries from China, Japan, Siam, South Africa, Australia, and Poland, and from Czechoslovakia, and Yugo-Slavia, new countries carved from the now defunct Austro-Hungarian Empire that no one had ever heard of before.

"I think I see President and Mrs. Wilson," Michael pointed the First Couple out to her. "It's shocking, I'll have to admit. But there they are getting out of that black limousine."

Dora had to agree. It was strange enough to be a tourist on the Continent in times like this. But a sitting President of the

United States on European soil was another thing all together!

"It's never happened before," Michael's eyes looked as if they might pop out of his head. "Imagine, traveling beyond the boundaries of the United States while holding office! What if a crisis were to occur back home? How would he communicate? Just by cable?" he shook his head. "President Wilson would be cut off. No wonder Congress threatened to impeach him before he left the country."

"We're not looking for Wilson!" Dora stomped her foot in frustration. The French seemed overenthusiastic to greet the American President. Huge banners strung from one building to the next blared:

VIVE WILSON!

"Did anyone give you a clue as to the whereabouts of the elusive Colonel Lawrence?" Michael pressed.

She shook her head "no". "All I've been able to gather is that an American producer named Lowell Thomas is staging a multi-media play about the Colonel called *With Lawrence in Arabia.* It opens this August in London. Only a few theater people were able to tell me that much."

Dora and Michael returned day after day, sometimes with umbrellas, sometimes without. They stood vigil twice daily, once in the morning to see the conference convene and once in the afternoon to see it break up. They watched as the delegates filed out and were driven in limousines back to their hotels, residences, or embassies.

Eventually they were able to pick out the major players at the Peace Conference – Prime Minister David Lloyd George, the French leader, Georges Clemenceau, and Vittorio Orlando of Italy aside from Wilson and his second wife, Edith. There was no trace of an Anglo-Saxon in Arab robes.

"Maybe he chickened out," Michael suggested. "After all, how many men would show up among dignitaries dressed like a film actor in white robes?" he snorted.

"I don't think the Colonel is the type to chicken out," Dora insisted.

On the very last day of the conference she noticed a party of men standing on the steps in front of the French Foreign Office. They were posing for a camera shot in three rows. In the first row by himself stood an Arab man of dark complexion in black ceremonial robes. He wore a white cloth headdress with two runners that fell loosely down the front. In his sash was a sword. His hands were folded, and he looked solemn.

In the second row from left to right Dora noticed another Arab man wearing Western dress. A black wool coat was buttoned over his suit. He wore a headdress. Next to him stood another Arab in military attire. Then came an Anglo officer. Next to him stood a man in an odd outfit that her eyes at first passed over. He was flanked by still another Arab in military attire.

In the third row all by himself stood a young black man in a plain costume wearing a white headdress.

Her eyes returned to the man in the odd outfit in the second row. When she examined him closely, he was not only fair-complexioned but blond. His eyes were startlingly blue. He was dressed in an Arabian military uniform of a Sharifian officer inspired by the British. At the same time he wore an Arabian headdress of a dark color, a *kaffiyeh* head cloth, that came far down past his shoulders. While the others frowned or looked poker-faced, he was the only one smiling. His smile was all his own. Everyone else's face was blank by comparison. His was full of character. His very posture radiated confidence and purpose.

This had to be the "blond *shereef*" that Edward had described in so many of his letters. It couldn't be anyone else except the man she'd been waiting months to meet – Colonel T. E. Lawrence. It was hard to take her eyes off him. The man exuded a magnetic power, a certain sort of charisma.

After the picture session ended, Dora darted right over to him. But he had disappeared. "Was that Lawrence of Arabia?" she asked everyone she could see. The black man and the one in the front in the imperial robes, the one they told her was

Emir Feisal, son of King Hussein, had disappeared as quickly as Lawrence. She couldn't ask either of them where Lawrence was hiding.

Dora was ready to give up when someone touched her on the arm. "Madam, he will see you in this room over here away from the crowds," one of the Arabs whispered to her in an accented voice.

"Do you want me to come with you?" Michael hesitated, looking suspiciously from the Arab to Dora and back.

"The *shereef* will see the lady alone," the Arab pointedly informed the American gentleman.

CHAPTER 63

Michael whispered into Dora's ear, "If you need me, I'll be right here."

"Thanks!" she squeezed his hand.

Michael insisted upon standing outside the door as she was ushered into an out-of-the-way room inside the French Foreign Ministry that was dead still and silent. It seemed to be as far away from the crowds as one could get. At first she didn't see anyone else in the darkened room. The shutters were fastened. The drapes were shut. Only bare glimpses of sunshine filtered through, just enough to illuminate her way so she didn't run into a piece of furniture or a bookcase.

Gradually, as her eyes grew accustomed to the gloom, she became aware that there was a man sitting in the corner cross-legged on the floor. He was reading a book. She approached him slowly. He was the same one she'd seen at the photo session, the white man wearing an Arab headdress.

"Do you know who I am?" Dora asked, clutching her purse in both hands.

"Yes, Miss Benley, I do," came the terse answer in a clipped British accent. He didn't so much as glance in her direction. He kept on reading.

"If you know who I am, you must know why I am here."

She'd imagined what she would say to Lawrence for weeks now. She'd dreamed about it. But Dora hadn't counted on how hard it would be to address him once alone with the famous man.

"Sorry," he put his book away and leaped up with the ghost of a smile, "but after years on a camel I find furniture uncomfortable. The British War Office told me you've been trying to meet me for months," Colonel Lawrence said without offering to shake her hand or approach her more closely.

He wasn't going to make this easy for her. "Did – did you hear what happened to Sir Adolphus Ware?" she asked after a few moments of awkward silence.

He nodded, frowning, and strode away toward a small window at the back of the room that didn't have shutters. She hadn't seen it at first. The drapes were closed, but he was peering out a crack.

"Do you have any idea why – why he killed himself?" she followed the Colonel with her eyes.

He didn't answer. He just looked out at the passing throngs in Paris.

"I – I figured if anyone alive knew, you would."

"I'm amazed that Sir Adolphus, with his excitable disposition, lasted this long. He never could keep a secret. He always had to be prattling about something."

Dora opened and shut her mouth in amazement. She hadn't expected such a confession. She'd always imagined that she'd have to force it out of him, that it wouldn't be this easy.

"I've had nothing else to think about for a whole year now, ever since I got Edward's last letter from Petra," she tried to make Lawrence understand her situation. "I went through so much before that. I don't know if Edward told you, but I was –"

"A survivor of the *Lusitania,* I know," Lawrence acted all-seeing and all-knowing.

Dora wasn't sure how much time the busy man would allot to her. She had to get on with what she had to ask him. It appeared he knew everything she knew and a lot more, too.

She wanted to ask about Edward. Now that she was face to face with the man, for some reason she shied away from that topic. She kept putting it off. She thought to ask about everything else first. After coming this far, her nerve was failing her.

"Was it because of the humidor? Was this why Sir Adolphus killed himself and why his gardener, Ali, was after me? Was this why Asalah, died? You do know who she is, don't you?"

Lawrence nodded enigmatically, again while looking away from her.

"I overheard a conversation between Leonard Woolley and Sir Adolphus back in May of 1915 at Ware House. It was late at night. Sir Adolphus said he'd thought he was safe. It had been three years. Leonard Woolley reminded him that he would never be safe. They said something about how you, sir, had been the one to start it all," she paused.

Lawrence broke out laughing so suddenly it made her jump. He was always acting unpredictable. He smiled at her, "You sound like the Ottoman Turkish press, miss."

"Oh, I see," she fumbled with her bag again.

He strode right up to her. Funny, but on the other side of the room he'd looked much taller, like someone with far more presence than a slim, five-foot-three man would have. "I owe you a full explanation for everything that's happened to you in the past . . . oh, four years," he said.

She nodded.

"I was very young at the time, just out of Christ's College, Oxford. Woolley invited me to Carchemish. Sir Adolphus was an old chum of Woolley's. We traveled the whole Syrian Desert. We even visited Petra, 'the rose-red city half as old as time,'" Lawrence intoned the words like a poet. His eyes flashed with the memory of the place.

Dora stood spellbound. She'd hated and resented Colonel Lawrence for years. She had never thought to stand tongue-tied in front of him, hypnotized by his strange powers of elocution and persuasion. Was this what had drawn Edward to him, bound him by loyalty never to leave his side until the mission had been accomplished? It seemed that her whole life had led her to this minute.

"We stumbled upon King Abdullah's tomb by chance. I was curious. I lowered myself down into it. The others waited above. Then I called Sir Adolphus down since he had the better camera. I'd discovered some ancient texts next to the bier of the king himself. They dated to the time of Muhammad."

She nodded, glad that Lawrence was doing all the talking.

"It turned out to my amazement that they were

original texts of the *Koran*. What was even more interesting and significant, they didn't seem at first glance to correspond exactly to the one all Moslems use nowadays. I didn't have time to translate the scrolls on the spot. Neither did Woolley. So I had Sir Adolphus take photos of them for later examination."

"I – I see," she remembered how handy Sir Adolphus had been with a camera.

"Just as we were finishing up in the tomb, one of the local residents discovered us and put out the call for warriors."

"Why?"

"Nothing if you are rational thinking," Lawrence explained. "The Shereef of Mecca, King Hussein, that I have the privilege to represent here in Paris, would understand. There are darker forces in the Arab world who don't – such as Ib'n Saud."

She shuddered, remembering Prince Ali, one of Ib'n Saud's sons.

"We wouldn't have made it out of Petra alive except that Asalah, a daughter of Ib'n Saud who happened to be visiting friends near Petra, helped us. We escaped dressed as women in long black abayas that she provided. After that she couldn't return to her father's house. Sir Adolphus agreed to spirit her away to safety in England."

The Colonel got out the humidor. It seemed to appear from the shadows. The last time she'd glimpsed it she'd been saying her goodbyes to Edward while standing on the pier in Liverpool in late May of 1915. Now here it was in Paris. That elaborately carved wooden box with the Hittite characters seemed to have a thousand lives.

Lawrence was holding it out to her. He was trying to make her take it. She stepped back. It made her fearful.

"It won't bite, Miss Benley, I assure you," he said with a note of sarcasm.

He pushed it into her hands. It burned her fingers. She wanted to drop it but didn't dare. Even in May of 1915, when she'd last seen this humidor in person, she'd never actually handled it.

"Tell me what you notice about it, Miss Benley.'

She held it up to her eyes, turning it in all directions. The Hittite script was still scrawled on the bottom. She looked up at Lawrence.

"We added that as a distraction, a trick if you will," Lawrence explained. "It was supposed to mislead the curious, as it seems to have misled you."

She blushed.

He reached out and removed the cigars from the box. "I don't want these to distract you," he stuffed them into his pocket.

She kept looking at the humidor from different angles. "I'm sorry, but I don't get it," she apologized.

He took the box back from her. "No one has yet guessed the trick of the humidor, not even Mohamed when he thought he'd cheated me out of it in the desert for ten new cigars."

"What – what is the trick?" Dora edged closer.

He reached down to the bottom of the box and pulled up a trap door. Standing next to a table, he poured out about twenty small cannisters with lids on them. They rolled around on the table top until he made them stop with his hand.

She stared at him in disbelief. "You – you thought of that, didn't you?" It reminded her of Lawrence somehow – all the trickery, the scheming. He had fooled the Turks at Akaba, too, and the Turks and Germans at Petra. He was a very cunning fellow.

"Most people don't associate anything with cigar boxes except cigars. But I've dug up ancient boxes built of elaborate materials such as gold, jade, and ebony – all with false bottoms. Howard Carter wrote me about the most elaborate boxes of all found in Egyptian tombs in the Valley of the Kings. There's one from a royal's tomb that doubles as a sarcophagus for a pet bird at the same time it is also a backgammon board with all the pieces tucked neatly away. They are so tightly packed together that you can't hear them when you move the sarcophagus. You have to slide open the drawer of the sarcophagus and take the pieces out. Have you ever played backgammon, Miss Benley?"

Lawrence slipped all the film cannisters back into the humidor and jiggled it to show her it had been built with the same idea.

She shook her head "no", astonished at the way his nimble mind worked.

"I highly recommend it once you get back to America. It diverts the thoughts enormously. So we commissioned a woodsmith and told him the general idea of what we wanted. We didn't, of course, tell him what we wanted it for. I had the idea to build a decoy in case we needed it. That was the one that Sir Adolphus so foolishly sent to your father before you boarded the *Lusitania.*"

She nodded, thinking that Lawrence didn't allow for the human foibles of mere mortals like poor Sir Adolphus. He couldn't understand how scared Edward's father had been.

"After the followers of Ib'n Saud started tracking us, they suspected everything we did. Prince Ali was sent to the dig at Carchemish to watch us. We often smoked and carried the humidor with the film cannisters about. So Ali at once thought we were concealing something inside it. The tragedy for him was that he never discovered the trick about the false bottom. An iconoclast doesn't make for a very good archaeologist."

Dora gazed at Lawrence. Her awe in his presence was beginning to thaw just a little. "You're – you're a very clever person, Colonel."

"I have to be, Miss Benley," he strode across the room. "Don't you think?" he turned around and faced her. "Seriously, I mean?"

"You hide film inside a humidor the way you – the way you lured the Germans and Turks into the Siq and then opened fire on them."

He nodded.

"But – but your cleverness has cost Sir Adolphus his life." She wanted to add, *And may have killed Edward, too!* But she still couldn't get up the nerve to mention her fiance.

He sighed, "Miss Benley, I wish your eyes could have seen what my eyes have." He paced away from her to the small window in the back of the room and looked out as he spoke to her. "I have seen towns that Turks have pillaged and plundered. They have left dead women and children on the ground. They have beheaded boys. They have fed corpses to dogs and left others to rot in the sun – things that I shouldn't even talk about in front of an American or British lady." He sighed. He gripped the window sill and shook it as if he wanted to bring the whole building down. "That's why I wanted to fight this war and win. I wanted to give twenty million Semites a chance to hold up their heads among nations. I thought it was worth a few lives."

Her mouth fell open at the grandeur of what he was sketching for her.

"I thought I would succeed. We won the battles," he started pacing again. "The Turks signed the Armistice. But this Treaty of Versailles that will be signed to end this Paris Peace Conference won't give either Hussein or Feisal a united Arab country to rule. I have failed. That has strengthened the forces of darkness in the Arab world – and I mean Ib'n Saud. Now they will hunt us down worse than before."

She thought of the curse of the Five Generations that Ali had told her about before he died.

"But we will prevail in the end, and that's where I want to ask you a favor, Miss Benley."

"Me?" she was astonished. It was beyond imagination for Colonel Lawrence to ask a favor of her. "What – what could I possibly do?"

"It's your chance to participate in something larger than yourself, larger than all of us." He stopped in front of her and looked straight into her eyes, transfixing her with his stare. It was impossible to look away.

His voice echoed through her mind. It consumed it like a whirlwind out of the desert, leaving nothing else standing. She wasn't aware for some minutes that Lawrence had taken her hands. He was shaking them to make his point. He handed her the humidor. "I want you to keep it for me, along with its precious contents."

"But aren't – aren't you the one who can best defend it?"

"That's when I was the head of an army. Now I'm just a private citizen, or soon to become one," he sighed and strode away from her again. "Since I've failed to establish a state for King Hussein and Prince Feisal in Paris, they can't defend me either. These valuable film cartridges won't be safe with me, I'm afraid. They'd be far safer in distant America hidden discreetly in your attic or perhaps in another box or container. If I think it's safe to study them in Europe someday, I'll send for them."

She nodded.

"This sort of progress in the Arab world is what Edward gave his life for, you know. If someone can translate the *Koran* and show that it doesn't really justify *jihad,* and is instead a religion of peace, it could change the world," Lawrence came about as close to her as he could get. "It could also explain why the old translation resulted in the wreck of the Ottoman Turkish Empire."

Tears streamed down her cheeks. *Edward gave his life . . .*

"What's wrong, Miss Benley?" he asked, taken aback.

"So Edward's dead, isn't he?"

"Didn't I hint at that in my letter?" he headed off towards the window again.

"How did he die? I at least have the right to know that, don't I?" she dabbed her eyes.

"I was trying to soften the blow for you by saying that he'd been lost."

"Yes – yes, I sensed that," she gulped to have her suspicions so quickly confirmed.

"He was found two days later in the desert. He'd been shot. It was an assassination style killing," he said quickly as if it were very disagreeable to him to talk about it. "They took his money and ran. Very sad. Very tragic, if you must know."

She tried to see the scene before her. "What about his body? Are you going to send it to his mother at Ware House?" It was tragic she'd come this far just to make Edward's funeral arrangements.

He threw his hands out to his sides. "Miss Benley, when a man dies in the desert, most frequently he's left lying there for the jackals. It's not pretty, but we have only camels. They carry the supplies for the living."

She stood there holding the box weeping.

"Miss Benley, will you please take the humidor and go. I'm sure that the gentleman waiting for you outside, Mr. Byrne, if my assistant Abdul informs me correctly, will be perfectly happy to escort you back to your hotel."

She put the box down on the nearest table. "I – I can't take the box that killed Edward. I – I just can't."

"Would it help to tell you that Edward would want you to do as I request?"

She shook her head "no" again.

"Would it help to tell you that he told me so himself before he died?"

"No."

"You won't help me honor his memory?" Lawrence pressed.

Dora turned to go. She could barely see to walk she was weeping so. She could never remember later just how far she got.

"He's telling you the truth, you know, Dora. I do want you to help Lawrence," came a voice out of the darkness that Dora thought she'd never hear again as long as she lived.

CHAPTER 64

Atall young man with a pale complexion, freckles, and red hair, now cut very short, advanced upon her in a British military uniform, wearing what must be his Victoria Cross. He looked very different from when she'd last seen him at the pier in Liverpool four years ago. He was no longer a smiling young boy. He looked grave and serious –- and much older.

For a moment all she could do was stand stock still. She raised her hand to her throat and gaped at him. "Edward! Is it – is it really you?"

He stopped some distance from her.

She threw her arms around his neck and hugged him to her, the young man she hadn't felt in the flesh since that late May day in 1915 almost four years before.

He wasn't hugging her back.

"Edward?" she looked up at him, realizing that Lawrence had removed himself discreetly from the room. "What's – what's wrong? Why – why were you pretending that you were dead when you're alive? Why didn't you tell me? Why didn't you write to me?" she ran her hands along his cheeks as if she couldn't get enough of him as tears ran down hers.

"Mohamed was ready to finish me off," he turned and stalked off. "Lawrence appeared to save my life just in the nick of time – for whatever that's worth."

"What's wrong, Edward?"

He paused with his back toward her. "I wanted so much to come home to you, Dora, and now I never can."

"But you're here now, aren't you?"

"I'm going to work on Colonel Lawrence's staff. He's going to serve under Churchill and help administer the British territory in the Syrian Desert. I'm not going back to Ware House. I'm not going to live the life of an English country gentleman like my father did before he shot himself."

He sounded bitter somehow. "Are you angry at me?"

she burst into tears.

He turned toward her, "No, Dora, I've longed for years to feel your lips against mine, to be together with you again like we were in London." He looked at her with such intensity that she knew it must be true.

She advanced upon him with her arms outstretched. She took one of his hands and kissed it. Then she took the other and rubbed it against her cheek. "What's to prevent London from happening again right here in Paris? Today? Tonight?"she whispered low.

He winced and looked away. He hesitated for so long she wondered if he was ever going to speak to her again. "Could you love a man who couldn't love you?"

"Don't talk like Lawrence. Don't make puzzles as you speak."

He put his hands on her shoulders. He looked down into her eyes from his towering height. He lowered his voice to a mere whisper, "I mean, I can't father children."

She gave him a blank look.

"You remember when I wrote to you about the Arab women ululating?"

She nodded.

"Well, Mohamed handed me over to his wives to torture before he killed me. They . . . well . . . They knew it was like a living death. After they'd done their worst, that's when Lawrence showed up. He killed off Mohamed and Osama. He chased the wives away. But he couldn't undo what they'd done to me."

Dora crossed her brows. She knew vaguely what Edward was alluding to. She'd read the *Arabian Nights*. They mentioned eunuchs. She'd heard vague rumors about corrupt practices of the Ottoman Turks. No one ever explained the technicalities in print. She wasn't sure she understood them even now.

Dora took his cheeks in her hands and brought his lips down to hers. Suddenly she felt him kissing her back. She slipped her arms around his waist. His arms went around hers.

In triumph she said, "See, you do still love me! You do! You do!"

"Dora, that's not the point if I love you or you think you still love me," he held her away. "It's not fair to you. I can't give you any children."

"We could adopt them then."

"Mr. Byrne could give you children. Remember your parents? Don't they deserve something?" he spoke with his arms still around her crushing her against him.

"Edward, this doesn't sound like you to be so . . . well, noble . . . You used to be so irascible, so irrepressible . . . so full of life . . . so . . . so . . . " she took hold of his uniform's lapels and shook him.

"There's something else, too, Dora," he finally let go of her.

She knew this must be the real reason. She hung her head.

"What they did to me makes me want to continue to serve with Lawrence. I want to straighten out the Arab mess. Then my sacrifice, our sacrifice, won't be in vain. You can't be happy any place besides America. I don't blame you. Europe is a shambles. I must serve in far off places around the globe. Our paths won't cross often."

She sniffled. She finally understood what he was saying.

He put his finger under her chin and made her look up at him. "That's why it's so important to do what Lawrence wants. I want it, too. It would be the best way to get back at Ib'n Saud and triumph in the end." He picked up the humidor and gave it to her.

"I'd do anything for you, Edward. You know that."

Their lips met over the top of the humidor. They clung to each other for a second. Then he turned and left the room. He stopped at the door. She waved good-bye. He blew her a kiss. For a fraction of a second, that old smile played about his lips.

She walked toward the door in the direction she'd come

hours before. Only now she felt like she was marching. Today she'd been recruited into a kind of army herself.

"Miss Benley?"

Dora turned.

Lawrence's lips turned upward into a full smile as he beamed at her from the room she'd just left. "We will fight the good fight!" he flashed out his sword and raised it into the air. He saluted her with it. "That's all that anybody can do who is human."

She put her hand on the door knob. For the first time she could appreciate Lawrence's real courage – and Edward's too. Edward was standing beside him. For the very first time Dora thought it was the good fight.

"Miss Benley, white men underestimate the Arabs at their own cost. You saw what they could do on the *Lusitania*. You will probably see what horrors Ib'n Saud and his Wahabbis can wreak, tearing down rational thought and going back to the Middle Ages. This so-called Paris Peace Conference could mean rebellion and assassination for the next five generations. It's really up to your children and your children's children to do something about it and make it right."

Dora thought, *Five generations* . . . Only now she was impressing it on her mind and soul. She realized it was up to her and Michael to produce them.

She put her arm through Michael's. She looked back. Edward was already gone. Lawrence had disappeared, too.

They had vanished like a mirage in the desert.

CHAPTER 65

Dora and Michael took a steamer across the English Channel, and returned to their London hotel. Dora called Rita, who also happened to be in London visiting friends. She was invited to Dora's and Michael's wedding. They didn't wait for bridal dresses or matron of honor outfits. Dora got married in her traveling suit before they booked passage back to America on the *Tuscania,* one of the first ocean liners to be reinstated into regular passenger service after the war.

As soon as they settled in their stateroom on the first-class Boat Deck, a florist shop delivered two dozen red roses. "How lovely!" Dora sniffed them. "It says from my parents. Congratulations."

"I told them when we left a year ago that we were eloping and would be going on an extended honeymoon," Michael admitted. "I thought Edward was dead and you only needed to find out for yourself. I never dreamed what we would learn in Paris."

She kissed his cheek. "Thank you, Michael."

Just before the last call for visitors and guests go ashore, a letter arrived for Dora. It was addressed to her in a mysterious hand:

Dear Miss Benley, or Mrs. Michael Byrne as I should now say:

All men dream: but not equally. Those who dream by night in the dusty recesses of their minds wake in the day to find that it was vanity: but the dreamers of the day are dangerous men, for they may act their dream with open eyes, to make it possible. This I did. I meant to make a new nation, to restore a lost influence, to give twenty millions of Semites the foundations on which to build an inspired dream-palace of their national thoughts . . .

But what I dreamed is all now dust. The British have failed. Their empire has failed. It may be that the future now belongs to you Americans. Go forth and fight the good fight. I'll be rooting for you, if only in spirit. And if you hear someday that I am felled while fighting the good fight, don't spare me a tear. It is my destiny.

Yours truly,
Thomas Edward Lawrence

She handed the letter to Michael. She intended to keep it, the letter from Lawrence of Arabia, close to her heart just as she always intended to wear Edward's Crusader ring. She would keep it pressed into an album beside the roses that a very dear well wisher had sent her earlier today along with some photos that he had developed in Paris.

She briefly glanced at the photos. The first made her frown. It was of her sitting in bed looking surprised, holding the sheets up over herself in Queenstown. The second was of her standing there in Mr. Byrne's suit in Ireland. It was the photo that Edward said he kept of her by his bedside, the one he talked to. The next was of her sitting beside Edward in the garden at Ware House the day she and her parents had arrived. Then there was the shot of her and Michael the morning he'd come to Ware House to pick her up and take her to Liverpool to board the *Philadelphia*.

Then there was the photo that Lawrence had directed Edward to take from the heights of El Deir. The whole city of Petra was spread out before her, including the Siq where the famous battle had been fought. The fifth and last photo was of a fair-complexioned young man wearing a white headdress. He also wore a white, flowing robe. It was Lawrence himself.

"Michael," she said to him on their wedding night as they climbed into bed, "we will name our first son Edward, won't we?"

"I wouldn't care if you called him Attila the Hun at this point," Michael sighed. "I'm just glad that you turned out to be Mrs. Michael Byrne in the end. While I waited for hours outside that room in Paris, I thought you were going to turn out to be Mrs. Lawrence of Arabia!"

"Oh, Michael!" She didn't know whether to laugh or cry – perhaps a little bit of both.

"These Europeans, these English – constant intrigue! Constant machinations! I'm sure glad we're headed back to the good old USA."

As the *Tuscania* steamed into New York Harbor six days later, Dora and Michael were at the rail. They passed the Statue of Liberty. Dora could begin to make out her parents in the cheering throng on the dock. She turned to Michael. "Five generations from now . . . What would that be?" she asked.

He thought, "About a century from now, I guess, give or take a few years."

"The Great War began in 1914. It would be about 2014," she said, "a new century once more. Only by then it would be the twenty-first."

"Yes, and a new millennium," Michael added.

"I wonder if the great-grandsons of Ib'n Saud will still be at it, looking for the missing rolls of film hidden inside the humidor," she whispered low.

"Or if some other assassin will want to get revenge for the lack of an Arab state in Paris," Michael shuddered.

"O-o-o-ops! I never thought of that!"

"I intend to hide the humidor up in our attic," Michael said. "If one of our great-grandchildren wants to take the rolls of film out and study them, let them!" he pulled her close. "We survived the Great War. That's enough for one lifetime."

2014 . . . Dora tried to imagine what it could be like all those years from now. But they were coming into port. And, after all, that would be someone else's story. Michael was right. They had earned a little peace – at least for the moment.

AFTERWORD

T.E. Lawrence wrote on June 20, 1927, in his letter to John Buchan: "My two-year expedition in native dress is also fiction. All my walking tours in Syria were done in European clothes: and four months was the longest. I only wore Arab kit on one or two short treks after forbidden antiquities." Lawrence meant to deny a rumor about how he wore native dress for long periods of time before World War I. But he confirms what we suspected: he couldn't resist meddling in native antiquities.

For purposes of simplicity T.E. Lawrence is called "Lawrence" or "T.E. Lawrence" before Edward's first letter arrives from the Syrian Desert. After that he becomes "Colonel Lawrence", again for simplicity's sake. He didn't actually attain the rank of Lieutenant Colonel until March of 1918.

Leonard Woolley (later Sir Leonard Woolley) joined the British Army himself in 1914. While serving as an intelligence officer in the Mesopotamian theater, he was captured and was held as a prisoner of war for two years by the Turks. In the novel he is on leave long enough to visit Ware House in May of 1915.

About the Authors

L inda Cargill has written numerous thriller and supernatural novels. Among her titles are *The Surfer* and *Pool Party* published by Scholastic USA. She wrote *Hang Loose* for Harper Collins. Scholastic UK has published her series *The Dark I* and *II*. She has no fewer than forty-eight titles in print by the German publisher Cora Verlag. These include: *Face in the Falls, The Raven, She Who Watches, Volcano, The Spiral Staircase, The Louvered Window, Note in a Bottle, One Perfect Rose, The Lighthouse, River of No Return, The Oldest House,* and *Murder in Yellowstone,* among others. *Those Who Dream By Day* is her third title by Cheops Books after *To Follow the Goddess* and *The Black Stone.*

Linda Cargill currently resides in Tucson, Arizona with her husband, Gary, who has a law practice there and who co-authored the novel *Those Who Dream By Day.* He served as an historical consultant about World War I and American Isolationism, which is an underlying theme of this novel. He helped with plot twists and rewriting.

They live with their son, Kenny, a student at the University of Arizona. Also at the same address are her Labrador Retriever, Sabaka, and her two cats, Ramses and of course Spooky.

You may reach the authors through their websites and email addresses. Linda's author's website is www.lindacargill. org. Her email address is lindabcargill@cox.net. Gary's website is: www.garycargilllaw.com. His email is: garycargill@cox. net. Both can be found at the Cheops Books website: www. cheopsbooks.org where Linda has a blog.